Praise for *The Gray Ghost Murders*

"This is a truly wonderful read. In an old and crowded field, Keith has created characters fresh, quirky, and yet utterly believable, then stirred them into a mystery that unfolds with grace and humor against a setting of stunning beauty and danger. Stranahan, the fisherman sleuth, breaks free of the old clichés and delights with his humanity, vulnerability, and love of cats. Yes, cats. Keith has written a book that speaks to women and men regardless of color or background. The only downside of this book is that we must wait a year for the next one."

—Nevada Barr, *New York Times* bestselling author of the Anna Pigeon mysteries

"McCafferty skillfully weaves Big Sky color, humor, and even romance (in the form of Sean's stunning new girlfriend, Martinique, who's bankrolling veterinary school by working as a bikini barista) into the suspenseful plot as it gallops toward a white-knuckle . . . climax."

—*Publishers Weekly*

"Think big-city CSI teams have it tough? Their examinations of crime scenes are hardly ever interrupted by a grizzly bear like the one that sends Deputy Harold Little Feather to the hospital. . . . Irresistible."

—*Kirkus Reviews*

Praise for *The Royal Wulff Murders*

"Keith McCafferty has pulled off a small miracle with *The Royal Wulff Murders*—a compelling Montana-based novel that will please both mystery readers *and* discerning fly-fishers."

—C. J. Box, *New York Times* bestselling author of *Back of Beyond* and *Force of Nature*

"Keith McCafferty hits a bull's-eye with Sean's story in his debut novel, *The Royal Wulff Murders*. . . . Like bacon and brownies—Stranahan's odd mix of painter, P.I., and fly-fisher *works*. . . . Add the backwoodsy feminism of Sheriff Martha Ettinger, and the mystery is a good fit for enthusiasts of Nevada Barr who have read through all the Anna Pigeon novels. Packed with wilderness action and starring a band of stalwart individualists, *The Royal Wulff Murders* will have readers begging McCafferty for more."

—Tom Lavoie, ShelfAwareness.com

"Keith McCafferty's *The Royal Wulff Murders* is the mystery fly anglers have been waiting for. Finally, an author who knows the crucial difference between 2X and 4X tippet! But it's not just the fishing details that make this novel so enjoyable: it's the rich characters, the robust sense of humor, a sadly topical plot, and a writing style that is as gin-clear as a Montana trout stream."

—Paul Doiron, author of *Trespasser* and *The Poacher's Son*

"*Wulff* is fun . . . with sharp dialogue between characters . . . [and] fishing scenes that read right. . . . [McCafferty is] *Field & Stream*'s survival editor, and that savvy shows in subtle and satisfying ways."　　—*Fly Rod & Reel*

"[A] muscular, original first novel. McCafferty is one of the country's most convincing writers on survival and life in the wilderness, and this mystery is an impressive foray into fiction—taut, often highly amusing, filled with memorable characters like the lady sheriff and the former private eye who paints and fly-fishes—and it's a real page-turner."

—Nick Lyons, author of *My Secret Fishing Life*

"The last time I fished the Madison River it was high, fast, and dirty—words that come to mind for parts of McCafferty's tangy debut mystery. But there are also episodes of angling wonder and Montana beauty, rendered in prose so gorgeous they make this book a truly rare catch, the page-turner that doubles as a poetic meditation."

—Mark Kingwell, author of *Catch and Release: Trout Fishing and the Meaning of Life*

THE GRAY GHOST MURDERS

Keith McCafferty is the survival and outdoor skills editor of *Field & Stream*. He has written articles for publications as diverse as *Fly Fisherman Magazine*, *Mother Earth News*, and the *Chicago Tribune* on subjects ranging from mosquitoes to wolves to mercenaries and exorcism. Based in Montana, he has worked on assignment around the globe. McCafferty has won numerous awards, including the Robert Traver Award for angling literature and has twice been a finalist for a National Magazine Award. His first novel, *The Royal Wulff Murders*, was a finalist for the 2013 High Plains Book Award. A former nightside crime and catastrophe reporter, he holds a bachelor's degree in zoology from Duke University, a master's in journalism from the University of Michigan, and a PhD in child rearing, animal rescuing, and general derring-do from the school of hard knocks. He lives with his wife in Bozeman, Montana. This is his second novel.

THE
GRAY GHOST MURDERS

KEITH McCAFFERTY

PENGUIN BOOKS

PENGUIN BOOKS
Published by the Penguin Group
Penguin Group (USA) LLC
375 Hudson Street
New York, New York 10014

USA | Canada | UK | Ireland | Australia | New Zealand | India | South Africa | China
penguin.com
A Penguin Random House Company

First published in the United States of America by Viking Penguin,
a member of Penguin Group (USA) Inc., 2013
Published in Penguin Books 2013

THE LIBRARY OF CONGRESS HAS CATALOGED THE HARDCOVER EDITION AS FOLLOWS:
McCafferty, Keith.
    The gray ghost murders : a novel / Keith McCafferty.
        p.   cm.
    ISBN 978-0-670-02569-5 (hc.)
    ISBN 978-0-14-312438-2 (pbk.)
    1. Fly fishing—Fiction.   2. Murder—Investigation—Fiction.   3. Madison River Valley (Wyo. and Mont.)—Fiction.   4. Mystery fiction.   I. Title.
    PS3613.C334G73 2013
    813'.6—dc23   2012037086

Printed in the United States of America

To the Madison River Liars and Fly Tiers Club—
Bill Morris, Steve Dunn, and Keith Shein

God makes some men poets. Some He makes kings, some beggars. Me He made a hunter. My hand was made for the trigger . . .

—Richard Connell, "The Most Dangerous Game"

No man ever steps in the same river twice, for it is not the same river, and he is not the same man.

—Heraclitus, "On Nature"

ACKNOWLEDGMENTS

Although I give four Brewer's blackbirds credit for helping me finish *The Gray Ghost Murders* on deadline, many featherless friends also deserve mention. I wish to thank my brother, Dr. Kevin McCafferty, for acting as my medical adviser with respect to the illnesses that afflict several of the novel's characters. Kevin also is largely responsible for tearing me away from the desk so that I might renew my spirit on the magic carpets of rivers. Other companions of the rod, past and present, to whom I am grateful for their friendship and good humor include my son, Tom; my nephews Brent and Brandon; Mike Czaja; John Davis; Bob Bullock; Bill Morris; Steve Dunn; and Keith Shein. Also Tim Crawford; Bud Lilly, that great champion of the trout; and Joe Gutkoski, my wilderness mentor.

Parts of this book were written at Café Francais des Arts in Bozeman, where Francoise Manigault bakes the best *pain au chocolat* outside Paris. My thanks to Francoise and her family—Bernard, Alexandre, Andrew, and Ashley—for making me feel so at home.

None of this would be possible without the loving support of my wife, Gail Schontzler, or without the love of stories instilled in me by my mother, Beverly McCafferty.

I have had the good fortune to work with many fine editors whose guiding hands can be seen in these pages. At *Field & Stream*, among those who helped shape me as a writer were Jean McKenna, Slaton White, Anthony Licata, Mike Toth, Dave Petzal, Sid Evans, Duncan

Barnes, Colin Kearns, Dave Hurteau, and the late Peter Barrett. My editor at Penguin Books, Kathryn Court, has taught me in her margin notes more about writing novels than I could have gleaned by obtaining an MFA. Associate editor Tara Singh also provided suggestions while keeping a firm hand on the tiller of the novel, steering it toward publication. Finally, my thanks to editor Beena Kamlani, who has the last word on the finished manuscript. She's simply the best.

To be successful, a book needs to stand out in a crowd, and I believe that the jacket designs for both *The Royal Wulff Murders* and *The Gray Ghost Murders* are among the most inviting and striking of any books published over the past decade. The Penguin designer Jim Tierney deserves all the credit, not only for his tremendous talent but for his patience in working with me to get the details of the flies right.

An unexpected source of help has been the actor Rick Holmes, who read *The Royal Wulff Murders* for Recorded Books. He not only did a terrific job, but caught several inconsistencies that I was able to correct in the final days before the book's publication. I feel lucky to have him on board for the audio version of *The Gray Ghost Murders.*

The prerequisite for writing acknowledgments is obtaining a publisher and so having a book to write them in. I might well have written this novel without the help of my agent, Dominick Abel, but there's a very good chance you wouldn't be holding it in your hands right now.

Last, I want thank two legendary fly tiers who now fish those celestial waters where a well-presented cast is never refused by the trout. Lee Wulff's series of hairwing dry flies acted as the hook upon which the *The Royal Wulff Murders* was crafted. Lee was one of the greatest ambassadors the sport of fly fishing has ever known. Carrie Stevens of Upper Dam, Maine, designed the Gray Ghost streamer in 1924. In her first hour on the water fishing this most elegant of fly patterns, she caught a six-pound, thirteen-ounce brook trout, which won second place in the *Field & Stream* fishing contest. I have not yet equaled that catch in any river with any fly, but as nothing makes a fish grow bigger than almost being caught, I'm sure I have lost a few.

THE GRAY GHOST MURDERS

PART ONE

THE GRAY GHOSTS

The hands shook as the watcher adjusted the focus ring of the binoculars. In the circular field of view, he saw that the driver of the Pinto wagon looked older than the time he had seen him last, back in spring. Or rather his walk, as he climbed out of the car and moved into the shadow cast by the pylon of the river bridge, appeared hesitant, as if the driver was unsure of the footing. The simian slope of the forehead, the tight gray curls and liquid brown eyes over the broad nose and cleft chin, he could not see clearly from such distance. But the swinging-armed walk, the man bent forward as if his brothers had only recently left the security of the trees, would identify him anywhere.

For several minutes the driver was out of sight under the bridge and one of the hands that shook on the binoculars moved to the dog, the fingers digging under the collar to worry the fur. Maybe he had hidden the envelope too well. But then the man reemerged and it was plain to see that he was holding something. The driver got back into the wagon and from his vantage in the pines the watcher heard the Pinto cough to life.

After the vehicle disappeared, heading south up the river canyon, the watcher set down the binoculars. He felt the fish that had been swimming in his veins slowly subside. It would happen. The man still looked strong enough. The man would be worthy.

He lowered his eyes to the dog. He watched, a bystander to his own body, as his right hand jumped on the dog's neck. It was the same involuntary grasping that came more often now, that reminded him, as if he needed reminding, that the family nightmare had not died with his father's passing, but was beginning again.

Prologue

Katie Sparrow didn't think she'd be back tomorrow. Knowing a bit about men and one kind in particular, she didn't think the hiker that search and rescue was looking for was lost, or even that he was on Sphinx Mountain. She'd figured it for a "bastard search" from the get-go, ever since Lothar lost the man's scent—his common-law wife had contributed a well-seasoned Bon Jovi undershirt—back at the trailhead. To Sparrow, this meant that instead of putting one foot in front of the other as he'd promised, Gordon Godfrey had parked his vehicle at the trailhead to erase suspicion, then had climbed into another rig. In this assessment she was in agreement with the wife, who had reported her husband missing. Godfrey, a schoolteacher with a scratch to itch that lay south of his belt buckle and a history of women cutting his face out of photographs, had left a note to the effect that he had backpacked up the Trail Fork of Bear Creek for an overnight fishing trip for cutthroat trout. He'd written that he'd summit the Sphinx if he got a "wild hair" up his ass. That had been three days ago. As he had not discussed the trip with his wife and had previously shown little interest in fishing, or in climbing anything steeper than the stairs to the second floor, she suspected a ruse. She thought he was with "that bitch" and told the deputy who had taken her call that if this proved to be the case, he had her permission to shoot them both and save her the cost of the ammunition, what with 180-grain Federal "Vital Shok" loads in .30-06 going for forty-five dollars a box.

"Now what the hey, Lothar . . . ?"

Katie Sparrow cocked her head upon spotting her dog, who had curled his tail and stiffened his back. The shepherd froze for several moments before turning in a half circle and lying down beside a boulder. He looked at Sparrow with his own head cocked, the faces of handler and canine showing similarly quizzical expressions, then he settled his chin onto his outstretched forelegs. The signal or "alert" was one that Katie had taught him, but for a moment she had a hard time comprehending. Godfrey, if in fact he had hiked here, might well be dead. Mountains in Montana could kill a man at any month and in any number of ways. But buried?

Still, there was no second-guessing Lothar. As a search-and-rescue K9, he was a bona fide triple threat—a Class III wilderness air scent dog who also had certification as a tracking/trailing dog and a human-remains detection, or "cadaver," dog. Back at the trailhead, Katie had worked him in trailing mode with his nose to the ground, but after he lost Godfrey's scent only a few yards from the vehicle, she had taken him off leash and worked him as an air scent dog. That is, she had signaled Lothar to search generally for human odor, not a particular one, which he did with his nose elevated to catch particles of scent, consisting of sloughed-off skin cells eddying in the air. Dropping his head to the ground could mean anything—to a dog the world was a wonder of distracting odors. But lying flat with his head on his forelegs could not be misinterpreted. There was a human body underneath the earth where Lothar was lying.

Sparrow's VHF radio crackled as she turned up the volume and pressed the transmit button.

"Jase. This is Katie. My dog just gave me an HRD alert."

In the Incident Command trailer on the skirt of the mountain, some twenty-three hundred feet below and five miles to the west, Jason Kent set his coffee cup on the fold-down tabletop.

"Body, you're saying."

"That's a ten-four. He's lying on it."

"Above or below ground?"

"Buried. Earth's torn up in the vicinity, but the disturbance looks old. Like frost heaves, maybe. I suppose a bear could have dug it up a few weeks ago and scattered the remains, but I don't see bones."

The radio went momentarily silent as Kent digested the news. He ran blunt fingers through his crew cut.

"You there, IC?" Katie looked at Lothar and mouthed the words "Good dog."

"I'm here. It isn't Godfrey. Walt found him down in West Yellowstone at the Three Bears Motel. Very much alive. A little depleted in the prostate department, if you know what I mean. He was with a woman. Name of Marcy Hardy. We called off the search."

"I didn't get the relay."

"This just happened. I was about to notify the wife."

"That ought to be an interesting call."

"Oh, yeah."

"So whatcha want me to do?"

Kent thought a second. "It's too late to get a recovery team there tonight. Mark the waypoint and get off the mountain. FWP says there's a sow grizzly with two cubs reported up the Trail Fork. I want you checked in with me before dark. Call with a progress report every thirty minutes. Are you packing pepper spray?"

"Always."

"Keep your finger on the trigger."

"Okay, I'm out."

She holstered the radio. Carefully picking her steps, she worked around the places where the earth looked scarred and sat down next to Lothar. Katie Sparrow was a sun-streaked blonde with a wrenlike face and eyes as blue as an October sky. She looked quite small on the mountain, sitting beside a German shepherd that was bigger than she was. Crossing her legs in a lotus position, she fingered the brass locket under the neck of her damp T-shirt. For a little while she was on another mountain, far away, then she was back. She pulled a dog biscuit out of her shirt pocket. She broke off half to offer it to Lothar.

"You're such a good dog." Her voice had become the voice of a young girl. "You're my boyfriend. Yes, you are."

The shepherd gave her a soulful gaze and laid his head on her lap. Katie reached down and switched off the GPS unit strapped to his collar. She bit a piece off the remaining half of the dog biscuit and chewed it thoughtfully, wondering just whose bones she was sitting on.

CHAPTER ONE

Montana Metrosexual

Sean Stranahan winced when his client, sitting on the elevated swivel seat at the front of the raft, came forward with his fly cast. He whistled and slapped a hand to the side of his head.

"Oh, shit," the client said. "My bad. Did I hook you?"

"Only in my ear," Stranahan said, forcing a smile. He rowed the raft to a cut bank and told the client, a hairstylist who owned a salon in Baton Rouge, Louisiana, to hop out and hold the raft steady.

"Careful," Stranahan said. "Don't move your rod." He pulled a small nail clipper to the extent of the elastic coil that tethered it to his fly vest and snipped off the leader in front of the two-inch-long salmon-fly pattern.

The client, Kenneth Winston, tied the raft to an exposed root. He waded through the shallows to inspect Stranahan's earlobe, from which the fly dangled like a cockroach earring.

"I say, Captain, this could be the beginning of a new fashion trend in angling," Winston said. Long black fingers pinched the lower part of the lobe. At Stranahan's instruction, Winston passed a loop of monofilament leader material under the bend of the hook. He grasped the ends firmly.

"Steady now," Stranahan said. "Don't be shy about it. Yank it out quick." He felt a brief sting as the fingers abruptly jerked the loop of monofilament, backing the hook out.

"Good thing we were fishing barbless." Winston chuckled. "Here." He dabbed at a ruby droplet of blood suspending from Stranahan's lobe. "Now you know what it feels like to get your ear pierced." He touched the diamond stud in his own left earlobe. "You want," he said, "I could hook you up with one like mine and we could forget about the guide fee. Turn you into a Montana metrosexual."

"Thanks anyway," Stranahan said.

"Really, I *am* sorry. I'm a better caster than that. Let me make it up to you. Who cuts your hair?"

"I do," Stranahan said a little defensively.

"I was afraid that might be the answer. Perhaps we can do something about it. The fishing's slowed down, anyway."

"Here?"

"Why not? I'm like Paladin in, what's that old TV western, *Have Gun Will Travel*? I'm always packing—in my case, just about as fine a set of Bucchelli barbering tools a man can buy." He rummaged in his Simms waterproof duffel and pulled out a folding leather wallet, which opened to reveal three neat rows of combs and glistening cutlery.

"These picks and snips are what brought me to your fine state," the stylist said. He slipped a pair of scissors out of a leather loop. "Every summer I line up workshops near rivers I want to fish. Last year it was Pocatello, because I wanted a piece of that cutthroat action on the South Fork of the Snake. This year you're the beneficiary of my expertise. See, what I do is teach white barbers how to cut hair so a black man doesn't end up looking like a poodle. You get away from cities east of the Mississippi, you'd be surprised how many brothers can't find anyone who can cut their hair.

"Now you"—Winston stroked his pencil mustache thoughtfully as he waded around the boat to examine Stranahan's head from different angles—"I'm thinking an unstaggered part, swept-back wings over the ears. I'm thinking George Clooney, I'm thinking Clark Gable. Something simple, but classic. Your haircut says, 'I'm a man's man, I wear a plaid shirt, but I can rock cuff links and a tux.'"

So it was that Sean Stranahan found himself getting a hundred-dollar haircut from a man whose business card read "Hot Hands," while sitting in a swivel chair on the rowing frame of a secondhand raft in the upper reaches of the Madison River. Had someone told him this would be the agenda of the afternoon, he would have said he was crazy.

Or maybe not.

In the fourteen months since he'd come to Montana—"moved" was too strong a word for an artist slash fishing bum slash guide who didn't know which way to turn the wheel after the ink on the divorce papers dried—Stranahan had been duct-taped to a chair, stabbed, and nearly drowned. It was a long story and, to say the least, an interesting chapter in his life. But not an especially profitable one. Like most Montana immigrants, he had found that while he could eat on one job, he needed two more to pay rent and feed gasoline to his rig, a '76 Toyota FJ40 Land Cruiser that was as conspicuous in its boxy antiquity, even on Montana back roads, as a rhino in a Thoroughbred paddock. Having once worked as an investigator for his grandfather's law firm in Boston and subsequently done private snooping under his own shingle, Stranahan had picked up a few odd jobs in Montana, operating illegally under an expired Massachusetts PI license. That's what had got him into trouble the summer before. By comparison, painting watercolors for the angling clientele and escorting sports down blue-ribbon rivers such as the Madison were quite safe, if not entirely predictable.

"So what do you think?" Winston had slipped a mirror from a pocket in the leather wallet and held it in front of Stranahan's face.

Sean took a look at the suntanned visage staring back, the dark blue eyes set in ovals of pale skin where his glasses rested, above them his usually unkempt shock of black hair swept back from the temples and knife-parted on the side.

"That's the best haircut I've ever had," he said, and meant it. "I look like Black Bart . . . whoever Black Bart was."

"Of course you do," Winston said. "Considering who cut your hair before, it shouldn't come as a shock. But I'll still take it as a compliment."

Winston climbed into the seat at the front of the rowing frame, swiveled around to face Stranahan. He smiled. "What do you say we call it a morning? We've seen the sun rise over the mountain, pricked a few lips. Let's just kick back and eat some ribs and drink a little of that Moose Drool Ale you've been talking about." Unlike most clients, who expected the guide to provide lunch, Winston had let Stranahan know he'd be bringing the vittles, as he called his homemade coleslaw, short ribs, and Cajun spice deviled eggs.

"So you want to hear what happened last month at the salon?" Winston asked. He delicately nipped the last meat from a shingle of five-alarm ribs and sucked the bones clean. "Should I toss this on the bank or are we going to pack it out?"

"I'll pack out the rest, but I suppose you can leave that one for the coons."

Winston tossed the ribs onto the bank.

"There's this guy," he said, "always hanging around outside the salon. Older gentleman. Sort of a disheveled dignity in his carriage, remind you of Morgan Freeman if he fell on hard luck. So one evening"—Winston held out a deviled egg, Stranahan shook his head— "so one evening everybody's gone but me and I'm about to lock up when in he walks. First time across the threshold. I say, 'Sir, are you thinking about getting a haircut?'

"He considers the question. 'No,' he says. 'I'm *going* to get a haircut. I'm *thinking* about pussy.'"

Winston shook his head. "Gentleman was dead serious. I tried not to laugh, but couldn't, you know. Would have fallen out of the chair if I'd been sitting down." Winston was laughing.

"Of course I have to tell everybody in the salon. And ever since, we'll be snipping away, any time of the day, and somebody will say, 'Sir, are you thinking about getting a haircut,' and the whole place falls apart."

Winston wiped a hand across his eyes. "Oh man. The human comedy, you know. The things people do." He took in a deep breath and exhaled. He looked at Stranahan, shook his head. "Great day to be alive," he said. "Great *place* to be alive."

Stranahan tied a new salmonfly imitation onto Winston's monofilament leader and added a golden stone dropper. He looked doubtfully at his client.

"Try to direct your casts at the fish from now on," he said, mock seriously.

"You got it, Captain," Winston said, and they pushed on down the river.

An hour later, a mink, slipping like oil through the rose bushes along the bank, came upon the discarded ribs. He cautiously sniffed at the bones. He hesitated. The scent was enticing, but he preferred raw meat to cooked, hot blood to cold. He continued on his way.

CHAPTER TWO

Ursa Major

The grizzly sow wasn't picky. She'd attempted to dig up the human body earlier in the spring, when the surface of the earth at nine thousand feet was as hard as a pool table slate. Her two cubs were no bigger than furry basketballs then. Now, grown to the size of border collies and with as much restless energy, they watched with twitching noses as their mother wrenched the decomposed body from the earth. Though it could only charitably be called flesh, even one putrid mouthful was worth a dozen mountain voles and had the great advantage of staying still. She greedily tore at the tatters of clothing, exposing the sickening parchment of the skin. She bent her head to jerk out a section of haunch.

Suddenly she swung round to face downslope, one huge foreleg poised on top of the rib cage, which cracked abruptly under her weight. She lifted her nose, questing, then with a woof bounded into a screen of undergrowth, closely followed by the swarming, up-and-down shuffle of her cubs.

Harold Little Feather was the first to crest the rise of land. He'd heard the bones cracking, which from a distance sounded like a small-caliber rifle shot, and had climbed with great caution until reaching the lip from which the timbered bench lowered into view. Immediately registering the mangled remains of the body, he turned and put a finger to his lips. Sheriff Martha Ettinger, a few steps down the ridge, raised her eyes.

Little Feather pressed down with his hand. *Stay low*. He tapped his nose. "Bear." Just mouthing the word.

Ettinger signaled the recovery team below her to stay put. Katie Sparrow, twenty feet down the slope, squatted to place a reassuring hand over Lothar's neck. The wind, which had been drifting uphill when the sow caught the dreaded human scent, had changed its mind, and the odor of the bear was thick in the nostrils of the shepherd. Katie could feel the cabled neck muscles quiver under her hand.

Kneeling behind her, Sheriff's Sergeant Warren Jarrett drew back the bolt of his .338 Winchester Magnum to chamber a cartridge. He hadn't wanted to pack the nine-pound rifle up the mountain, but protocol dictated a heavy-caliber weapon in areas of high bear activity. The modified Mauser action, worn slick after thirty elk seasons, made a barely audible click as the bolt closed on the round. Doc Hanson, the Hyalite County medical examiner, was the straggler of the group. Having struggled with the altitude all morning, he placed his hands on his knees to breathe deeply. The hairs of his walrus mustache, more salt than pepper, drifted slightly with each exhalation.

Martha Ettinger popped the safety tab off her canister of UDAP pepper spray. Impatient by nature, she looked hard at the back of Little Feather's head, as if she could will him to turn around and explain the holdup. *Is the bear in sight? What about the crack that sounded like a gunshot?* She hated not knowing. She wrinkled her nose at the cloud of odor invading her nostrils—the sour dog smell of the bruin coupled with the putrid tang of the decomposed body.

Ten minutes passed, a heartbeat at a time.

Finally, Little Feather turned and hooked a finger. Ettinger climbed up the ridge, gave him a *what's up?* look.

"Bear excavated the body, winded us, left. Probably halfway around the mountain by now. Was best to stay patient, make sure he was gone."

"Ursa Major or Ursa Minor?"

Little Feather picked up a stick and walked forward a few steps, tapping it on the ruptured earth.

"Not a black bear," he said. "Griz. Sow, she's got a cub. No, two cubs. Good thing about the wind giving us away. Come on her unawares—well, you know how perturbed mama grizzly bear can get."

"Should I call up the troops?"

"Bring them to the lip. No farther 'til I work out the tracks. Probably only human print is Katie's yesterday. Still, I'd like to be sure before everyone mucks it up."

They'd been conducting the conversation in whispers, not so much because of the bear but because it was the way hunters communicated, and this was a hunt in the sense that they were working out tracks, trying to solve a riddle etched onto the surface of the earth.

Ettinger turned and called down the hill. "Come on up."

The words sounded jarringly loud and she immediately regretted them, feeling as if she had breached an unwritten code of conduct. She turned back to Harold to gauge his reaction, and as she did there was a popping sound from the screen of brush to her left. She knew it was a bear chopping its teeth before she saw the head bulge out from the tangle of downfall. In the time it took her to shift her eyes to Harold, the bear was on him and Harold was down as if struck by a bat, the bear shaking him, issuing horrible grunting sounds as it worried his left arm. Ettinger fumbled the canister of bear spray out of the holster, inadvertently pressing the trigger before it was withdrawn and spraying the ground in front of her. The cayenne mist brought her to her knees. But then Katie was flashing by, right through the red cloud from Martha's canister to empty all eight ounces of her own spray into the face of the bear. Below them, thunder crashed as Warren Jarrett shot his rifle into the air as a diversion.

And like that it was over. The bear, a blur, then a crashing in the underbrush, gone from sight. Martha gasping. Katie flat on the ground, having inhaled enough pepper spray to discourage an elephant. Little Feather lay curled on his side, his right hand behind his head in a protective posture and his left hand a bloody claw of fingers, sticking out at a grotesque angle from the forearm.

Warren Jarrett took the last steep steps at a run. He instantly inventoried the carnage and had just started for Little Feather when he was brought up short by a rasping sound. One of the grizzly cubs had started backing down a lodgepole pine tree thirty yards away. He could hear the mother chuffing from somewhere beyond the tree, encouraging the cub. Jarrett froze, knowing that if he put the cub back up the tree, the sow would return and then God knows what would happen. The last thing he wanted to do was have to shoot her and orphan two cubs. The cub reached a fork in the lower limbs of the pine and stopped. Again, Jarrett heard the chuffing.

"Come on, little bear. Come on," he said under his breath. He deliberately kept his head down, not looking at the cub.

Again came the rasping sound. Jarrett, his eyes watering from the cayenne mist that permeated the air, didn't look up until the cub had reached the ground and shambled off, encouraged by more chuffing from its mother. Jarrett took the remaining five step to Harold Little Feather and bent over him.

Doc Hanson arrived on the bench, his legs shaking and his breath stentorian.

"My God, Warren. Is everybody all right?"

Later, much later after the Air Mercy chopper had evacuated Harold Little Feather to Hyalite Deaconess and he'd been the beneficiary of a blood transfusion, the puncture wounds to his upper chest drained and dressed, his broken radius set, his left shoulder relocated into its socket, his body pumped full of antibiotics, and his condition downgraded from serious to stable, Hanson would live to regret the comment. The four who had accompanied Little Feather on the body recovery, plus Janice Inderland, Harold's sister from Pony, and Sean

Stranahan, who had befriended the Blackfeet tracker the previous summer, were crowded into room 223B. Seven hours had passed since the bear attack and the gray mood had just lifted, as Harold emerged from a drug-induced stupor to utter labored words of thanks to those who effected his rescue. The crowded room smelled herbally of smoke. Janice Inderland had burned a braid of sweetgrass and conducted a smudge ceremony to cleanse her brother's body of bad spirits.

The nurse, a hips-forward, severe-looking woman who clipped her words, had to shush them twice. Under ordinary circumstances she would have booted them out, allowing no more than three or four visitors at a time. But the patient was Native American. Chanting, sweetgrass incense, and standing room only were cultural norms that the hospital staff recognized.

Martha Ettinger added her signature to those already decorating the cast on Harold's left forearm and hand. She hesitated, then followed her scrawl with an X in the red felt marker. Harold squinted at his arm.

"Is that a kiss you put on it, Martha? How about one for my cheek."

Martha kissed him brusquely, then tossed her head back to cover up the burn in her face.

"Picture this, Harold," she said. "Old Doc here's last to arrive on the scene. There's blood over a ten-foot radius. There's bodies on the ground, two of 'em aren't moving. Then there's this human skull the bear dug up like something out of a nightmare, staring up with empty eye sockets. And Doc says—what was that you said, Doc? Oh yeah: 'Is everybody all right?'"

The coroner tugged at the wings of his mustache, his cheeks bright cherry. He muttered something about the power of positive thinking.

"Don't let them get to you," Harold said thickly. "I know who kept the blood from leaking out of me. I get to thinking straight, I'll give you a proper Blackfeet name. Right now I want to know what happened up on that bench."

"Well, I believe the sow would have taken off," Warren Jarrett said, "but one of her cubs went up a tree. When Martha called down for us, she read threat and reacted. Just being a grizzly. If Katie hadn't come through—"

Little Feather cut him off. "No, I mean the body. What did you find out?"

"We didn't find out anything. We haven't been back," Ettinger said. "If I can clear my morning, we'll make another climb tomorrow. But it's a cold case, literally. Doc thinks the body's been buried since freeze-up last winter."

"The mountain might tell you something, you let it talk to you."

"Maybe, but without you, who's going to know what it says?"

"Take Sean. He took the man-tracking school I taught up in Great Falls. Come to game sign, he's damned near savvy as I am."

"I'll consider it."

The nurse's Crocs clapped down the hall.

"Everybody out," she said. "You know the visiting hours. You can come back tomorrow."

She flared her nostrils at the smoke scent. "You want to chase any more spirits, make your fire outside. This man was dying, I'd make an exception."

She smiled with her eyes at Harold, shifting gears. "How are you feeling?" Her voice, minus the edge, had gone up an octave.

"Like a man who made the mistake of climbing into bed with a she-bear. You think you can put a little more of that white man's candy into the drip?"

Outside the hospital, Ettinger and Stranahan lingered until everyone else had left. They had been bumping into one another and lingering right through the March thaw, through the April rains and the pale leaves of June, without either of them working up the nerve to acknowledge the arithmetic of coincidence.

"Good thing Nurse Ratched threw us out," Martha said. "The smoke was getting to me."

"I think she has a soft spot for Harold," Sean said. He leaned back against the driver's side door of his Land Cruiser.

"I can't blame her."

"I know you can't." The words were out before Sean could stop them. Martha's reaction was to pull her head back, as if dodging a blow.

"What's that supposed to mean?"

"Sorry. It's none of my business."

A silence fell between them. It was a small town. Like everyone else, Stranahan had heard the talk. There had been talk, just the other day, about Martha and Harold being spotted in the Painted Horse Cafe, their heads bent to each other. There had been talk, last autumn, about a horseback hunting trip up along the Two Medicine River that each had mentioned without mentioning the other, one and one making a suspicious two, and there had been a lot of talk in the spring about Harold's rehiring onto the county force as deputy and resident CSI. The fact that Harold was Indian with a strong face and an ebony braid just added spice to the conversation. "She been touched by a feather," was the way some people put it. Stranahan didn't know any more about Martha and Harold's relationship than anyone else did, and had told himself the same thing he'd told her, that it was none of his business. Except it was. It was hard to fathom where he stood with Martha without knowing where she stood with Harold.

He stared off at the southern horizon, the sun pegged high this close to the solstice, despite the evening hour, the ridges still carrying puzzle pieces of snow on the north slopes.

"So how about it?" Martha said, bringing him back to the present. "You want to climb a mountain tomorrow? Or do you have a client?"

"I do and I don't."

"Good. Oh-six hundred. Parking lot at Law and Justice." She strode off toward the white Jeep Cherokee parked a few cars away.

Stranahan smiled at her back. Typical Martha.

He called after her. "So does this mean you're going to deputize me?"

Ettinger gunned the Cherokee to life. She regarded him from the open window.

"Nah. I can't have you getting a bigger head than you've got. And last summer, that was a breaking crisis. I don't have the authority to deputize a citizen unless it's a breaking crisis."

"You're the sheriff, Martha. You can do anything you want."

Ettinger fought back her own smile and drove off, leaving Stranahan to glance once again at the sun.

"Time to go fishing, Rusty."

He smiled to himself. Naming your truck was one thing, a western eccentricity and no more said. But talking out loud as if it could hear, that was the mark of a man who needed a woman.

CHAPTER THREE

The Graveyard

The warning shots that crashed off the limestone walls of Sphinx Mountain echoed into silence. Warren Jarrett ejected the last of the three spent cartridges, pocketed the brass for reloading, and removed his foam earplugs.

Sheriff's Deputy Walter Hess, whom Martha had drafted for the recovery after Doc Hanson begged out of making a second climb, took his fingers out of his ears.

"Ought to do the trick," Hess said.

Stranahan and Ettinger followed suit, lowering their hands from the sides of their heads.

Jarrett said, "I'm betting that sow never came back. But better to play it safe, let her know we're up here."

"We don't want no déjà vu," Hess agreed. He turned to Martha. "That means—"

"Yeah, Walt, I know what déjà vu means. You've told me before."

"Well aren't we Miss Testy?"

She exhaled. "Damn that's a hard climb to revisit on a day's rest. Warren, take point with that blunderbuss of yours until we lip over."

A few minutes later the team reached the elevation where the slope flattened into a bench, a half acre of scattered trees and conglomerate boulders that were cordoned off with marking tape. All eyes immediately sought the backpack that Jarrett had suspended from the limb of a Douglas fir tree the day before yesterday. In it were the two plastic evidence bags, one containing the rib cage and skull that the bear had excavated, along with tatters of rotted clothing and the few odd bones that had been strewn across the bench, the other a jellied mass of dark tissue and organ matter. Doc Hanson had been in favor of packing the remains down in the Air Mercy flight for examination at the lab, but Ettinger had been adamant about studying the crime scene, if indeed a crime had been committed, with the evidence intact. Hanson's objection, that a bear had already disrupted the scene, fell on deaf ears.

Ettinger's hands went to her hips.

"Doesn't look like anything's been disturbed." She swept her hand, the gesture taking in the extent of the bench. "Okay, here's what we're going to do. Warren, Walt, take down the pack and put those bones back exactly where we found them. Here's the surface scatter sketch we made yesterday." She fished in her breast pocket for the paper drawing and handed it over, along with a half dozen prints developed from the scene photos she'd taken with her digital. "Then we stand back, eat our lunch, and let Sean work the bench."

She looked at Stranahan, one eye lifted as if appraising a plug horse with rain rot scabbing its coat. "Though what you think you're going to find this long after that man went into the ground is beyond me. But I'm going to humor Harold and let you have your shot. That tape marks the boundary of our involvement yesterday. The chopper landed in the meadow I pointed out to you down at the trail junction; they took Harold down to it in a game cart with a motorcycle tire—you can see the tread mark from here."

Stranahan nodded.

Martha went on: "Beyond the tape, anything farther up the mountain, anything to north or south, none of us went there. Once you've cleared the area inside the tape, we're going to go in with the gas probe to outline the position of the body before the bear dug it up, grid it off and collect any evidence still buried. Between you, me, and the walls of this mountain, I think if we learn anything at all it's going to be at a forensic level. Still, let's treat it as a crime scene with the blood still wet. Okay, any questions?"

"How far afield should I conduct a search?" Stranahan said.

"Go from here to Canada if you want to."

Walter Hess pinched his Adam's apple. "Jeez, Marth, that's like two hundred miles, give or take."

"Oh come on, Walt. It's called hyperbole."

"Just saying it's a far distance, that's all."

Martha looked at him—he had to be kidding, right? She wasn't sure she wanted to know the answer.

"I'll try not to get lost," Sean said.

While the bones were repositioned, the atmosphere on the mountainside changed. A cloud had been hanging on the peak when the team left the trailhead, the temperature dropping during their climb, producing an upslope fog as the air cooled to the surface dew point. One minute it was crisp, clear, cold where the sweat had dried on Stranahan's shirt; the next minute he was enveloped in mist. The boulder where the bear had dug up the body shone dully, like a tombstone. Sean glanced at the skull, encrusted with dirt, a few strands of gray hair over one eye socket. A chill flushed through his veins, sifting the hairs on his forearms.

"Give a fella the willies," he heard Hess say behind him.

Sean tapped the ground with a stick, emulating Harold Little Feather, who claimed that isolating a track by tapping next to it helped focus the concentration. The soil, still damp from early summer snowmelt, offered a yielding surface for tread impressions, and Sean easily isolated several distinct patterns. The heavy impressions of the bear, where they had not been tramped over by the recovery team and later the EMTs, were unmistakably grizzly, the front claw indentations a full three inches beyond the toe pads. The ground, a tone darker where Little Feather's blood had seeped into the soil, smelled of sheared copper. He noted Lothar's paw impressions and suspected the corduroy ribbing pattern beside a rending in the earth was where the tracking dog had lain down, marking the position of the body before the bear had unearthed it.

Stranahan focused the camera that had been in Little Feather's effects when he was admitted to the hospital.

"What do you think you're doing?" It was Ettinger, standing impatiently at the edge of the bench, a half-eaten elk meatloaf sandwich in her hand.

"Being thorough."

"Be thorough faster."

Sean ignored her and snapped close-ups of the individual tread marks. Little Feather had once told him that Martha worked a case like a dog worked a deer bone, gnawing constantly until it was gone. "But you watch that dog," he'd said, "you'll notice sometimes he'll lay his head sideways to get more leverage, like so"—he mimicked a dog gnawing a bone with his incisors—"and he'll have his eyes closed. Dog's got focus, but at the cost of his vision. Martha, she's always gnawing that bone. I'm not saying she's not a good investigator. But her strength is her focus. You want to complement her work, you keep your eyes on the edges of the case. You might pick up a detail she's being too Martha to notice."

"Now what?" Ettinger flicked a bread crust to a gray jay perched on a spruce branch. The jay, waiting for a shot at the bones, hopped onto the ground and pecked at the crust, nervously jerking its head.

Stranahan had removed a clipboard from his pack and was sketching the imprint of a sole with an air bob tread onto a standard print form. He used a tape to take measurements and made a notation on an irregularity in the tread, where one bob had failed to leave a mark. He glanced at the jay, which an old-timer would call a whiskey jack, then caught the eyes of the sheriff. She gave him a taut smile.

"When we get back," Sean said, "I'm going to need the boots worn by everyone who tracked up this place, including the Air Mercy crew. For matches, so I can rule them out."

He sketched for another thirty minutes, filling out six more print forms with impressions that ranged from entire tracks to half a heel from a cowboy boot.

"Five of you from Tuesday, plus the two EMTs. The pilot stayed with the chopper, you said. That makes seven on this plot, if I counted right."

"You counted right," Martha said.

"Then I have at least a partial from everyone. If there's another track here, I can't find it."

"What did you expect? There probably hasn't been anyone up here in months. You're just going through the motions."

"Is there anything about the bones I should know, besides their positions?"

"No sign of foul play, if that's what you're getting at. But the skull's caked with soil so we won't know until it's cleaned. And the rib cage is a partial. He could have been shot in the chest and the bullet could be in the guts of that grizzly for what we know. Doc says there's freezer burn on the upper surface of the chest. You dig down very far, the ground never freezes solid, so that means he was probably buried face up, sometime before the freeze last winter. Victim was male. Doc thought past sixty. We have teeth and we'll have DNA, no problems there."

"We just need a missing person," Warren Jarrett pointed out.

On the hike up the mountain, Ettinger had mentioned that a records search failed to reveal anyone missing in the Madison Range, body unrecovered, since the late 1960s. The closest match had been a ranch hand who had disappeared in the Tobacco Root Mountains while hunting elk, but that had been in 2009. Too distant, too old, plus the hand had been in his twenties.

Stranahan was studying the remnants of clothing that clung to the rib cage. The victim had been wearing a wool jack shirt in a camo pattern. No other clothing but a dark, solid-colored undershirt; Sean guessed spun polyester. There was a femur naked but for a wrap of skin, crinkled like elephant hide. What looked like the other femur, a part of one, lay alongside. The pelvis had been cracked by the teeth of the grizzly. Smaller bones were scattered. Radius? Ulna? Metatarsals? He didn't know his anatomy well enough.

"No hunter orange," he commented.

"No hunter orange, but that doesn't mean he wasn't a hunter," Martha said.

"No," Jarrett said, "he could have had an orange vest and the bear ran off with it before we arrived. Or ate it. We've known that to happen."

"What, bears fancy orange?" Martha looked skeptical.

"'Member the mountain lion attacked that mushroom picker up at Hungry Horse Reservoir?" Walt said. "He pounced on the fella, ripped off his backpack, and took off with it like he was toting a bowling trophy. Guy didn't have a scratch."

"There's another possibility," Stranahan said. "He was bowhunting. You don't have to wear orange in archery season, but you do wear camo."

"I ran that by Doc," Martha said. "Bow season closes early October. He thought there would be more decomposition if the body had two months to age before the ground got cold." She squatted down, her elbows on her knees. She made a steeple with her fingers and scratched her chin.

"Katie, you haven't said a word."

Katie Sparrow was sitting with her back to a tree, dwarfed by the shepherd that sprawled across her lap. She looked up, shrugged, and kissed Lothar playfully on the nose.

She said, "I empty my head when I run dogs. Most handlers try to get inside someone's mind. What's this guy thinking, where is he going? But lost people, they're lost in the first place because they aren't thinking logically, and then when the panic sets in, they're running wherever their feet take them. The panic is predictable, but where the panic leads them is unpredictable. But the dog doesn't care what a guy's thinking. All he cares about is the scent. The scent tells the truth. So when I'm up here, I try to be like a dog, stick to the grid, just work out the tracks. Me and Lothar, we let you guys do all the figuring."

"Well, thank you for that insight," Martha said. "That's more sentences strung together out of your mouth than I think I've heard before."

"Glad to be of help." The woman smiled, wrinkling the corners of her eyes. She bit the ear off a dog biscuit.

"But if you had to guess?" Martha persisted. The sheriff had worked a dozen missing hunter/missing hiker SARs with Sparrow and knew the petite handler possessed a keen mind. She seldom offered an opinion, but what little she did say was carefully weighed and logically presented.

Sparrow sucked at the water hose of her Camelback backpack. "I think you're looking at murder. Either that"—she capped the hose intake—"or it was a hunting accident. Someone fired at movement, took the fella for an elk. Then panicked and buried the body. The other possibility is a bear. Bears will bury a carcass. But I don't think so."

"Why not?"

"Because I've been around bears all my life and haven't known one yet to bury a carcass and not come back for the rest of it. Not if undisturbed. And if this bear killed him late fall, early winter, he's trying to fatten up for hibernation. He'd have eaten him up, bones and all."

"Warren?" The sheriff's sergeant was the most practical person Martha had ever met.

"I agree with Katie. If a bear buried this man, he'd have been recycled through its gut system eight months ago. I think we ought to be careful exhuming the rest of the body. I think we should bring in the roots from a radius around it. If somebody cut clean through them with a shovel, then we get Harold back on his feet and he might be able to confirm it from the scarring."

"That's a good point."

"What about me? You didn't ask my opinion." It was Walt, an injured note in his drawl. The former Chicago policeman had affected western speech patterns and mannerisms since moving to Bridger five years previously. It was his cowboy boot, a crocodile Tony Lama, that had made the heel imprint Stranahan found at the scene.

"Okay, Walt, I'm asking."

The deputy looked at his watch. "It took almost three hours to climb here, it's going to take another two to work the body, and then we got to hike down with the evidence. I'd like to be back for supper. Its chili night at Josie's and ESPN's got the Cubs at Wrigley. This is going to be their year."

Ettinger slowly nodded her head. "You know, you're right, Walt. We're thinking when we should be working. Sean, you're free to roam. Do you want Katie's help? Otherwise, she's going to just sit here and further her unnatural relationship with that animal. I can't have her probing and sifting evidence. It's against policy."

"I thought if she was law enforcement, that was okay."

"A park ranger is federal, we're county. It's complicated. Do you want her help or don't you?"

"Sure I do," Sean said. "Maybe she can help me figure out what I'm looking for."

"That's your problem. The only reason you're here is because Harold asked."

"Something you've made clear," Sean said.

"Martha, I have to say something." Warren Jarrett was pulling on latex gloves. "I know your ways well as anyone. I know your manner. Every one of us respects the heck out of you, so we take the whiskey with the wine, as my grandmother used to say. Myself, I wouldn't have you any way but what you are. But today's a little rough, even by your standards. You're treating Sean like he's the guy put the body into the ground. What's eating at you?"

Ettinger made a bubbling sound with her mouth and blew out a breath. "I'm sorry I've been short with you. With all of you. I've been mad at myself since Harold got mauled. If it means anything, I've been even shorter with myself."

"What the hell, Martha?" Walt said. "It wasn't your fault there was a bear in the woods."

"No, but when I called down to Katie and Warren to come up, my voice triggered the attack. If I'd just been quieter, the sow would have moved off. And then when she charged, I couldn't even get my damned spray out of the holster. I'm the reason Harold's where he is and not here where we need him. Warren, you said it yourself. The sow read my voice as a threat and it triggered her attack. And the damned thing is, I knew as soon as I spoke that it was a mistake."

Jarrett shook his head. "No, you're wrong there. As long as that cub was in the tree, mama wasn't going to leave. There's a better than even chance she would have attacked even without the provocation of your voice. We got too close, that's all."

Ettinger made a show of pulling at the cockleburs that had hitched to her pants cuffs. "Thanks for the support. I mean that. I just wish it made me feel better. So what do you say, let's get to work. I'll try to keep my tongue in my mouth."

"About time."

"What was that you said, Walt?"

"I said it's time to work." Both he and Jarrett had carried heavy backpacks containing the gas probe and power pack, as well as tools and evidence bags for the remains of the corpse. Walt unzipped his pack and rummaged around.

"Walt, while we get to work, you consider this," Martha said. "The Cubs aren't going anywhere but the sewer, this season or any other."

"How 'bouts if they're a .500 ball club at the All-Star break, you buy me the bison porterhouse at Ted's Montana Grill."

"And if they aren't?"

"If they aren't, I'll buy you frog food over to that French joint in Bozeman. All the foie de la grass and pig intestines you want to eat."

"You have a deal."

Sean looked at Katie. "I'd like us to have some time looking before Lothar tracks it up."

Sparrow stood up and pressed her palm down. The shepherd immediately obeyed the down stay.

"Your wish is my command, sire."

She smiled, her eyes shining, letting him glimpse the young girl in her, the one who had disappeared for years and just recently come back.

When Sean Stranahan was a little boy, he loved tracking animals second only to fishing. Both offered the intense pleasure of immersion in the moment, of seeking a treasure that in one case was buried beneath the reflective surface of the pond at his grandfather's house in upstate Massachusetts, and in the other behind the wall of birch and maple trees that rimmed it. He could still recall the moment, when tracking a deer, that he had spotted ivory fingers poking above a bush. The buck whitetail, oblivious to the boy's presence, stepped into the open, his antlers tall and heavy. He tensed, his nose questing for scent. Sean was so close he could see the expression of the deer's face change when a shift in wind brought the human scent to him. The buck had wheeled and bounded away, waving its white flag of a tail.

Sean had run back to the farmhouse with his heart pounding. But when he told his father and grandfather what had happened, he watched their faces change to incredulousness, just as he had seen the deer's face change when it scented him. Clearly, they didn't believe that a seven-year-old had tracked a deer for a quarter of a mile, especially without snow on the ground to show the hoofprints, and their indulgent smiles told Sean that his description of the buck— "bigger than that one on your wall, Grandpa"—was a product of the vivid imagination for which he had often been scolded. He had walked away muttering to himself, "But it was a ten pointer. It was."

After that, the thrill of finding a flesh-and-blood animal standing at the end of its tracks was his secret alone. Harold Little Feather was surprised that Sean's skills had not been learned with a rifle in his hands, but instead with the aid of an instinct at once as powerful as the hunting impulse and uniquely human—simple, burning curiosity.

"So whatcha looking at, bunch a woodpecker holes?" Katie Sparrow peered at the lower trunk of a Ponderosa pine. The cambium under the bark, oozing sap, looked as if it had taken a charge of buckshot.

"They were made by a three-toed woodpecker hunting for bark beetle grubs. Either a three-toed or a black-backed."

Katie rolled her eyes.

"What?"

"Nothing. I'm impressed. You impress me, sir." She smiled widely.

"*You're* in a good mood today."

Sean had worked a search with Katie the summer before and remembered her as being cordial but distant, preoccupied with the working of her dog. Her manner was friendlier now, almost flirtatious. There could be other people around and she would find his eyes and arch her brows in bemusement, creating a bond of light intimacy.

"You don't know what you're looking for. Admit it," Katie said.

"No."

"I thought so."

"What would *you* be looking for?"

"Besides tracks?"

"Besides tracks."

"A bullet hole."

"Ah." *Why didn't I think of that?* Stranahan asked himself.

"You figure," Katie said, "that if the guy in the ground was shot, then maybe the bullet went through him and hit a tree trunk. Or maybe, if there was more than one shot, there could be more than one hole in more than one tree."

"We don't know that he was shot. And even if he was, he could have been killed somewhere else and the body carried here. The bullet could be in the wall of a garage for all we know."

"Um-hmm, um-hmm. But short of draping the carcass over the saddle of a horse, how do you get him this high up the mountain? See what I'm saying? It doesn't make sense he was killed anywhere else. And if I was the one who pulled the trigger, I wouldn't spend a lot of time dragging the body around. I'd get him in the ground soon as I could."

"Which means," Stranahan continued the thought, "that the bullet is close by, if it was a through and through." He looked around. "There are an awful lot of trees."

"That's my point," Katie said. "A bullet couldn't go very far without hitting one. How about you look for tracks and I stay in line behind you, looking at wood? Work a zigzag pattern, keep heading uphill. That's how I work Lothar. But I'm just along for the ride. It's your show."

"No. That sounds good as anything else. It's a long shot, though."

"Well everything's a long shot, this far after the event. But I'd rather be with you up here than sifting bones down below with that crew."

They worked in silence for a time, Sean, his stick tapping the ground, Katie following. They were out of sight of the bench, the intermittent voices of the team fading behind them. Above, the slope climbed steeply into an area Katie identified as a microburst, where gusting wind had rendered the pines a haphazard pile of matchsticks. Every step was up and over deadfall.

Looking at the back of Stranahan's head, Katie said, "Somebody made you a little more human than last time we met on a mountain. Did you get a haircut?"

"Yes," Sean said, "a client. It's a long story."

"I can listen to a story and look at trees at the same time."

"So, this guy's a barber, a hairstylist if you will." Sean told her about his client, then began to tell the stylist's story about the man who wanted a haircut, his eyes never leaving the ground.

Katie interrupted him. "Who's Morgan Freeman?"

"He's a famous actor. You don't know who Morgan Freeman is?"

"No, I don't have a TV."

They had lipped onto a bench much smaller than the lower one, just a place where the slope caught its breath before angling up sharply. Sean was bent over, studying an oddly shaped stone with a pocked surface. The stone had lichen growing over it, pinpoints of scarlet and gray.

"What's that?" Katie came up alongside him.

"I thought it was a rock, but the more I look at it . . . Could it be the end of a bone?" He tapped it. "It's got knuckles like a femur."

Katie nodded. "About the right size to be human. But look how old it is."

"If the rest is underground . . . What are we looking at, Katie?"

"Part of that guy?" It was a question. "Maybe the bones were buried in different places and the frost heaved this one. I don't know. It's weird."

"There were two femurs back on the bench."

"You sure?"

"Pretty sure."

"Then . . ."

They looked at each other for a moment. The moment stretched. The fog covering the mountainside had become a presence, the pines seeming to lean forward to listen.

Sean's voice was a whisper. "Is this a graveyard?"

Katie Sparrow turned down the hill and brought two fingers to the corners of her mouth, breaking the eerie stillness with a shrill whistle.

CHAPTER FOUR

The Price of a Fly Fisherman's Soul

For years, Sean Stranahan had told anyone who cared to ask that the reason he went fishing was to think. On the river, thoughts didn't pile on top of each other the way they tended to on land. Rather, his mind became elastic, adapting itself to the creative demands of catching trout. Sean would never make an important decision without turning it over first with a fly rod in his hands. But lately, it seemed, he came to the river for the opposite reason. He fished to erase the burden of thought, to immerse himself in the moment, and to find recognition in his reflection on the surface of the water—to see there the boy he had been. For the wonder of a trout had nothing to do with its spots or the sheen of its flanks, but its ability to pull the angler back though time until he was no longer what the world had made of him, but who he was when that world was new.

On this evening, stopping to fish the Bear Trap Canyon of the Madison River on the drive back from Sphinx Mountain, Sean tried to relax into the rhythm of casting, to let the tension in his mind ride out through his hands while his heart hitched a ride with the fly. He tried to put behind him the long hike back to the trailhead, carrying an evidence bag containing bones from the second gravesite. But a vision kept coming back. It was the first skull that the recovery team had unearthed. When Ettinger gingerly examined it, her latex-sheathed thumb poked through the crust of soil to reveal a nickel-sized hole in the temple. Turning the skull over, her fingers scooped dirt from a second hole, this one as large as a beefsteak tomato. She had glanced up at the gathered heads of the crew, her expression grim.

"Gentlemen, something bad happened here," she had said.

Stranahan had thought yes, and more than once, and months or perhaps even years apart, if the eroded bones of the second body were an indication.

He felt his line tighten. He'd been pulsing a slim marabou streamer fly through a current seam that held fish in high water, and this one was out of the river as soon as it felt the steel. It ruptured the quicksilver surface, then ruptured it again, and once more. He let the trout have its head, listened to the click of the old Hardy Perfect reel as the line sung out, and after a couple short runs was able to lead the trout into a shallow cove.

"How 'bouts you let an old hound have the honor."

The man walking up the bank was backlit in the slanting rays of a dying sun, his face cast in shadow, but Sean would have known the lumbering gait anywhere.

"Sam. What the hell are you doing here?"

"I had an afternoon float from Papoose to Palisades and got to the ramp late. Saw your rig. Figured you were such a fuckup you might need my help."

The big man stepped into the water in his sneakers and bent over, ringlets of coppery hair falling forward and his silhouette stretched thin as a heron's. He deftly unhooked the trout and kissed it on the nose, sending it on its way without ever lifting it from the water.

He grinned, straightening up. Now that he was facing the sunset, Sean could see the grooves in the front teeth where Sam Meslik had nipped the tag ends of a few thousand leader tippets, too impatient to use fingernail clippers. Meslik, who was known in the angling community as Rainbow Sam, had given Sean his start in the profession—it was under Sam's outfitter's license that Sean guided—and he was Sean's best friend west of the Battenkill River in New York State. That's the way he thought about it. All Stranahan's reference points were mountain ranges or trout streams.

Sam sloshed out of the water, muttering something about his "goddamned Reebok shoes."

"Took your bud out this evening," he said, "the black barber fella. Good angler, had me laughing to split a gut. Offered me a haircut. Told him I was like Samson. I'd lose my strength if somebody cut my locks."

"Why didn't he book me?" Stranahan said. He made a face as if he was hurt. He was a little hurt.

"His flight was canceled, so he didn't know he could go 'til this morning. Told me he tried your cell. But I think he just wanted somebody who could actually put him into some fish."

Stranahan nodded. "I was out of reach this morning." He wanted to tell Sam about the discoveries on Sphinx Mountain, but knew Martha Ettinger would frown upon it, even though the cops reporter at the *Bridger Mountain Star* would have the story in the morning.

"Did Mr. Winston tell you about the guy who came into the salon to get a haircut?"

"He tried to. I told him the last time I heard that joke it was a Swede farmer walking into a car dealership. 'Are you thinking about buying a Cadillac?' says the salesman."

A short silence.

"Sean, you're such a gullible trout. You were had, my man."

Stranahan nodded up and down, then shook his head. "I'm a rube," he said.

"Come on, rube. Let's go shoot eight-ball at the Inn. Maybe some cowgirl will like that haircut so much she'll have a wardrobe malfunction."

Twenty-four hours later, no wardrobe malfunctions but a persistent seam leak in the crotch of his waders, Sean Stranahan was standing behind an easel in his studio at the Bridger Mountain Cultural Center, exercising his second love on a twenty-by-twenty-four-inch canvas. The previous summer, a vintner from California's Santa Ynez Valley had hired him to paint eight watercolors and four oils for his riverfront mansion on the upper Madison. No pens being handy, the contract was signed in Montana fashion with a handshake and a tumbler of whisky—Johnnie Walker Black Label, as Stranahan recalled. Richard Summersby would be arriving at his summer residence on the first of July, leaving Sean little more than a week to complete the last of the paintings, which was slated to hang in the master bedroom.

He dipped his paintbrush into a Mason jar of turpentine and stirred it absently, the paint thinner clouding while he stared at the canvas, a riverscape of British Columbia's Copper River dressed in the rich palate of autumn. The angler in the painting was casting a Spey rod in a run called Silver Bear, gold rocks reflecting light from the riverbed, the broken teeth of the Telkwa Range buttressing the horizon. In the interests of verisimilitude the man did not have a fish on. In steelhead fishing you almost never do. It is like an agnostic's prayer in that regard, hoping that there is reason to hope.

Sean knew this firsthand, for Summersby had paid for him to fly to BC the previous September. Sleeping in a rental car and fishing with an old single-handed eight-weight fly rod, he had hooked exactly one steelhead in four days casting. It had bulked out of the river, flipped upside down, and smacked the surface with a tail as wide as a bear's paw. There are some fish that your heart knows you'll never land, that are placed in the path of your fly only for the memory. It was such a fish.

Recalling the sinking sensation in his chest when the leader parted from the fly, Stranahan touched the tip of a #2 Filbert brush onto the sienna and cadmium yellow mix on his palette. He had poised it to add a dab of color representing a rock on the riverbed when there was a rap at the door. The travertine floors of the cultural center echoed as loudly as marble, something Sean knew all too well, for the futon in the corner served as his bed. But he had not heard the faint-est footstep and was so surprised by the knock that he inadvertently jabbed the canvas, fortunately in the exact spot he'd intended to.

"Come in."

Kenneth Winston entered. "Captain," he said.

Sean switched his brush to his left hand and came around his easel extending his right. The slim hairstylist was wearing cherry red sneakers; perhaps that's why he hadn't heard him arrive.

"Sam told me your flight was canceled, but that was yesterday," Sean said. "I thought you'd be in Louisiana by now."

"Well, so did I. So did I. But here I am, still in White Castle."

"White Castle?"

"You know, the Caucasian Kingdom."

"Ah. Well, what brings you to my door? For that matter, how did you find me? I'm not in the book."

"Sam Meslik told me a little about you on our float yesterday. Sounds like you've led quite the life since moving here."

"I won't argue," Sean said. "But hey"—he raised a finger—"I don't know if I ought to be talking to you after you pulled that joke on me, took advantage of my naivety. Don't look innocent. You know what I'm talking about. 'Sir, are you thinking about getting a haircut?'"

"Oh now, where's the harm? All I did was tell a little story, and as I recall you laughed hard as I did. I wasn't taking advantage of you, it was just part of my effort to make your day enjoyable. You want to know what a man's true worth is, money aside? It's how many people did he make happy. Saint Peter asks for my credentials at the Pearly Gates, I want to be able to say that I put a smile on someone's face every day."

Sean had to smile. "So what can I do for you, Kenneth? You didn't come to book me tomorrow, did you? I'm free. Have boat, will fish. You buy the gas, bring some more of those ribs, this time we forget the guide fee."

"No, I'd like that, I really appreciate the offer, but I'm on my way to the airport. I'll be in Baton Rouge in time to get lucky or watch Conan, depending on the whim of the wife."

"Well, sit down then." Sean dropped his brush into the jar of turpentine and took a chair opposite Winston. He put his hands behind his head.

Winston was examining the canvases on the walls. "You are a fine painter. Very fine if I say so, and I do."

"Thank you. But you didn't come here to look at art."

"No, I didn't."

Sean followed Winston's eyes as they roamed over the room, his gaze falling on a tea saucer by a small hole in the corner of the wall.

"Are those crumbs I see? Sean, tell me you're not feeding a mouse."

"I'm not feeding a mouse."

"Yeah, and I'll bet it doesn't have a name, either."

Sean brought his arms from behind his head and leaned forward, his elbows on the desk.

"Okay, okay." Winston held up his hands. "I'll come right to the point. I lost a fly box out of my vest last night, after fishing with Sam Meslik."

"Sure it didn't fall out in Sam's truck? You could hide a dead Doberman in there and not smell it for a week."

"Well, that's the thing. Sam gave me a ride back to my rental after we fished, and there were a good three hours of light left so I drove up to Three Dollar Bridge to see if there was a hatch. I had the vest on, I was wearing it. I didn't open the box but I patted the outside of my pockets, you know how you do that to make sure everything's there"—Winston waited for Sean to nod—"and I remember feeling it there, the shape of the box."

"But you never unzipped the pocket to look at it."

"No, I was fishing caddis pupa and I keep them in a small box in the right lower pocket. The box with all my good dries is in the left, so I never had occasion to open it."

"When did you notice it missing?"

"Only about an hour ago. I was packing up."

"So what are you thinking? The pocket was unzipped and you dropped it along the river?"

"I must have. I fished until dark, about ten I'd say, and I was at least two miles below the bridge. When I waded out of the river I took a leak before hiking back up."

"And you have to take your vest off to pull down your waders," Stranahan prompted.

"You got it, Captain. I'd have hung it on a bush if there was one. But I don't think there was. I think I just laid it in the grass."

"So where exactly were you?"

"You know that log mansion that's on the west bank, set back in the creek basin? There's a break in the bluffs. Not the first break but the second. It's maybe the third house you see when you hike down the river. You really can't miss it. There's a little cottage below it, a couple hundred yards away, that's closer to the river."

"You mean that old homestead cabin that's held together with baling twine and prayer."

"I think somebody must have fixed it up. I was fishing below that cabin, maybe a five-minute walk."

"So you're asking me to go down there, huh?"

"I'd do it myself if I had the time. I called the airlines soon as I saw it was missing and tried to change my flight. But it's getting close to the Fourth, all the flights in and out of Bridger are booked. And I have to open the salon tomorrow."

"What kind of box is it?"

"It's a Wheatley. Early twentieth century. I found it in an antiques store in Kemnay, Scotland. Cost me sixty pounds. It's worth at least three hundred dollars to a collector."

"I can see why you want it back."

"It's not just the box. I must have two hundred dries in it—PMDs, tricos, Callibaetis, you name it." Winston shook his head. "Each fly worth about three bucks if you bought them at a shop, plus the box, I got more than a thousand dollars lying on the riverbank. But what makes me sick is I tied those flies. When I think of the man-hours I spent putting together that box, you can't put a figure on it." Winston took in the disorder of Stranahan's tying desk. "You roll your own, you know what I'm talking about."

"I suppose it would be too much to ask that you put your name on the box."

Winston sighed. "I've thought about it, one of those little water-proof tape labels. Good intentions, you know." He shrugged. "I'll pay you, of course. What's your day rate?"

Sean waved a hand. "Tell you what. You front me fifty dollars for gas, another fifty for taking me away from my brushes, and I'll drive down this afternoon. There's a good chance nobody's hiked that far from the bridge today, so if the box is there I ought to be able to find it."

"I really appreciate it."

Winston stood up. He drew a slim brown wallet from his hip pocket, the movement so fluid and quick it was reminiscent of a gunslinger drawing his Colt. Counted out the money with a flourish of his long fingers, added a business card to the stack, and fanned the bills on Sean's desktop.

"I'll bet you deal a mean hand of poker," Stranahan said.

Winston chuckled. "Let's just say more than one gentleman's lost the graces of a good woman finding out. I slipped a few more Andrew Jacksons in there, by the way. Thought you might need the incentive to keep your eyes on the ground. Wouldn't put it past a man of your nature to pocket my money and go down to the river and fish."

"Why Kenneth, I wouldn't even think of carrying a rod. You didn't just buy my time, you bought my soul."

"Your soul comes cheap," Winston said. He glanced at his watch. "Shit. I got to hit the road. You can bet some TSA queen's going to pat me down so thoroughly we'll have to share a cigarette at the gate."

He extended his hand. "Call me tomorrow?"

"Either way," Stranahan said.

When Winston had left, Stranahan rubbed the fingers of his right hand. Shaking the hairdresser's hand was like grabbing the steering wheel of his Land Cruiser on a July afternoon.

Maybe it's why they call him Hot Hands, he mused.

CHAPTER FIVE

The Cat Lady

Stranahan handed one of the twenties Winston had given him to the bikini barista at the coffee kiosk at the south end of town. The tall brunette who pressed her breasts against the sill had caramel skin and wore a name tag that read "Martinique." Sean had been working up the nerve to ask her to dinner for a month, spending money on coffees he couldn't afford.

She smiled. "I was just about to close. The usual?"

Sean nodded.

"I never asked where you are from, Martinique."

"Seattle," she said. "That's where the company is."

"How do you like working in Montana?"

"The hats are bigger but the tips are smaller. It doesn't rain here so much."

"Yeah, but it must have got pretty cold this winter." He was stalling, as usual.

"They gave us one of those electric oil heaters. They had to or we would have to cover up and then it wouldn't be 'Lookers and Lattes,' it would just be 'Lattes.' It stayed pretty warm. Except for my feet. I'd have to dance around to keep the blood moving."

"If I promise not to wear a big hat, will you go to dinner with me at the Cottonwood Inn this Saturday?"

There. It was out. Sean felt a constriction in his throat and swallowed. He'd started stopping at the kiosk for the same reason other men who never gave a damn about coffee found themselves driving two miles out of their way. And until Martinique there had never been anything personal in the exchange, a couple minutes' proximity to a half-naked woman for an overpriced java in a B, C, D, or DD cup, with or without a splash of cream called a "Happy Ending." An eye-opener of a different sort. But whereas the other baristas were artificially friendly, Martinique surprised him with her honesty and seemed open to the point of vulnerability. There was a touch of melancholy in her voice, a sadness in her eyes that made the smile she greeted him with seem brave.

He held her eyes while she regarded him levelly. She said, "This isn't who I am, you know. Most people think we're all strippers from Teasers, but some of us aren't. I'm in pre-vet studies, senior year at MSU."

"I'm not asking you because you wear lingerie."

"Of course you are." She put her elbows on the sill and rested her chin in her hands. "Aren't you?"

"Okay. I'm attracted to you. But you seem nice and you have a good smile. It's genuine. I get a mocha from you and the rest of my day looks brighter."

"Are you married? It's a yes or no question. You'd be surprised how many men can't seem to grasp that."

"I'm divorced."

"Legally?"

"Legally."

"How do you like cats? Men in Montana seem to hate cats. I see a bumper sticker every day. 'Ten things to do with a dead cat.' That kind of stuff."

"I've always had cats. I just don't have one now because I wasn't sure I was going to stay. But I don't seem to be going anywhere."

"You're not just saying that?"

"No, I like cats. Dogs." He shrugged. "I like all animals."

"Do you have ten minutes?"

"Yeah, sure." Sean switched off the engine. He had expected to be turned down and thought he'd be on his way to the Madison by now, talking out loud to himself and kicking himself for being stupid. Instead, he felt a little flutter in a vein in his neck, as if it had momentarily kinked and the blood started up again.

"Come on in."

The woman stuck the "Closed" sign on the window and shuttered it. She held the door open on the other side of the kiosk for Sean to step inside. He noticed a marmalade cat curled up in a cardboard box in the corner of the cramped kiosk. It regarded Stranahan through slitted eyes. He squatted down and slowly reached his hand out to let the cat sniff it. He drew his fingers along the line of the cat's jaw. It withdrew its head and Sean held out his fingers again. This time when the cat sniffed them, it allowed Sean to scratch its cheeks. It began to purr.

"What's her name?"

"Ichiro. It's a he. Poor old pussy. He's been through all nine lives and is into extra innings."

"You named him after the baseball player?"

"Ichiro was pretty big in Seattle. He was my dad's favorite player. The cat's name was Chester, but when Ichiro came over to the Mariners, Dad gave him a new name. I inherited him when he died. Poor old guy has to have subcutaneous fluids every day. All sorts of pills, too. And the medicine's expensive and I don't have the money but I do it because he needs me. When I moved out here, all I wanted was for him to live long enough to sit in the sun and see one more summer. Do you think I'm crazy?"

"Not at all."

"Will you help me do his fluids?" She indicated a drip bag apparatus suspended from a J-hook screwed into the fiberboard ceiling. "I can do it on my own, but it helps if someone distracts him. What I'll do is sit down and hold him and slip in the needle. You just keep doing what you're doing. Talk to him in a calm voice."

"But I'm a stranger."

"No, he likes you already."

Sean stood up while Martinique settled herself in a lotus position on the floor and scooped the cat into her lap. She was wearing the sexy cowgirl outfit today, cutoff shorts below a lavender halter top with white polka dots. Sean knelt down opposite her and scratched the cat's cheeks while Martinique pinched up a tent of skin between its shoulder blades and inserted the slim needle. As the fluid dripped, the cat developed a lump under its skin. It took about ten minutes and all the while Martinique talked soothingly to it.

"It's okay, Ichiro. This will make you feel better. I know you don't like it but you're my sweetie and this nice man is helping us and I don't even know his name.

"I don't even know your name." She looked up at Stranahan with a shy smile. A wing of hair had fallen forward and she brushed it back with her hand. It had been a strangely intimate ten minutes. She wasn't just the pretty woman at the kiosk anymore.

"Sean. Sean Stranahan."

"Sean. Isn't that a nice name, Ichiro? Sean is our new friend. It's all over. No more poking. What a good kitty you are.

"Thank you," she said. "You never got your coffee." She stood up, clutching the cat to her chest.

"I didn't really want it. It was just an excuse to come by. I've been meaning to ask you out for at least a month."

"Do you still want to? I mean, I'm twenty-nine and here I am, already a cat lady." She kissed Ichiro on the top of his head and placed him on the floor. She stood very close to Sean, her eyes nearly even with his, though Sean was six feet and a bit.

"It's only one cat," he said.

"There's two more where I live."

"I don't care."

"I have some other baggage."

"I have some, too."

She locked her hands behind his neck and regarded him very seriously.

"I'll go out with you, Mr. Sean Stranahan who's nice to cats."

"Good," was all he managed to say.

CHAPTER SIX

The Madison River
Liars and Fly Tiers Club

Stranahan listened to the engine tick down in the grassy parking lot at Three Dollar Bridge. He looked for some ones to slip into the rusted box that the landowner had tacked onto a fencepost, realized that he'd never got change from the bill he'd handed to Martinique, and smiled. She'd kissed him on the cheek when they parted, the act no more suggestive than when she had kissed the cat, but still . . .

He scrounged a couple quarters that had been wedged into the tread of the floor mat. "Next time," he muttered, clanging the change into the tin box, and came back to the Land Cruiser, shrugged into his fly vest, and slipped the old bamboo rod his father had made from its case. He breathed in the tung oil smell of the rod sock.

"That's something you don't get from graphite," he muttered.

He fitted the German silver ferrules together and strung the rod with a double taper line. True, he'd assured Kenneth Winston that he wouldn't carry a rod while looking for the lost fly box, but what if he found it right off the bat? He'd be on one of the loveliest stretches of the Madison River with nothing to do about the circles the trout made but watch. A fly fisherman's Hades.

Along the fisherman's path, Sean resisted the urge to drink in the beauty of the afternoon, nodding off into purple blues on the ridges and deep greens in the valley, and kept his eyes on the ground. Not only for the fly box, which could have dropped out of Winston's vest anywhere in the two miles, but so he wouldn't step into a badger hole. They were everywhere, freshly turned earth to mark the new additions, and yet one almost never saw a badger. Sean did spot a small garter snake and picked it up. After it calmed he held it in front of his face and let the questing forked tongue tickle the end of his nose. He watched it slither away and looked behind him, up a draw through the bluffs. The mansion Winston had mentioned was built from blond logs in a hexagonal design, with a wraparound porch and peaked windowpanes looking toward mountains at each point of the compass. Closer to the water and downriver was the old homestead cabin, freshly chinked with a large picture window facing the river. The newly constructed porch was a long fly cast from the riverbank; there was a picnic table on the porch, slatted Adirondack chairs, a couple old oil lanterns hanging from nails driven into the logs.

Sean hated to see development of any kind along his favorite river, but the structure was reminiscent of fishing huts he'd seen in Maine and had a down-home feel he could relate to. Mercifully, the "No Trespassing" signs that Sean had come to see as the state motto weren't in evidence. Although Montana had the best stream access law in the West, permitting anyone to wade, hike, fish, or float a navigable river, the stipulation being only that one had to stay within the high-water mark, many landowners, especially the new gentry from out of state, posted their property and hassled anglers anyway.

He picked up his pace, hiked past the little bungalow, and ten minutes later turned around, facing back upstream. He could see the minute figure of a fisherman who must have strolled down from the cabin. Sean started back up, zigzagging across the path, his eyes glued to the ground. The grass was up past his knees and he realized that finding the box would not be as easy as he originally thought. He searched slowly and methodically, lifting heavy grass tufts with his wading staff to peer underneath them, his shadow lengthening so that it reflected on the water, the river sparkling under the low-angle eye of the sun. Caddis flies swarmed the wild rose bushes on the bank. Pale Morning Dun mayflies batted their wings, rising and dipping in flight. Trout kissed the surface in the slicks behind the boulders. Sean looked wistfully at the parachute Adams hooked to his stripping guide.

"Just my luck," he said out loud. He was so preoccupied looking at the water that he didn't notice the approach of the fisherman, who had a hitch to his walk and was wearing a tweed fedora. *Shit*, Sean thought. *He's going to bawl me out for walking above the high-water mark.* A welcoming smile disavowed him of the presumption.

"You wouldn't be looking for a fly box, would you?" the man said.

"I sure would be." Stranahan briefly explained the circumstances that had brought him to the river.

The man nodded. "I was half hoping you wouldn't show. I found it this morning. It's hard to part with a box as nice as that one. My name is Patrick Willoughby, by the way."

Stranahan took the outstretched hand. Just for a moment the man looked down, showing a bashful expression. A portly fellow with a moon face and thin lips, he reminded Sean of the late newscaster Charles Kuralt, who also had been a Montana fly fisherman.

"Do you own the cabin?" he said.

Recovering from his brief inability to hold Sean's eyes, Willoughby peered up at him through the thick lenses of his glasses.

"It's a joint ownership by our club," he said. "When the estimable Weldon Crawford of yonder mansion bought the old Anderson ranch, he financed the construction by selling off a few parcels. When this one came on the market, we pounced."

"You mean Weldon Crawford Jr. from Kalispell? The congressman who introduced the bill to reinstate hunting for grizzly bears?" Bears were a polarizing issue in Montana. Crawford's efforts to remove federal protection and turn management over to the state had drawn national media attention.

"He does make waves," Willoughby said. "But to tell you the truth I've not had the pleasure. Oh, we've said hello a few times and Polly Sorenson was invited up to the house for dinner last year—Polly is one of our members—but I've been here a week this summer and seen no sign of the man. The congressman, I mean."

They had arrived at the cabin porch, having followed a small rill of water up from the river. Sean read the lettering burned into a piece of driftwood above the door: THE MADISON RIVER LIARS AND FLY TIERS CLUB.

Willoughby stepped out of his boot-foot waders, hung them from one of a series of pegs driven into the wall, and slipped his feet into sandals on the porch. He hung his hat on a nail.

"You can leave your rod beside mine here in the rack," Willoughby said. "Who made it, by the way? I'm something of a student of vintage bamboo rods. You don't see them anymore, at least not many that catch anything but the dust over a mantelpiece."

"My father, actually."

Willoughby peered at it through his glasses. "Looks a little like a Thomas Payne rod. That's a compliment, by the way. Does it cast a nice line?"

"You have to settle into its rhythm, but once you get used to it, it casts a very nice line."

"Mr. Stranahan, I can see you are a man after my heart."

He opened the screen door and ushered Sean inside.

"Don't you want me to take these boots off?" Sean said.

Willoughby made a dismissive gesture with his hand. "We go in and out of here in waders all the time." He reached along the wall inside the door. The candle-tip bulbs of a chandelier flared. He hit another switch and a half dozen copper sconces cast the room in a warm amber glow.

The front room, consisting of the living area with a small kitchen alcove, was paneled in light wood and except for an ornately carved stool and two wicked-looking spears crossed over an African shield was furnished in American hunting lodge motif—slat-back couches and stuffed chairs with ducks in flight, casually arranged around a glass-topped coffee table littered with fishing magazines. On the shelves of matching bookcases were miniature glass domes like those used to display pocket watches. Classic British salmon flies tied with exotic feathers stood on clear pins protruding from the walnut bases. Other flies, mostly dries, were housed in custom-made wall display boxes that reflected prisms of light from the elk antler chandelier. Against the south-facing wall were a fireplace and chimney built from smooth river stones. The skull and horns of a bison were mounted above the mantelpiece, a tuft of dried grass protruding from the nasal cavity.

Willoughby followed Sean's glance.

"Sweetgrass is a Cheyenne good-luck charm, hoping for bountiful vegetation," he said. "With the rains this spring, the grass here is higher than I've ever seen it, so I'd say the homage we've paid our predecessors has paid off. Though not entirely to our advantage. The river is taking its time dropping into shape. Most stretches I couldn't wade if I wanted to."

"What is that chair?" Stranahan asked.

"It's a Chokwe throne. A tribal chief was said to have ruled from it. One of our members imports African artifacts."

"Mmmm." Through the screen door Stranahan could hear the undertone of the current, sinking into bass notes as the evening erased the polish from the surface. He turned to face the picture window, before which a rough-hewn table ran nearly the entire length of the room. Desk lamps of varied designs—gooseneck, banker, Tiffany—presided over a half dozen fly-tying benches. Feathers, furs, and other tying materials littered the tabletop.

"Bunkhouses and the bathroom are in the back," Willoughby was saying. "We can sleep eight here with the new addition, though there are seldom more than four or five of us at any time. All the necessities as you can see, including a humidor and the bar. I'm going to have a branch water and bourbon in a tin cup, which is the only way.

Would you care to join me? The water's from the creek outside the door. We run it through a filter pump. There's no worry about giardia."

"Sounds good to me."

"In that case I stand corrected. I suggest you do get out of your waders. It's too good of a drink to hurry."

Sean sat in one of the Adirondack chairs on the porch to remove his waders. The outside walls of the cottage were hung with framed quotations.

If fishing is interfering with your business, give up your business. Sparse Grey Hackle.

Game fish are too valuable to be caught only once. Lee Wulff.

There's more BS in fly fishing than there is in a Kansas feedlot. Lefty Kreh.

"This place reminds me of a Catskill fishing lodge," Sean told Willoughby when he had rejoined him inside. "Like Sparse Grey Hackle wrote about in *Fishless Days, Angling Nights*."

"Ah yes, what was it he said? Something about not wanting to be in any club that would accept him as a member. Which was a falsehood. I met old Alfred—his real name was Alfred Miller—oh, I think it must have been in the early seventies. He was a friend of my father's. On the river he gave the appearance of a basset hound. A jowly face and a big chin, wore a porkpie hat and smoked a pipe. Always had mischief in his eyes. *Such* an erudite writer. It heartens me to know that a young man like yourself recognizes the name. So many fishermen today, all their gung-ho talk about Jedi sticks and hot fish and so forth, why when I floated the Gunnison last year the guide clicked the number of strikes on a digital counter!" He shook his head. "I'm afraid I'm showing my age, but when you begin to count trout you've lost sight of the reason to go to the river. It reminds me of something Henry David Thoreau wrote, men fishing all their lives without knowing that it is not the fish they are after.

"Here, have some of this. Consider it Viagra for the mind."

Sean sipped at the whiskey. It was nectar.

"That may be the best bourbon I've ever had."

"It ought to be. George T. Stagg is better than Maker's Mark Gold Label in my humble opinion."

"Well, here's to good whiskey and a well-tied fly." They tapped cups. "If you don't mind my asking you, where are the other members of your club? On the river somewhere?" Sean had noticed a couple pairs of waders hanging on the porch besides those that Willoughby had taken off.

"Polly Sorenson was the pilot fish this year. He came on the twenty-second, beat me by a week. He's in town today. The core membership arrives tomorrow. It sounds like I'm talking about a committee, but these are my best friends. We're all disciples of Sparse Grey Hackle in a sense. By which I mean men who understand that how many you catch is not nearly so important as who you sit around the fire with after. Speaking of which, would you so terribly mind if we took our drinks to the hearth? I've been on my feet about as long as I can today." He tapped his right thigh. "I took a bad spill this spring. I wish I could say I slipped in a trout stream, but it was the front step of my house. Hairline fracture of the femur. Apparently I inherited a chemical deficiency that did not allow the bones to properly knit. My doctor made me promise that I would fish from the bank and not attempt to wade the Madison."

"When I saw you, you were wearing waders," Stranahan pointed out.

"Was I?"

"I seemed to notice they were wet, too."

"Just freeing a snag, my dear man. I didn't want to lose the fly." Willoughby winked, then settled himself into one of the stuffed chairs and heaved a sigh of contentment.

Sean looked at him, smiling, and for just a second Willoughby looked away, the quick dipping of the eyes that Sean had noticed when they met. He frowned inwardly. Patrick Willoughby seemed to have stepped from the pages of a book. A fox-eared book of the history of American fly fishing in which Catskill anglers who were only a few generations removed from the clubs of London fished bamboo rods in rivers with names like Neversink and Beaverkill, using flies called Hendrickson and Cahill. He had the manner cold: the self-assured, self-deprecating patter, the diction and enunciation that belonged more to a Yorkshire chalk stream than a Montana freestone river. It was a pat performance, but Sean suspected it was still a performance.

He sat down opposite Willoughby, wondering when the man intended to hand over the fly box, which he had made no further reference to. He decided to test the waters of his suspicion.

"Mr. Willoughby?"

"Patrick to you."

"Patrick, I don't want to make you get out of your chair, but I drove down here from Bridger and lifted about a thousand tufts of grass looking for a fly box that I have yet to see. I'm beginning to wonder if it actually exists."

"My dear man, if you would look in the second drawer of the desk over there, the left-hand side."

Sean returned with a vintage Wheatley fly box with a pewter surface. Maybe he had been wrong about Willoughby.

"Take a close look at the flies, Sean. How would you characterize them?"

Sean reached into the breast pocket of his fishing shirt and removed a pair of half-glasses with a 3X magnifying lens that he used to knot Griffiths gnats and other will-of-the-wisp flies to his leader tippet. He carried the box to the fly-tying table and found the switch for a goosenecked lamp. He peered through the clear lids of the spring-loaded compartments, where the dry flies stood at attention on their hackle tips. He took the glasses off.

"They're exquisite. I had no idea that Kenneth Winston—that's the name of the man who lost the box—was such a talented tier. He's a black man who runs a hair salon in the South. Seems an unlikely candidate. You don't see too many black fly fishermen in Montana, or anywhere for that matter."

"Kenneth Winston is in the upper tier of the best fly tiers in the United States." Willoughby announced it as a fact.

Sean smiled. So he had been right. He said, "Mr. Winston didn't lose this fly box on the river, did he? That was just the excuse to have me come down here to meet you." He snapped shut the box and placed it on the coffee table. He waited, listening to the crickets rubbing their legs together outside the cottage. He supposed he should feel like a fool for falling for another of Winston's lies, but whatever the reason for his being lured here, it had to be more interesting than the simple recovery of a fly box. And he *was* interested.

Sean realized, as he took a sip of his whiskey, that he had been leading a largely pedestrian life since the previous summer. He painted pictures and he guided anglers. The day-to-day provided a living, albeit a tenuous one sans health insurance and proper sleeping quarters, but it didn't elevate his heart rate. The bodies on the mountain engaged his fascination, but Martha Ettinger had made clear that his involvement would remain marginal. The one case of investigation he had taken on since the spring had not tested his abilities. He'd solved it with two gallons of gas and a knock on a door. Waiting for Willoughby to explain, he remembered that day.

The client, a trust fund hobby architect named Garrett Anker, was very grateful to discover that his one-night stand had not resulted in a progeny he would be obligated to support. The one-night stand was very happy to inform Stranahan that she had flushed the entire incident from her mind, right down the toilet with the blue strip of her pregnancy test. Why hadn't the bastard called her himself if he was so fucking worried? Stranahan didn't have the heart to tell her that his client had forgotten the woman's name, along with where and how he'd met her. All Anker had given Sean to go on was something a friend had said about seeing him, Anker, outside the Molly

bar with a "skank" who was wearing a pink sweatshirt with puppies
or maybe kittens on it. The friend had noticed the sweatshirt only
because he suspected it concealed a pair of "swinging hoochie mamas." Anker did recall that the trailer where the woman led him
must have been right by the railroad tracks. The trains thundering
by literally shook the bed. It had seemed erotic enough at the time,
right until she threw up into her toilet. The gagging had made his
own gorge rise and he had stumbled out the door to vomit on the
grass. From there he could see some lights from a restaurant that
looked like a log cabin. It was the only business in the town. "It was
nowhere, man," Anker had said. "I don't know how the fuck I drove
myself back." Sean had thought: Logan, the Land of Sirloin Steak-
house. The second trailer door he knocked on, a woman opened
it. She had bloodshot eyes in a smoker's face, the pupils shrinking as
she peered skeptically at Stranahan or maybe just at the daylight in
general. She said, "Was it you?" Then: "No, I don't get that kind of
luck at two in the morning.

"Well, shit," she had said. "You drove all this way. Come in. Take a
load off." Stranahan had declined the offer, though it looked like the
friend had been right about the hoochie mamas. She could have held
up a bank with them.

"Sean, you seem to be somewhere else." Willoughby peered at him
with his eyebrows arched.

"I was thinking about the amnesia of alcohol. When I was an investigator, I found I could make a living off it."

"What exactly did you investigate?"

"Wrath. Greed. Sloth. Pride. Lust. Envy. And gluttony."

"Ah, the seven deadly sins."

"What sin is it that caused you to seek my help?"

"Avarice or envy. Possibly both."

"Why don't you tell me about it? And why the mystery? You could
have called. I'm not hard to find."

"Quite right, maybe I should have. But I didn't know your name until yesterday. And then when Kenneth suggested that we engage your services, I felt I needed to ascertain your suitability for the club. If you agree to help us, it would mean that you would have quite a bit of interaction with the members. We are on vacation here and we—and I speak for all of us—are determined that the problem that has arisen does not detract from our time together. Frankly, none of us with the exception of Kenneth are young. We don't worry the small stuff anymore, or even the big stuff unless it involves a matter of health. I would rather not resolve this issue if your presence proved disruptive."

"So this evening was an audition. To see if I met your standards?"

"Yes. But to tell you the truth, as soon as I saw the stem of that pipe sticking from your pocket and the bamboo rod I knew you would be the best possible fit."

"Kenneth," Stranahan said, as if the word were new to the tongue. "I'm not sure he's told me the truth about anything since I've met him."

"Kenneth is exactly who he told you he was. When he booked you to fish, that's what he wanted to do, fish. Then when he found out who you were from your friend, Mr. Meslik, we came up with a plan to lure you down here. It was the club's money Kenneth paid you. I thought if we brought you here under false pretense, you deserved to be compensated regardless of the outcome."

"So those really are his flies in the box?"

"Indeed so. Sean, when I say Kenneth is in the upper tier of our country's fly tiers I mean the top twenty, the top three if you limit the discussion to the Catskill school of tying. If you agree to take our money you will meet a couple of his peers who are much better known. You may recognize the names."

Sean swallowed the last of his whiskey.

"Let me refill that." Willoughby came back with the two tin cups. He leaned forward in his chair, his owl-like eyes narrowed as he fixed Sean with a look of scrutiny. No downward glance, no bashful expression now.

"What do you know about collecting fishing flies? Let me put that another way. What would be the most sought-after flies for a collector?"

Sean searched the dusty drawers of his mind for a name. "Dame Juliana Something-or-other. The English nun. Wasn't she the first person to write about fly fishing? Back in the fifteenth or sixteenth century? I remember a rumor about her tying flies with the fur of her cats. I think one of her flies would bring an awful lot of money."

Willoughby was nodding his head. "One of Juliana Berner's flies would indeed bring a pretty penny today. Unfortunately, the good Dame's existence may be as much a rumor as her method of tying. She is given credit for writing *A Treatise of Fishing with an Angle* in the second edition of *The Boke of St. Albans*, in 1496. But there are no records of her in Sopwell Abbey, where she was supposedly a prioress, so it may well be that Dame Juliana only exists because we want her to. She is fly fishing's Eve, as the historian Paul Shullery said. She gives our sport a tidy source of origin."

"If not her, then what about some of the fancy salmon flies, or a trout fly tied by someone like Rube Cross."

"You bring up two distinct categories of collecting. First, collecting with regard to beauty and intricacy of construction, such as salmon flies. A Green Highlander or Jock Scott from a classicist such as Polly Sorenson is a work of art incorporating exotic feathers and requiring several hours to tie. The second category are flies tied by famous fishermen, such as Lee Wulff or Art Flick. Who would you say is the most famous trout fisherman our country has produced?"

"That's easy. Theodore Gordon."

"You know your history. Gordon, who was tubercular and somewhat of a hermit, took English fly patterns and reinvented them to match the hatching insects in New York's Catskill rivers. Wrongly or rightly, he is considered the father of American dry fly fishing. He was quite secretive about his tying methods, and most of his flies disappeared in the lips of trout or in the trees banking his beloved Neversink River. He died in 1915 in the Anson Knight House, which today is buried several hundred feet beneath the surface of the Neversink Reservoir. If there were any remaining flies in that house they rusted away seven decades ago. His most famous pattern is the Quill Gordon, tied to represent the *Epeorus pleuralis* mayfly. Few of verifiable provenance have ever been offered at auction."

"If one did surface, how much would you expect to have to bid?"

"Seventeen thousand five hundred dollars," Willoughby said without hesitation.

Sean took a sip of bourbon, set the cup down, and walked over to the bookcase. On the wall above it, several flies were displayed in shadow boxes under pictures of the men and women who had tied them. He found what he was looking for, a grainy black-and-white photo of a waiflike, mustachioed man standing calf deep in a trout stream, wicker creel on his hip and a cane rod in his hand. Under the photo was an inset for a fly but no fly in the inset, and under the inset the words *#12 Quill Gordon tied by Theodore Gordon, circa 1910.*

"How long's it been missing?"

"Since Sunday. There's another fly missing as well." He indicated a box on the wall near the doorway. It also displayed a photograph, this one of a woman with curly hair. The inset for the fly was empty. "A vintage Gray Ghost tied by its originator, Carrie Stevens from Upper Dam, Maine," Willoughby said. "She was a self-taught tier of the mid-twentieth century who developed many streamer patterns that are still fished today. This particular Ghost has sentimental value. It isn't as valuable as the Gordon fly, but as it is irreplaceable, the loss is equally disturbing."

"Did you report the thefts?"

"What good would it do? It would just go into the police log and then the paper would pick it up and maybe our club would come to the attention of someone else with a larcenous heart. We don't like to draw attention here." Willoughby had crossed over to the bookcase. He handed Sean his whiskey cup.

"You drew someone's," Sean said.

"We did. We'd like you to find who that was."

CHAPTER SEVEN

Valley Fever

"**Y**ou didn't have to come down. It will be in my report in a couple hours."

"Trust me, Doc, when a cadaver dog sniffs out two John Does buried in Hyalite County, I don't wait for information to cross my desk."

"I know you don't, Martha. But what you're going to see doesn't wash off in the shower. Put it this way. If you had any romantic plans tonight, you might want to tell your beau to hold the Viagra. You aren't going to be in the mood."

"I'm a big girl, you know that."

"Then go ahead and gown up. You know where."

"You want me to scrub?" Ettinger's voice came from the morgue changing room.

"We reserve that for patients with a pulse."

Ettinger's feet in the blue paper slippers made no sound on the marble floor. Doc Hanson was bent over two stainless steel trays set on a long counter, at one end of which squatted the matte black microscope that dated to his childhood. In one tray lay a spongy, tube-shaped organ about ten inches long, with a tail-like protrusion. The other tray displayed a puddle of revolting tissue, purple-gray and gelatinous. The antiseptic chemicals that gave the room a tart Mr. Clean scent couldn't overcome the smell of offal.

"Before we start," Hanson said, "the freezer burn on the epidermal tissues supports a death before freeze-up. Otherwise, the body could not have been buried. Decomposition is fairly minimal. I'd guess late fall. Quite frankly, if it was much older than that, even the bears would have given him a pass."

"Just so we're on the same page, you're talking about John Doe the first, the body unearthed by the grizzly."

"I'm sorry. I should have made that clear."

"Cause of death is gunshot, right?"

"Well, the holes in the skull are consistent with a gunshot wound. But I found no traces of copper or lead indicating passage of a bullet. That isn't conclusive. If the bullet remained intact, it could have passed through without leaving a trace; in fact, one would expect it to. The holes also could have been made by the teeth of that grizzly. Speaking of which, the bear ingested approximately half the chest, much of the buttocks, and the left thigh, so possible evidence sites of other wounds are missing. The skull has the two craters you inadvertently uncovered." Hanson peered at Ettinger over his glasses. "Next time I trust you'll be more careful."

"Yeah, yeah," Martha said.

"Would you like to see it?"

Ettinger nodded. "Maybe I'll get a better sense of what this guy looked like when he was walking around."

"Of course. I'll be just a minute."

Martha walked to one of the shuttered windows that looked out onto Gallatin Avenue. She pinched back several slats of the blind. Outside, two male finches engaged in a war dance of fluttering feathers, fighting over position at a bird feeder suspended from the limb of a mountain maple.

"Feeling claustrophobic, are we, Martha?"

She released the slats and the rectangle the sun's rays had inscribed on the floor vanished. "Just reassuring myself that life goes on."

Doc Hanson nodded. "My wife wonders why I insist on being outdoors on the weekends. She thinks we've reached an age where joining a book club or inviting the friends for cards are more sensible options. She thinks canoe trips through the White Cliffs of the Missouri are evidence of a midlife crisis. I tell her I'd rather have a new truck than a Ferrari and I don't need assurance of my virility by having an affair. But I do insist on spending as much time as I can under that big blue dome, whether it's with a fly rod in my hand or a Sawyer canoe paddle. Have you read *This House of Sky*, by Ivan Doig? The title says it. Truest words about this state ever written."

Suddenly Hanson looked away. He took off his glasses and rubbed a blue latex fist in his eye. Ettinger could see his walrus mustache quiver.

"Are you all right, Doc?"

"I'm just turning goddamned sentimental in my old age. I seem to get on the verge of tears for no reason. I'm sorry, Martha. Where were we?"

"Under this house of artificial light. You were going to show me a skull."

Hanson indicated a third steel tray that he'd set on the counter. "Better brace yourself," he said.

It was worse than she'd thought.

"I liked him better up on the mountain, when he looked deader," she said.

"Strange, isn't it? He still has his skin, what was left of his hair. He doesn't look dead a week, let alone six months."

"What he looks like is a head on a stake."

Hanson ignored the comment. "He has good bone structure, his teeth show top-quality dental work, the eyes are wide-set, chin is strong, he has an aquiline nose. You wouldn't think it, but I would guess this was a good-looking man, even distinguished. Moderately receding hairline. Still some brown in with the gray. Good muscle tone. I did some bone measurements. About five-nine, in the neighborhood of a hundred sixty pounds."

Ettinger swallowed.

"You've seen enough?" Hanson looked over his glasses again.

She nodded. "How about this other stuff? What's up with the goo?"

"The goo, as you so eloquently put it, consists of the pancreas"—Hanson pointed to the tray containing the corrugated, tubelike organ—"and"—he indicated the purple-gray puddle—"what remains of the left and caudate lobes of the man's liver."

"You could have fooled me," Martha said.

"Have a look through the microscope."

"You like to prolong the agony, don't you?"

"What, Martha? Is everything all right?"

Ettinger blew out a breath and chuckled. "Okay. I deserved that. Now, are you going to tell me something that brings us closer to identifying these bodies, or aren't you?"

"The best I can do is point you in a direction you can further explore."

Ettinger took a seat and bent her eye to the lens. "Is this a biopsy sample?"

"Yes. You're looking at cells from a lymph node near the tail of the pancreas. You'll notice that several of the cells look abnormal. That indicates a cancer."

"So was it malignant?"

"Without getting too clinical about it, I also found tumors in the liver. Cancer that begins in the pancreas and spreads to other organs is called metastatic pancreatic cancer. It's malignant and it's incurable."

"How do you know it wasn't liver cancer that spread to the pancreas?"

"Because the cancerous cells in the liver resemble abnormal versions of cells found in the organ of origin, the pancreas. The spread occurs when clusters of cancer cells are carried through the bloodstream or lymphatic tubes to other organs. Pancreatic cancer commonly metastasizes in the liver."

"I'll take your word. So what's the story?"

"The story is that we're talking about a man, probably in his sixties or seventies, who had a life expectancy of less than a year."

"Could he have climbed halfway up a mountain?"

"Cancer patients are up and down. That's not intended as a pun. He may have been at a point where the bad days predominated, but on a good day, if he was otherwise in decent health—and from what I can see he was—I would say yes, it is possible."

Ettinger put her chin in her hand. She noticed that she was no longer smelling offal. It was there only if she thought about it. "So tell me about the other victim," she said. "I'm assuming it's a he."

Hanson nodded. "Late middle age. Shorter than the first victim, about five-seven. But powerfully built. An injury to the ribs on the lower left chest quadrant, in fact a rather large hole."

"Too big for a gunshot wound?"

"Not at all. Gunshot trauma is possible, but after this much deterioration, it may be hard to prove. However, there *is* something about the body I find very interesting, and unlike the rib injury, it's definite." He led Martha to the examining table in the middle of the room. He switched on the overhead ultraviolet lights and drew back the sheet.

"Mother of mercy."

"Do you need to take a minute?"

"No, I just have to remember to breathe through my nose." She studied the naked skull, the careful arrangement of rib cage and bones, including the exposed femur covered in lichen that Sean Stranahan had found. The bones weren't the problem. It was what passed for flesh, a clingy organic gauze that stretched across the skeleton.

"Are you going to torment me, or can we just cut to the chase?"

Hanson was unfazed. "I want to draw your attention to the skin." He pointed with his probe to a raised, weltlike line on the right upper thigh. "Dermal lesions can be difficult to distinguish after this much decomposition, but"—he moved the instrument—"the spinal column and skull contain evidence of permanent bone damage—right under the probe here, see? These lesions are much more apparent and very telling, if you know what you are looking at. This is unusual stuff, Martha."

"What is it, some rare cancer?"

"No, not cancer. This damage was caused by a severe fungal infection, I'd bet my license on it. But if I hadn't done my internship at Kern Medical in Bakersfield, I'd be scratching my head."

"But since you're not scratching your head . . ."

"Have you heard of valley fever?"

"You mean what those girls who go to dude ranches come down with when the local cowboys saddle them up? No, Doc, of course I don't know what valley fever is. In fact, you can just assume that any question you give me, the answer's going to be a 'no,' so why don't you just tell me what you're going to tell me without the interrogation. The sooner you put the sheet back over this table the better."

"I didn't know I was interrogating you, Martha. I mean Sheriff."

Martha blew out her breath. "Do I have to say I'm sorry? It seems like I'm saying it all the time lately."

"No, Martha, you don't. Just like Warren said, 'When it comes to you, we take the whiskey with the wine.'"

"How do you know he said that? You weren't there that day."

"It must have been a bird that told me."

"Yeah, a bird about five foot ten who calls himself Walt and used to be a cop in Chicago. Maybe that kind of bird?"

"Or another."

They looked at each other across the pile of bones that was John Doe the second.

"We'd have made a good married couple," Hanson said. "We bicker like one."

"Oh, you couldn't have handled me."

"That's just it. I wouldn't have tried."

"Well, hell, Doc, where were you fifteen years ago?" Martha felt that they had breached a barrier. For the first time in the decade she'd known Doc, she was really talking to him, not just sparring or extracting information. The bones no longer seemed to be in the room.

"I was already twenty years married," he was saying. "Either I was born too soon or you were born too late."

Martha's voice was reflective. "That's the story of life, isn't it? Timing's never been my strong suit."

"So how are you really doing? Are you happy? Is this thing you have with Harold going anywhere?"

"I don't know, Bob. It isn't so much the cultural difference. Harold moves back and forth from the reservation with a lot less baggage than most Indians. But we've both been divorced and had our share of disappointments. You grow older, you get set in your ways and it's harder to bend. You know what I mean?"

"I do." He paused a moment. "That Sean Stranahan seems like a fine young man. Calls me 'sir.' And he's so damned handsome he makes me feel like a cactus. But I can't say I know him."

"Sean is . . . different. He comes across this one way, friendly and, I'm looking for a word—self-deprecating. He seems so open, but he keeps a lot back. I think there were things in his past that haunt him. I know he was pretty young when his father died . . . but you wouldn't think so when you're around him because he's got this youthful optimism. And he's like a magnet. It's uncanny. I walk out of Law and Justice, go around the block, maybe a dog poops in a yard. Sean takes a walk, a tree falls on someone, he's there in the middle of it, blood up to his elbows. He's just one of those people who open the door and things happen to them." She stopped, a look of perplexity crossing her face. "Jesus, Doc, how the hell did we get started on Sean Stranahan?" She permitted a smile. "I must be getting to be an old-timer like you, shooting the breeze while people are rotting under my fingers."

"Martha, I love you for all your warts and graces."

"Who said that? Some poet I ought to feel bad about not knowing, right?"

"I did. Let's talk about valley fever."

Valley fever, Hanson explained, was caused by a soil fungus breathed into the lungs after being stirred up by wind or, particularly, by agriculture. The initial symptoms were flulike—headache, fever, cough, chills, night sweats. Rashes might appear, typically on the legs. In more severe cases, the victim could experience weight loss, expel blood-tinged sputum, and develop severe chest pain, not dissimilar to tuberculosis. In the worst cases of valley fever, the infection spread beyond the lungs to other parts of the body, into bones, the heart, and notably into the meninges, the membranes that protect the brain and spinal cord. The lesions Hanson had found on the spinal column and skull indicated a severe case of spinal meningitis. He showed Martha where the hair clinging to the lower skull looked to have been shaved away. Hanson said the site was where a doctor would typically perform a cistern tap, removing spinal fluid and mixing it with antifungal drugs for reinjection. The drugs were toxic, with the worst being amphotericin B, known as "Ampho the Terrible." For some patients there was no end in sight for the painful procedures, the chronic pneumonia and tuberculosis symptoms, the aching in the bones, and quality of life greatly suffered. The suicide rate among advanced cases was high.

"So exactly how does this point me in the right direction?" Martha said. "I was hoping for a relationship between the victims."

"There is one. They were both older men who could still get around, but had nothing to look forward to but pain and suffering."

"So you're thinking this was some kind of suicide pact? A burial ground for the walking dead, like an elephant graveyard kind of thing? That sounds macabre."

"I'm just pointing out that their conditions and outlooks on life may have been similar."

"I wish there was more."

Doc Hanson smiled. He felt guilty, but couldn't help saving his most important discovery for last.

He said, "I told you I interned in Bakersfield, California. The only reason I know so much about valley fever is because the infections are specific to the Southwest. Bakersfield has the highest incidence, but clusters of infection also occur in Tucson and Phoenix. There's a very good chance that your victim contracted valley fever in or around one of those three places."

"It would be nice if we could narrow that down."

Hanson held up a hand. "I'm not done. Valley fever is still fairly rare, given the incidence of exposure to the fungus. No matter where they live, almost everyone who seeks treatment for an advanced case sees the same doctor, Boyd Mathis. Boyd is the chief of infectious diseases at Kern Medical Center in Bakersfield. He was one of my supervisors when I was in residency. The man we're looking at is probably in his records."

Martha let the information sink in.

"Doc," she said, "I could kiss you but I'm not going to."

"I still might make you change your mind about that," he said. "Valley fever is much more prevalent among blacks and Latinos than the Caucasian population. The strands of this man's hair lack pigment at the temples, but on top of his head they are jet black with perfectly round structure. That's a very common hair type for many Latinos." He held up a finger. "Nothing definitive, understand, we also can have jet black hair, but in whites the trait is recessive. And valley fever only discriminates to a degree. Particularly the elderly, asthmatics, and people who have suppressed immune symptoms are vulnerable, regardless of heritage. But the nature of the disease, its locale, and the hair make it fairly likely that this man was Latino."

Martha stroked her fingers down the left line of her jaw. "Can you put a date of death on this guy?"

"Assuming he was underground the entire time? You take into

consideration rates of decomposition of bone, organs, and dermal tissues, seasonal temperature swings and so forth, it points to some-time last summer. Boyd treats a lot of people, but he might remember a late-middle-aged Latino patient who disappeared last summer. I could give him a call."

Martha moved her fingers to her throat, feeling for the pulse. It was a habit she had when she felt scared or inadequate, but as she had become more certain of herself, she also sought the reassurance of her heartbeat when she was excited, when she felt on the cusp of discovery. If she could ID this body, the dominoes would start to fall. It was like hunting elk, finding a fresh track after days of old sign. The elk might be miles away, but it was there, standing at the end of its tracks. You just had to work out the trail.

"What are you thinking about, Martha?"

"Come here," she said. "I'm going to plant a wet one right on the corner of that mustache."

CHAPTER EIGHT

Quest for Metal

Stranahan stumbled to his desk for the phone.

"Who is it?"

"It's Katie Sparrow." A moment of silence. "You know, Katie the dog handler."

"Yes, Katie." Stranahan glanced outside his gallery window, a wafer of pearl showing above the Bridger Peaks. The old cottonwoods on the grounds of the cultural center were frozen in silhouette, the night still grappling for purchase.

"I know it's early—"

"Five a.m.," Stranahan interrupted.

"—but you didn't seem like the kind of guy who sleeps in."

"It's no problem, Katie. What's up?"

"I got to thinking, you and me, we make a good team. I got today off and thought maybe we could climb the Sphinx. I have an idea how we could find a bullet up there. You could meet me at the trailhead up Bear Creek in an hour or so. Unless you're guiding, I didn't think about that."

"I'm not guiding. What did Ettinger say?"

"I didn't call her. I thought just you and me, a couple enterprising civilians, we could go on a treasure hunt. It's not like it's a crime scene with ribbon around it."

"Actually, it is."

"You know what I mean. The trail's cold. Martha's going to work the forensic end, but with Harold in the hospital there's no reason for anyone in the department to make the climb again. So whatcha think? You wanna?"

Stranahan thought a second. Sam had booked a guide trip for him tomorrow and he'd been invited to dinner at the Madison River Liars and Fly Tiers Club later that evening, to meet with the other members who would be flying in. The only mark on his calendar today was a date at seven with Martinique.

"Yeah, I wanna."

"So what's your bright idea, Katie?"

The dog handler was sitting in the cab of her pickup at the trailhead at the Bear Creek Forest Service Station, Lothar riding shotgun. The skirts of the mountain slept in the deep shadow cast by the Sphinx's subordinate sister, a towering eruption of striated limestone known as the Helmet.

"It's in my pack." Katie rummaged around behind the seat of the F-150. Sean glanced at the protruding handle of the black metal tool.

"What's that, a metal detector?"

"It's a Bounty Hunter Tracker. I went out with a guy who fancied himself a treasure hunter. He was always looking for battlefield bullets, like in the Powder River country, or up in the Bear Paws where Chief Joseph surrendered. After that last little incident that we won't go into, he didn't have the nerve to come back and ask for it. He knew Lothar would rip his throat out." She clicked her fingers and the shepherd bounded out of the truck.

"Rip his throat out?" Stranahan said.

"As in kill the motherfucker."

"You sound dangerous to be around."

"Not as dangerous as Julie Godfrey."

"Who?"

"Julie Godfrey. She's the wife of that asshole we were looking for when Lothar found the body. You didn't hear?"

Stranahan shook his head.

Katie reached down and scratched Lothar's ears. "You're anxious to go, aren't you boy? Let's get going. I'll tell you up—"

The shepherd barked, then bolted from Katie's feet and raced up the trail.

"Whoa!"

The dog abruptly obeyed, but his nose was still pointed away. His whole body quivered.

"Heel." In three seconds Lothar was back at Sparrow's feet, his head bowed and his tail down.

"Bad dog." And to Stranahan. "It's all in the tone. That counts more than the words." She spoke to him in a tone that said he was the one who had chased the cat up the tree, not the shepherd. For that was what had happened. Lothar had treed a large, long-haired cat that was now peering down at them with alarmed eyes from twenty feet up a Ponderosa pine.

"How the hell did a cat get out here?" Stranahan said.

"'Cause somebody got tired of him and didn't have the guts to pull the trigger. So they drove him up here and threw him out. It happens every day. Get tired of your cat, throw it to the coyotes. Get tired of your dog, throw it to the wolves. That's folks for you. That's why I stick with animals."

She directed her speech at the shepherd. "Except for you, lover. A Class Three ought to know better than to chase a cat. You're in the doghouse.

"Come on," she said to Stranahan. "Let's get up there before the sun gets too hot. That cat's not going to come down until we're gone."

This early in the summer, the path up the Trail Fork of Bear Creek was a slog, requiring four creek crossings in the first two miles. It was cool and misty in the timber as Sean and Katie navigated puddles looking at their boots, while the shepherd, chastised, obediently followed at Sparrow's heels. Lothar's tongue was hanging out by the time they reached the trail junction in the big meadow from which a hiker has his first glimpse of the Helmet's red pinnacle, and farther east, bulking immensely against the skyline, the limestone extrusion that is the Sphinx.

At the junction, Sean and Katie took the 326 trail to the left, which ascended in switchbacks for another three miles before reaching a saddle between the two great mountains. To the right of the saddle, a shoulder of the Sphinx rose in a series of small benches to the timberline, above which the slope inclined steeply toward the peak. It was on one of the upper benches, grown over in scattered pines and strewn with great rocks, that the grizzly had unearthed the first body. The crime scene tape had torn in the night wind and was strung across the ground.

"Spooky, isn't it?" Stranahan said. They were sharing one of the sandwiches he had made and swapping swigs of iced tea from Katie's Nalgene bottle.

"Nah, it's just woods." Katie released the drawstring of her pack and extracted the metal detector. She pressed a keypad and pointed the four-inch-diameter coil at Sean's jaw. The detector buzzed, picking up the fillings in his teeth.

"Yeah," Stranahan said, "but can it find a bullet buried in a tree trunk? I thought these things could only isolate metal if it was buried shallow, a few inches under the ground."

"Well, you figure the bullet makes a hole going into the tree, right? Unless the tree healed up, you'd have a clear path to the bullet."

Stranahan looked skeptical. "Didn't they already use a metal detector the day we found that bone?"

"They only used it where the bodies were buried. Come on," Katie said. "I thought you were an optimist. Have a little faith."

She started fiddling with an adjustment device on the tool. "This is your basic model," she said, "but I can tune it to discriminate metals. Like, if you know the bullet you're looking for has a copper jacket,

you can weed out other metals. That can save a lot of time at an ur-
ban crime scene. But I figure up here there's not going to be a lot of
trash, so we'll just set it to all metals."

"Do you have a plan?"

"Hey, I brought the detector. I'm going to leave it to you to come
up with the plan."

"There's too many trees to try to search every one, so I think we
should start here at body one and conduct a diameter search, working out, say, thirty yards or so, then move on to body two and do the
same thing."

"Let's do it."

Two hours later, they had exhausted Stranahan's plan, including
broadening the search area to a fifty-yard diameter around each
burial site, and had found only one piece of metal, a discolored gold
band that had prompted them to utter the same words—"wedding
ring." The ring had been buried under several inches of loose duff at
the base of a spruce tree, on the upper-level bench where they had
unearthed the second body.

"Were either of those guys wearing rings?" Katie said. She blew a
sweat-damp strand of hair out of her eyes.

Stranahan shook his head. "I'm not even sure the second guy had
fingers."

"It's something, though. See, this wasn't for nothing like you were
thinking it was going to be."

In fact, Stranahan was thinking about dinner with Martinique. It
was already early afternoon and they'd need to get going fairly soon
if he was to make it back in time. He slipped the band over his ring
finger and slipped it off.

"He had big fingers," Katie said.

"Like a rancher," Stranahan said.

Katie drew a dog biscuit out of her shirt pocket and snapped off an
ear for Lothar. She snapped off the other ear, cracked that one in
half, and handed a piece to Stranahan.

"Come on, take it. They're gourmet." She popped her half into her mouth.

Stranahan bit off a corner. A little dry, not much flavor. But it wasn't bad.

"I suppose you've heard they call me 'Dog Breath,'" she said, "'cause I eat biscuits. I say if you really want to find out, all you have to do is kiss me."

It was an awkward moment, for they were standing far enough apart that one or the other would have had to step closer to be in range of a kiss, and as the moment passed, Katie made light of the situation by saying, "You know, in the interests of science and all."

"Oh," Stranahan said, "I doubt you'd have anything to worry about."

"You ever want to find out for yourself, I promise I'll keep my dog from tearing your throat out." Now she was teasing him.

"So what was it you were going to tell me about Gordon Godfrey's wife? Before Lothar chased that cat up the tree?"

"Oh, that. If I tell you, it might put you off kissing women for good."

"Tell me."

"Okay. So, Julie finds out her husband was cheating on her with the woman in West Yellowstone, right? He's buying her flowers, sleeping on the couch like a good boy, promising it was nothing and will never happen again, he's just been under all this stress. Yada yada. And after a few days pass, this would be the day before yesterday, she acts like she's going to give in and they share a bottle of wine and he thinks, you know, makeup sex, he's going to get lucky. What he doesn't know is that Julie went to the antique store in Ennis and bought the biggest branding iron on the wall. It was from a ranch called the Triple Star R and it's got three stars circling a capital letter R, the whole thing being like, yea big." She made a circle the size of a soccer ball with the thumbs and forefingers of both hands.

"How do you know all this?"

"One of the neighbors breeds Aussie shepherds. She's friends with the woman. Do you want to hear or not?"

Stranahan faced both hands up—*go on*.

"So anyway, they drink another bottle of wine and she takes him to bed and they do the nasty, 'cause she knows it will make him pass out afterward. Plus like she's feeling sorry for him knowing what's going to happen and he deserves a goodbye fuck, the fucker. Once he's snoring she turns the main water supply off in the basement. Then she builds a fire in the woodstove and sticks the iron in it. She leaves it there while she drinks another glass of wine and contemplates the shitty state of her marriage. When it's glowing a bright red she straddles good old Gordon and brings her hands over her head and hesitates—the heart or the belly? She decides belly 'cause she's afraid he'll have a heart attack if she aims high."

Katie made a downward stabbing motion with one fist on top of the other. She made a sizzling sound.

"He sits bolt upright like someone stuck an adrenaline needle in his heart. I mean, you can imagine. Then he starts running around the house, screaming. He turns on the shower, figuring to stop the burn with cold water, but there's no water. And the wife, standing at the door, says, 'Gee, Gordon, I wonder what happened? Somebody must have turned the water off.' By now he's like making animal sounds and people on the block are turning on the lights, wondering what's going on. They see this naked man running in circles around his yard, keening like a skunked puppy. Finally he finds a little ditch that's damp 'cause it rained the day before and he flops himself down in it. Somebody 911s and when the medics arrive they see this guy with his bare butt sticking up and a bunch of people standing around in PJs."

Katie paused. "Anyway," she said, "she branded the bastard. She says the thing she'll never forget was the smell. When she stuck the iron on him it smelled like the neighbors were having pork barbecue."

"Jesus," Stranahan said.

"I knew I shouldn't have told you."

"What happened to them?"

"He's up in Deaconess. Julie was arrested, but old Gordon said he didn't want to press charges. If he did it would be public and everybody in town would know. But pretty much everyone does anyway. So"—she bent down and rubbed her face against the muzzle of Lothar—"are we done here? Those clouds look like hail to me. I don't think we're going to find a bullet."

"I have one more idea," Stranahan said. "So far we've just searched the vicinity of the burial sites. But where the second guy was buried, it's so thick up there you can't see the spot until you're standing on it. But that aspen stand on the left is more open. Maybe that's where the shooter saw him, and he shot him and the guy ran into the timber where he died. The bullet would be buried in the open ground, the one place we really haven't looked."

"You're thinking like an elk hunter," Katie said. "Not a murderer."

Stranahan shrugged. "It wouldn't take long to sweep it."

"You just want more of my company, admit it."

"Humor me, as Martha would say."

"She's a piece of work, isn't she? I thought she'd be like, more human once she was getting laid regular. But Harold doesn't seem to have made much of an inroad. She's still wound tight as a tick."

Stranahan didn't want to talk about Martha and Harold. "If you don't mind my asking," he said, "what's under your shirt that you're always rubbing between your fingers?"

"That's my sweetie," she said, pulling out a worn brass locket. She opened it so Stranahan could lean close and see the photo.

He was embarrassed. The man in the picture was young, hardly more than a boy. He'd heard that Katie Sparrow had had a boyfriend who drowned in an avalanche. The story was that watching the avalanche dogs work as they looked for the body was what had spurred her interest in search and rescue, and she'd become a handler as a result.

"I'm sorry, Katie, I didn't know."

"It's okay. It was a long time ago. Colin's my good-luck charm. He keeps me safe when I'm in the mountains. Him and Lothar."

"He looks like a nice young man."

"He was a sweetie," Katie said. She offered up a smile, her eyes far away for a moment, and dropped the locket back under her shirt.

Fifteen minutes later, Sparrow's detector buzzed as it passed over a knuckled aspen root that had spread into the open area, twenty feet from the treeline.

She swept it back—*buzz*—and forth—*buzz*.

"Jiminy Crickets." She fell to her knees and began to dig into the root with the knife of her multitool.

"I'm shaking," Katie said. "Feel." She put Stranahan's hand on her arm. "We might really have something here, you know it?"

After a minute she sat back. "Damn, that root's tough as bear hide."

Stranahan, squatting beside her, said, "Can you see a place a bullet might have gone in?"

"There's a bunch of scars. But they're all healed up."

"Can you fine-tune the detector to get a more specific location?"

"Not really. It's getting me within a few inches. Maybe we should dig around and expose the whole root."

"Do you have a saw on your Leatherman? We could cut out a cross section."

"That's a good idea," Katie said.

Ten minutes later, she handed Stranahan a ten-inch section of heavy root. It was as big around as a softball. She passed the detector around the root to make sure the metal that set it off hadn't passed through to lodge in the ground. The signal indicated it was there, buried in the root. Katie took the instrument and turned the discrimination adjustment so that it would only react to copper. The coil passed across the root, passed back, nothing.

She squinched up one side of her face. "Most bullets have copper jackets," she said. She adjusted the dial to isolate lead. Again, nothing.

"Then it's not a bullet," she said. "Goldang it. I was sure we'd found one."

"Keep fiddling with that thing."

A minute later she had isolated the source of the reaction. It was steel.

"Bullets that don't expand have steel jackets. Like military bullets, right?"

"Yes." Stranahan's voice was skeptical. "But even steel-jacketed bullets have a lead core. The detector should have picked it up. But it could still be evidence. As much as I'd like to dig it out, I'm thinking we're already in trouble for climbing up here on our own. We probably should hand it to Martha as is, rather than dig into it and take a chance on damaging something."

"Now you sound like Warren Jarrett," Katie said. "I've been on like a hundred searches with him and I swear the man has a balance scale in his brain. He balances everything out before making a decision. I can't remember a single time he didn't do the prudent thing. It drives me crazy." She made a face. "But yeah, you're probably right. You're going to have to take it in, though. I got to wear my pointy hat for the next four days."

"I'll give you full credit. It was your idea."

"You're such a stand-up guy. Isn't he a stand-up guy, Lothar?"

"Now you're teasing me."

"You know you like it. Come on, let's get off this mountain before it rains."

CHAPTER NINE

A Night in a Grain Elevator

"**M**y name is Doris. I'll be your server tonight." The woman who had bustled over to the corner table in the dining room of the Cotton-wood Inn extracted a pencil from the tangled curls of her hair. She cocked it over an order pad.

"Well?"

"Aren't you supposed to list the specials?"

The woman looked at Stranahan and pulled half her face into a frown. She said, "I'm sorry, I forget my manners. For the appetizer tonight we have sautéed turkey gizzards in a red wine reduction. The dinner special is a rattlesnake sashimi wrapped in lightly steamed poison oak leaves, served with a bitchin' hot wasabi."

"'Bitchin'?"

"That's what it says on the blackboard. I'm just the messenger."

Beside Stranahan, Martinique shifted in her chair, her lustrous hair swinging forward over the musculature of her shoulders. She looked curiously from one to the other.

"Aren't you going to introduce me to this tall drink of water next to you, Stranny?" the waitress said.

"Doris, this is Martinique. Martinique, Doris. Doris is the first person I met in Bridger. She thinks she's my mother."

"That's because you need one," the waitress said. She pressed the hand Martinique offered between both of hers, leaned down close to her, and whispered, "He thinks he's doing okay, but I grew up on a sheep farm and I know a lost lamb when I see one."

Sean acted as if he hadn't heard. "Doris, Martinique is studying to be a veterinarian."

"Good for you. I never knew what a people doctor was until I had my first baby. If somebody got sick, we just called the vet."

When Martinique lowered her head to look at the menu, Doris got Stranahan's attention, rolled her eyes to the side, and mouthed the word "wow." She took their orders, stuck the pencil back into her hair, wheeled on her heel. When they were alone, Martinique said, "Thank you for taking me here. This place is really beautiful."

Stranahan told her that when the Cottonwood Inn had been built in the 1920s, it served as a gateway hotel to Yellowstone Park, a ninety-mile stagecoach ride up the Gallatin Canyon. Located on a spur of the Chicago, Milwaukee, and St. Paul Railroad, it had been constructed in Spanish style with arched windows and Polynesian mahogany wood-work and had once been named the country's most romantic inn by a bed-and-breakfast association. Which was ironic considering that for most of its history it also had been a whorehouse.

Stranahan stopped, realizing that he was talking just to talk. The fact was it had been years since he'd had an actual date with a woman and he was searching for topics to fill gaps in conversation. The evening hadn't started that way. When he'd knocked on the door of the converted grain elevator out on the road to the Bear Trap, Marti-nique had greeted him with a soft kiss on the corner of his mouth while her fingers sought the snap breast pocket of his print cowboy shirt, the only shirt besides threadbare Sears work shirts that Sean owned.

"What's this?" he'd said, patting the pocket.

"That's your twenty. You never got your coffee or your change."

The inside of the grain elevator was poorly lit and haphazardly furnished. Martinique had told him that a couple from California were planning to renovate the interior next year, making it into a five-story dream house; they had given her lease of the place through January.

An old Formica table with mismatched art deco chairs and a sofa constituted the living and dining quarters. There was a dish of dry cat food with "Attack Cat" scrawled on the side, a water bowl, a litterbox. The only wall decorations were a calendar four months out of date—a snowy landscape photo with a fluffed-up cat sitting atop a weathered fencepost—and a framed photograph of a man and a gangly girl of ten or so standing on a cold-looking beach, "Say cheese" smiles on their faces. The man was holding a bucket; the girl had a shovel in one hand and was extending her other arm, holding what could have been a chip of driftwood.

"Your father?"

She nodded. "I grew up in Grays Harbor. That's a razor clam."

"Idyllic."

"It really was."

But she hadn't elaborated and a few seconds ticked away and then a few more and the silence became heavy. Suddenly they were awkward with each other.

"You promised me cats," he had finally said.

"They're on the bed in the loft." She glanced up, then drifted a hand in the air.

"It's not much," she said, assessing the living space. "But all I do is work and go to class." She turned away to pick up a shawl lying on the sofa and for just a moment her shoulders sagged. The smile she gave Sean on turning around was one of her brave ones.

The awkwardness had continued while they drove to the inn, and now it was there when they were finishing dinner. At his prompting, Martinique had opened up about her background, telling him that she was one-quarter Fulani on her father's side; his father had been a French diplomat who married a Fulani woman from Senegal, Senegal having been a French protectorate. Her mother was a U.S. citizen of Welsh heritage, born into an extended family of Olympic Peninsula loggers. She said if you added up the missing fingers at a family reunion, there would be enough to make two hands. After high school,

Martinique had enrolled at UW, but had left to take care of her father when he became ill. The roundabout route that found her in a bikini in a coffee kiosk and in a bad relationship that made her reevaluate her life wasn't worth going into. She had moved to Montana at a friend's prompting and decided to establish residency, go back to school, and apply to the WICHE program that allowed Montana students to pay in-state tuition at veterinary schools in the Northwest. She'd been accepted at OSU and would be moving to Corvallis, Oregon, to complete her studies next February.

But speaking had been an effort. She had wound down and hadn't seemed interested in Sean's story about moving west. He'd been tempted to fill the void by talking about the mystery piece of metal in the root. But that was police business and he could envision Martha Ettinger's reaction to the disclosure, having withstood his share of withering looks from the sheriff in the past year.

He decided on a more circumspect disclosure, told her he'd been painting and had seen a cat up at the edge of the wilderness. "Like the one on your calendar," he said. "But it was feral and its hair was matted. It had a wild look in its eyes."

It was maybe a Maine coon cat, she said. "Poor thing." Then her shoulders dropped as they had back in her apartment and she closed her eyes, and when she opened them, the irises were glistening. She said, "I'm so sorry for not being good company. I shouldn't have come out tonight. But you were nice and I thought maybe it would do me some good and help give me the strength to face the next few days . . ." She sighed and put a crumpled napkin to the corner of her left eye.

"After I saw you yesterday, Ichiro had a seizure. I took him to Svenson Veterinary and he said I'd done all I could, giving him the fluids, but his kidneys were finally shutting down. Now he won't eat and he had another seizure this morning. And I don't know what to do, have the doctor put him down or just try to keep him as comfortable as I can while he dies. He'll try to hold on, cats that have bonded with you try to hold on, he could live for another three or four days. I was up all last night with him and I don't know if I can take it. So I want you to take me home. I never should have left him, even if it's just a couple hours."

"Yes, of course," Sean said. He placed bills on the table to cover the dinner and Doris's tip and Martinique leaned against him as they walked to the Land Cruiser.

When they got to the grain elevator, she asked him to come in while she checked on the cat. To get to the loft, she had to use the outside stairs, and she was back after a couple minutes to say that Ichiro was sleeping. "All he does is pull himself to the cup of water on the bedstand to drink. He's just going on instinct, trying to dilute the poisons building up in his body. I could give him more fluids, but it would be cruel. It would just draw out the suffering. I'm going to ask you a big favor, Mr. Sean Stranahan. I'm going to ask if you will sleep on the couch tonight. I'll lock Mitsy and Miss Daisy down here where they can sleep with you. Ichiro needs to be alone, and I need to be alone with him. Do you think maybe you could do that for me? I don't have a sleeping bag or anything . . ." She took a big breath, her shoulders falling as she exhaled.

"I have a sleeping bag in the rig," Sean said.

So he lay on the couch with a gray tiger cat in the crook of his knees and a sealpoint Siamese stretched across his neck. He didn't get much sleep and was up at five, having to meet his clients at the Ennis Café in an hour. He was quiet dressing and was lifting the tailgate of the Cruiser when Martinique appeared at the door in a flannel nightgown.

"He's getting weaker," she said. "He wants to be on the floor, so that's where I slept with him. I'm not going in to work. Could you stop by the kiosk and tell Kristin? She'll get a substitute."

"Sure. I have a day float and then I have something else up the Madison. I could stop on my way back, but it could be really late."

"I'd like that. I'll put the key under the mat . . . or here, just take it."

She tucked the key into his shirt pocket and kissed his neck, the gestures not so different from when he had knocked on the door last evening, when she'd kissed the corner of his mouth and it was money she put in his pocket. But there was no space between them now and she clung to him afterward in the half-light of dawn, smelling like Martinique.

CHAPTER TEN

"A Theft of History"

Stranahan was picking up his raft trailer at Sam's place when his cell vibrated. He'd resisted getting one for more than a year, Montana being a state where you could cross three county lines without passing in range of a tower. But now that he worked on call, taking on clients for Sam, he'd had to cave.

"You have some explaining to do." It was Martha Ettinger.

Stranahan put the phone on speaker and set it on the ground. He had dropped off the package with the desk sergeant at the Law and Justice Building last evening, after the sheriff had gone home. He'd been expecting the call.

"Didn't you read my note?" He dropped the tongue of the trailer over the ball hitch.

"I did. And I quote: 'Katie Sparrow and I used a metal detector to find these items near body removal sites on Sphinx Mountain. Unidentified piece of metal buried in root.' End quote. There seems to be something missing here, like permission from the appropriate legal authority."

"As I recall, you told me I could go to Canada if I wanted. All I did was broaden a search we'd already initiated. But Katie gets the credit. The trip was her idea. And the metal detector."

"I'll have a word with her when she comes off park patrol."

"So what was in the root? The metal detector isolated steel."

"That's police business."

Stranahan hooked up the safety chains under the chassis of the Land Cruiser.

Finally: "Where are you?"

He told her.

"Come to my office tomorrow morning. Don't bother to dress. I can find a state-issue jumpsuit in just your size."

The Oglethorpe twins, proprietors of a Ford dealership in Petoskey, Michigan, traded bad casts and finished each other's sentences all day. They gave Stranahan a fifty each for the tip, not bad considering that neither had felt the rod bend since the elder brother—by seven minutes—boated a fifteen-inch brown on the first cast of the morning. It was the closest Stranahan had come to taking a skunking, at least in a professional capacity, and he came off the water knowing a hell of a lot more about the woes of the auto industry than he had at the launch. He hand-cranked the raft onto his trailer and was parking on the grass behind the Madison River Liars and Fly Tiers clubhouse a little past six.

"No trouble finding the place?" Willoughby asked, coming around the corner of the cabin.

Stranahan shook his head. "That's a heck of a house I passed driving off the bench."

"It makes our place look like a shotgun shack. Please join us for drinks on the porch."

Two men rose from Adirondack chairs as Sean climbed the steps. Jonathon Smither was darkly tanned with white teeth and a hail-fellow-well-met smile that went with a two-handed handshake. Ruggedly handsome with dark hair parted to the side, he looked like a '60s cigarette model hunkered before a campfire, rough hands cupped to the flame of a match. Sean placed him in his midforties. By comparison, Robin Hurt Cowdry was sunburnt, sandy-haired, and very slender. Both his voice and age were hard to place.

"Robin is from Zimbabwe," Willoughby said. "He runs a safari outfit in the Okavango Delta, in Botswana. The African artifacts you saw in the clubhouse are his."

"Have you met Joseph Keino?" Sean asked. "He's a Kenyan who owns a bed-and-breakfast in Bridger; it's called the Aberdare."

"I know that old Kikuyu camel thief. I traded him an ironwood sculpture of a Cape buffalo last year for a fine-condition Masai shield. Got the better of him for once."

Stranahan remembered the night he had spent in the little cottage behind Keino's Victorian inn. Vareda Beaudreux, the Mississippi riverboat singer with whom he had done some bartering of his own—his heart and his reason for an awful lot of trouble, he thought wryly—had pinned a note for him under the buffalo's hooves while he slept.

"I saw that sculpture," he said.

"Small world," said Cowdry.

The last club member Willoughby introduced Sean to was bent forward over one of the fly-tying benches at the long table indoors. He peered at Sean through magnifying lenses folded down over his glasses and inclined his head. Returning his attention to his vise, he put a half hitch on a half-tied salmon fly and with some effort rose to his feet.

He said, "I used to be able to tie a fully dressed Green Highlander in just over two hours. Now it takes all afternoon. Strange thing to do, don't you think? Spend that much time on a single fly when you may only have a few years left." He rapped his knuckles on the tabletop.

"Now there, Polly. We'll have none of that talk in here." Patrick Willoughby shook his head.

"Patrick thinks that if we don't mention the elephant in the room—I'm talking about COPD—then it doesn't exist. I knock on wood because a few years is the hopeful outlook for someone at my stage of the disease, given that I have complicating factors that already impaired my lung function." He was a kindly man with thinning hair who looked to be considerably older than the other club members, but to Stranahan he appeared very fit, except for the apparent arthritis in his knees and a slight laboring of his breath.

"Do you know what COPD stands for, Mr. Stranahan?" the man said.

"I don't."

"Be glad that you don't." He measured Stranahan with slightly wavering hazel eyes. "So you're the private detective Kenneth Winston found. Now Kenneth, once he gets his materials sorted and matched, he can tie a Highlander in an hour and a half and better than I can in four."

"Polly, that's simply not true," Willoughby said.

"I'm afraid it is."

"Polly Sorenson is the foremost dresser of classic salmon flies on our side of the pond," Willoughby said to Sean. "When that Highlander you're looking at is finished, it will sell for five hundred dollars and reside in a glass display case."

"That's nonsense, this one's going to catch a trout in the Madison River," Sorenson said. He looked at Sean with a mischievous twinkle. "These old Victorian patterns were designed to catch the eyes of fishermen, not fish. But I've found the wings slim down in water to resemble small baitfish and will snag the occasional trout. Of course, you destroy the value the first time the feathers touch the water. As I am a house husband, what the French call a man of the hearth, as opposed to Tennyson's vision of the sexes—'man for the field and woman for the hearth, man for the sword and for the needle she, man with the head and woman with the heart.'" Sorenson paused. "Where was I? Patrick, help me here. I've lost the thread."

"You were talking about how you are a man of the hearth."

"Oh, yes. My wife does not approve of me fishing with flies that could contribute to our retirement. As far as she's concerned, when I cast one into the river I might as well say goodbye to five suppers at a Parisian bistro. Which"—again, he rapped on the tabletop—"I still hope to enjoy someday."

Dinner was a bourguignon of elk rump and morel mushrooms, courtesy of Jonathon Smither, who told Sean he had burned out as a crime reporter for the *San Francisco Examiner* and now wrote a series of mystery novels featuring a sleuth who was a "nose" for a perfume company. He traveled the globe, bedding beautiful women and solving crimes with his superior olfactory organ. The books sold particularly well in France. "God bless a country that isn't ashamed of its noses," he said, touched glasses with Stranahan, and refilled his wineglass.

None of the members seemed the least interested in broaching the subject of the missing trout flies, at least not until after the evening hatch. Sean wadered up and fished with Smither for a while, or rather Smither insisted that Sean have the honor, and whistled appreciatively when Sean made a perfect parachute cast that dropped a PMD cripple into the feeding lane of a butterfat brown trout. But shortly after he released the fish, a cold wind whisked down the valley, blowing froth off the tops of the riffles and tilting the wings of the delicate mayflies that sailboated on the surface. Stranahan hiked upriver by himself as the sun dipped, swapped out the cripple for a streamer fly, and took a heavily striped rainbow that walloped the river with its tail. He had hooked and lost an even better one when Patrick Willoughby walked up the bank.

"I've had my eye on you. What are you using?"

Stranahan held up the slim marabou streamer. "I hope I haven't broken a club code by fishing wet," he said.

"I won't tell if you won't," Willoughby said.

Stranahan adapted himself to Willoughby's hitching gait as they walked back to the clubhouse, accepted a whiskey and branch water and sipped it on the porch while the others trickled back, shucked waders, put their feet up on the rail, and, except for Sorenson, lit cigars. Theirs was the easy camaraderie of men who had nothing to prove and talked without weighing the impact of the words. The proposition they put to him, punctuated by the glow of the cigars, wasn't long in coming. The club would like to hire him for a week and invite him to use the clubhouse as his base. Willoughby had not volunteered the details of the theft on Sean's first visit and filled in the blanks. The Quill Gordon dry fly had been presented by its originator to Roy Steenrod, Theodore Gordon's friend and frequent fishing companion on the Neversink River, and had been in a private collection for nearly seven decades. In May, it had been offered through Gray's Auctioneers in Cleveland, its provenance having first been authenticated by the curator of the American Fly Fishing Museum in Manchester, Vermont. Willoughby, acting on behalf of the club, had raised the paddle and purchased the fly in its shadow box display frame, draining the club coffers to the tune of $17,500. The hammer price was more than triple the estimate, but, as Willoughby put it, "all of us but Kenneth would be fertilizing Kentucky bluegrass" if they had waited for another to come onto the block.

Who else had bid? Stranahan wanted to know. Willoughby said both the Federation of Fly Fishers and the Bud Lilly Trout & Salmonid Initiative at Montana State University in Bozeman were aware of the Gordon fly and had expressed interest in its acquisition, but only as the beneficiaries of donation. The three bidders who pushed the price had used agents, preserving their anonymity.

"I see where you're going, Sean," Willoughby said, "but as much as a private collector might have wanted the fly, do you really think anyone would follow me out to Montana and break into the clubhouse?" He shook his head, his jowls wagging.

Sean had known avarice to take many forms, with consequences ranging from petty theft to murder, but didn't push an argument.

"What about the other fly, the Gray Ghost? You mentioned it had sentimental value."

"Yes. Carrie Stevens gifted the fly to my father only months before her death. She had written to him that this particular fly had two additional feathers in the wing with a blue tinge, which made it more attractive to landlocked salmon. The letter is in the box. Sean, you can't buy that kind of provenance."

Stranahan asked Willoughby to take him through the days leading up to and following the thefts. Willoughby said that he had packaged the majority of the club's fly collection and sent it via UPS to a friend in Montana for safekeeping until his arrival the previous week. The half dozen frames displaying the most valuable and rare patterns, including the Quill Gordon and the Gray Ghost, he had wrapped in bubble wrap and put in his carry-on, not trusting them to checked luggage. After Sorenson had picked him up at the Bozeman airport and they arrived at the clubhouse, he had hung the frames on the wall overnight and then the next afternoon taken them apart, removed the flies, and placed them in a large fly box that he kept zipped in his wading jacket.

"Why not leave them in the display cases?" Sean asked.

Willoughby seemed embarrassed. "The truth be told, I wanted to touch the flies, particularly the Quill Gordon," he said. "I suppose it would be the same for a concert violinist given the opportunity to cradle a Stradivarius. Not even dreaming of playing it, mind you, the way I would never dream of fishing with a fly tied by Theodore Gordon. But Polly and I were alone here. It was two days before Kenneth flew in and nearly a week before anyone else arrived. We'd be fishing, buying groceries in West Yellowstone, we'd be in and out. I just figured the flies would be safer on my person. We were going to have a ceremony when everyone arrived and hang the cases in their place of honor."

"What if you'd fallen in the river?"

Willoughby said the box was sealed inside two Ziploc bags. He laughed. "I thought if I drowned, then at least I'd be leaving the flies for posterity."

Stranahan turned his attention to Sorenson. "So you examined the flies also?"

Sorenson nodded, the flip-up magnifying lens attached to his glasses reflecting bright moons of light from the porch lanterns.

"Yes, but my priorities were different than Patrick's. It was the Ghost that held my interest. Carrie Stevens accented the heads of her streamer patterns with a few turns of red thread, and I wanted to put the fly under a magnifying glass to examine the wraps. It was her signature."

"Did anyone else see them?"

Sorenson seemed to hesitate and Stranahan gave him a questioning glance. But before he could probe further, Willoughby spoke up. "Kenneth came in Saturday. He saw them. As a tier of the Catskill school, he was probably more excited to examine the Gordon than I was."

Stranahan probed for detail. When exactly had Willoughby discovered that the flies were missing? Willoughby said that would have been Sunday, when he'd had the urge to examine the Quill Gordon in natural light. He'd taken the box from his vest and opened it on the tying table.

"And there's no possibility Kenneth took them?" Stranahan thought that a storyteller of Kenneth Winston's caliber would have no trouble feigning surprise over a couple missing flies that his own larcenous fingers had filched the night before, while Willoughby slept.

"Mr. Stranahan"—it was the first time Willoughby had referred to him by his surname—"the members of the club are beyond suspicion."

Sean backed off. "Show me the box," he said.

During his exchange with Willoughby and Sorenson, neither Jonathon Smither nor Robin Hurt Cowdry had uttered a word. They seemed as entranced by the mystery as Stranahan was. He watched as the long ash on Cowdry's cigar dropped onto the porch floor. And why wouldn't he be concerned? Sean thought. As the five club members had contributed equally to the fly's purchase, each had lost an investment of more than three thousand dollars.

They gathered around the tying table, Willoughby's Wheatley fly box opened under the intense halogen eye of a goosenecked lamp. The box layout was similar to the one belonging to Winston that Sean had seen on his first visit, with lidded compartments on one side and steel clips to hold wet flies and streamers on the other.

The club president pointed to the only empty compartment. "That's where the Gordon was."

"It was the only fly in that compartment?" Sean asked.

"I didn't want to crowd it and mash the hackles. The Gray Ghost was in one of the large clips, this one to be precise." He tapped a clip with his forefinger.

Sean scanned the box. Most of the compartments contained several flies. Together with the flies in the clips, the box could easily hold a couple hundred. "Are any other flies missing?"

"None of the collectibles. About the rest, I couldn't say. I don't count them each time I go fishing. But if more than a couple dozen were gone, I'd like to think I would notice."

"What about the rest of you? Has any gear disappeared, not just flies?"

"What are you getting at?" Jonathon Smither said.

"There are two ways to look at this," Sean said. "First, as the theft of two valuable flies. If that's the case, someone had to know what he was looking for, have a good idea where to find it, and then—and this is key—be able to recognize the flies when he saw them. It limits the scope of the investigation to people who would know their value. Besides Kenneth Winston and the four of you in this room, and maybe the mystery bidders for the Quill Gordon, I don't know who that could be. Once Patrick transferred the flies from their display frames, which identified them as antiques, they become trout flies like any other. You see what I mean?" He went on, "But if you look at this as part of a larger-scale burglary—rods, reels, fly boxes, cameras . . ." He shrugged. "Then the flies become part of the haul and whoever took them doesn't know what he has."

Willoughby shook his round head. "I must be getting old," he said. "I honestly never considered the angle that the specific flies weren't the target."

"But why just take one or even a couple dozen flies out of a box?" Cowdry asked. "Why not take the whole box?"

Sean frowned. "Maybe because a missing box would raise more suspicion, although that points to theft of a very petty nature. But to get back to my original question. Have any of you suspected that any of your gear was stolen since you built the clubhouse?"

Nobody had. Then Sorenson, even as he was shaking his head no, said in a reflective voice, "But the damnedest thing happened last summer. I put my Orvis in the rack on the porch and the next morning it was gone. I thought I must have broken it down and cased it, and you guys were hurrying me along—it was that day we fished Willow Creek—so I grabbed my six-weight Sage and got in the car. Then when we got back, I found that the Orvis was in the rack, all strung up and right where it was supposed to be. How had I not seen it there in the morning? Honest to God, I thought I was having a senior moment. I didn't tell anyone because it was embarrassing."

"We're all getting there," Willoughby said.

Sean didn't know what to think about Sorenson's story. Who would steal a rod only to replace it in the rack the next day? But the incident called into question the vulnerability of the cottage, which was only a short distance from the riverbank. Was it customary for the members to leave six-hundred-dollar graphite rods in an outside rack overnight?

Willoughby spoke for the group. "I know it looks like we're inviting someone to steal, but honestly we haven't had a problem. It's against regulations to fish this stretch from a boat, so there aren't many floaters, and anyone who hikes this far from the public access doesn't strike me as the kind of man who would swipe someone else's gear. And you've seen how hard it is to drive in here."

The latter remark was in reference to the two locked gates that led to the development, which until a dozen years ago had been a sprawling ranch. Stranahan had been loaned a key to the first gate, three road miles downriver at the entrance to the development, and given a four-digit combination to the second lock on the spur road that led to the clubhouse.

"You never left your vest hanging outside on one of those pegs, did you?"

"Oh, gosh no. Whenever I wasn't fishing, I hung it on the chair you're sitting on. I was careful to lock the place when I left."

"Did you ever return and find that it was unlocked?"

"No. I would have noticed that."

"Who has keys?"

"All of us here. Then there's the caretaker of the development, who used to be the ranch manager back when it was one. His name is Emmitt Cummings. These are mostly summer homes, so someone has to be able to get in if there's a fire or gas explosion or something of that nature. The only other person who has a key is Geneva Beardsley from Ennis. She's the cleaning person who opens the place up before we fly in and closes it back up in the fall. Her husband is sort of a jack-of-all-trades, keeps up the grounds, drains the pipes before the cold weather sets in. The inside of this place falls well below zero in the winter. You can leave whiskey or a bottle of vodka in the liquor cabinet, but last winter we forgot a couple bottles of zin and there wasn't enough alcohol to keep them from exploding."

"It was Maryhill Proprietor's Reserve, too," Jonathon Smither said.

"Jonathon has an interest in a couple Argentine wineries. You could call him the club's sommelier. The wine you had with dinner was a Malbec."

"From the Lujan de Cuyo in Mendoza Province," Smither added.

"Sean," Willoughby said, "at the risk of coming across as self-satisfied bastards, we're all of us comfortably well-off. We're not concerned about the monetary loss. This is not a theft of money. It is a theft of history. Come stay with us this week. You'll get paid for having a good time, if nothing else. Meals and drinks included."

"And if you need to get your mind right, we have some wicked bud, mate," Cowdry added.

"Christ, Robin." Willoughby shook his head. "Sean's going to think we're a bunch of old hippies."

"And that would be wrong?"

"I like to think of us more as Renaissance men."

"You had me at 'wicked bud,'" Stranahan said.

He had one more question about keys. Was there a hidden spare? Willoughby said he'd show him on his way out. He led him around the side of the clubhouse, past a woodblock used as a base for splitting firewood. The key was under a glass electrical insulator in the shape of a bell. The insulator was on top of the electrical meter, a little above head height. It was maybe the third place a prospective burglar would look for a key, after lifting up the front doormat and turning over the big stone beside the steps.

"I know," Willoughby said. "It probably expands the pool of suspects, huh?"

To anyone with half a brain, Sean thought.

Instead, he just said good night and walked to his Land Cruiser, his mind already having traveled sixty miles up the road, to a grain elevator with a cat calendar on the wall.

As he pushed open the door, Stranahan saw that the lamp on the end table was on, with the shawl Martinique had worn to the Inn draped over the shade. She was in her print nightgown, sitting at one end of the couch with the two cats, Mitsy and Miss Daisy. Her sad smile told him that Ichiro's suffering was over.

"He died a couple hours ago. I gave him some kitty Valium and he was peaceful, he just slipped away. I hoped maybe you could help me bury him tomorrow, maybe take a drive somewhere in the country."

She patted the couch. "Come sit with me. I can't go back up to that bedroom tonight."

"I'm sorry it's so late," he said.

"That's okay. I should be exhausted, but it's a relief now that it's over."

She rearranged herself so that she was leaning into him and rested her head on his shoulder. "Tell me about your day."

Sean did, feeling the comfort of her body pressing softly into him and the rhythm of her breath, and realized that what Martinique offered was a tranquil envelope of life that he had never really known. He had been caught in the snare of infatuation before, and in the course of his troubled marriage the phases of deeper love had opened like doors before him, and had shut behind him, isolating him in rooms that more and more he'd just wanted to escape from. By comparison, Vareda Beaudreux, the riverboat singer he'd fallen for last summer, was a burning fire; her passion was the tail of a comet that he was still riding. But Martinique, Martinique was a warm scent and a slow heartbeat and a window wide open.

Martinique turned her face up to kiss him, and kissed him warmly and then more urgently as she twisted into his lap and pressed her breasts against his chest.

But when she pulled back to look at him there were tears in her eyes.

"I'm afraid I'm going to ask you to go home," she said. "There's part of me that wants to love you all up, right here on this couch. It would be an affirmation of life that I really need. But this isn't the way for us to start, with me crying and you wondering what kind of crazy you've gotten into. You come back tomorrow morning, though. I'll make you breakfast."

Sean was in time for last call at the Cottonwood Inn. He took his draft beer to the pool room, empty except for Sam Meslik, who was practicing rail shots on a battered Brunswick.

"Kimosabe," Sam said. "Doris told me you were here last night with a lady friend. Said the two of you looked like Branga-Fucking-Lina. I didn't have the heart to tell her she sold mochas with her ta-tas."

"How do you know who she was?"

Sam cocked his face sideways, his head down over the cue. "Bro, there can't be two Martiniques in the state of Montana. *If* that's her name."

He rammed the two-ball into a side pocket.

"I got to go drop a few buckeyes," he said. He ambled off to the men's room.

When he returned, Stranahan picked up the conversation in stride. "I'm going to disappoint you, Sam," he said. "All I've been doing is sleeping on her couch."

"Why don't you just borrow an apron and wash her dishes?" He lined up another shot and handed Sean the cue. "Get your head down over the ball. Now stick your butt out. Farther. Farther."

Sean raised his eyebrows.

"What?" Sam held up his hands. "I just thought the position ought to come natural for you."

CHAPTER ELEVEN

The Bullet and the Betrothed

"I told you to be here this morning."

Sean glanced at the clock on the wall of Ettinger's office. Eleven fifty-four.

"It is morning, Martha."

"Uh-huh."

"I was helping a friend bury a cat."

"Uh-huh." Ettinger looked at him with her mouth downturned.

"I think I know that look," Sean said. "So, did you cut that piece of metal out of the root?"

"First things first." She unbuttoned the breast pocket of her khaki shirt and withdrew the ring Katie had found with the metal detector. "Take a look at the inside of the band."

He canted the ring to catch the light. The etching was shallow, but clear. *For Fidelia. From This Day Forever.*

"It's pronounced Fie-de-leya," Ettinger said. "Spanish origin."

"So we're looking for a guy who had been married to an Hispanic woman?"

"We don't know if the ring belongs to the body, but if it does, then yes, probably." She told him about the hairs Doc Hanson had examined.

"Katie and I weren't wasting our time up there, were we?"

"No, you weren't. But next time, go through the channels and call me first. Okay?"

Sean nodded. "It was covered by a couple inches of dirt. On the upper bench where we found the second body."

"Why do you suppose the ring was buried?"

"Maybe the man knew he was about to die and didn't want whoever killed him to have it. Or maybe it was a farewell gesture, he kissed the ring and buried it as a way of saying goodbye to his wife."

Ettinger, nodding, set the ring on her desk and reached into her pocket for the bullet. She flicked the nose of the bullet with her forefinger. It spun around on the desktop. When it stopped, the nose pointed at Sean's heart.

"Pure steel?"

"Steel jacket. Lead core. The detector only registered the jacket."

"Hmm."

"That's what I told myself when Doc cut it out."

"It's an awful big bullet."

"I hunt elk with a .30-06," Martha said. "The diameter of the bore is .308. The bullet weight is 180 grains."

"And this?"

"Four eight eight. Five hundred grains. No deformation, even after hitting the root. It's a solid, like an armor-piercing bullet."

"What's it from?"

"Without the cartridge case it's hard to say. You'd think a heavy handgun, like a .44 Magnum. But the diameter doesn't exactly match any handgun caliber and the bullet is way too heavy. Walt thought it might be from a military rifle. A long-range sniper gun with a tripod, like you see in the movies. But they weigh about thirty pounds. Not the kind of gun you carry up the face of a mountain. But we haven't had much time to look into it."

"I was hoping maybe there would be some residue on it, like skin tissue," Stranahan said.

"Doc managed to scrape some matter out of the grooves at the base of the bullet and sent it to the lab. The bullet also could have transferred tissue as it went through the root."

"So with a little luck you'll have DNA?"

"So with a lot of luck we'll have DNA."

"Why tell me? You made it clear my part in the investigation is over."

"Yet here we are with a ring and a bullet you dug up. Take me through it from start to finish."

Ettinger put her fingers to her throat as she listened. "What an enterprising young woman our Katie is," she said. She put her hands behind her head and leaned back, staring at her office door. Stranahan glanced at her wall calendar. Not cats. Dogs.

Ettinger refocused.

"When I say we haven't had much time to look into this, I mean we don't and we aren't going to. Walt's flying back to Chicago for his sister's wedding at the end of the week. Warren's off starting the Fourth for the next five days. Harold's on indefinite leave. I want to put names on those bodies, and I want to put a name on who put them there, and I can't do that with a skeleton crew. I wondered if you wanted in."

"I thought it had to be a breaking crisis before you could deputize me."

"I'm not deputizing you. I'm hiring you as an outside investigator for special projects. There's a discretionary fund I can dip into that I've never dipped into. We can't match your day rate, but I think we could work something out to your satisfaction."

"There could be a conflict." He told her about the Madison River Liars and Fly Tiers Club.

"The 'Case of the Missing Ghost,'" she said. "It sounds interesting." The tone of her voice said it wasn't.

"It's important to them."

"All right. Here's what you do. Go on down there this week, find your precious Ghost and that other fly . . ."

"Quill Gordon."

"Quill Gordon. You're what, fifteen, twenty miles from the base of the Sphinx? If you can get free, hike back up there and have another look around. Use your imagination. I don't expect you to find anything, but then you found the bullet, so . . ." She shrugged. "Then check back with me after the Fourth and we'll go to work, just us probably and Harold once he's up and around. He was released from Deaconess this morning." She pursed her lips and looked off for a second. "I don't know that it's relevant, but the bodies, they were older gentlemen. Doc says they had terminal illnesses."

She held up a hand as Sean began to speak. "I'll tell you about it next week. Hopefully, we'll know more then."

"I was going to ask if you have any advice about finding the trout flies."

"Sure. If what this guy—"

"Willoughby," Sean prompted.

"Will-oh-bee. If he's telling the truth, then it sounds like an inside job. For some reason, one of the members isn't as far above reproach as Willoughby thinks he is. Maybe the barber fellow. Or Willoughby himself could be guilty." She fingered her jawline. "He could have acted as agent for a third party. Buy the fly, say he lost it, and then get paid back the dollar amount by whoever he turned it over to. Walk away with the shares his buddies put into the purchase. Fourteen, fifteen grand, it isn't chump change."

"I think it's more likely he lost the flies out of his box and is just too embarrassed to say so."

"Could be," Martha said. "If that's what happened, then your flies are blowing in the wind, like the song says."

"Or . . ." Sean sat back in the chair, compressed his lips.

Martha flicked the backs of her hands at him. "Shoo," she said. "Do your thinking on somebody else's dime. I'll see you next weekend. But give me a call if you find anything up on that mountain."

When Stranahan left, Ettinger steepled her fingers and rested her chin on them. She looked at the blinking light on her phone. A message had come in while they were talking. She cocked her finger like a gun and punched the button, then grimaced when she heard the

voice of Gail Stocker, the cops reporter at the *Bridger Mountain Star*.
Did she have the autopsy results? Had they revealed any clues to the
identity of the bodies? Stocker was a snip of a woman, barely five feet
tall, but she was a badger once she got her teeth into a story. Martha
had grudging respect for her, but she hated dealing with the press.
She knew the questions that would be asked and always jotted down
notes to set the parameters of her responses. Then she'd go off point
and say something stupid. Either she said something she regretted or
she grunted and stonewalled, neither of which endeared her to the
public. She slid the autopsy report out of the top drawer of her desk
and reluctantly picked up the phone.

"So these guys were pretty sick, huh?" Stocker said after Ettinger
had filled her in.

"They had terminal diseases, yes."

"So what's the cause of death?"

"That's yet to be determined." She had withheld mention of the
bullet and any trace DNA evidence that might have clung to it. If
there was a killer out there, she didn't want him destroying evidence.

"But you said the one guy had a hole in his head that is consistent
with a bullet wound."

"No, I said he had pieces of skull missing that might have been
caused by any number of things and which may or may not have
been the cause of death. You're the one who introduced the word
'bullet.'"

"But you aren't ruling it out?"

"We're not ruling anything out at this point in the investigation."

"Including suicide? It sounds like these guys might have been looking for a way to check out. Maybe they had some kind of deal going
where they buried each other."

"That's speculating."

"If you're holding something back, we can talk off the record."

"All I know for sure," Ettinger said, "is there's a couple of . . ." She
paused, thinking back to her conversation with Stranahan about the

missing trout flies. "A couple of old gray ghosts up there haunting that mountain, and I'm not going to be satisfied until we've put them to rest."

In the newsroom, the reporter jotted in her notebook. *Gray Ghost Murders? Ghosts of Sphinx Mountain? Mystery of the Gray Ghosts?*

Ettinger hung up the phone, not realizing that she'd just provided a headline for the next day's front page.

CHAPTER TWELVE

Knocking on Heaven's Doors

Stranahan didn't expect that anyone would answer his knock, let alone the estimable Weldon Crawford Jr., the state's sole representative to Congress. Dressed in creased Carhartt jeans and a snap-up black shirt with red piping in a lasso design, he looked like a page in a western wear catalog, right down to his snakeskin Larry Mahans. He smiled, the creases at the corners of his eyes running back into silver wings framing a full head of jet black hair that looked real enough, even though Stranahan knew from the papers that the congressman was in his midfifties. From camera front, the politician's view, Crawford was one of the handsomest men Sean had ever seen. From the side, his head was shaped like an egg with a golf-ball-sized bulge under the right ear.

"Congressman," Sean said, "I'm sorry to disturb you. I'm from the Liars and Fly Tiers Club, the cabin down by the river."

"Yes, of course. I sold that property. They did a first-rate job of fixing it up."

"We had a break-in last week. I thought I'd let the neighbors know and see if anyone else was hit. You haven't had any problems, have you?"

"No. I've only been up for a couple weekends this summer, but I'm sure E.J. would have told me if there'd been any trouble. Emmitt Cummings, he's the caretaker of the property. Would you like a drink, Mr. . . . ?"

"Sean Stranahan."

Crawford winked. "It's five o'clock in"—he glanced at his watch—"well it's five o'clock somewhere, after all. Oh, come in, come in. The family won't be arriving until the Fourth and I'm all alone in the house. In a place this size, you begin to feel small."

Sean doubted that the congressman would feel small even if he was alone in the Governor's Mansion in Helena, to which he was said to have aspirations. He followed the man's nickel-diameter bald spot into a vast living area paneled in light wood with massive log support beams. A Shiras moose peered down at him from one wall, a bull elk with its mouth open to bugle from another. Over the mantelpiece, incongruous with the western theme, presided the shoulder mount of an enormous African Cape buffalo with a scabby black hide.

"M'bogo, that's the Swahili name. An old dugga boy from the Ruaha River. I shot him in full charge. You can see the crease under the right eye where the bullet went in. He was all cut up from fighting off lions. Scotch and soda's my poison."

"That sounds fine."

Crawford busied himself behind an antique zinc bar.

"Are you a hunter?" he called out.

Sean answered no, but now that he lived in Montana he was thinking about it.

"I can't hear you."

He brought the drinks, indicated chairs for them to sit.

"'Hakuna matata,' as they say in Kenya. No worries." They touched glasses.

"I'm hard of hearing, so you have to speak to my left ear. My right eardrum burst in 1969. I was riding an elephant in the Terai. That's the belt of tall grass that runs under the Himalayas. We were beating the cover for tiger—this was just weeks before Indira Gandhi outlawed hunting—when the man sharing the howdah let go with a .375 Holland and Holland, the muzzle about six inches from my ear. He said he'd seen a cobra, but nobody else saw a snake. I rode that elephant the rest of the day while the side of my head swelled like a football. Long story short, a doctor in Delhi drained a quart of fluid that had collected in the abscess. People think I'm vain because I turn my left side to face them, that I'm hiding my reminder of that day—it's what doctors call a benign mass—but I just want to hear what they're saying."

"Could you have it removed?"

"The mass? I see you have no experience in Montana politics. I was cursed by being born with a symmetrical face. Each side is the mirror image of the other." He showed Sean by turning his head. "It's actually quite rare. Among movie actors, Denzel Washington and Kim Basinger have such faces. No one would disagree that they are very attractive people. But very few can pull off a perfect face. It brands them as effeminate, or in my case"—he made quote marks with his fingers—"a 'pretty boy.' A rancher from eastern Montana sees this face on TV and he thinks twice. He wants to cast his vote for a feedlot manager with a crew cut, a tire around the middle, and a lopsided grin. The lump under my ear is my lopsided grin."

He regarded Stranahan with shrewd eyes. "Are you a Republican, Sean? Or are you a granola-grazing liberal donkey who lies down with wolves? I like to know when I've invited an enemy into the camp."

"I'm a fisherman."

"Nicely played, but I have my answer all the same." He stood up. "I'm keeping you from making the rounds. What was taken, by the way?"

Stranahan had anticipated the question and decided that he'd go with honesty.

"A collectible fishing fly. Two, actually. They're quite valuable."

"I had no idea there was such a thing before meeting Polly Sorenson. He's the one member of your club I've gotten to know a bit. I'll admit I'm a spin fisherman myself. A number 9 jointed Rapala in a rainbow trout pattern is my go-to. A black number 6 Panther Martin with a gold blade if the water's muddy. I like to catch big fish that are eating the little fish that are eating the flies."

"You're just saying that to appeal to people who can't cast a fly rod," Stranahan said.

Crawford wrinkled the corners of his eyes. "Maybe you know more about politics than I gave you credit for."

Stranahan felt himself smiling along with the man, despite disagreeing with nearly everything he stood for. "Congressman, it's been a pleasure." He pointed to the Cape buffalo mount on the wall. "Do you mind telling me what gun you used to stop the charge?"

"A .470 Nitro double rifle built by John Rigby in London."

"What weight of bullet does a gun like that shoot?"

"Five hundred grains."

Sean set down his drink glass, trying to cover any expression of surprise.

"That Woodleigh solid," Crawford said, "it's a stopper."

As Stranahan settled behind the wheel of his Land Cruiser, he frowned inwardly. A little more than two hours had passed since Martha Ettinger showed him the bullet. You didn't just knock on a door on an unrelated matter and find the man who owned the rifle that shot that bullet. And that man a U.S. representative. Still . . . how many cartridges could there be that fired a five-hundred-grain bullet, and how many men owned a rifle that fired that cartridge? In, say, a hundred-mile radius of Sphinx Mountain?

He looked across the valley. The lion-headed mountain was just visible above the escarpment, its peak cut off by a layer of cloud. He heard a raindrop ping off the hood of the Land Cruiser and then another. He turned the key.

The rest of the interviews—of the half dozen doors he knocked on there were three answers—weren't so revealing. No one had reported a burglary. No one had noticed anyone suspicious driving or walking about on the posted land. But then, Stranahan hadn't expected anything. The break-in at the club—he had taken the liberty of exaggeration—had been an excuse to assess the neighbors as possible suspects in the theft of the fly. Which, with respect to the events of the morning, seemed much less interesting than they had the night before. He had turned onto the spoor of a much more dangerous animal than one who had taken a liking to a trout fly. But he had made a commitment to the club, and unlike Sheriff Ettinger's promise of money, the club's check was already in his wallet. Willoughby had cut it for the full amount when Stranahan had driven down in the afternoon.

His last stop was the house belonging to Emmitt Cummings, who Crawford said oversaw several of the neighbors' properties and, as the development's only year-round resident, acted as its unofficial watchdog. Cummings's twenty acres were set on the westernmost section of the old ranch property and included the original ranch dwelling set in a copse of gnarled aspens. As he pulled up the dirt drive, he saw a man wedging a peeled rail into an age-blackened jack fence that zigzagged along the toe of the hillside.

The man acknowledged Sean's wave with the tip of his hat and walked bowlegged down the hill, passing a chestnut quarterhorse that turned to follow him. Cowboy head to toe but not out of a catalog, the real thing, sweat-stained Stetson cracked in the crown crease, chambray workshirt with two pearl snaps missing, Levi's bought hard and blue-black and never washed. A belt buckle embossed with a bucking bronc winked in the sunlight that had opened a hole in the rain clouds. Cummings smelled of sweat and horseflesh.

"I'm sure as hell happy to meet you," he said when Sean introduced himself. "I'd be amenable to shaking hands with a polecat this time of day. The old Swede who put up this fence was spit and vinegar on the outside and boot leather underneath. Or maybe 'tother way around."

The left side of the man's face clenched in an odd expression and quickly relaxed. The eyes were a startling blue like cerulean, set in a network of deep creases. He pinched the crown of his hat and tipped it forward off his head, ran a hand through short sandy hair, wiped the sweat on his jeans. He got down on one knee and set the hat over the other knee, plucked a stem of grass and chewed it, his mustache working like a restless rodent.

Sean squatted down to be at the same height. The quarterhorse dropped its head and nuzzled the top of his head.

"Don't mind Sally. She's my air conditioner. Licks your hair and you feel cool enough for five minutes. 'Bout all she's good for anymore. Now what can I do for you?"

"Uh-huh, uh-huh," he repeated as Sean went through his spiel. "You don't say? Why, I haven't heard of a burglary in this development since the sale went through in '02. No, sir, I haven't."

Sean felt himself drawn to Emmitt Cummings as he had been drawn to other ranchers he'd met since moving to Montana. They were conservative to a man, resistant to change and wary of strangers, having developed a second skin to keep the first from getting burned. But polite if you weren't telling them what to do with their property—salt of the earth, roll up their sleeves and do anything they could for you.

"So this fly you're looking for, it's collectible you say?"

Sean told him how much it had brought at auction. Cummings whistled, high-low.

"Now, I can see the value of a good cutting horse or a fine firearm, yes I can, or one of them museum paintings though I lean to western art myself. Gary Carter, that man's painting just gets me. But a nickel's worth of feathers tied on a hook? But then it takes all kinds to make a world, doesn't it?" He spit out the stem of grass, plucked another.

Sean learned that Cummings had been born the sole son of a ranch manager and had managed ranches himself since he was twenty, had borrowed heavily to buy his own place up on the Milk River,

650 acres with another 450 in grazing rights, small outfit but a working cattle ranch with senior water rights on Hardy Creek. He'd lost his shirt in an outbreak of blackleg disease that claimed half his yearlings and sold out for a song, but maintained the mineral rights. Went back to ranch managing and outfitting, taking horseback hunters up into the Bear Paws for elk and mule deer in the fall, moved south when there was an opening to manage the Anderson spread, stayed on after the ranch was sold and subdivided. Lived a mite too close to the bone until a silver mining company bought the mineral rights up on the Milk property. Put the money toward the twenty acres the old homestead was built on. Now he was setting pretty enough what with the development stipend and the outfitting dollar, but would really like to get back to working cattle, it was where his heart was. Married, now a widower, his wife dying of breast cancer, two children, the son a groundskeeper for a couple North Dakota golf courses—"that there's what I mean by saying we live in changing times"—his daughter married into a ranching family out of Roundup—"good people but the place is sliding south, they wouldn't know to stand up a tipped sheep." A ten-minute history of his forty-two years on the planet, then ten minutes with the grass stem bobbing as Stranahan told his own story—"uh-huh, now ain't that just how it is, yep, I remember something about that, that was you, why I'll be, life sure can be funny"—not an out-of-the-ordinary conversation between strangers squatting opposite each other in wide-open country in Montana.

They stood up, Cummings put his hat on and said he'd keep an eye out, he smiled with his cerulean eyes, and then hitched away in his bowlegged gait, the horse following. Sean walked back to his rig thinking rivers, sky, and people—*this is why I'll never go east again*—and drove back in time for supper with the club members without having learned a single useful piece of information concerning their missing trout fly.

What he did learn that night, lying in bed in one of the two spacious bunkhouses, was that Willoughby snored like a dragon and Robin Hurt Cowdry spoke to himself in his sleep, in what he'd later learn was a Zulu dialect called Ndebele. He woke up to the patter of rain against the windows and hiked up the riverbank after breakfast, fishing to take advantage of an on-again, off-again blue-winged olive hatch and talking to everyone who came by, which amounted only to a half dozen anglers. Three were buddies from Oregon who were camping up on the West Fork and had hiked down from Three Dollar Bridge. Two were local anglers and the last was a boy who cast a wet noodle fly rod as if he were whipping a Thoroughbred and asked Sean if he had permission to trespass on the property.

"My uncle says fishermen don't stay under the high-water mark. He says they want to fish the river they ought to pony up and buy their own property."

"Let me guess," Sean told him, "your uncle's from California. Either California or Texas."

"We're from Abilene," the boy said. "What's your name?"

Sean told him.

"I saw you catch three fish." The tone was accusatory.

"And three more downriver," Sean said.

"What are they biting on?"

Sean showed him the size 18 crippled parachute Adams hooked to his stripping guide.

"What's your rod made out of? I didn't think they made wood rods."

"It's bamboo."

"Can you help me pick out a better fly?" He pulled a foam fly box out of his hip pocket—he was wading wet and didn't wear a vest. Sean examined the mishmash of flies, a couple dozen that were well tied alongside a couple dozen cheap, general-store patterns, thread and tinsel unraveling, none of them properly dried after fishing so that the hooks had rusted, streaking the white foam copper and staining the bodies and wings of the patterns. He snapped the box shut and handed it back, snipped off his own Adams, knotted a fresh 5X tippet onto the boy's leader, and tied on the fly. He coached him into a small trout and then a fairly good one, which the boy lost. The boy had thorough command of the proper idiom to use upon losing a good one, managing to stain the air over the river with a number of epithets. He said his name was Sid, "not Sidney, which is gay." Sean gave him a half dozen of his own flies when they parted.

"Will you be fishing tomorrow? My uncle doesn't fish so I don't have no one to go with."

"I think so. But only if you promise not to swear on the river."

"Okay, mister, I'll keep it clean. I'll see you."

Sean walked back to lunch and told Willoughby he'd met the Huckleberry Finn of the Madison River.

"Huck Finn was a watermelon thief if memory serves me right. Did he steal our flies?"

"He's rough around the edges, but I wouldn't go as far as calling him a thief. I think I'm going to be a good influence on him."

"I'm glad you're putting our money to such a philanthropic endeavor."

CHAPTER THIRTEEN

Shifting Polarity

The week progressed; Sean's investigation didn't. He canvassed the neighborhood one last time on Saturday, purple storm clouds riding the teeth of the Madison Range, and checked off two more of the neighboring properties. One belonged to an air traffic controller from Reno, Nevada, named Bart Glenn, who like Senator Crawford was a big-game hunter and had a spacious living room hung with elk, Coues deer, and javelina trophies, the mantel of honor presided over by a full curl desert bighorn. Glenn had Sean by five inches, combed his thinning silver hair straight back, and had an air of authority bordering on arrogance. Sean noticed a glass-front gun cabinet that had racks for six long guns with only one in attendance, a scoped bolt-action rifle with a diamond-shaped inlay in the stock. When Sean inquired on the pretense of being a gun nut himself, Glenn said it was a .300 Weatherby. His family was up only through July—his wife and younger daughter had driven into Ennis for the rodeo—but he'd be coming back the last week in October for an elk hunt, and had booked Emmitt Cummings to act as his guide.

"I met Emmitt yesterday," Sean allowed.

"Let me tell you something about the man," Glenn said. "I hunted with him last fall up on Specimen Ridge and never heard so many 'Yes, sirs' and 'No, sirs' in my life, and I'm USMC retired. When I missed a shot at a bull that we'd put a two-hour stalk on, E.J. just placed his hand on my shoulder and said don't let it bother you, these things happen, we'll get a chance at another. And by God we did." He held up his thumb and jerked his hand over his shoulder so that the digit pointed toward a six-point bull collecting cobwebs on the stucco wall. "Why if I had an unmarried daughter, I'd do anything short of throwing her under his belt buckle to get 'em hitched. Money isn't everything, Mr. Stranahan. Instead, my Mary Jen took up with a goddamned divorce lawyer who has billboards plastered up and down Virginia Street. I got three rules when it comes to marriage. One, never marry anyone who has more troubles than you do. Two, never marry a twin. Three, never marry anyone who would put his boot to an animal. This lawyer fellow—I never let the bastard's name cross my lips—is an alcoholic, a compulsive gambler, and I've personally seen him kick his dog. Now if I was to learn he had a twin, I'd be on a plane tomorrow and give him one in the balls with the Weatherby. As it stands, he's just making my daughter miserable, running all over the strip and sticking his John Henry into any keno girl who will lie still for it, and there's not a goddamn thing I can do 'cause Mary won't listen."

Glenn seemed to have assumed that Stranahan had knocked just to introduce himself as a neighbor. When he stopped talking long enough to learn the real reason he was there, he looked around for something hard to pound his fist on and had to walk ten feet away to the dining room table.

"I can't abide a thief," he said. "That's rule number four, by the way."

Sean left by the front door, noting an NRA cap hanging on the antler tines of a mule deer skull that served as a hat rack and mentally marking an X by Bart Glenn's name.

The last house on Stranahan's circuit was built of blond logs below a metal roof sun-blanched to a robin's egg blue. Aside from the original ranch house, it was the smallest of the structures on the old Anderson spread and stood on the bluff closest to the hexagonal mansion belonging to Congressman Crawford. Though a million-dollar property in its own right, it could easily have been mistaken for the politician's detached bunkhouse. Sean noticed a cheap fly rod standing in a corner of the porch, with his fly still tied to the tippet. At his knock, the boy Sid cracked the door and beamed a smile, then called out that the man who had helped him catch a fish was here. Sean heard the oak floorboards creaking. The creaking stopped, then picked up again, and stopped just inside the door. Sean heard a wheezing sound as a man caught his breath.

"Tell that gentleman, 'Come on in.' I ain't hiding no wetbacks on the premises."

The man who extended his hand had a smile plastered on his face that exposed a row of small, very neat bottom teeth. John Deevers— "everybody calls me J.D."—was of medium height, fortysomething, sloppy around the middle and sloppy in the face, with a red wine complexion under a shining pate that reflected the light streaming in the east-facing windows. Sean had seldom so disliked a man on sight and for a moment stepped back from himself to ask why. It wasn't just the racial slur. It was the transparency of expression, the shrewd pig eyes in the fat folds of flesh, the nearly hairless lids that narrowed to assess Sean's ethnicity, and his ascension of the totem pole in order that he might place him in the pantheon of acceptable acquaintance. In the depth of those eyes, Sean saw himself falling short of the mark. There was just too much infusion of Mediterranean blood under his sun-darkened skin for him to sit at table with the gatekeeper of strict Deevers society.

"Sidney, I thought I tol' you skedaddle on down to the mailbox."

"But the mail don't come on Saturday, Uncle John."

"But the mail do come on Friday and it's still setting there. Git now, 'fore I unbuckle this belt."

When the boy had dashed out the door, Deevers said, "That's my brother's boy and I can't blame him for his father's shortcomings. But some of these kids ain't worth a shit today. I just say ignore him he bugs you on the river. He got into a wrong crowd. Caught selling that Mary Jane, the boy not even ten years old. I had to twist a woman's tit 'til she pulled down Judge Dawkins's zipper, else that boy would be stewing in juvy. I took him up here to tone him down a notch."

He showed Sean his bottom teeth again, then hollered for his wife to get their neighbor a beer. Sean made a mental sketch of the wife before she appeared and was off by no more than a brushstroke. A proper lady at a glance, with a pleasant face under a Laura Bush hairdo, but a bit of tremor in her jaw and eyes that never quite settled. She handed Sean a Coors in a can and stepped back, hovering at the periphery of her husband's theater of hands as he punctuated his opinions on everything Texas, specifically taxes, private property rights, and immigration. He allowed, just one good American to another, mind you, that every time he swerved the car to smash an armadillo, he made the sign of the cross and said, "By the grace of God, there goes another 'Meh-he-can.'"

Sean thought of Mrs. Deevers as a fighter who danced around the ring. She stayed out of reach and covered up the best she could, but probably got caught with hard hands nonetheless. Stranahan felt his antipathy for the man grow. He understood that alpha males were the norm in ranchette country. You had to have money to move in when the natives sold out. And with money came self-importance and power. But the men who looked north to Montana for a summer home came because they liked to fish, or to hunt, or simply to turn steaks on the grill, sit with their feet on the porch rail, and toast their kingdom of mountains and sky. They might not be as affable or deferential as an Emmitt Cummings, but they appreciated life, and liquor tended to make them happy, not mad. Sean had friends who fell into the category. They were the bread-and-butter clientele who hung his paintings. Throwback bullies like Deevers seemed out of place.

Out the window, Sean could see Sid scuffing back up the drive. The boy opened the door, dropped a few pieces of mail on an end table, and walked with his head down to a stuffed chair at the far end of the living room. He flopped down and looked at his hands. Sean took his leave a few minutes later without looking in that direction, sensing in Sid's body language a plea for him to make no further reference to their meeting on the riverbank.

When Sean glanced back at the house from his rig, Sid was standing at the front window. Sean pointed down the hill toward the river—*I'll meet you there*—but the boy didn't smile back and he didn't come down to the river that afternoon.

On Sunday, the club members had booked guides to float the Big Hole, a blue-ribbon tributary of the Jefferson River some one hundred miles in the direction of the sunset. The famed salmonfly hatch had run its course, but golden stoneflies and caddis were still in enough abundance to make the trout kiss the surface. Willoughby made a pouty face when Sean declined his offer to join them, on the basis that it would require the club to book a third boat. Besides, he'd been hired to do a job and had one more avenue to explore concerning the missing flies.

"You cut me to the quick," Willoughby said.

"You'll think otherwise if you find those flies mounted on the wall when you get back," he said, regretting the remark as soon as he'd said it. True, he had thought of another avenue to explore, but harbored scant hope it would pay off.

The members were up before daylight. Sean waited until the headlights were glancing over the sagebrush, said "Sorry boys" under his breath, and began a detailed search of the clubhouse. He had not bought Martha Ettinger's assertion that it was an inside job any more than he had bought his own earlier suspicions of the same, but having eliminated most of the nearby residents as likely suspects, his eyes had drawn a closer focus.

Before the sun discovered the surface of the river, Sean learned that Willoughby suffered from hemorrhoids, that Jonathon Smither powdered his nose—if the substance in the folded wax paper was what Sean thought it was—that Robin Hurt Cowdry was reading an espionage novel by Steve Pieczenik, and that Polly Sorenson's toilet bag contained two nitroglycerin inhalers. He opened various fly boxes that were strewn across the tying table, stacked on shelves, crammed into duffels. Willoughby had shown him a photograph of a Theodore Gordon–tied dry fly in a book, had pointed out the forward cock of the wings ahead of the hackle and the squarish bend of the vintage iron hook. None of the flies he examined came close. Feeling dirty after rummaging through his friends' personal belongings, for friends were what Willoughby and the others had become as they fished together and played wee-hours poker, he shifted mental gears and laced up his hiking boots. Forty minutes later he was clucking to the long-haired cat that Katie Sparrow's dog had run up a tree a few days before. The cat retreated into a clump of serviceberry bushes when the Land Cruiser pulled up, and regarded Sean with alarmed eyes. At the first step he made in its direction, the cat vanished.

Stranahan noted two rigs parked in the campground adjacent to the Forest Service station and another three at the trailhead turnaround: a mud-spattered Dodge Ram, a Subaru Forester, and a vintage Volvo wagon with a peace sticker that Sean pegged for out-of-state even before glancing at the California plates, based on the fact that diesel fuel without the proper additive turned to jelly in Montana winters. As he grabbed his pack and rod case, two women trailed by a terrier with his tongue lolling came clomping down toward the trailhead, bear sprays holstered on their hips. The women were "XX Montana hardbodies," as Sean had heard Sam Meslik brand the type—crinkly-eyed, small-busted, hold-the-makeup women with ropy muscles and year-round tans, who weren't afraid to show sweat or a stubble of underarm hair, and who trekked like sherpas in summer and skied like bats out of hell all winter. They were the granolas who had arrived in the big immigration waves of the '70s and '80s and '90s, and came to include Montana's waitresses, receptionists, and hairdressers, as well as her doctors, attorneys, fly fishing guides, and university scientists. They came, they stayed, they worked, they played. They might have the same problems with the men in their lives as the sisters they had left behind, but the rivers were their Xanax and the mountains were their wine, and the sun that leathered their faces kept their hearts supple. If the idealism with which they had crossed the border was tested by the staunch conservatism of the old guard, it had not disappeared so much as been replaced by pragmatism. Theirs was a world with an environment worth fighting for, and they had learned how to fight for it. Sean thought the state was better for them, smiled hello, greeted the panting terrier, and started up the trail.

It was an hour hike to the trail junction in the meadow, where Sean paused to flick a grasshopper fly here and there in the Trail Fork of Bear Creek. It was too early for hoppers at this elevation, but trout that eked out a living in the pocket water of mountain streams didn't have the luxury of discrimination, and Stranahan caught and released a half a dozen six-inch rainbows that were silver as minted coins. He was breaking down his fly rod for the long hike up to the saddle when a sensation that was like a wind tickling the skin below his ear caused him to jerk his head up.

Stranahan had spent enough time in bear country that he had developed mental antennae similar to those of prey animals, who could not only scent, hear, and see the minutest indications of danger, but also could feel it as a shifting of magnetic poles. In the fall, fishing the Copper River in British Columbia, he had hesitated to walk downstream to the next good steelhead run, and questioning his reaction but not disobeying it, had watched as a boar grizzly with silver guard hairs emerged from a willow thicket fifty yards below him, then ambled down the bank in search of dying salmon. Here, experiencing the same sensation, he felt for the safety tab on his bear spray and looked around him. To his right was the creek bottom where he'd been fishing, to his left rose a long timbered ridge near the top

of which was an outcropping of white rock, behind him was the timbered canyon he'd climbed through. He felt the hairs on his bare
forearms briefly pimple with dread. He could actually hear his heart
beating. Then the wind that was not a wind subsided, the urgency
vanished, and he told himself he was just being foolish.

PART TWO

THE ARRANGEMENT

Three times before, the watcher had experienced the disturbance in the bloodstream that accompanied the sight of his brother man on the field from which one or the other would never emerge. He had come to think of these encounters as the "arrangements." But when the hiker had stopped in the meadow to break down his fly rod, the watcher, focusing his binoculars, saw that the hat that the man removed and hung from the trail post was the wrong color and that his hair was black, not the gray curls that framed the face of the simian man he'd observed at the bridge. Now that the watcher knew he'd been mistaken, the hands on the binoculars were quite steady. The fish that thrilled his veins had stopped swimming.

Although the distance from his vantage at the top of the rocky outcrop was too far to note a person's facial features, something about the hiker struck a chord of familiarity with the watcher—the posture perhaps—and for a moment this bothered him. Then he thought no, it didn't matter, for whoever this man was, his presence in the country was innocent. People hiked the Trail Fork nearly every weekend. But the country was big, an accordion of ridges in an evergreen sea, and the small timber benches where he had already buried two bodies were invisible until you were standing on them. The watcher doubted that more than two or three people set their boots on that shoulder of the mountain in a given year, and they were hunters climbing through snow, not hikers in July.

And so what if someone heard a shot today? Shots meant nothing in the high country. They were as common as thunderclaps, forgotten before their echoes rang into silence off the walls of the Sphinx.

The watcher placed a hand over the back of the dog that curled by his side. The sun was up and a few minutes after the hiker had continued up the trail and was out of sight, the watcher stood, moved into the shade of a Douglas fir tree, and sat back down, the dog following. Three hours passed. The shadow moved away from him and he felt sweat bead at his temples under the brim of his hat. He got up, stretched, and sought the shadow. He knelt on one knee and wiped the sweat with the back of his hand. His eyes were drawn to a yellow butterfly that was spotted like a leopard. It was beautiful and he smiled, surprised for a moment that he still had that capacity for wonder. The butterfly flew away.

By the time he raised the binoculars, the dark-haired man had emerged onto the trail and looked to be swiftly striding in the direction of the trailhead. He was leaving. He glanced at his watch. The man with whom he had the arrangement was late. But he might still be coming. There might still be time for death with honor.

CHAPTER FOURTEEN

The Realm of Gods

The young couple who had backpacked to the top of Sphinx Mountain had planned the trip to coincide with the woman's peak hours of fertility. If they conceived a boy in this realm of gods, they would name him Arden, which in Greek means "to lift up high." If they conceived a girl, they would call her Skye.

The man had packed a double-wide sleeping bag and they were zipped snug together at sunset, their tongues tasting each other's freeze-dried dinners—Mountain House Turkey Tetrazzini for him, Chicken Saigon Noodles from Backpacker's Pantry for her—when the shot rang out. Because they were from California, the echoing *kerrawang* that rang back and forth between the walls of the mountains came as a shock. At least to the young woman. She broke off the kiss and jerked her head up.

"What the hell was that?"

"Nothing," said the man. "It's Montana. People hunt here." He'd already had to calm her down once, when they heard what they thought was a wolf howling. He put his hand on her neck to pull her down on top of him.

At the second shot, the woman sat bolt upright.

"I'm calling 911," she said.

"The echoes make it sound closer than it really is." After climbing some forty-four hundred vertical feet, class three difficulty at that, he was seeing the mood slip away.

"I don't care. I'm calling." She reached for her backpack and fumbled for the cell in the top pocket.

"You'll never get reception."

"Hello. This is Mandy Clark . . ."

The young man sighed.

Martha was in bed with Sheba, the brittle-whiskered Siamese, on one side of her and Goldie, her Australian shepherd, on the other side, when the phone rang. Sheba stretched her claws out and kneaded them into Martha's side.

"Ouch, goddammit."

She reached for the phone, heard the voice.

"Walt, what the hell are you doing in the office? I thought you were flying to Chicago tomorrow morning."

"Well, this is morning, if you want to be technical about it. It turned into today about, ah"—she heard him fumbling with something— "an hour ago. Now Chicago time, that's central—"

"Walt!"

"Yeah, okay. Here's the thing. I'm not in the office, but Judy, she worked evening shift and got a call about nine forty-five. Some woman who was camping in the Madison Range 911'ed to report rifle shots."

"What's that got to do with anything?"

"That's exactly what I told myself, but then Judy said where and I thought I oughtta call. This woman, she was backpacking up on Sphinx Mountain. She and her fella, they're spending the night on the peak. Could be anything, but, you know, that's no more'n a half mile or so from the bench where we found those bodies. As the bullet flies, that is."

"Jesus. Why didn't Judy call me right away?"

"She's off last week, remember? Out of the loop. A shot in the mountains, it's just a notation in the log. I wouldn't be too hard on her if I was you."

Martha was thinking, why would Judy be telling Walt about a shot in the mountains after he left the office? It dawned on her.

"Are you sleeping with Judy? For Chrissakes, Walt. You're her boss."

There was a silence. She could hear Walt breathing.

"It just sort of snuck up on us."

Martha told herself to focus. "What exactly did this backpacker say?"

"Just what I told you. She heard a couple shots before dark and got worried." His voice rose an octave. "Was there anything else, Judes?"

Martha heard a female voice. She couldn't imagine anyone in bed with Walt. It was simply unimaginable.

"She said they'd heard a wolf howling earlier. You want, I could call in to Dispatch and get that number for you. The woman told Judy they'd be up there all night."

Martha thought, *He's still there, too. Whoever put those bodies in the ground, if he's killed again, then he's got the shovel out. He's digging the grave. He's got the blood on his hands right now.*

CHAPTER FIFTEEN

The Houndsman

"**H**ey, Irish. It's for you."

Stranahan faced his cards down on the fly-tying table and reached for the receiver that Jonathon Smither extended.

"It's a woman," Smither said, and raised his eyebrows. "Calling this late at night? Booty call. Got to be a booty call."

He pulled the phone back just out of Sean's reach and grinned, a big wolf grin.

"Tell her to come on down," Robin Hurt Cowdry said, his voice slurred. "I'll bet her for her clothes. If it's that barista of yours, there shouldn't be too many layers to peel."

Sean hadn't spoken to Martinique since they had buried the cat in the countryside. She'd been melancholy and they'd parted with no definite plans. Maybe it was her. He found that he wanted it to be her. He wrenched the receiver from Smither's hand.

"Hello."

"Your friends have loud voices." It was Martha Ettinger.

"We were just playing poker."

"Are you sober enough to drive?"

"Right now?"

"Right now."

"Sure."

"Do any of your buddies have a gun? I know you don't."

Sean repeated the question to the table, everyone gathered there but Polly Sorenson, who had gone to bed after losing a Silver Doctor

salmon fly, the equivalent of a high-dollar chip had they been playing for money instead of intricately tied feathers.

"I'm always packing," Smither said. He looked at the surprised
faces at the table. "Somebody's got to protect you assholes from the
natives." Were they all so old they didn't remember that he'd brought
a shotgun last year to hunt pheasants? It was in the eaves.

Stranahan drove the last five miles with the running lights, the
mountains bulking in the foredistance, erasing constellations as he
drew closer. He wiped the sweat from his palms as the engine ticked
down at the trailhead. Ettinger had been brusque on the phone,
sketched the details in thirty seconds, the possibility of another killing, the fact that he could beat her to the trailhead by forty minutes
and she wanted him there to take note of any vehicle leaving the
scene. The shotgun was a precaution. Under no circumstances was
he to play hero by trying to detain anyone from driving away. She
said she'd meet him there and hung up before Stranahan could tell
her that he'd been hiking the trail himself only a few hours before.

He switched on his headlamp and jotted down the plate numbers
of the two vehicles in the campground and those at the turnaround,
the same Dodge pickup and Volvo wagon that had been there when
he had driven out that afternoon. Returning to his rig, he slipped the
Beretta over and under from the mutton-lined leather case, jointed
the barrels onto the action, and dropped a couple shells into the
chambers. He walked up the trail a few hundred yards to the first
creek crossing, which consisted of a single log hewn flat on top, and
edged back into the trees. He sat down on soft duff under the branches
of a spruce, wrapped his hands around the barrels of the shotgun,
and listened to the silence settle about him. He was close enough to
the trail to get at least a vague impression of face and stature, should
anyone pass by in the dark.

The night was chill, and after twenty minutes he started to shiver.

He stood up to get his blood moving and heard a faint yelp—a dog? He sat down out of sight of the trail and waited.

And got nervous. Had it been a dog? If it was, it would scent him and investigate, likely as not followed by its master. He tried to think of excuses for being found there. A twisted ankle? No, he was too close to the parking lot. It would be tough to explain his presence, even if he ditched the shotgun. He could retreat farther from the trail, but that meant giving up any chance of seeing the hiker clearly enough to identify him later.

He heard the yelp again. Now he was sure it was a dog. Making up his mind to leave, he took the trail at a trot and arrived at the turn-around five minutes later with a plan. Opening the hood of the Land Cruiser, he used a box-end wrench to loosen the cable nuts on the battery terminals, hefted the battery out, and replaced it with a half-dead battery that he'd been hauling around in the back of the rig, meaning to get it charged up at the Exxon station. He tightened the nuts to secure the cables to the posts of the old battery, covered the good battery with his sleeping bag, and got behind the wheel.

He didn't wait long. When the flashlight beam bobbed into sight and swept over the vehicles at the trailhead, Sean cranked the ignition without putting his foot on the accelerator. The motor ground away without catching. He tried again—*urr, urr, urrrrr*—and climbed out to peer under the hood. The skin on his back crawled as the light swept over him from behind, illuminating the engine block.

He turned around, said, "Must have left the dome light on. I keep trying it every hour, trying not to run it down any more than it is. If you could give me a jump I'd be obliged. I've been here 'bout half the night." Falling into the drawl that came so naturally in barbed-wire country.

He tilted his head so that his headlamp flashed on the face of the man who approached him. The face was canyoned with shadows where the light glanced across at right angles. It was a lived-in face, skeptical, the eyes unfriendly slits under a felt Stetson. The man's cheek muscles flexed, pulling up the corners of a mustache gone to seed, the kind he'd once heard a woman call a "molest-stache."

"You picked a bad place to run out of juice. A fella could wait here a while, all right. Shit, let me get this pack off my back. And take the goddamned light off my face." The voice was as hard as the expression.

Sean said, "Sorry," and watched the man's back as he walked to the pickup. He was followed by a hound with a triangle silhouette, its deep chest tapering to a belly no thicker than an Irishman's wallet. The stout, short-barreled bolt gun strapped on one side of the man's backpack shone dully in the lambency.

Just stay calm, he told himself. Knowing, for reasons he had never understood, that the admonition wasn't necessary. He had always managed to keep his heart in his chest when the world around him began to spin. As a reaction to potential danger, it wasn't exactly the same as absence of fear, nor was it courage. Courage, in Stranahan's book, required an active summoning of will in a situation where the natural response was flight. Sean's composure was innate and required no summoning. Percy McGill, the retired Boston police detective who had headed investigations for Sean's grandfather's law firm, had witnessed the character trait on several occasions. "Most guys"—he'd jabbed a finger at Sean's chest—"it takes them years on the beat to grow your kind of nerve. But by then they have the experience you don't. Nerve without experience, that buys a man his tombstone."

Sean heard the engine start up. The truck idled down, coming to stop a few feet from the Cruiser's front bumper. The man brushed aside Sean's offer of help and hooked up the cables. "No offense, but I don't know you from Adam. I seen a battery explode once. Took a man's face off, half of it, per' near. You just turn the key when I gun the engine."

Where the hell was Ettinger?

Sean turned the key and the engine coughed and caught.

"So who am I thanking?" he said.

The man threw the cables into the back of the pickup and stood by the open driver's side door, the dog at his feet.

"I gotta hit it," he said. "My hound here, he took after a lion and I spent half the goddamn night running him down, trying to get to him before a wolf did. I caught up to him down at the crick, I come this close to putting a bullet in his head. And this dog, this is a dog never done a wrong thing in his life before."

Sean reached down to pat the dog's head. His arm was trapped in a vise grip halfway through the movement.

"Son, don't you never put your hand to a lion hound lest you have a mind to lose it. Judge here, he's a Walker dog and got a mild temperament, but if this was my ridgeback, my kill dog, Bear—Bear'd take that hand right off'n you."

The man whistled the hound into the cab and climbed in behind it.

"I heard a couple shots earlier," Sean said. He hadn't, but Ettinger had told him about the 911 call. "Was that you?"

"You're full of questions, aren't you? But yeah, I emptied a couple trying to pull Judge off the track." He touched the brim of his hat. "I hope you learned a lesson tonight," he said.

CHAPTER SIXTEEN

Field of Stars

"**S**o you had a conversation with this man and somehow managed not to get his name? Is that the size of it?" The half of Martha Ettinger's face that was illuminated looked tired.

"He wasn't the kind of person who said anything he didn't want you to know. I got the impression he liked anonymity."

The two vehicles, Ettinger's pickup and Jason Kent's Chevy four-by-four, had driven up the access road a half hour too late to intercept the houndsman. They were gathered around a six-volt lantern set on the hood of the Chevy. Kent spread his big hands on the hood for warmth. Warren Jarrett was working a toothpick. Harold Little Feather scratched under the cast covering his left forearm. In the hard glare of the lantern light he looked like a zombie, with a blood-stained gauze forehead bandage half hidden underneath a tattered red bandana.

"Like old times," he said.

"Don't remind me," Martha said. The last time they had pow-wowed around the hood of Kent's truck was a little more than a year ago, night two of the manhunt for a murderer named Apple McNair. He had managed to escape the net.

"What I'm saying is, being back, it wasn't a guarantee," Harold said. "It's a nice feeling."

Ettinger felt the cell vibrate in her pocket. One bar of reception, a short conversation consisting mostly of *huh*s.

"That was Katie. She'll be here in forty minutes." She unscrewed the stopper of a metal thermos and poured a cup of coffee into the cap. "I've got paper cups in the truck," she said.

Jarrett stopped working the toothpick long enough to say, "No thank you."

"Unless you know something I don't," Kent said, "I can't see why we aren't done here. At least 'til daylight when we can turn the dog loose and see if he finds a fresh-turned grave. We've accounted for the Volvo. Pickup's gone. We got a plate we can run and an eyewitness who can make the ID."

"Uh-huh," Ettinger said. She lifted her chin toward Stranahan. "Would you say this man was evasive because he had something to hide, or because it was his nature?"

"I think if he was trying to hide something, it was running lion outside the chase season. He came up with a cover story of his dog bolting just in case someone from FWP asked me about it later. But the guy seemed awful unconcerned for someone who'd just committed murder. I don't see him with a shovel in his hand."

"You never do," Martha said. She blew out a breath. "Look, we're here. It's only a few hours 'til dawn. Let's kick it around. I don't expect all of you to add this to your workload, certainly not you, Jase"—Kent nodded—"but I'd like everybody in the loop."

Warren said, "Is Katie bringing donuts? Or is she going to feed us dog biscuits?" He looked at Sean. "She did that once. She was supposed to bring donuts and handed out these biscuits shaped like hearts. 'They're gourmet,' she said. She got offended when we passed on them."

Martha said, "I told her to get the donuts when I called her from Bridger. She said she would."

"Then I'll have some of that coffee," Warren said.

While they waited, Ettinger took them through the case developments, starting with the autopsy results for the second body. Doc Hanson had contacted Boyd Mathis, his old residency supervisor at

Kern Medical, who had records of a sixty-four-year-old Hispanic patient with degenerative bone and nerve damage from valley fever. The man had been reported missing in mid-July last summer. Mathis had recalled sitting down with the distraught brother, with whom the patient lived, and discussing the very real possibility of suicide. But because a body had never been found, Mathis wanted to consult with the medical lawyers about confidentiality issues before discussing the patient in detail. He did say that he would get in touch with the brother, to pave the way for Martha speaking to him directly. She said she was cautiously optimistic. The age, ethnicity, and time frame were on the money.

"We get a DNA match with the brother, then we work the phones and see who this man was in contact with. It could lead to a relationship with the first victim, or maybe to whoever killed him."

"If it wasn't suicide," Jarrett said.

Ettinger rubbed her front teeth over her lower lip, thinking. "We have two men with terminal illnesses dead four months apart, buried within two hundred yards of each other, one with a big hole through his skull. Plus we have a bullet in a tree root from the vicinity. I think this is murder. Somebody lured these men to the mountain to kill them. If it isn't the lion hunter, then it's someone else with roots in the area. He's killing people in his backyard."

"Awful big backyard," Little Feather pointed out.

Katie Sparrow arrived, Lothar with his ears perked, sitting shotgun. She walked around the hood of the truck, holding out the donut bag like she was offering a bucket of candies for children at Halloween. She came to Sean last.

"And one for you," she said.

He took a bite of a powdered cake donut.

"I like a man with a white mustache," she said, and winked at him.

Martha caught the wink and said, "Hunh-uh. No office romances."

"I'm federal and he's a private citizen. I can jump his bones if I want to."

Warren said, "Martha's just upset because she found out about Walt and Judy."

"You've got to be kidding," Katie said. "Isn't that, like, unnatural or something?"

"Or something," Martha said. "Can we focus here? Katie, you found the bullet. Take us through the process of discovery."

When Katie had finished, Sean said, "About the caliber. I met a man who has a rifle that shoots a five-hundred-grain bullet. He used a solid in that weight to kill a Cape buffalo."

Ettinger looked at him. "Really," she said.

All eyes turned to Sean as he related his meeting with Congressman Crawford.

"Why didn't you tell me?" Martha said.

"Because the caliber's wrong. The congressman's rifle is a .470. The bullet Katie found is .488."

"Caliber designation isn't always the same as bore diameter," Jarrett said. "A .270 Winchester mikes out at .277."

Martha was shaking her head. "Bullet, no bullet, I can't see Crawford as a suspect. He's an asshole who's set the image of our state back forty years, but I don't see him as a murdering asshole. He would have been in office at the time these two men were killed. Still, why don't you look into this, Sean? Arrange for another meeting, feel the man out. And nail down the bullet discrepancy. Find out exactly what kind of gun it is we're looking for."

Jarrett abruptly stopped working his toothpick. Feeling his eyes on her, Ettinger explained Stranahan's temporary hiring as an outside investigator for special projects. Sean watched the faces register the news—Katie raising her eyebrows in bemusement, Kent nodding slowly, Jarrett starting to work his jaws again with no change of expression. Little Feather said, "Sean showed good judgment tonight. He managed to talk to this guy without arousing suspicion. I say welcome aboard. I can always use another pair of eyes on the ground." Stranahan realized his status in the group had changed over the past year. He was accepted now, if not as an equal, at least as someone who didn't need hand-holding.

Ettinger said, "Yeah, well, we're shorthanded. I thought it was in the department's best interest. Sean seems to be able to step in shit even if there's only one cow in the pasture. Jase"—she worked her chin with her fingers—"why don't you go home, bolster what's left of the troops. You can take off after I get back. It doesn't look like we're going on a manhunt this morning, at least not for anyone above ground." She pursed her lips. "Warren, you run down that lion hunter. Don't mention the bodies. Just bring him downtown for question-ing. Let him think it's something to do with chasing cats out of sea-son, a wildlife infraction. I want him in the chair, face-to-face, when I drop the M word on him."

Jarrett nodded and climbed into the passenger seat of Kent's Chevy.

After the truck had grumbled away, Stranahan said, "So I guess my job is to step in shit."

"What about me?" Katie said. "What do I get to do?"

"Besides being chipper for no reason?" Martha looked west across the valley. The sky was midnight blue over India ink, a field for a thousand stars.

"It's your show. Lead the way. If we start now, it will be light when we reach the saddle."

For two hours Katie worked Lothar off leash, uphill into the sink of the chill morning air that flowed down the shoulder of Sphinx Mountain. When the sun was up and the flow shifted, she skirted around to the top of the microburst and worked down through the deadfall from the upper bench to the lower one, clearing grids as Martha, Sean, and Little Feather sweated through their shirts, search-ing the country to either side.

They reconvened at noon before hiking back to the trailhead. No one was in the mood to joke. Katie had found fairly fresh grizzly tracks in the disturbed earth where they had excavated the second body, mama bear and her cubs just making the rounds. But if someone had been shot and buried, it wasn't here. Katie suspected from Lothar's elevated attention that a human had passed through the area within the past twenty-four hours, but she couldn't be sure. When Martha pressed her to be more specific, she said flip a coin.

Sean reminded them that he had spent an hour or so in the area yesterday afternoon. It could have been him that aroused the shepherd's nose.

"Fiddle-dee-fucking-dee," Martha said.

It was a weary procession that switchbacked down from the saddle to the meadow at the trail junction, where they stopped for a water break. They rested awhile in the shade of some boulders near the creek and had just started walking again when Harold motioned them to a halt. It was the exact place where Sean had had an impending sense of danger the day before, but Harold didn't look concerned, just attentive as he canted the angle of his head and turned first one ear to the east, then the other.

"Bear bells. Probably that man and woman who called from the Sphinx."

In a minute they saw the couple clomping down the trail under bulky packs. They stopped, chests heaving, the man with a beatific expression on a face framed with damply curled long brown hair and a Jesus beard; the young woman's face just looked relieved. She was pretty in a hippyish, Joni Mitchell way, a willowy blonde with sea foam eyes, her untethered breasts tenting a T-shirt that read THINK GREEN under a stenciled frog. They took off their packs and sat with their arms around their knees, reliving their night on the Sphinx.

"The wind wouldn't stop," the woman said. "It howled all night."

The man agreed. "It was wild."

Martha questioned them to fix the timeline. When did they hear the wolf? About seven, after they had peaked. Was it a wolf? For sure, the man said. The woman drew her shoulders together and shuddered. Scary, she said. Just one wolf? One drawn-out howl, followed by another about an hour later. The woman said no, the wolf had howled a third time, but it was faint because the wind had picked up. But all from more or less the same place. Location? The man pointed toward the saddle. But hard to tell. Two shots? No disagreement on that. About an hour before dark. Close together. Not *bang bang*, but *bang . . . bang*. Where? Really hard to say. From the place where the wolf howled? Maybe, but the man thought more north and from lower elevation, down toward the Middle Fork Trail. Had they by any chance heard a dog barking or baying, like a hound would bay? The woman might have. She'd thought it was coyotes. It came and went. It was in the middle of the night. She hadn't managed much sleep. The young man shook his head. He hadn't heard anything after the shots.

Martha noticed that the man looked only at her and seemed unable to meet the eyes of either Sean or Harold, both of whom were indelibly stamped by their masculinity and utterly relaxed within their bodies, setting their feet on the planet wherever it occurred to them to set their feet. *He's just a boy trying out his beard*, she thought. The young woman kept glancing at Harold. When she stood up and shouldered her pack, her damp T-shirt stretched tight and she spent what to Martha seemed an inordinate amount of time adjusting the sternum strap.

"I need her like the ax needs the turkey," Harold said after the couple had gone.

Sean said he knew what he meant.

"Grow up," Martha said, feeling her face flush under the brim of her hat.

CHAPTER SEVENTEEN

Dark Continent, Light People

"I wanted to hear your voice. Are you at work?"

"I just sold a decaf C-cup to a guy who must have been eighty. He told me I looked like Paula Prentiss. Do you know who that is?"

"Some actress? The name's familiar."

"He said I should take it as a compliment. I watched him drive around the block twice before he worked up the courage to stop. I *do* think the gentleman has a crush on me."

It was the first time Sean had caught a note of playfulness in her voice.

"It looks like I have competition," he said.

"You better hurry back is all I can say."

"I have another job that will keep me through the afternoon. Then tonight the boys at the clubhouse want to have a going-away party for me."

"Did you find their fly?"

"No."

"Some detective you are."

"Do you want to drive down after your shift? Everyone would like to meet you. I call them the boys, but they're older. You'd find them entertaining, I think."

"I've had enough old men looking at me today."

"They're not like that. Besides, I want to show you off. It would do you good to get out of the house."

"Okay . . . Let me think about it."

Sean heard a clacking noise. Martinique's voice was faint. "Welcome to Lookers and Lattes. What can I get you today?"

Sean heard a man's voice and held the phone out, discovering that he didn't really want to hear someone talking to her whose eyes were directed at her body. Outside the phone booth, an anvil cloud jutted its jaw over the Gravelly Range. He could smell rain coming.

"I'm back," she said. "Okay, I'll come. Where should I meet you?"

After using the phone at the Blue Moon Saloon, Sean drove across the West Fork Bridge, headed upriver and then down the grade from the bluff to the Crawford mansion. He sat a minute after switching the motor off, looking down the draw past the clubhouse to the trees and the river beyond. The surface was pelted pewter by the rain. Sean had always had luck fishing in rain, darting a marabou streamer and then letting the line slide through his fingers so that the fly drifted, the minnow it represented vulnerable for just a second before he stripped it again. The trout hit during the pauses, and if the take wasn't as visually exciting as seeing a trout sip a dry fly off the surface, it had the element of surprise. It sent a shudder right up the arm holding the rod. But he was too exhausted to think about fishing now, and he walked to the door licking the rainwater off his lips and half hoping the congressman wasn't home.

"Come in, come in. Just don't shake yourself like a Lab or I'll have to get the mop." Crawford held the heavy door open, a querulous look on his symmetrical face.

"Thank you, Congressman."

"There aren't any congressmen here. The congressman resides in Kalispell. In Hyalite County, I'm Weldon. Drink?"

Sean nodded.

"To what do I owe the honor? You're not still looking for those trout flies, are you?"

"Yes, I am, but with less hope. The fact is I'm here because of that guy." He pointed to the Cape buffalo brooding on the wall. "I've always wanted to test myself against one of those and finally sold enough paintings to do more than dream. I thought maybe you could give me some advice about safari rifles. If you have the time. I know you're a busy man."

"I always have time to talk guns," Crawford said. "Where are you going to hunt—Botswana, Tanzania, Namibia? Namibia's an arm and a leg. Tanzania's your pecker, too. For my money the best bet for buff is the Cahora Bassa in Mozambique. You'll track bulls in mopane scrub, every day all day. You'll earn your buff. I wouldn't hunt with anyone but Tony Tomkinson. He's the best PH in the business. I'd be happy to help you book your hunt."

"I'd appreciate it. I'm thinking about sometime next summer."

"Our summer's their winter. I'd suggest July, not as hot then." He walked to the bar. "Scotch suit you?" Stranahan nodded.

"'God is good, but never dance with a lion.' Old African proverb," Crawford said, and they touched glasses.

"So what do you think about a rifle?"

"How much money do you have? A Ruger .375 will set you back a grand. That's the least you can expect to spend."

"I'd like to shoot a bullet as heavy as the one you took that bull with."

"Then you want a bolt-action in .458 Lott, but only if you can handle the recoil. The classic route is a double rifle in a caliber like .470 Nitro, but if you have to ask how much one costs, you can't afford it."

Sean wanted to bring up the diameter of the bullet he and Katie had found in the root, but didn't know how he could without alarming Crawford. Just keep him talking, maybe. He shrugged. "I'm asking."

"Twenty grand for a boxlock made during the golden years between the world wars, and as high as the sky from there. I've owned a handful, including a .577 that weighed thirteen pounds and God help the man who shoulders it, but most of my collection's back in Kalispell. The only double I have here is the .470 I took the buff with. I'll just go into the library and get it. You haven't touched your drink."

When Crawford came back, he set an oak and leather gun case with brass corners on his dining room table. The outside of the case was battered, the scuffed leather stamped with faded railroad and steamer ship tickets—Bombay, Mombasa, Pretoria, Ceylon. He opened the lid. Nestled in faded burgundy billiard felt was the rifle, its barrels in one compartment and the stock and action in another. A parchment trade label glued to the inside lid read JOHN RIGBY & CO., GUNMAKERS, LTD. BY APPOINTMENT TO HIS MAJESTY THE KING.

Crawford fitted the barrels onto the action. "Made in 1927 for the Maharaja of Sonepur. Rising bite action, shuts up tight as a bank vault." He passed the rifle to Stranahan.

Stranahan eased the top lever to crack the action. He squinted down the gleaming bores, which were as big around as his ring finger.

"You'll notice some minor throat erosion," Crawford said. "Those old Berdan primers were corrosive, but she'll put both barrels into a playing card at fifty yards."

Stranahan said seriously, "I never really thought about a rifle as being beautiful before. But this is a work of art." He turned it in his hands, admiring the flawless marriage of the stock to the action, the crisp diamond-point checkering on the pistol grip and scroll engraving on the sidelocks and steel buttplate. The twin black barrels looked as deadly as mambas.

"What's this?" Stranahan said, tapping the buttplate.

"That's a trapdoor operated by the recessed lever here. Actually, a steel buttplate is a bit out of place on a double rifle; most have a rubber pad to absorb the recoil, but the Maharaja must have specified the buttplate."

Crawford shrugged, but his voice had betrayed a touch of nervousness.

"Is there anything inside it?" Stranahan asked.

"No," said Crawford quickly. "I mean yes, there is, but not what I'd hoped for. The rifle was in India, so I was hoping for rubies. Alas, there was nothing but an extra set of firing pins."

"It's a beautiful piece of wood," Stranahan said.

Crawford nodded his head. "That's Circassian walnut. The oil finish alone is a half-year process. I could put this rifle up on a website like Champlin Firearms and pad my retirement account by eighty thousand tomorrow." Confidence was back in his voice. "I kid you not."

"You said you own more doubles like this?"

"I've bought and sold over the years. Lately I've sold, so my collection isn't what it used to be."

"What's the bore diameter of a .470?"

"Point four seven five."

Sean felt a letdown. The diameter of the bullet in the root was .488. He could pry further about specific guns the congressman owned, but knew he'd be pressing his luck. He tried a different tack.

"What made you want to hunt buffalo? It's a question I've been putting to myself, that's why I'm asking. Why can't I just be content to track elk in these mountains?"

"I can answer that one without saying a word." Crawford opened the lid of a compartment in the gun case and extracted a red-and-gold package of Kynoch cartridges. He extracted one and held it up, the brass case with its protruding bullet the size of a Panatela cigar.

"An elk's antlers are impressive, Sean. But elk don't bite back and they don't require a cartridge this size." He pushed the brass right up to Sean's nose, and as he shook it Sean saw a cloud pass across Crawford's face. Then it was gone and the sun was back in the man's eyes, but in that brief instant the concentration of dark energy was palpable.

Sean found that he was looking down on himself from a distance. It was as if they had become actors in a play.

"Hunting dangerous game is a rush," he heard Crawford saying. "It makes you come alive in a way you didn't know existed. Until they legalize grizzly bear hunting, the only place I can get my fix is the dark continent. If you were a reporter I couldn't say that because of the connotation—dark continent, dark people. But I mean in the sense of Africa as the last blank spot on the map. And that caliber of wildness, forgive the pun, it's still there, even if you have to turn over more stones to find it. I'm envious of a young man like you taking his first trip. You face a buffalo charge, you'll find out what makes you a man."

"Sort of like going to war, I guess," Stranahan said.

"I wouldn't know about that. In 1973, my draft number was fifty-six. But that was the last year of fighting and they took only to eleven. As a good Montana boy I'd have gone, of course, and as a 'Nam vet I'd be a more successful politician than I already am. Give a man vet status and he jumps fifteen points in the polls." He gave short laugh. "Unless your name is John Kerry."

Crawford drained the amber liquid out of the squat, square glass. "Another?"

Still on his feet after thirty-six hours, neat whiskey was the last thing Sean needed.

"I don't suppose you could make me an Irish coffee." He was back within his weary body, the senator so close he could smell the after-shave.

Crawford said, "I'll take that as a challenge."

"You look like a man who'd rather lay his head on a pillow than the saddle fork of a woman," Crawford said. He handed Sean a glass of black coffee and Jameson.

"We played poker to all hours in the clubhouse."

"Invite me next time. I can hold bad cards with a straight face, it comes with the territory. Really, I've enjoyed the members I've met. Polly Sorenson, especially. Willoughby, isn't he the president?"

"He is. But our game might not be rich enough for you. We don't play for money. We play for flies. A caddis fly would be a dollar, say. A streamer, five dollars. The more elaborate the fly, the more it's worth in the pot. They indulge me, letting me bet my own flies even though I'm not on the same skill level as a tier. Some of the flies that change hands, the salmon flies, are worth five hundred dollars."

"Sounds like fun."

Crawford indicated a stuffed chair under the glowering bulk of the buffalo mount.

"You know the great thing about Montana?" he said. He settled himself into a chair identical to the one he'd indicated for Sean and leaned forward across a coffee table. He placed the cartridge on its base between them. "It's that people from all walks of life walk together. What I mean is, you go to Washington, anywhere East, and you find that people stay within their own socioeconomic class, within their own political circles. If you're from Boston, Irish, blue-collar roots, vote the Democratic ticket, most of your friends are more like you than they are different. Am I right? But here, you take a rancher who is land rich, who's as conservative as Limbaugh, and his best friends might include a doctor, a professor with an Obama sticker on his bumper, a mechanic, and a waitress. In the East, to be a politician who claims to be a man of the people means you have your picture taken with them. But here, I can meet someone like you, or your friend Willoughby, or a movie star who owns land in the valley, with an old ranch hand like Emmitt Cummings thrown into the mix, and we can become friends on a level playing field. I have guys I hunt deer with who can't pony up the gas money to drive forty miles and back. In camp I'm just Weldon to them. We're at the same eye level. If all the country was like this, we'd understand each other and work to find common solutions. Now I'm sounding like a politician."

"No," Stranahan said. "I've noticed the same thing." He was surprised to find himself in tune with the congressman on at least one subject. There was a charm behind the man's bluster and Sean found himself liking him despite his very real suspicions.

"I've been thinking about your trip to Africa," the congressman went on. "I don't think I explained the thrill of hunting buffalo adequately. Let me ask you. Have you ever heard of a story called 'The Most Dangerous Game'?"

Sean brought his head back just a fraction of an inch. He was wide awake now. He said, "That's about the guy who gets shipwrecked on an island and meets some count or somebody. The man plays a life-and-death game with him. I had to read it in high school."

Crawford nodded. "Actually, he's a Russian aristocrat who traps shipwreck victims and hunts them down—man is the most dangerous game, you see. The premise is that the Russian, Zaroff, has hunted big game all over the world, but it got to be boring. So he searched for a more dangerous game. He came to the conclusion that it was man, the only animal that could reason. But there's a flaw in the story. Zaroff sends his victims into the jungle with a knife, where he gets to track them down with a gun. How fair is that? Now, if two men were equally armed—say you and I went at each other with big-game rifles. We agreed to a field of play. We hunted each other until one was dead. Now that would be a fair fight, and I'd just as soon go that way as another."

Sean found himself leaning forward until the men's faces were no more than a foot apart. The darkness was back in Crawford's face. It was as if he exuded a magnetic force that drew Sean forward.

Crawford rolled the cigar-sized cartridge in his fingers.

"Now you take a Cape buffalo, you wound him, he goes off, he circles back on his trail, he waits, one ton of armor-plated m'bogo. He's sick in his stomach, he has hate in his heart. All his life force is directed at destroying the man with the stick that sounds like thunder. He's twelve feet long and he's black as midnight, but he can hide in the tiniest patch of thornbush. When he comes, he comes with his nose out, the boss of his horns flat, he comes with all the fury and menace in the world. It's true, you got your PH by your side. But believe me, in that moment you find out what you're made of. You've got maybe three seconds to raise your rifle, and if you don't get one into his spine or his brain, he'll knock you flat, he'll hook you in the guts, he'll pound you with the boss of his horns until you're a red smear on the ground. Each year, professional hunters and clients die in buffalo charges. The danger is real. It's a hell of a lot more real than tracking down a man who's holding nothing but a knife." He rapped the cartridge on the table and set it back upright.

Sean, sipping his Irish coffee, felt his fingers shake on the glass. What had he heard Crawford say? For the past few days, he'd been trying to paint a scenario that ended with two bodies buried on Sphinx Mountain. Could it have been a deadly game, or two of them, with the victor ensconced in his home, sipping whiskey from a square tumbler under the eye of a buffalo? But if it was, if Crawford was involved, then why did he feel free to talk about it, even if he didn't know about Stranahan's relationship with the sheriff's department?

"Weldon," he said, "what do you think about those bodies found on Sphinx Mountain?"

"I read about it. Sounds like foul play hasn't been ruled out. But who knows? Bodies turn up in the backcountry now and then. People underestimate the power of nature." He shrugged. He didn't seem concerned. "Would you care to stay for dinner? I'm fending for myself tonight. I could rustle up a T-bone from the freezer."

"I'd like to, but I have to drive to Bridger this evening."

Crawford saw him to the door. The rain clouds had broken up. Every grass stem glistened. "I've got a range on the back acreage," he said. "Come out day after tomorrow, say late morning. You can shoot the .470."

"Sounds good."

"No, I mean it. If I'm not here, just follow the sound of the gunshots. You won't mistake them for a .22." Crawford stuck out his hand. Sean took it, still thinking about their conversation, the big cartridge standing at phallic attention between them on the coffee table.

CHAPTER EIGHTEEN

A Study in Pointillism

Even conservatively dressed in jeans, cowboy boots, and western shirt snapped high enough to remove any hint of provocation, Martinique was a hit with the members of the Madison River Liars and Fly Tiers Club. Sean had never seen her in a social situation and was surprised to find her outgoing, quick to laugh, and able to stand her ground when the conversation on the porch turned to African politics, Robin Hurt Cowdry's perspective colored by his experience growing up in Zimbabwe during colonial rule and then having his family's farm confiscated when Robert Mugabe initiated his fast-track resettlement program, Martinique's by her Fulani heritage.

"Yes, but of the two of us I'm the real African," Cowdry said. "My family's been on the continent five generations, since it was Southern Rhodesia in the 1890s. We're buried in African soil."

Martinique had told him to extend his forearm along hers. "I rest my case," she said.

When Sean went inside to call Sheriff Ettinger on the club's landline, he doubted anyone on the porch would notice his absence. None of the members had taken their eyes off Martinique since she stepped out of the Land Cruiser. Ettinger picked up on the first ring. Without preamble, Sean sketched in the details of his conversation with the congressman. Her response—"hmm"—was followed by a half minute of silence. He could envision her rubbing her chin, staring into the middle distance. Then she said she also had some news, how about he drop by her house in the morning.

Patrick Willoughby was showing Martinique the proper way to

grip a fly rod—"like you're shaking its hand, thumb on top," he was telling her—when Sean rejoined the group outside. "My good man," Willoughby said, "with your permission, Polly and I are going to spirit this young woman down to the river and teach her to flycast. It's always best to learn from someone who is not in the family, don't you agree, Polly?" Polly agreed. Martinique gave Sean a covert wink as they walked away.

"You might have argued you weren't part of her family," Jonathon Smither said. He was turning a pheasant on the grill.

"I don't think it would have done any good."

"Probably not. Just be thankful it isn't me teaching her how to cast." He gave Sean one of his wolf grins. "I'd be teaching her about gripping something other than a cork handle."

Cowdry, sitting in an Adirondack chair, smiled briefly. He was sipping a glass of Scotch and didn't look up.

So Sean fished alone in the hour before dinner. Above him was one of those summer skies that people who live in the East can't believe are for real, the light over the Gravelly Range lavender bleeding to pink, the clouds rimmed with golden light from the setting sun and the river a study in pointillism, as wavelets bounced colors back and forth and trout made quick swirls to take caddis pupae from the surface film. Sean felt the bamboo bend a dozen times before he heard the old iron triangle ringing from the porch. As he walked downriver to check on Martinique, her saw her sitting on the bank with Sorenson, engaged in deep conversation. Willoughby had apparently gone back to the clubhouse ahead of them.

"What are you two talking about?" he asked.

"Only the meaning of life." Sorenson patted Martinique's hand. "I wouldn't let this one get away if I were you."

Martinique stood up, her jeans wet from the grass. She gave Sean an impulsive kiss and they helped the old fly tier to his feet.

After dinner, when they said their goodbyes and were driving in the Land Cruiser toward Ennis where Martinique had left her car,

Sean said, "Kissing me in public. I might have a chance with you after all."

"I don't know," she said. "You're used to the couch and the cats. Maybe you'll be content to stay downstairs tonight." But she put her hand on his thigh as she said it. Then, in a wistful voice, "Poor Polly Sorenson, he doesn't know whether he has two months or two years. It's a reminder we don't live forever. We can't count on tomorrow."

"He mentioned something about his health to me last week, having OPED, initials like that. He didn't say anything about it being that serious."

"It's COPD, chronic obstructive pulmonary disease. For most people it isn't a death sentence, but he has some scarring between his lungs and chest wall from an old injury that compound the symptoms. Basically, his lungs are filling up with fluid. He's dying of asphyxiation and the only thing the doctors can do is slow down the progression with medication. He says he's lived a full life and made his peace with dying. He just doesn't want his last hours to be spent in a hospital bed, fighting for breath. I'm afraid I didn't learn much about fly casting from him. He opened up to me right away, he said I reminded him of somebody he knew once, some girl he fell in love with after the war and he always regretted they didn't marry. So"— she squeezed Sean's thigh—"in the spirit of no regrets, I don't think I'm letting you out of my reach tonight."

After he had dropped her in Ennis and was following the taillights of her car north toward the converted grain elevator, he thought about what she had said. Many people suffer from debilitating diseases that end in prolonged, painful death. The fact that Sorenson shared a similar prognosis with the men whose bodies had been found on Sphinx Mountain could not be considered anything but a coincidence. What made Sean frown inwardly was something Willoughby had said at their first meeting, about Polly Sorenson being the only club member who had spent any time with Congressman Crawford. He had even been invited up to the mansion for dinner.

Was that, too, a coincidence? He was too tired to think straight, and then he was on the driveway to the grain elevator and Martinique was waiting at the door, having beaten him there by five minutes.

She had already changed into a black silk kimono embroidered with red hibiscus flowers. She waited until they were inside before putting her arms around his neck, the loose sleeves of the kimono sliding up to her shoulders. She held him at arm's length the way she had the first time, in the coffee kiosk, when she had said, "I'll go out with you, Mr. Sean Stranahan who's nice to cats." This time, she didn't say anything.

In the morning she served him cheese grits, saying that it was her father's favorite breakfast and he'd always told her that no one could make them the way she could.

"I take it you were a daddy's girl," Sean said.

"I was."

"Did he name you Martinique?"

"No, that was my mother. Martinique is an island in the West Indies. It was discovered by Christopher Columbus and the story of the name is that when his ship was coming in the women on the shore called out 'madinina, madinina.' My mother always wanted to go there, to any tropical island really. But the closest she ever got was listening to Jimmy Buffett sing about them."

She put down her coffee cup and took Sean's hand.

"My mother wasn't easy to live with. After Daddy died, she overdosed on lithium. She wasn't trying to kill herself, it was just that she got into the habit of taking a couple extra pills to treat her depression. I found her lying on the couch. That was March last year. Two years watching my father die and then that happens. It changed me. Last night I was afraid I would start to cry while we were making love, and you're so nice and you'd see me sad and you'd get yourself all dragged down with me and then you'd leave this morning and never come back and I couldn't blame you. And just look at me, I'm crying now." She wiped at the tear track below her left eye.

"I'm still here, Martinique."

She nodded, her eyes shiny. She tried to collect herself.

"Can I get you another cup of coffee? There's only a little."

"I couldn't handle any more than a B-cup," Sean said.

"Now you're making fun of me." But she was smiling in spite of herself. "The guy who hired me asked me if I'd consider a boob job. He said I couldn't sell snow cones in the Sahara with these breasts."

"Then why did he hire you?"

"He liked my face. He said when I smiled, it was so sad it made men want to take care of me. Some smile, huh?"

She stood to get the coffee, but Sean didn't let go of her hand and pulled her around to him.

"Do we have time? I thought you had to go see the sheriff."

"The sheriff can wait."

CHAPTER NINETEEN

For Love of Fidelia

Martha Ettinger was walking up the hill from the creek, wearing hip boots. A fly rod poked in front of her, the tails of her plaid flannel shirt were tied in a knot, there was a wicker creel on her hip. Stranahan rolled down the window of the Land Cruiser and told her she looked like a Norman Rockwell painting.

"I didn't know you fished, Martha."

"I also know how to tell time," she said. "You're late. I'll see you up at the house."

When she met him on the porch, she opened the lid of the creel. Three brook trout with jade flanks patterned by creamy spots rested on a bed of ferns. The backs of their heads were starting to discolor where she had whacked them with a stone.

"Don't tell me you're one of the those fly fishermen who doesn't believe in killing a trout to eat," she said.

"I have nothing against eating trout, especially brookies."

"Good answer, 'cause that's what I'm frying up for lunch."

"You're not mad at me for being late?"

"You mean for the second time this week, and this time you being on the county nickel and all. No, I'm not going to let anything spoil my mood on my day off, especially not a man at such loose ends he feeds a mouse just so it keeps him company. You're still feeding that critter, right?"

"Mickey," Sean said. "Or maybe it's Minnie. And I have a girlfriend now, a human one. At least I think I do."

"Katie? She's only making a play for you, that's obvious as mud.

You don't watch out, she'll put a collar around your neck and start telling you 'Fetch.'"

"It isn't Katie."

Martha looked at him, raised her brow. Sean said nothing.

"Then don't tell me. So what do you say we drink iced tea on the porch and bat this thing around?"

They talked about the congressman's penchant for guns, his admiration for "The Most Dangerous Game." Martha wasn't familiar with the story. Neither could make Crawford as a murderer, even if he had painted a credible scenario for the way the men on Sphinx Mountain were killed.

"This thing about Polly Sorenson. Crawford makes a point of getting to know the one member of the club who's seriously ill?" Stranahan made it a question, drank his tea as he watched Martha consider.

"Well, I don't know what to say about that," she said. "It ties in in the obvious way, the bodies on the Sphinx, those men having terminal illnesses. That's why I wanted to talk to you this morning, to tell you we ID'd one of the victims."

"Really? That's good work."

"It's all thanks to Doc. The second body, the one you and Katie stumbled across, the guy had valley fever. It causes degenerative bone and nerve damage. Doc recognized the scars on the tissue and bones right away." She sketched in the details of the disease and its prevalence among Hispanics.

"It sounds horrible," Sean said.

"It is. There's a very high suicide rate. Anyway, it turns out one of Doc's supervisors in med school pioneered treatment for the disease. He had a patient who fit the description. The man bailed on his treatments last July and disappeared."

Sean rattled the cubes in his tea glass. "Wouldn't you have to run a DNA match to know? From what you told me, there must be hundreds of Hispanics who have the disease."

"There are, but only one had a wife named Fidelia."

For a second Stranahan drew a blank.

"The wedding ring," he said.

"I called the missing patient's brother. He confirmed it. Those bones belonged to a man named Alejandro Gutierrez. Called Aleko. From the brother's information he was born in a region called the Sierra Tarahumara in Mexico. There were originally three brothers, but the oldest fell off a cliff in the Huachuca Mountains on the Arizona border, trying to cross. The other brothers were luckier and ended up as pickers in the San Joaquin Valley. The one I spoke to, Diego, he's the youngest. The story is that he and Aleko worked their way up to being managers of a big ranch in Kern County. They got their citizenship and bought some land from the owner to get their start. The Gutierrezes' is one of only a handful of Hispanic ranches in the valley. They live in a hacienda, grow almonds, grapes, apricots, you name it."

"How did our guy wind up in Montana?"

"The brother doesn't know. He says after Aleko got sick, he'd walk up one of the ranch roads, go into the foothills, and sit under the live oaks and read the Bible. Sometimes he'd walk back and sometimes he'd have his brother drive up and get him because he was in too much pain to walk back. One day last July, Aleko goes on his walk, he doesn't return. A vehicle the pickers use is reported missing, so naturally Diego suspects his brother might have taken it. A week later he gets a call from Bakersfield police. They've run the license of an abandoned vehicle. The truck was parked two blocks from the Greyhound station."

"If he left on a bus, you ought to be able to trace the ticket."

Martha shook her head. "You have to show state-issue ID to pick up a ticket if you've reserved it online. But if you buy your ticket over the counter, you can ride from Bakersfield to Bangor, Maine, without having to produce identification."

"So the truck in Bakersfield is the end of the trail."

"It seems so. But there's more to the story. After Aleko's wife died, the brother says, he went downhill fast. Diego got him into a group therapy program up in Modesto, where he could meet other gravely ill patients. He also encouraged him to log on to an online therapy site. But Aleko seemed to lose heart after a few weeks. Then a few days before the disappearance, Aleko asked his brother very seriously what he thought about assisted suicide. Did he think that was a sin? Diego told him that he didn't know what was in God's heart, but that the family loved him and would take care of him, please don't think about such things. Aleko said, 'You don't know what it's like. I'm not the person you used to know. The person you crossed over with is dead.'"

Stranahan exhaled with a whistle. He said, "The congressman's idea of men hunting each other, it doesn't seem so far-fetched, does it? This Gutierrez is a guy who might have welcomed a bullet."

"I think that's a stretch."

"Not a long one."

Martha nodded. "Maybe."

"So where do we go from here?"

"We check records. Even if the bus company doesn't have paper on him, he could have rented a car or checked into a motel once he got here. Or bought a rifle, for that matter. If we can pick up his trail, a name might turn up along the way."

"It would be nice to ID the other body and see if the profiles match," Sean said. "Find out if anything else in the history correlates besides disease. Hunting, group therapy, death of a loved one, a car parked by a railroad station, whatever."

"Yes, it would, but so far we've gone nowhere with the first victim. By the way, Warren ran down that lion hunter in Big Timber. I let him stew an hour in the interview room. The first rule of law enforcement is, 'Everybody lies to the police.' Some 'cause they're guilty, some 'cause they're trying to protect somebody, and the rest just do it to get on my nerves. The second rule is, 'Anybody who goes to sleep in the box is guilty.' You take a guy who's wrongfully accused, he's jumpy as a bug. This guy put his head down on the desk and fell asleep. But then, what's he guilty of? My guess is nothing but a game violation. He claims he didn't know anything more about the bodies than he'd seen on TV. Said it was a coincidence they were buried in the same district where he outfits. Warren had already checked that part with Fish and Game, and he's licensed to guide in District 360. So he's telling the truth there. My guess is he's a dead end. What? You look dubious."

Stranahan drank the last of his tea, watered now that the ice cubes had melted in the Mason jar. "Doesn't it make you suspicious, Martha? I mean, who better to look at for this than a guy who hunts the area with paying clients? He knows the forests around Sphinx Mountain better than anyone. Plus he runs hounds. Maybe he uses the dogs to track the old guys down. That's what the count in the story does."

"And he gets men of sound mind to agree to it? No, I don't buy that."

"Still, I think he's worth looking at. You want me to ask around?"

"No. I'll have Warren do it. This guy put one and one together and knew it was you who ratted him out at the trailhead. His word. He told Warren the next time you meet, he's going to stick your head in a toilet bowl."

"Should I be worried?"

"Probably not. But I thought I'd tell you."

"What's his name?"

"Buster Garrett. He's one of those guys who always has a bone up his butt about something. I'd stay out of the Road Kill Saloon in McLeod. That's where he and his buddies do their drinking."

"You don't think I can take care of myself?"

"Can you?"

"My father was South Boston Irish. He had me in boxing clubs from when I was ten. I placed second in my weight class at a tournament called the 'Silver Mittens' in Lowell. Got to shake hands with

Micky Ward. I might have gone on and boxed Golden Gloves but my dad died and we moved to the country."

"I didn't know that about you. All the same, though, I don't want you mixed up with Garrett. You run down the bullet, the rifle that fired it, like we agreed on."

She stood up. "I'm going to fry those trout. Then I'm going to tell you about a few acres down the road you might want to consider buying, so you don't have to keep thinking up excuses to see my pretty face."

When he crossed the bridge below Ettinger's place after lunch, his cell was ringing. It was Sam, telling him he'd lined up an evening float with an old client, someone Sean knew. They'd be putting in to float the lower Gallatin at six.

"You want to spell me with the oars?"

"Who's the client?" Sean said. He was thinking of Winston, the barber from Mississippi. Willoughby had said that Winston would be coming back to spend a week with the club later in the month.

"It's Frankie Dibacco."

"Oh." He hesitated a moment. Dibacco was an affable angler who looked like an NFL linebacker a few years and a few pounds out of the game. But Sam would have been his next stop anyway. Sean wanted to ask his help in pinning down the kind of rifle that had shot the bullet Katie's metal detector found. Sam knew everyone in the valley. If anyone knew who might have such a rifle, other than Congressman Crawford, it would be Sam.

"Yeah, okay."

"You don't sound so enthused," Sam said.

"No, let's do it."

"Meet me at that VFW access in Logan. We're going to wade the good runs. Be a chance to get your dick wet. Better odds than you've got with that woman who sells stripper coffee. Dominique or whoever she is."

"Martinique."

He heard Sam laughing and the click as he hung up on him.

When Sean pulled the Land Cruiser up to the boat ramp, Sam was rigging rods and regaling Dibacco with an exaggerated account of Stranahan's kidnapping the summer before. The client buried Stranahan's hand in his giant paw. "I didn't know I'd be fishing with a celebrity."

"Sean isn't a celebrity so much as a dipshit," Sam said.

So it was old times, the men laughing their way down the river, Sam outfishing the others three to one where they stopped to wade.

"You couldn't catch goldfish in a toilet bowl tonight," Sam said, when he and Sean were shooting pool at the Cottonwood Inn afterward. "Seemed like you were off somewhere in your head and it wasn't the river. That woman must really have you by the nads."

"It's not her." Sean lined up the six and scratched.

Sam caught the cue ball before it rolled into a corner pocket. He took the stick out of Sean's hands. "You can't fish, you can't shoot. What's on your mind?"

"You are, Sam. I'm trying to find a gun that chambers a particular bullet and I wonder if you can help." He'd cleared broaching the subject at lunch with Ettinger, finally convincing her that Sam had the pulse of everyone in the county and could be an asset to the investigation. "He's the biggest bullshitter in the county, too," she'd reminded him, but had relented on the condition that Sean tell Meslik no more than necessary; specifically, he was not to mention that they had ID'd one of the bodies. She was holding back that information from the newspaper, fearing that it could compromise the investigation if someone local was involved and knew a cold trail had grown warmer.

Sam shrugged the heavy slabs of muscle on his shoulders. "I'm afraid I can't help you, my man. I just buy Winchester Western loads off the shelf for my .270. I don't know squat about ballistics."

"It was worth a try," Stranahan said.

"I said I couldn't help you. I didn't say you couldn't help yourself.

There's this thing called the Internet, been around a while now. Come back to the trailer and we'll boot up the Mac. You'll have your answer before I can make you a Bloody Mary."

Stranahan wondered what he'd been using for brains half his life.

Sam's time frame proved to be wishful thinking. They batted around in cyberspace for half an hour before Sean found a site called Nitro Madness, which included a forum on big-bore rifles. He registered as a new member with the user name "Simba Sean," finished Sam's V8 cocktail waiting for the moderator to email him his password, then logged on and started a thread. "My friend bought a bullet from a collector at a gun show. Diameter—.488. Weight—500 grains. He forgot what the collector told him about the cartridge and the gun that fires it. Help, anyone?"

"Watch," Sam said, after Sean hit the submit button. "These boys are like ranch hands who chain up their half tons and drive down the road hoping to winch somebody out of a ditch. They'll fight each other to help." He was right. The first response came within five minutes, under a postage stamp photo of a fat white man holding a spear. His handle, "Masai Warrior," sounded optimistic.

"The warrior believes the cartridge you're looking for is the .475 No. 2 Nitro Express. It's a rimmed cartridge developed in the early 1900s by W. J. Jeffery, a top-tier London gunmaker. Ballistically, the cartridge is similar to the better-known .470 Nitro, except shooting a bullet a few thousandths of an inch bigger around. Jeffery double rifles are highly sought after for African big-game hunting, particularly for buffalo and elephant."

"There you go," Sam said. "Four seven five numero dos." He scratched the bridge of his crooked nose. Sean clicked off the search engine, Sam's computer reverting to a screen saver photo of a bikini blonde wearing hip boots, a rod in one hand and a salmon in the other, the fish days dead and the model's expression only slightly less so.

Sean rubbed the ears of Killer, Sam's big Airedale, who lay beside him on the upholstered booth seat in the kitchen nook.

"So are you going to tell me what this is about, or do I have to guess?" Sam said.

"I can tell you this much. The bullet was found with a metal detector on Sphinx Mountain, near where those bodies were unearthed. There's no proof that it has anything to do with the deaths, but we have to check it out. There's a guy in the valley who has hunted in Africa with rifles that are chambered for similar rounds."

"Close but no cigar, you're saying."

"No, not the same. But he's a collector, he might have a .475 No. 2. If he does, then he becomes a person of interest because these rifles are expensive and very rare."

"Just ask the fucker if he owns one, that's what I'd do."

"The man doesn't know we have the bullet. If he hears the caliber mentioned, he'll know we found evidence and get rid of the rifle."

"Did you get DNA off the bullet? If you didn't, then you can't tie it to the body except by proximity. Proving it came out of a particular rifle will put this guy at the scene, but he can just say he was shooting at an elk." Sam saw Sean's expression.

"What? So I've watched a few episodes of CSI. Who hasn't?"

"No, you make a good point." Sean hesitated. He said, "I've already told you more than I was supposed to, but I'm going to go with my gut on this. Most crimes are solved because people can't keep their mouths shut. You're a guy who hears everything about everyone. But you have to promise, this is just between us."

Sam held up his hands. "Never leaves the trailer, Kimosabe."

"About the DNA, that's confidential. And I'm not at liberty to tell you anything specific about the bodies. But all along, the question's been: What were these men doing up there? Were they killed by someone? Or did they commit suicide and have someone bury them? These were older guys who were sick and weren't going to get better, so they may have deliberately been looking for a way out. It isn't out of the question that they died in some form of paintball warfare, but with bullets and not paint. That last is my own speculation. Nobody else seems to think much of it."

"All right, I'll keep my ears open. Be an excuse to hit a few more bars than I already do. Can I run a tab with the department?"

"You wish. Let's boot up your computer again. There's something I'd like to Google."

By the time he reached Martinique's, it was past midnight. He let himself into the darkness and felt one of the cats rub against his leg. Martinique had told him she had an anatomy test tomorrow and Sean had intended to sleep at the cultural center. But when he left Sam's, he'd hesitated only a moment before driving to the grain elevator. It had nothing to do with physical desire. He just wanted to be near her, had found that the studio only reminded him of how long he'd lived alone. Sleeping on his futon with the second-floor windows open, he'd listen for the distant trains and feel the loneliness of the other solitary sleepers to whom love was a faint murmuring of those who passed in the dark and might have been, if only you had met them.

At Martinique's, he lay down on the couch and drew up the Indian-print buffalo blanket. Toward morning he was awakened by her opening the back door, where the outside steps led to the loft. He heard her moving about, her feet padding into and out of the bathroom, then coming close. She took his hand and led him back outside and up the steps with the moon watching, and in the bedroom she wriggled back against him so that they lay like spoons. He placed his hand over one of the breasts that couldn't sell snow cones in the Sahara. When he woke up again, she was gone. Her note said, "Feed the cats." A heart drawn in pen. The scripted initial "M." He folded it into his shirt pocket, could imagine Sam seeing it, his eyes rolling.

CHAPTER TWENTY

Charging Buffalo

"I thought you'd forgotten," Weldon Crawford said.

He handed Stranahan a pair of shooter's earmuffs. "Have a seat in back of the spotting scope. Focus on the fifty-yard target."

Stranahan squinted into the eyepiece. Behind the target, a bank overgrown with sagebrush served as a backstop.

"You on it?"

Sean nodded.

"Okay, as soon as you see where the first bullet strikes, say 'Got it.' Don't tell me where the bullet struck, just say 'Got it.' After I fire the second barrel, then you can tell me where each barrel hit the target."

The congressman's head jerked backward violently with the recoil from the first shot, violently again at the second clap of thunder. He opened the breech of the rifle. Smoke poured out of the twin chambers. He set the big double down and removed his headgear.

"How'd I do?"

"Your first barrel is one inch high of dead center. The second"—Stranahan slightly adjusted the focus knob—"is an inch and a hair high and an inch and half right."

"Good enough is good enough. A bull buff is a ton on the hoof. You don't have to drive tacks. Here, you shoot the next two."

Sean hadn't shot a rifle since he was a kid, when his grandfather helped him shoulder the heavy eight-millimeter Mauser that he'd confiscated from a dead German infantryman at the end of World War II. The Mauser had a reluctant trigger pull and when Sean finally got the sear to fall, the recoil had knocked him down.

"Don't crawl the stock," Crawford said. "If you slide your head too far forward, the recoil will knock your teeth out." Crawford coached him into proper form, reminding him to hold the butt of the rifle tight to his shoulder. When Stranahan pulled the front trigger, the comb of the stock smacked into his cheekbone and the barrels jerked up and to the right. He brought the sights back in line and fired the left barrel.

"She hits with authority, doesn't she?"

Stranahan grunted his affirmative. "It feels like I took a one-two from George Foreman."

"Your bullets are three inches apart, but it's easy to hold steady when you're shooting paper. Now that you've popped your cherry, let's see how you do with something coming at you."

Crawford led Sean to a pulley apparatus strung between two Ponderosa pine trunks. A life-size cutout of a Cape buffalo bull was wired to the rope cable. Crawford showed him how the pulley system worked to draw the buffalo forward in a simulated charge. He said, "I'll go first so you see what you're up against. When I say 'Pull,' you haul on that rope fast as you can. I'll start with an empty rifle, load two cartridges as he comes, and see if I can get one in to stop him." He held the rifle at port arms across his body, two gleaming brass cartridges protruding between the middle and ring fingers of his left hand.

"Pull!"

As the buffalo sped toward him in jerking starts, Crawford pushed the top lever to open the breech, dumped in the two cartridges, snapped the action shut, raised the double, and fired. He brought the barrels down out of recoil and fired again as the target swung in on him from only a few yards away. Sean stopped hauling and they examined the target. The first bullet had cut a hole in the buffalo's chest, just under the nose; the second had hit over the massed boss of the horns, where the neck merged with the swollen hump ahead of the shoulders.

Crawford nodded his satisfaction. "He would have stumbled at the first, gone down with the second so close I'd feel the earth shake. Think you're up to facing a charge?"

Sean wiped his palms on his jeans before taking the heavy rifle. He felt sweat crawling down his right armpit. *This is absurd*, he told himself, *it's just a poster stapled to a piece of plywood.*

Crawford had pulled the target back to its starting position thirty yards away. "Robert Ruark said a buffalo looks at you like you owe him money. You ready? Here he comes."

Sean managed to open the rifle. He tried to fumble one of the cartridges into the breech and dropped it, tore his eyes away from the rushing target just long enough to make sure he chambered the second, threw up the rifle, and fired. He stepped to the side an instant before the target swung past where he'd been standing. He went down to one knee and fumbled for the cartridge he'd dropped.

"Too late," Crawford said. "I saw where the bullet hit his boss. You gave him a hell of a headache, but he's trotting away with your guts hanging off his horns. Now are you still sure you want to hunt buffalo in Africa?" Crawford was standing over him, smiling down. But his eyes were not smiling and once again Sean felt the concentration of dark energy that seemed to lie just under the surface of the man's skin. An intensity that both attracted and repelled.

Stranahan got to his feet. He deliberately calmed himself. He cracked the breech open and blew a wisp of smoke from the barrel he'd fired. "Oh, I don't know," he said. "That was my first time. Let's run it again."

This time, he put two into the buffalo's chest before it had crossed half the distance that separated them.

Crawford grunted. "Not bad. A little off center but not bad."

"I did some Internet shopping last night," Sean said. "I searched a few of the gun websites—Champlin Firearms, Westley Richards, Cape Outfitters. Came up with three possibilities, a William Evans double in .450/400, a Cogswell & Harrison .470, and a Jeffery in an odd designation, .475 No. 2, if that sounds right." He never took his eyes from Crawford's face and would have caught the slightest change of expression if there'd been one. There wasn't.

"I've owned double rifles in all those calibers," Crawford said. "I'd tell you to get the .470 because you can buy cartridges over the counter and the other calibers you have to handload, but Cogswells are a mixed bag. Some good guns and some so-so. The .475 No. 2 is a great cartridge, but the Jefferys I've handled in that chambering run a little heavy to carry all day." Crawford unjointed his rifle and fitted the barrels and stock into the gun case. He looked off into the distance. His voice was quiet.

"So those flies you were looking for, they're still missing?"

"Yes."

"And you're looking out of what, the goodness of your heart? I ran into Willoughby. I know you're not a member of the club." He fiddled with the straps on the gun case.

"I never said I was," Stranahan said.

"No, but it was implied, wasn't it?" Crawford raised his eyes from the case. Frown lines had worked deep into his forehead. "When I'm here in the valley, Sean, I tend to let my guard down. I like to think I'm among friends. It's foolish of me. A man in my position can never be too careful. There's always somebody trying to turn a joke I shared with a receptionist into a one-night stand, or trying to twist my brother's promotion in the highway department into nepotism. Looking to unearth any skeleton to bring me down. Some men are wolves in sheep's clothing. I took you at face value. I'm a good judge of faces. Maybe I was wrong."

"You weren't wrong. It was Willoughby who asked me to help find the fly. I'm friends with Kenneth Winston, one of the club members."

"So why you?"

Stranahan had no idea what Willoughby had said and so had no choice but the truth. "I used to be an investigator at a law firm in Boston."

"And you just happened to knock on my door?"

"When something's missing, you look at the people closest to the victim of the theft. Not just friends and relatives, but those who live nearby. I didn't suspect you. But you're wealthy. Your place is vacant a lot of the year. It's a cat burglar's Shangri-La. If you'd also had a break-in, it would help define the perpetrator, depending on what was missing. It was a long shot."

"Then forgive my asking," Crawford said. "I thought it was possible that you had worked your way into the confidence of the club to get to me. A reporter, or an investigator for the Democratic Party who could retain plausible deniability. I hate to think that way, but it's part of the hand you're dealt when you assume public office."

"I understand."

"Still friends?" Crawford held out his hand.

"Still friends."

"If you decide to move on one of those doubles, let me know. Most dealers offer a three-day inspection period and I'd be happy to appraise the condition."

Again, Crawford had surprised him, this time by what appeared to be genuine vulnerability. So Sean took the offered hand, and the irony of feeling like the heel in their encounter wasn't lost on him. The congressman might well have skeletons buried in his past, but Stranahan was having a harder and harder time believing that the bones of two men on Sphinx Mountain were among them.

CHAPTER TWENTY-ONE

Resting the Trout

A quarter mile down the draw, the Madison River Liars and Fly Tiers clubhouse looked deserted, the two rental cars gone and all but one of the pegs where the members hung their waders unoccupied. Stranahan had looked forward to dropping in, perhaps having dinner, and flicking a CDC emerger into the slicks afterward, for it was a still, overcast day, with an emergence of mayfly duns a promise.

He walked around the side of the porch to get the hidden key off the meter box. He reached above his head, fingered the key from under the glass insulator, found the front door unlocked, and paused with the door half open. Something was ticking at his brain. Following his instincts, he walked back to the side of the porch. The members split firewood here and the floorboards were littered with chips and sawdust. His eyes mentally swept the floor, registering where the heavy chopping block had been pushed several feet to a position underneath the meter, then pushed back to nearly but not quite its original position, scraping the sawdust clear from its path. It had occurred so recently that the pollen from the cottonwood trees, which covered the other surfaces of the porch in a snowy dust, had yet to settle over the drag mark. The only logical reason someone would move the block, Stranahan reasoned, was to use it as a step to reach the key on the meter. Stranahan reached up to replace the key. He was a hair under six-one and it was an easy reach. The members of the club were of average height, but still, none would have needed the block. Only a small man or woman would have to make himself taller to reach the key. Or a child.

A tight smile flickered across Stranahan's lips. He went inside the clubhouse and glanced around. Nothing appeared to be missing, but if he was correct about the identity of the person who had used the key, he didn't think there would be any sign of obvious burglary. That the recent intruder was the same person who had taken the flies last week Stranahan had no doubt. He noted a couple fly boxes on the fly-tying table. An unfinished salmon fly was clamped in one of the tying vises. A Jock Scott, Stranahan thought, from the toucan feathers tied to the rear half of the hook. One of Polly Sorenson's five-hundred-dollar creations. The voice mail button under the telephone was blinking red. Stranahan punched it.

"Kimosabe, if you get this, meet me at the Palisades take-out at five. I couldn't get you on your cell, figured you might be here. I heard something guaran-fucking-teed to give you a hard-on. Adios."

Stranahan scratched at his three-day beard. He found a scrap of paper in the kitchen with a grocery list written on it, rustled drawers until he found a pencil stub. He turned the paper over and scrawled. *I've got an idea who took the flies. I'll try to work out how best to retrieve them and get in touch. Sean.*

He started to slip the note between the jaws of one of the fly-tying vises on the table, then on second thought crumpled it into his pocket. No sense raising heart rates until he was sure. He was turning to leave when the door of one of the bunkrooms opened behind him. It was Polly Sorenson, his hair disheveled.

"I'm sorry I woke you," Sean said. "I thought the place was empty."

"I heard the answering machine," Sorenson said. He took his glasses from his shirt pocket and peered up at Stranahan. "I overdid the fishing this morning. A part of me still thinks I can do whatever I want. Father Time and Dr. Nesbitt assure me otherwise." He walked to the table and sat before the vise holding the half-tied salmon fly. He folded down his magnifying lenses over his glasses.

"Can I get you anything, Polly? A glass of water, a cup of tea?"

"I'm fine." He waved a hand. "Be gone with you. You were about to leave and I don't want to hold you up. I hope it's to see Martinique. Love is too often wasted on the young. Don't you make the mistake of taking her for granted."

Stranahan wanted to ask Sorenson about his relationship with Weldon Crawford without appearing as if he was investigating the congressman. He took a chair at the table and asked if it was okay if he watched.

"Absolutely. I wish I had secrets to reveal, but I use the same tying techniques Kelson and Scruton pioneered in the nineteenth century." He continued to talk as he married strands of turkey feather and kori bustard for the wing assembly. When he paused to rest his eyes, Sean saw his opening.

"I've just been up to Congressman Crawford's place on the bluff. He said you two had met."

"That would have been last summer." Sorenson spoke with eyes closed. "He was out for a walk and I was the only one here that week. A man that rubs you two ways at once. He invited me for dinner and I went, though I was less interested in the prospect of his company than I was in seeing the house. Impressive. The man, too, in his way. What were you doing up there?"

Stranahan told him.

Sorenson grunted. He opened his eyes and inspected the fly in the vise. "I'm afraid we've seen the last of them, the Quill Gordon and the Ghost."

Stranahan sought to bring the conversation back to Crawford. He said, "What did you mean by Crawford rubbing you two ways at once?"

"I mean you like him and you don't." Sorenson turned his attention from the fly to Sean. "The man's a blowhard. And he's a bully. But his interest in you seems genuine and you find yourself talking to him almost against your will. He noticed me breathing—I walked up to the house with him and even a short hike like that can be taxing some days—and he asked about it. And . . . I told him." Sorenson glanced down, as if he was ashamed. "I hadn't told Patrick or any of the other members at that point. They thought I just suffered periodic bouts of bronchitis. After my doctors and my wife, this near stranger was the first person to know I had COPD. He asked me all kinds of questions about it, even told me he could pull some strings to get me seen at the Mayo Clinic. He'd pay the airfare and any medical bills my insurance didn't cover."

"Did you take him up on it?"

"I would have if I thought it would help. And it might have, if I hadn't fallen climbing the bank of the Miramachi River ten years ago. I broke my ribs, punctured my right lung. Now there's scar tissue where the oxygen leaked out between the lung and chest wall. That puts a lot of strain on my respiratory system, not to mention my heart. You add it to COPD . . ." He shook his head. "I'm afraid the Mayo Clinic can't do much for me at this point."

"He probed into my personal life, too," Stranahan said. Crawford hadn't and Sean felt guilty for the remark, knowing he'd made it only to gain Sorenson's empathy. He pressed on. "I found him strange. He wanted to talk to me about an old short story called 'The Most Dangerous Game.' It seemed to mean a great deal to him."

Sean saw recognition come into Sorenson's eyes.

"Yes, yes," Sorenson said. "Someone hunting people on an island. Man, the most dangerous game. He tried to get me to read it. I said it didn't sound like my cup of tea. He said that when his time came, he'd rather be carried out on his shield than die in a hospital. He wanted to lend me his copy of the book, told me he'd had it since he was a child. He wouldn't take no for an answer. So I took it to be polite. Returned it the next time I saw him. Never did read it."

"Did he bring it up again this summer?"

"No. He knocked on the door here the day after I picked Patrick up at the airport. Patrick was out fishing, so it was just the two of us. I invited him in for a drink and haven't seen him since."

"Did you show him the flies, the ones that were stolen?"

"I might have. I really can't recall." For an instant, Sorenson glanced away. "But if what you're getting at is that he could be a suspect in their disappearance, I would disabuse you of the presumption. Weldon Crawford could buy the best fly collection on terra firma if he wanted; he has no need of ours." Sorenson folded the magnifying lenses back over his glasses. "I'm sorry, Sean, but I have to get back to this fly if I'm going to finish it. At my age, I can't work without a lot of natural light."

It was still two hours before he was supposed to meet Sam. Stranahan stayed in his chair. It was fascinating to watch a master tier like Sorenson. The livered, old-man hands that trembled holding a tin cup of bourbon were absolutely steady before the vise. The final touch was the horns, two matched fibers of blue macaw slightly crossing at the rear of the fly. Sorenson painted the head with lacquer and sat back and removed his glasses.

"My eyes are swimming," he said.

"You tie a beautiful fly, Polly," Sean said.

"It could be better. The underwing is about a millimeter off center, and it has to be perfectly vertical before you add the overwing or you're doomed." He shut his eyes. "I'm doomed."

Was he talking about the fly or himself? Maybe it was both. Sean's heart went out to the man.

Sorenson said, "I'd think twice before putting it up for sale with my name on it. But I won't have to, because I'm giving it to you."

"No, I can't accept that, Polly."

"You can and you will." He blinked his eyes. "I'll apply several more coats of lacquer and it will ready for you the next time you come down. I'd say it was something to remember me by, but that sounds rather ghastly, doesn't it? Just accept the fly as a gift from an old man to a younger man, wishing him tight lines and loose women. I joke."

Stranahan saw Sorenson's mouth tremble slightly and realized how hard it must be to turn a brave face to the world while the hourglass lost sand.

"Thank you," Sean said. "I'll treasure it. Do you mind my asking you what your favorite river is? Someday I'd like to paint you into a picture."

"It's the one outside this window. But if you ask what river made the deepest impression over the years, that would have to be the river Dee in Scotland. Jock Scott, the man who first dressed this fly, wrote about fishing the Dee. As legend has it, his original pattern included a hair from a Titian beauty. I fished the Dee once and it's as gorgeous as the day it was made. Unfortunately, I did not catch a salmon."

"Who knows, Polly. Maybe you'll return."

"That's kind to say, but I don't need to. I'm one of those lucky men who fish in their dreams. Some people have Paris. They shut their eyes and they have Paris. Others it's London or Rome. I have the river Dee."

Twenty minutes saw Sean to the Palisades boat take-out. The sun had worked through the clouds and was heavy on the nape of his neck. He felt a dull pain behind his eyes, the headache of the sleep-deprived. Too many hours on Martinique's couch trapped between cats. He glanced at his watch. Sam wouldn't show up for at least half an hour. He got a sleeping pad out of the Land Cruiser and found a shady spot under the riverbank willows. He lay on his side with his head on his old felt hat. A merganser with a late brood of brown fluff balls scooted across the river surface. One of the ducklings was perched on the hen's rump feathers, hitching a ride. The other three looked to be jerked along by colorless ropes. The sound of moving water was like a drug. Stranahan shut his eyes and fell asleep.

"Fucking A, would you look at that? This is what happens to a river when you let the riffraff on it."

Stranahan opened one eye. He saw Sam towering over him. A few feet away, parallel shadows ended at the wadered feet of an older man; beside him stood a woman with Medusa hair in gray-blond.

ringlets. The couple wore matching straw cowboy hats with chin straps.

Sam shook his head. "This sorry sack of bones was a pretty fair fly fisherman once. Crawled down the bottle like a true Montanan. Urine must be running a hunnerd proof. Piss on your campfire and watch the whole forest shoot up in flames."

Stranahan stood up. He walked to the river and splashed water onto his face. He came back and stuck out his hand. "Sean Stranahan."

The man and woman each had hearty grips. A John and Lou Anne Callishaw from Solvang, California.

"I know someone from Santa Barbara who had a vineyard near Solvang," Stranahan said. "His name's Summersby. He has a home up the valley, across from Slide Inn."

"That's who we're staying with," Lou Anne said. "Richard and Ann are old friends. Sam told us we'd be meeting you. We'd like to talk about commissioning a painting. We think the work you did for them is just outstanding, especially the watercolor of the Madison in the Bear Trap Canyon. So stark, but . . . beautiful." She had intense green eyes that vibrated a little.

Stranahan made the appropriate self-deprecating remarks, ingratiating himself in his accustomed manner while inwardly shaking his head at his behavior. Selling yourself was the part he hated most about trying to brush out a living as an artist. The couple exchanged cards with him and made a tentative plan to meet Sean at the Summersby home upriver, a week from Friday. It reminded Sean that he still had to complete his oil of the Copper River in British Columbia.

Sam slapped Stranahan on his back after the couple had driven off, their car already having been shuttled to the take-out. "Thought I might bring you a little business," he said, "you being such a fuckup as a fishing guide."

"Well, thanks." The money would be welcome but Stranahan felt let down. When he'd heard Sam's message, he'd thought that the big man had learned something that might help solve the riddle of the bodies on Sphinx Mountain. He told Sam as much.

Sam scratched at a new tattoo on his right upper biceps—Sylvester the cat licking his whiskers while eyeing a brown trout in a fishbowl. On Sam's left biceps was a fly fishing Mickey Mouse hooked up to a leaping rainbow trout. He rolled his waders to his waist—"THE BEAT-INGS WILL CONTINUE UNTIL MORALE IMPROVES" was stenciled on his T-shirt. He sat heavily on a cottonwood drift log on the bank.

"You know Peachy Morris," he began.

Stranahan sat down on the cut bank where Sam's driftboat was tied off and nodded. Morris was a fellow guide he'd met a couple times on the water.

"Peachy couldn't catch the clap in Copenhagen, but not for lack of trying if you get my drift. I don't know what it is about that boy, whether he can lick his eyebrows or just 'cause he's such good people, but any woman plants her cheeks on the casting chair leaves a snail trail. Hell, half the *guys* who fish with him are ready to go Brokeback Mountain before the day's over. You pass by Peachy's driftboat tied up along the river and no Peachy, no client, you know he's back in the bushes with his waders rolled down to the ankles. 'Restin' the trout,' he calls its. You drift by, nod to yourself—old Peachy's resting the trout. I mean you gotta hand it to the boy . . . Hey, you wanna split a beer, I only got one left."

Stranahan said sure. This was Sam. Sometimes you didn't know where he was going or what the point was once you got there, but it was never less than an interesting ride.

Sam fished a Silver Bullet from the cooler in his driftboat, popped the tab, and handed it over. "That dude ranch up Willow Creek, the Double D? The one out of Pony, you pass the gate on the way up to the Tobacco Roots? There's this teachers' convention there, goes on all this week. The ranch runs a guide service for the guests, Peachy and some other guy. Peachy has a cabin there. These teachers, you figure like ninety percent of them are women trapped in a room with a bunch'a little monsters nine months of the year, putting dinner on the table for the old man who doesn't appreciate 'em, run ragged by a couple brats of her own, the ranch must be like Vegas—'What goes on at the Double D stays at the Double D.' Peachy gets so much action he says he has to eat liver and oysters for a month just so he can build up his stamina."

Sam took the half beer Stranahan held out and knocked it down in one swallow. He crumpled the can in his fist and tossed it into his boat.

"So yesterday he's going to float this chick from the convention, like forty years old, a cougar. Harriet with some Kraut last name. She's like an annual fuck, comes every summer, talks about her family, hauls Peachy's ashes like she's shaking his hand—casual about it, a very European lady. So yesterday she's booked him to float from MacAtee to Varney. Peachy says she's a good fly fisherman for a chick, casts a candy-cane line. He pulls up to her cabin towing his driftboat and they're rigging rods when this older guy walks up and asks what they're biting on. They talk a bit and the man asks if he can go with them. Peachy looks at Harriet; she shrugs. 'Sure,' Peachy says. He and the cougar had been resting the trout the night before, so it's not like Peachy's upset they'll have company. He's tired and figures he can use a few hours on the pins with nothing to do but tie on flies and shoot the breeze."

Sam used a forefinger to dig into the cowlick of chest hair sprouting from the neck of his T-shirt. "Anyway . . ." He let the word hang while he pulled off the shirt. He peered down at a dime-sized circle of blood over his sternum. "I got a fuckin' tick," he said. "Where did you come from, darling?" He pinched off the pendulous bug, bloated with blood, and flicked it away. He dug into the bite. He peered at his chest skeptically. "I look like a gorilla mainlining Rogaine. No wonder Darcy left me."

"Darcy left you because you're married to this boat all day and you're in the bar all night."

Sam grunted. "God love her," he said, dismissing the subject.

"So anyway, they're on the river and this guy starts yanking lips. Peachy says it's a miracle because he's a rug beater, slapping the water on his backcasts, throwing wind knots in his leader, he can't get a free drift to save his soul. But you guide, you know it can happen. Guy can't find his dick with both hands catches all the trout in the river. Like a gift from God or something. And the cougar's getting her rod bent, too, it's just one of those days. Then they pull over for lunch and all of a sudden the dude's got his head in his hands, crying. And this is when it gets interesting, because when Peachy asks what's the matter, the guy says he thought he'd be dead now. He says he'd *planned* on being dead. We're talking really distraught, so Peachy fetches the medicine kit from the skiff, mixes the guy a dirty martini, olives and all. Mixes one for the cougar. Mixes himself one. Peachy being Peachy, next thing you know they're passing a joint. The cougar gets in on the act; she puts her arms around the guy and pulls his head down onto her Marilyn Monroes, does everything but offer him a nipple. Turns out she's a school counselor with a master's in psych, she knows the buttons to push and they're sitting there on the bank and the guy comes out with the story. Weird-looking dude, Peachy says he looks like he belongs in a tree, got a face like a chimp . . . Yeah, I know, I digress.

"So the deal was, this guy took a fuckin' train all the way from Ann Arbor, Michigan. He was a professor at the U there, cultural anthropology, which is sort of apropos considering the mug. Spent a lot of time in Guatemala, some other places they speak español. Surfer dude, go figure. The waves are coming in, the world's a good place to live. Then one day he's with the girlfriend and can't get it up with a cantilever crane. There's Viagra so it isn't the end of the world, but other symptoms start popping up: chills, fevers, fuckin' delirium, man. Turns out he contracted some rare kind of brain malaria during a sabbatical year when he was surfing off the coast of Panama. He'd been taking malaria pills for years, but the side effects were so bad sometimes he'd stop for a while. Guy gets worse, guy gets a little better, guy gets a lot worse, guy gets only a little better. Doctor's pumping him full of antibiotics, but anybody can see where the arrow's pointing. This kind of malaria, there's no silver bullet. Skeeter drills that proboscis into you, you got a couple years losing your mind and wishin' you were dead, then the wish comes true. Shit, man, I need a smoke."

Stranahan's mind raced while Sam fished in a compartment under his rowing seat for cigarettes. This was Gutierrez's story with the names changed. Two strong men who'd seen a lot of life, deciding to check out on their own terms. Only the state and the symptoms were different.

Sam waded back to the log, a handrolled fag with a dogleg bobbing in the corner of his mouth. He flicked the head of a wooden match on his thumbnail and Stranahan could smell sulfur. Sam exhaled a lungful of smoke.

"I know, I'm killing myself. But I'm down to smoking only on fishing days." He thought about it. "'Course I fish every day."

"Finish your story," Stranahan said.

"I told you this would give your pecker a jolt. Shit, this is just the *beginning* of the story. So this guy, he's been in psychotherapy half his life, the kind of guy wakes up after a bad dream and figures he better see his shrink and find out what it was about. Okay, a little more understandable considering the circumstances. His shrink advises him to go to a retreat upstate, the U's biological station at a place called Burt Lake. This is just a couple months ago, before the summer session students show up—"

Stranahan interrupted. "How do you know all this?"

"I'm getting to it. So he goes to the retreat, it's a bunch of people like himself who are looking at the void and rehearsing for good

Saint Peter, and he meets this guy, a fellow patient. Guess where he's from."

"Montana?"

"Bingo."

"What's his name?"

"Wade."

"That's all?"

"They just go by first names. So the two of them, they take a rowboat out onto the lake to drown some worms, but considering the lateness of the hour, so to speak, they're not too interested in fishing. They start talking and find they're on the same page. They got no intention of dying in diapers with a tube up the John Henry and half a dozen brain cells between them. Wade, the Montanan, tells him about this short story he read as a kid, something about a count who hunts down these guys stranded on an island . . ."

"'The Most Dangerous Game,'" Stranahan said. His skin crawled. The sun had angled under the willows that shaded the bank and he felt a drop of sweat track down his spine.

"That's it," Sam said. "How the hell?"

"I have to call the sheriff," Stranahan said.

"Good luck getting reception. When we get back to Ennis—"

"No, I mean now."

"Keep your hay in the barn. She already knows. Peachy was going to call her after he talked to me. Shit, it was me who told him to. I tried calling you first, but when you didn't pick up . . . Are you going to let me finish or not? Yeah? Okay? Listen to Sam. So this guy tells him this story which you seem to already know about, and asks him if he'd like to play it with him, only with the sides being equally armed. Says, 'Let's go out like fucking men with rifles in our hands.' Calls it 'Death with Honor.' Anyway, Peachy wasn't real clear on the details, but the upshot, and I'm cutting the conversation short, is that the two of 'em plan to duel it out up in the mountains." Sam cocked his finger and pointed east and north across the river, where the striated peak of the Sphinx brooded under scuff marks made by a shoal of cirrus clouds.

"So comes the big day, Sunday being the Lord's day, or maybe it's Monday, and now I'm jumping way the fuck ahead 'cause there's the train ride to work out and this secret correspondence and a bunch of other crap so no one's to know, and the guy drives to the trailhead and punches in the GPS coordinates where they're supposed to go High Noon on each other. He starts hiking in, and about halfway up the mountain he's in a cold sweat with his heart jumping out of his chest and the chimp chickens out. Just fucking turns a puke shade of yellow. He books a room at the dude ranch and holes up in the cabin with his tail between his legs, trying to get straight with the Almighty who up to this time hasn't been such a big fuckin' part of his life, but I suppose a death sentence gives you religion. At dawn he still hasn't slept and then here comes Peachy towing his blue driftboat and he takes it as a sign, Jesus being a fisherman and all . . ."

"Sam, are you bullshitting me? Jesus. Really?"

Sam looked abashed. His chest heaved and he took the cigarette from his mouth and dipped the ash in the river. He slipped the butt under a curl of hair over his right ear and shook his head.

"I don't know what the fuck gets into me. I start telling it like it is and then all of a sudden I'm making shit up. I been doing it all my life and I'm not even aware of it half the time. I don't know, man. I just don't know. I was telling you the truth right up to the Jesus part, I swear. Well, maybe the halfway up the trail part. I really don't know how far he got or even if he left the fuckin' car before turning tail."

"Okay, Sam."

"Well, for *some* reason he decides to go fishing, and I've already told you he spills the beans to Peachy and the cougar. Well, the thing is the whole time they're on the water the guy's super emotional and the cougar, being a counselor and all, tells Peachy that he's at really high risk for committing suicide and she doesn't think they can just leave him off at the cabin. She says she thinks she should stay with him, eat dinner with him, and keep him talking. And on account of Peachy knowing the cougar like he does, he can take the hint, he figures it's only a matter of time before the old guy's plowing that good German earth. So he says good night and the next thing you know it's two in the morning and the phone in his cabin rings and it's the cougar, asking him if he's got any Viagra. Sure enough, she took the old guy to bed and he can't get it up. He hasn't flipped that switch for two years and the end's in sight whether he snaps a cap or lets God pull the plug, and now he's naked in her arms crying like a baby. Peachy says you know I don't need no Viagra. And she says I don't know who else to call, so Peachy hangs up and calls me."

"So did you have any Viagra, Sam?"

"Moi? I need Viagra like a carp needs collagen. Well, if you're talking technically true there was this night I got sort of down in the dumps over the sorry state of my affairs, looking at myself in the mirror and seeing a guy with grooves in his teeth who lives in a fuckin' tin can, and I'd picked up this swamp angel at the Cottonwood and something didn't unfold the way it should have, if you savvy, but she had these dreads that looked like a nest of rattlesnakes and anyway it was just the once. Even if I did have some pecker pills, I was an hour's drive away. So Peachy calls her back and she tells him to start knocking on the doors of the guest cabins to see if he can rustle some up. Peachy draws the line right there, he's got his reputation to uphold, so the cougar says then you come over to the cabin and babysit while I go looking. So, all right, Peachy goes over and by this time the gentleman has his pants on and he's sipping a cup of tea with his pinkie out, like he's at fucking Ascot. The cougar leaves and the guy says would you like some tea. Okay, so they drink their tea and Peachy's thinking sometimes a day doesn't end the way you think it will, three in the goddamned morning, and the guy, he's talking about surfing, no bullshit, like how he'd like to hang on until he can hang ten just one more time. Then the guy gets real serious, tells Peachy that Harriet saved his life and he'll never forget it, and he'll never forget

Peachy either, it's restored his faith in humanity, and he wants to hug it out and by this time Harriet's back so it's a group hug, the three of them. Turns out about the second door she knocked on this middle-aged guy peeks out. She says, 'Sir, you wouldn't happen to have any Viagra, would you? It's for a good cause.' The guy says no and he's shutting the door when there's this woman's voice in the background—'Have a heart, John, give her one of your blue magics. How hard would *you* be without them?' So they got the Viagra and Harriet gives Peachy a kiss and whispers in his ear, 'Don't you dare go anywhere but your cabin,' and a couple hours go by and Harriet knocks on his door to tell him pop went the weasel and the dude's asleep like for the first time in three days.

"'What do I do now?' she says. 'He thinks he's in love with me.'

"Peachy says, 'You're the psychologist,' and they're talking, standing outside with the birds starting up and Peachy remembers I told him to call back and he puts me on speaker. Knowing what you told me about the bodies, I tell Peachy to call the sheriff and that's when I called the club and left you the message."

"Where are they now?"

"Peachy? He had to float some sports on a half hour's shut-eye. I got no idea where the cougar's licking her paws, probably still at the ranch." While they were talking, Stranahan was helping Sam load the driftboat onto the trailer.

"Did I do good or what, Kimosabe?" Sam said as he wound up the winch and set the chock.

"You did. Thanks. You'll get your reward in heaven."

Sam clasped a callused hand on Stranahan's shoulder, so hard it tingled. "All this touchy-feely stuff's making me teary." He was smiling, a silver-capped incisor glinting in the sun. He heaved his bulk into the cab of his truck, the springs creaking as the truck canted under his weight. "Keep me in the loop." He jerked his thumb up.

Stranahan dug his fingers into his bruised shoulder.

CHAPTER TWENTY-TWO

The Simian Man

"I was wondering if you'd show," Harold Little Feather said. "Your buddy Meslik fill you in?"

Stranahan nodded. "He told me what he heard from Peachy Morris. Sam likes to exaggerate, but it sounds like a hell of a story even if half of it's true." He lifted his eyes to take in the sprawl of the Double D, the ridges that backdropped the ranch, Hollowtop Mountain forming a pyramid under the evening sky. He walked up where the sheriff was polishing the hood of the Cherokee with her elbows. She had her chin in her hands and didn't look up.

Little Feather inclined his head toward the row of peeled log guest cabins. "Mountain chic. Each cabin's named for a tree. The fishing guide came off the river 'bout a half hour ago. He went to park his rig down at his cabin. It's around the back. Called Limber Pine. He told us the man is still with the woman in Mountain Maple. That's the one catty-corner from the lodge. The woman is trying to sweet-talk him into joining us. Peachy will give us the word when she does."

"We're waiting," Ettinger said. "You can help us wait." She lifted her chin from her hands and drummed her fingers on the metal.

"White women oughtn't do that," Little Feather said. "It hurts the ears."

Ettinger blushed.

"I'm just kidding, Martha. You and I both know you got the rhythm." Ettinger blushed a deeper red.

"Very funny. You two have any bright ideas how we approach this?

The gentleman's in an emotionally delicate condition. He's become attached to this Harriet person. I'm inclined to think he might see another woman as an intruder, that maybe he'd rather talk to a man."

"Have Harold feel him out," Stranahan said. "This guy's an anthropologist. He'll like it that Harold's Indian. Plus he has a cast on his arm and can play the 'I was mauled by a grizzly' card. It's a conversation starter."

"Harold?" Ettinger raised her eyebrows. "Sean might have a point."

"Worth a try," Harold said.

While they waited, Ettinger recited the details of the story she'd heard over the phone from Peachy Morris. Most of it aligned closely, if not as colorfully, with the version Sean had heard from Sam.

Little Feather listened with his arms crossed. He nodded sagely when she got to the Viagra search.

"Woman sounds like an angel of mercy," he said. "Man can use a little mercy loving from time to time."

"Or a tramp." Martha scowled.

"Here comes Peachy," Stranahan said.

Peachy Morris was boyish-looking with lobster hands from rowing his boat under a boiling sun. He wore jeans low on his hips, a cowboy shirt with the sleeves rolled up over ropy forearms. His smile was warm, but his eyes looked tired.

"Ma'am, sir. I'm sorry to make your acquaintance under these circumstances." He acknowledged Sean with a slight nod. "Stranny." He wiped back a strand of lank blond hair from his forehead. His face carried the sweat sheen of someone who'd been awake for forty-eight hours.

He said, "Mr. Kauffeld says he'll talk to you, but he wants to have Harriet with him."

"Kauffeld?"

"His name's Melvin Kauffeld. He told us to call him Mel."

"I'll go see him," Harold said.

Ettinger turned to Morris. "This guy Kauffeld met at the retreat, what did he look like? Did he describe him?" She glanced at Stranahan when Peachy didn't answer at once. They were both thinking the same name: Weldon Crawford.

"I guess we didn't ask him," Peachy said.

"He had to have said something. Age. Build. Maybe a guy who has what looks like a boil on his neck. Nothing?"

"Only that he looked fit, not like most of them there. We mostly just listened. Or I did. Harriet drew him out. She said he needed a sounding board. He felt like he couldn't breathe and she thought if he got it off his chest it would be a release."

"A release," Martha said. She raised her eyebrows, an ironic smile playing on her lips. "I suppose you could call it that."

Morris looked levelly at her. "Harriet's a fine person. Mel has a gun. He might have pulled the trigger on himself if she hadn't been with him last night."

"Uh-huh," Ettinger said.

"What kind of gun?" Stranahan asked.

"Model 99 Savage. The stock's a piece of firewood, but the bore's shiny. He asked me to take it. I locked it in my cabin."

They were digesting this news when Harold whistled from the door of the cabin. He waved them over.

"He says he's willing to talk to all of us," he said in a low voice. "He's not who you'd expect and he might be putting on an act, it's hard to tell. I had a few words with the woman first. I believe her when she says she believes him."

"And what? I'm supposed to believe you that you believe her that she believes him?"

"Martha, I'm just saying listen to the man and don't roll your eyes. Like you're doing now, don't do that."

Stranahan saw Peachy Morris regarding Harold and Ettinger with bemusement. Peachy glanced sidelong at Stranahan. "Those two ought to get a room," he said.

The first thing that struck Stranahan about Melvin Kauffeld, who insisted on serving tea while they made themselves comfortable around the wrought iron table on the porch of the cabin, was his voice. It was a barrister's instrument, a rich baritone with a lot of authority behind it, not a voice that Stranahan would have thought for a man who'd cried a river over the past couple days. That the voice was the most arresting aspect of the man was all the more remarkable because his face was utterly singular. Peachy had told Sam that he looked like a chimp, and the simian resemblance was extraordinary, but if Stranahan had to pick an ape for comparison he would have chosen a male orangutan. Old, with moist brown eyes that had seen the end of the world coming and knew there was nothing to be done to save it. For all that it was a handsome face, the face of tribal chiefs of ages past, and not really sad so much as thoughtful.

"I'll say right off I'm not going to be pressing charges," Kauffeld said. "If that's what you're hoping for I won't do it, nor do I see what charges could possibly be brought. We had a gentleman's agreement, which I broke. I won't accept that Wade is anything but who he said he was."

"Who was that?" Harold asked. He would continue to take the lead as long as it earned results.

"A fellow traveler, I suppose. As we learned at the retreat, we're on a journey that most people never realize they have the opportunity to take. Most people let others make choices for them when they become gravely ill. The final breath is a formality; the essence of the human being has already ignobly departed the scene. It isn't the way either Wade or I wanted to go. We wanted to die with dignity, 'Death with Honor' as he put it, with our minds sharp and our hearts beating with adrenaline. When I started up the trail, I was more alive than I had been since 'Nam. I had every intention of following through and meeting my destiny."

"Then why didn't you?"

"For that very reason. I felt alive. You must understand how a diagnosis like mine affects a person. When a doctor tells you you have a few months and how it's going to end, you walk out of the room a changed man. I lost my nerve, I lost my hope, I lost grip of my soul. I could no longer work up any zest for life. I'm ashamed of the person I became. It wasn't until I met Wade that I started to *feel* again. I got up that trail to where I could see the mountain and realized that if I went any farther, I risked losing that sense of being alive. I sat down on a log and thought about it. What was the point of getting myself killed, or killing Wade—because it could have gone down either way up there—when for the first time in two years I was really enjoying living? Enjoying it so much I was afraid of dying. And fear of death, that is *really* living, let me tell you."

Stranahan saw Martha regarding Kauffeld skeptically. Kauffeld saw it, too.

He said, "You can find a contradiction in this if you want to, but you'd have to have lived in my skin to understand. I still want to die with all my marbles. But I may have a few months left before having to make that choice again. Today, tonight, tomorrow, I want to live with every cell of my being. I realized that as I walked off the mountain and then yesterday, yesterday when I met Harriet . . ."

He shook his head. "I got so high on that boat I felt like I was flying over the river and I got so low I felt like I was on the stones on the bottom. These wonderful people"—he had to collect himself—"this good woman . . ." He squeezed Harriet's hand. He caught his breath and shook his head again. He couldn't find his voice.

Stranahan shifted his eyes to Harriet Langhor. After introducing herself in the cabin—she had a slight but recognizable German accent—she had taken the chair by Kauffeld's side and had sat quietly but for her gray-blue eyes, which were intensely alive and darted from person to person. She had loose curls of light brown hair, an angular body with long legs and broad shoulders, and strong facial features—sculpted cheekbones under a prominent brow, deep eye sockets, a square chin. Her nose was hooked like a hawk's talon, with a knuckle in the middle. Altogether it was a vital, handsome face without being pretty in any conventional way. Sam's description of her as a cougar licking her paws, Stranahan thought, wasn't far off the mark.

Harold's voice was quiet. "Mr. Kauffeld, I won't pretend that any of us here know what you've been through. I understand it's hard not to be emotional, but this is a murder investigation. We have to know everything that happened since you first met this man. It's important that we take your statement. You can add to it later, but this way we won't have to put you through the pain of going through the story again at the department. In fact, you probably won't have to go into town at all. You can stay right here. Just tell us what happened in your own words. If you want, I can clear the porch so it's just you and me, and Harriet of course."

Harriet pressed her fingers into Kauffeld's arm. He lifted his head from his chest. He looked at her as if she were the only person in the world. She nodded. After a few seconds, he nodded back at her and then turned to Harold and forced a smile.

Harold pressed a button on his Olympus pocket recorder. "This is Deputy Harold Little Feather of the Hyalite County Sheriff's Department. It's seven-fifteen p.m., July the . . ." He checked the date on his watch and finished the formalities.

For a long minute there was only the sound of Willow Creek talking to itself down the hill. Then Melvin Kauffeld began to speak.

He said he'd met Wade on the second day of the five-day retreat at the university's Limnology Station on Burt Lake. The station was a barracks-style camp consisting of a lodge, Quonset laboratories where freshwater aquatic sciences were taught, and a couple dozen tent cabins reserved for graduate students during the summer session. The retreat was hosted by an organization called Living at Last, based in Oakland, California. There were morning workshops on coping with terminal illness, daily excursions to Mackinac Bridge and other places of interest on the northern tip of the Lower Peninsula, plus one-on-one consultations with the doctor who headed the program. But the value of the retreat was bringing terminal patients together to share stories and lend each other psychological support. Kauffeld had not met Wade in a rowboat, as Sam had said, but during a day trip to Petoskey on Lake Michigan, which included a stop at a gabled house where the famous author Ernest Hemingway had stayed in the fall of 1919. The facilitator from Living at Last who drove the van to Petoskey had read aloud a passage from a Hemingway short story, "The Killers," which mentioned the house.

It was when they were walking back to the van that Kauffeld heard footsteps behind him. The man following him introduced himself. Kauffeld said they probably would have met sooner or later simply because they walked faster than the others. He described Wade as being a little less than medium height, but fit-looking with short brown hair and a ruddy face. Like a man who worked outdoors, he said. Maybe forty, maybe fifty. It was hard to tell if the lines on his face were from age or just mapped by weather. He did notice a demarcation line on his forehead where a hat had rested, white skin above, tan below. As they walked together, Wade said it seemed rather odd to him that they had stopped at a Hemingway site. If he was not mistaken, Hemingway had ended his own life by wrapping a toe around the triggers of a double shotgun and blowing his head off. "I don't reckon these so-called facilitators consider suicide an acceptable end to our journey, do you?" he'd said. Kauffeld remembered the word "reckon," thinking the man might have been from the West. He said the irony was not lost on him, either.

"What do you think about suicide?" Wade had said.

"I don't know what I think," Kauffeld told him, "but I'm pondering the question."

"Aren't we all?"

It was the next afternoon, when they rowed out onto the lake to fish, that Wade had brought up the concept of "Death with Honor."

He said that he'd been a hunter all his life and that nothing else matched it for the adrenaline rush. If it was all the same to God, he'd rather die with blood pumping in his veins than a morphine drip. He didn't think he could pull the trigger on himself, the state of mind that accompanied putting a gun to your heart, the darkness of the soul, no thank you to that. He'd much rather go out on the horn of a rhino, but as they were hard to come by in Montana he'd settle for dying in the heat of battle. Preferably at the hand of a brother in arms who knew the score and wanted the same way out for himself. He'd looked at Kauffeld in a frank manner.

"Maybe that person is you," he said.

Kauffeld had reeled in his line and set down the spinning rod. He'd returned Wade's direct gaze.

"Maybe it is," he said.

Wade told Kauffeld he'd been thinking of it for a long time, waiting for the right person to carry out a "terminal arrangement," as he put it. He had a mountain in mind in southwest Montana. They agreed on a date in July.

Kauffeld interrupted his narration to lock eyes with Harold. "We hammered out the details like we were planning a heist, like we were burglars. It was our secret."

Kauffeld said Wade gave him a phone number that he could call at precisely midnight eastern standard time, one week prior to the date, if for any reason he couldn't make the arrangement or wanted to back out. If Wade didn't receive that call, it was on and one would die, the other would bury him where he fell.

"If I lose," Kauffeld had told him, "I don't just disappear without people looking for me. They'll trace me and find you. You could die in prison." Had Wade thought of that?

He had. He told Kauffeld that there could be no record of him traveling to Montana. He was to travel by Amtrak to Shelby, up on the Highline below the Alberta-Montana border, then catch a bus to Bridger. Pay for both tickets with cash. In Bridger, he'd find a Pinto station wagon parked on East Mendenhall Street, key under a rock at the base of the nearest tree; in the car would be camping equipment and a rifle with ammunition. He was to drive up the Gallatin Canyon on U.S. 191 to mile marker 59 and set up a camp at the Greek Creek Campground. Specific instructions for the assignation, including maps and GPS coordinates, would be in an envelope under a white rock beside the westernmost piling of the bridge over Squaw Creek, a few miles upriver at mile 66. The canyon was surrounded by national forest where he could hike to become acclimated to the altitude and check the sights on the rifle. If Kauffeld wanted to bring his own rifle, instead, of course that was fine.

"What if I'm the survivor?" Kauffeld had asked.

"Then after you bury me, maybe you make a similar arrangement with someone else. What do you think? Sound fair? I don't want you to think I'm setting you up."

Kauffeld had said it didn't sound fair, as Wade had the advantage of picking country he was familiar with and setting the rules. Wade replied that once Kauffeld received the instructions, he'd understand that if anyone had the edge it would be him. "Believe me," Wade had said, "this is a fight I don't want to win."

Wade had extended his hand. Kauffeld had taken it. Wade said he thought it best if they didn't speak again, as there was too much chance they would become friends, confusing the arrangement and making it harder to commit. He said he was leaving within the hour, the next time they met would be on the mountain. They rowed to shore and parted. It was the last time Kauffeld had seen him.

Kauffeld managed the slightest smile and shrugged. He looked at Harriet and squeezed her hand.

Harold glanced down at the notes he had taken during the statement.

"Did Wade say what kind of illness he had that would make him consider ending his life?"

Kauffeld nodded. "It was Huntington's. He said he still felt fine but the symptoms had started. It runs in the family, so he knew he was at risk. He'd seen what happened to his father in the later stages of the disease. There was no way he was letting it get to that point."

"Did he say where he lived?"

Kauffeld shook his head. "I assumed somewhere around here."

Harold glanced at Stranahan and Ettinger.

Stranahan said, "Did Wade have a mustache?" When he'd glanced his flashlight over the face of the lion hunter at the Bear Creek trailhead, he'd noted the mustache.

Kauffeld nodded. "It was very neat. Everything about him was neat except he had rough palms. Like shaking hands with sandpaper. I got the impression he'd lived a hard life. But he's a good man. He had tears in his eyes when we said goodbye at the lake. He didn't wipe them away." He turned to meet Ettinger's level gaze. "He's not a monster, Sheriff, as much as you might want to believe that he is."

Ettinger stared off a moment in the direction of the creek. She kneaded her chin with her fingers.

"Where was this arrangement going to take place?" she said.

"Noon on a slope of Sphinx Mountain. He said it would be about a three-hour hike, most of it uphill. I said I thought I could make it."

"Did he give you a map?"

Kauffeld looked off a second. "No, only the GPS coordinates. He said I'd know I was in the right place when I saw the shovel. He was going to prop a shovel at the coordinates."

"We're going to need that envelope."

"I don't know if I want to show it to you. We had an arrangement. If he could get in any trouble—"

"Mr. Kauffeld," Ettinger cut him off. "I have something I'd like you to take a look at." She unsnapped her breast pocket and turned two autopsy photos face up on the table between them.

Kauffeld swallowed his Adam's apple and turned his head away.

"This good man of yours," she said softly, "used his shovel to put these two people in the ground, probably within a few hundred feet of the coordinates where you were supposed to meet him. One of the men was dug up and eaten by a bear, that's why there isn't so much left of him. You weren't the first person Wade talked into meeting a bullet. Or the second. Or maybe even the third. I'll bet he omitted these . . . previous engagements. It's a graveyard up there, Mr. Kauffeld, full of sick men like yourself, and if you hadn't turned around, your grave would be the one where the earth hasn't settled."

Kauffeld seemed to draw into himself, his sloping brow drawing parallel creases above his eyes, which looked milky and unfocused.

"Here's what's going to happen," Ettinger said. "We're going to take a short break while you reconsider your, er, arrangement in the light of what this man was really arranging, which was your murder. In the meantime I need the envelope and the phone number. And the keys to the car you picked up. Where is it?"

Kauffeld's voice sounded defeated. "It's not here. When I came off the mountain I drove it back to town and left it where I'd found it. I got a cab to the airport. I was going to fly to Detroit, but I wasn't enthusiastic about the idea. Who was there to go home to? My parents are dead. My brother is dead. My wife divorced me twelve years ago. My colleagues? I didn't want to see anyone, or anyone I knew, put it that way. I figured I'm here, I grew up fishing in the Au Sable River in Michigan and providence had brought me to Montana; it's supposed to be the best trout fishing in the country. When the cabdriver dropped me at the airport, we were right behind a van at the curb that had the name of the ranch. It had a picture of a trout on the door. I saw a young man and a woman wearing cowboy hats, loading bags into it. I asked the man if there were any rooms available. He said he didn't think so because there was a teachers' convention, but he'd check on his cell. There'd been a cancellation. He said, 'Welcome to the Double D,' and I climbed in. It's like this whole trip, angels have been guiding me."

Ettinger nodded to Stranahan and Little Feather and they left Kauffeld on the porch with his latest angel. Ettinger radioed Dispatch to send a deputy to take custody of the car Kauffeld said he'd driven back to Bridger. She put a trace on the phone number Kauffeld had given her. Then she opened the envelope Kauffeld had retrieved from the bridge, which he'd produced from his pants pocket. The note inside had been folded and refolded until the edges were furred. The handwriting was right-slanting, very small, the occasional word struck, neat to start with but the hand not as steady toward the end.

"I'll just read it," Ettinger said.

Dear Mel,

When you feed the coordinates into your GPS you'll see it's just east of the saddle between Sphinx Mountain and another peak called the Helmet. That's the Madison Range, about twelve miles south of Ennis, give or take. There's a good trail up to the saddle, number 326. I'll be up on a ridge above the trail when you start hiking. Wear that red hat so I know it's you. I'm not trying to get the drop on you, but I have to have a vantage to be sure we're more or less alone in that country or too many shots might raise suspicion. It's wilderness designated by the federal agency but there's some yahoos around and hippies that just hike for the sake of it which I don't understand myself.

Anyway, you get on the bench above the saddle and find that shovel and settle in, then noon comes you hit the red-tailed hawk call I gave you. I'll hit you back with the same. After that it's each man for himself with the odds on your side of the ledger. On my end I'll be stalking, moving around and trying to close in. So you'll have the edge there looking for movement and can wait on me if you want. Another thing, I'll be carrying an old Sharps buffalo rifle, which is a single-shot, and you can have any modern repeating arm you want, though no military or black ops. We got to draw the line there. This is a game hunt not a firefight. I'll have the car there a week prior at least, so you can get up on the bench a few days early if you want and look around.

A couple things we got to trust each other on. No climbing above timberline where you can get a long-range shot looking down into the timber, and no waving the red hanky looking for a way out and then letting loose if I come in, I really think we have to be men about this. I know for me the chips are in the middle of the pot once I hear the hawk.

You can see by my hand that I been drinking whiskey. When the hitches come to remind your sorry ass what's down the road it's hard not to reach for the Jack. I know you got your good days mixed in with the bad, or maybe the other way around, so keep in mind our plan like we talked about on the lake. You learn to blow that call now.

Death with Honor. Yours truly, Wade.

45°9' 33.86"N
111°29' 52.23"W

Ettinger passed the note to Stranahan and shifted her weight from one foot to the other.

"Harold, what do you think?" Little Feather had stood during the recitation in his plaid flannel shirt with the sleeves cut off, his muscled arms crossed over his chest.

"Could be Mr. Kauffeld had him figured right. The guy didn't let on that this wasn't the first time, you set that aside and the rest has a ring of truth. Man's come up against a hard wall and trying to figure a way out that doesn't end in a hospital ward. Might not be your way or my way, but put yourself in his boots. There's no easy choices here. Maybe this Wade's a straight shooter."

"You mean maybe he shoots straighter?"

"Both."

"Hmpff."

Little Feather uncrossed his arms. "I was just in the hospital four days myself. That nurse you said had the hots for me? Was that 'fore or after she emptied the bedpan? Second floor of Deaconess is no place I want to be when it's time to chase the spirits."

Ettinger stared at him.

Harold said, "I'm not condoning what he's done. I'm just trying to understand it."

"Sean, do you agree with this . . . evaluation?"

Stranahan put down the note.

"Meaning you don't."

"Not for a second. I don't care how noble he comes across. This guy likes to kill people. But forget about what I think. I'm asking you."

"From talking with Mel and the tone of this letter, I tend to agree with Harold. We're trying to twist this into a predator-prey thing when maybe we should take it at face value. I'm not saying we shouldn't try to bring the man to justice, or even that he doesn't get off pulling the trigger. It could have started innocently in the sense that it was a fair fight and he killed the first guy and found that it stimulated him, that it gave him a purpose where otherwise he'd just be marking time and hitting the bottle."

Ettinger felt for the artery in her neck and pressed her fingertips against the steady throb.

"I don't know what I think," she said slowly. "Nor—and I'm thinking out loud here . . . Well, it doesn't matter what I think. We're trying to get into this guy's head when the first thing we need to do is ID the bastard. Between the registration on the car Wade left for Kauffeld—keep your fingers crossed that it's still where he parked it—and our witness, we've got a good shot at coming up with a name. But short of confession, there's nothing to charge him with. Doc says we should get the DNA workup today on the tissue on that bullet, and my hunch is we'll have a match with Ghost Two. That leaves the rifle. We need the rifle in possession. And for that we need a suspect and we need a warrant."

Stranahan raised his eyes from the note.

"I know what you're going to say," Ettinger said. "But Crawford doesn't begin to fit the description."

"No, but the rifle that bullet fits into, you don't find it just anywhere and there aren't many people who could afford it if you did. Crawford's owned similar weapons. And there's something I haven't told you."

"Then pray tell me." Ettinger set her hands on her hips.

Stranahan told her about his conversation with Polly Sorenson, Crawford's interest in the old man's malady and giving him the book with the short story in it.

"If he was four inches shorter, fifteen years younger, and had a mouse on his lip, I'd say you had something there," Ettinger said.

"Okay, Crawford doesn't fit the description Kauffeld gave us of Wade. But he still could be involved."

Ettinger walked to the window that overlooked the porch. "Then the good congressman is our next stop," she said. "It's forty miles. We'll give him an ice-cold knock as soon as we're done here."

Harold made a murmuring sound. "You really think that's a good idea?"

Ettinger turned around. "The silent one speaks," she said.

"What the hell, Martha?"

"I don't know what's with you two," Stranahan said.

"It's nothing," Harold said.

"Then I guess it wasn't anything to start with," Martha said. Ettinger and Little Feather seemed to be alone in the room. Then Ettinger put her face back on.

"You're right, Sean. Let's focus. Harold, you were saying . . ."

Harold shrugged. "Just a thought, but what if Wade acts as a recruiter? He travels to these retreats for the dying, looks for a likely victim, trots out his spiel. Earnest as a pallbearer. Then he sets up the arrangement and steps out of the picture, because he isn't the one holding the gun. He's setting up the confrontation for Crawford. You knock on Crawford's door asking about a gun, then any evidence that puts cuffs on him goes up in smoke. We'll never get closer to him than talking to his attorney."

Ettinger was looking through the cabin window. Stranahan followed her gaze to the couple on the porch. Kauffeld had his head in his hands.

"Look at him," Ettinger said. "I think it's finally sinking in."

"Did you even hear me?" Little Feather said.

"I heard. If this was a plot in a movie I'd be more likely to buy your theory. But what you were saying about Wade being a recruiter got me thinking that maybe there's another way to look at this. All along we've been trying to find a guy who talks people into standing before the barrel of his gun, when maybe we'd get farther if we looked at who he recruits. Think about it. I don't care how earnest and believable this guy is, you have to figure that nine out of ten men he approaches are going to think he's crazy. What if someone came up to you on the street and asked if you'd like to grab a gun and play OK Corral with them? What would you do?"

"I'd contact the police," Stranahan said.

"Maybe someone has. If we can't get an ID from the car registry, then I think the next step is to start contacting the retreats. Call this Living at Last organization and see if they had a get-together last summer in Bakersfield or Fresno, anywhere near where the Mexican guy, Gutierrez, lived. His brother told me he went to some kind of group therapy in Modesto. Doesn't have to be Living at Last, could be any group. We need to check that out. Any place our vic signed up, see if someone named Wade attended, too. Find out if a third party complained that someone who called himself Wade brought up the idea of squaring off on a mountain in Montana."

Ettinger's cell vibrated and she stepped away to unholster it, turned her back, listened. Mouthed the word "fuck" as she clicked it shut.

"That was Judy. The phone number was from a bar phone in Ennis, the Silver Dollar. And there's no car that fits the description on the two hundred block of East Mendenhall. They checked a four-block radius."

"We shouldn't be surprised," Harold said. "Man's had two days to recover it. You'd think as soon as Kauffeld's a no-show, first thing Wade does is collect his vehicle."

"Whose side are you on?" Ettinger said, but the bitter tone Stranahan had noted earlier was gone. Martha and Harold had had their moment, the strain had boiled to the surface, and they'd worked through it and were friends again, Stranahan thought, all while conducting their business.

Ettinger said, "Here's what we do. We'll take the rest of the statement, then you and I"—she cocked her hand at Stranahan—"are going to make a house call. Your objections aside, Harold, I think this is the right thing to do. If Crawford's innocent, he'll bend over to cooperate; he'll be happy to give us all he has if he thinks it will keep him out of the headlines. Maybe he lent a rifle to someone or sold it; he'll cough up the name. I'd have you come with us, too, if you'd reconsider."

Stranahan looked puzzled.

Martha explained. "After we're finished here, Harold wants to take another look at the scene."

"I do," Harold said. "I didn't get the chance when we went with Katie because it was the dog's show. I haven't had my eyes on the ground there since the bear asked me to dance."

"I'd remind you to pack your pepper spray, but then you'd accuse me of acting like your mother," Martha said.

Harold rolled his eyes. "Dating white women is a challenge," he said.

The rest of Melvin Kauffeld's statement revealed little. Once he'd arrived at the ranch, his story fell in line with what they'd already learned from Sam and Peachy Morris, from first cast on the river right up to, and including, his night of frustration and ultimate passion with Harriet Langhor. An emotional roller-coaster ride that had slowed long enough for Kauffeld to refill the well behind his tear ducts, but was far from over. Langhor was an odd one, Stranahan thought. According to Morris she was a green card immigrant who had left a husband and three children in Portland to attend the teachers' conference. For one week each summer she shut a door on what she claimed was a solid family life and opened one that included a sexual hookup with a fishing guide and, this year, an angel of mercy intervention with a stranger. A woman who could change lives like changing coats and who may well have saved the life of a suicidal man. But intriguing as she was, she was peripheral to Kauffeld's story and Stranahan shifted his eyes from the woman to his notes. He tapped Ettinger's forearm and pointed to his notebook.

She held up a finger to indicate she was getting to it.

At the next break in Harold's questioning, she said, "Mel, what did Wade mean when he wrote 'remember our plan' and talked about having good days and bad days?"

Kauffeld drew his eyebrows into a single line.

"He, uh, well we, all of us who have terminal disease, it's not like we're sick all the time. There are days we feel pretty good. But then there are days when climbing to the saddle of a mountain would be out of the question. He meant if I was having one of those days, I could come back the next day and he'd come back, too. A contingency plan, if either of us didn't feel up to it the day before."

Ettinger had caught the change of expression.

"So you could have gone back yesterday and he'd have been there?"

"He said he would."

"Is there anything else we should know about this?"

He shook his head.

"He also mentioned a hat in his note."

"I have it. It's just a red hat, so he could see the color from a distance and know it was me. I have the hawk call, too. They were under the rock with the envelope."

"We'll need them. Peachy Morris said you have a rifle."

"He has it. I gave it to him."

"I thought Wade was going to provide one."

"There was a gun in the car. A bolt-action rifle with a scope. Seven-millimeter Magnum. It's more powerful than my father's old deer rifle, but I was going to stick with a gun I knew. I learned that in 'Nam. I left Wade's rifle in the car."

"I still have a hard time believing this arrangement of yours. In my whole career in law enforcement, I've never heard anything like it."

"I can't help you there, Sheriff. It happened all right, or almost did. I'm surprised it doesn't more often. It's ironic if you think about it. You make this commitment, kill or be killed, and it takes that to give you the will to live. Wade did me a big favor."

"Some favor," Ettinger said. She made a cutting motion across her throat. Harold began the closing formalities of the statement, which Kauffeld seemed not to hear. He had turned to touch noses with Harriet Langhor, their profiles a reflection of the evolution of humankind since its Cro-Magnon beginnings twenty-five thousand years ago.

CHAPTER TWENTY-THREE

Worried Man, Worried Smile

"We need Walt here," Ettinger said as they ascended steps made of river stones embedded in cement that led to the porch of Weldon Crawford's mansion. "Walt has the best cop knock I've ever heard. He says you can tell by the wet stain on the pants if the guy's guilty. Well, here goes . . ."

The congressman opened the door to Ettinger's *bang bang bang* with his professional smile in place, which turned by degrees from perplexity into a sour expression directed at Stranahan.

Ettinger introduced herself, said she'd like to ask him a few questions.

"Do I need to call my attorney?"

"Actually, sir, we'd like your help. You're not under suspicion of anything, but there is a possibility that a crime may have been committed by someone you've met. May we come in?"

"Not him." Crawford would not look in Stranahan's direction.

"I understand your reluctance. You can believe it or not believe it, but he came to you honestly, thinking you might know something about a burglary in this neighborhood. He's an associate, but he was not working for the department on that occasion."

"It's true," Stranahan said.

"Fuck you."

"Mr. Crawford, please. He has a better understanding of some aspects of the case we're working on than anyone else. I'd prefer him to be present. Or we can do this at the department in Bridger in his presence. It's your choice."

Crawford hesitated. "Be my guest."

Stranahan could feel the man's heat as he pushed by him into the spacious living room.

Ettinger said, "I understand you're a busy man. This won't take long. Mr. Stranahan says you owned a rifle, a very expensive rifle made in England."

"I've owned a number of British firearms. What's this about?"

"You told me you once owned a .475 No. 2 Nitro Express," Stranahan said.

"So I did. It isn't a crime as far as I know."

"It may have been involved in a crime."

"That's ridiculous," Crawford said. "That rifle was made for a governor of the Kenya colony before World War I. It's a collector's item worth forty grand. I know. That's what I sold it for."

"Who did you sell it to?" Stranahan asked.

"It wasn't a private transaction. I commissioned it to the firm of Westley Richards and was told the man who bought it is named Jeffery, he's an oil executive for Texaco. Jeffery's the same name as the maker of the firearm. No relation, but he wanted a vintage double and found one in his name. If that man's guilty of anything besides picking your pocket at the gas pump, I'd be highly surprised."

"When did you sell the rifle?"

"A few months ago, but I commissioned it just after Christmas. Couldn't get the barrels to shoot to the same point of impact. I can't abide a double rifle that won't group. Bucky over at WR wanted me to reduce the price by ten thousand, but I stuck to my gun, you might say. My retirement will be a little softer because of it. I correct myself. Harder. I plan on using the money to hunt Africa next June, after the House recesses."

"Would you mind showing us your gun safe?" Ettinger said.

"I would mind."

"Mr. Crawford, we're anticipating DNA results that will match the tissue on a bullet that was shot from a .475 caliber rifle to one of the bodies found on Sphinx Mountain. At that point we will contact Mr. Jeffery and check your old rifle for a ballistic match."

"And at that point you'll be talking to my lawyer."

"Mr. Crawford . . ."

"Congressman to you."

"Congressman, I think you should reconsider." Ettinger's voice was reasonable. "The rifle you owned is likely the only one of its kind in the state, and you can see Sphinx Mountain from your picture window. You figure the odds. Wouldn't it be in your best interest to cooperate, rather than impede our investigation? You know how that would make you look."

Crawford's shrewd eyes narrowed. He turned, showing them the lump under his ear, and led the way through the living room into a study that harkened back to colonial Africa—zebra rug, the bleached skull and horns of a sable antelope, an African elephant carved out of ironwood with warthog ivory tusks. Against one wall was a built-in bookcase. Stranahan glanced at the spines, noting a copy of Robert Ruark's *Horn of the Hunter*.

"Seeing how you have me by my Rocky Mountain oysters . . ." Crawford ran his hand along one side of the bookcase, then reached behind and swung the entire bookcase into the room, revealing a walk-in gun cabinet with a rack across the back, three rows of felt indentations to stand shotguns and rifles. At least a dozen rifles and shotguns stood at attention in the rack. In addition, several cased firearms were stacked on the floor. Crawford switched on a light. The blue-black barrels of the heavy rifles gleamed.

"I thought most of your collection was at your home in Kalispell," Stranahan said.

"It is." One by one he opened the cases. "Satisfied?"

"How many people know about this safe?" Ettinger wrinkled her nose at the scent of tung oil.

"A few. My family, of course. A couple gun nut buddies whom I'd trust with my children. I suppose someone who broke into the house could stumble onto the safe, if he knew what he was looking for. But just getting in the front door wouldn't be easy. They'd have to know the combination to the community gate and it changes every month. Then there's the key code to the house; you have to punch it after unlocking the door or the alarm would ring in your office, Sheriff. And we have year-round residents like Emmitt, and Erik Janssen now, who keep an eye out for trespassers. Besides, nothing's missing. Nothing ever has been. As I told you earlier"—he glanced at Stranahan—"the only break-in I've heard of is the one you told me about, someone stealing trout flies." He finished restacking the cases and laughed. "I'll give you points for originality. It was a unique approach."

Stranahan let it pass. He said, "You also talked about 'The Most Dangerous Game.' Who else have you mentioned the story to?"

"You don't think . . ." Crawford paused as he swung the bookcase back in place and ushered them into his living room. He ran a hand up the side of his neck and scratched at the soft skin under the lump. "My word," he said. "I've mentioned that story to a lot of people."

"You told me you'd as soon die in a mano a mano in the mountains as any other way," Stranahan said.

"As a hy . . . po . . . . thetical." The congressman's voice went up an octave. "You can't believe I have anything to do with what happened up there."

"No," Ettinger said, "but we have a witness who's stated that a man approached him with just that in mind, a duel on Sphinx Mountain. The man who approached him also mentioned 'The Most Dangerous Game.' Can I see your copy, please?"

"It's in the bookcase under the A's for Anthologies. Now what the devil? Maybe it's under G, Charles Grayson edited the volume. The book is called *Stories for Men*. I haven't lent my copy out since last summer. It's not a first edition and the condition is fair at best, but it has sentimental value."

He was on his knees, running his fingers across the spine of every book on the shelves. "This really puzzles me. I know it was here"—he brought a hand up and touched his fingernails to his neck again— "well a month ago, for sure. I'll be damned." He moved his fingers to the bald spot on his crown and then drew them down the sides of his nose. "It was my favorite story when I was in high school. I've no doubt brought up the title with dozens of people over the years. Now I've heard someone has made a video game out of the story. Our leaders of tomorrow, killing each other on computer screens." He shook his head.

"How about people in this valley?" Ettinger said.

"That I've mentioned the story to? None that spring to mind. Certainly no one who could be involved in something like you've implied." He had turned to look through the window facing the river.

"When you see it from this angle," he said, seeming to speak to himself, "it really doesn't look like the head of a lion."

Stranahan and Ettinger moved to the window. They could see the deep saddle between the Sphinx and the Helmet, but not the bench of timber where the bodies had been buried.

"Do you mind?" Stranahan lifted a pair of heavy binoculars from the sill and searched the skirts of the slopes until he saw the trail-head road, a faint trace of gray. Something clicked and he said, "Do you know a man named Buster Garrett? He runs lion hounds." He lowered the glasses.

"I sure do. He guided me to a 180-pound tom, what was it, three or four years ago I'd say."

"Could you have brought up the story in his company?"

"Now that you mention it, I might have." Crawford nodded to himself. "Sure. Because of the hounds." He nodded again. "Hell, yes. I remember him asking me what kind of hounds there were in the story. Because he has Walkers, you see. Is Buster under suspicion?"

"How well do you know him?" Ettinger said.

Crawford looked thoughtful for perhaps half a minute. When he spoke all the animosity seemed to have seeped from both his expression and his voice.

"I don't know him socially at all, really. Oh, I've seen him around

Ennis, in the Dollar. The most he's ever done is tip a longnecked Bud in my direction. You didn't know him, you'd think he was cold for someone you'd spent a hard week with. Usually, you hunt with a man—and this was December mind you, snow so high you don't piss ten inches to make a hole—you get to know him pretty darn well. Know how he wears his hat. That's usually. Buster Garrett isn't 'usually.' He doesn't talk, not back and forth anyway. If you ask him a question, you'd think he didn't hear you and then maybe five minutes later he'll spit out his snoose and sketch in his thoughts on the matter. Spit out a few words that get straight to the point." Crawford snapped his fingers.

"Was he ever in this house?"

"Sure. A couple of times." He paused. "I think I see where you're going with this, and I'll say right now Buster Garrett never borrowed my Jeffery rifle."

"So what do you think, Weldon?" Ettinger said, and this time Crawford didn't correct her about using his name. "One thing about those men buried up there, the autopsies said they had terminal diseases."

"So I read."

"Did Garrett ever talk about having any physical problems himself?"

"No. But he's the kind who wouldn't if he did."

"What rifle did he carry?" Stranahan recalled the short-barreled gun strapped to Garrett's pack frame.

"One of those Remington 600s with the dogleg bolt. Three-fifty Magnum. He had me shoot it in camp. I think he wanted to impress me. It's got a kick like a Tennessee mule." He scratched under the boil. "Jesus H. Christ. Buster Garrett, you say. I'd sure like to stay out of this mess, Sheriff."

"You still might." Ettinger turned from the window. "Would you have any photos of Garrett from when the two of you hunted?"

"Sure, on my computer." He walked to his desk and scrolled down the list of albums in his iPhoto application to one labeled "Lion Hunt." Pictures of the cat treed, dogs lunging at the trunk, one of Crawford holding the dead tom up in a bear hug, blood on the lion's mouth where it had exhaled its ruined lungs.

"Here," Crawford said. The photo showed Garrett, wearing wool overalls with orange tree-marking ribbons tied around the cuffs to keep the deep snow out, cowboy hat centered and pulled down. He was sitting on a log with his right arm around the neck of a big, lean reddish brown dog. Another dog, one of the Walkers with brick saddles, sat to the other side of Garrett, looking out of the frame.

"That big hound is a Rhodesian ridgeback," Crawford said. "Buster's kill dog. He calls him Bear."

"Can you downsize that file and send it to my cell phone?" Ettinger gave him the number.

He tapped keys and a minute later saw them to the door. "Buster Garrett, it's hard to believe," he said, seeming to talk to himself. And to Stranahan, "I'm sorry about earlier."

"Thanks for your cooperation. We'll be in touch," Ettinger said. They started walking to the Cherokee.

"You notice he didn't name Polly Sorenson when you asked him who he'd mentioned the story to, people in the valley?" Stranahan said.

"Mm-hmm. I also noticed the way he distanced himself from Buster Garrett, got that look of 'maybe I didn't know the man after all' on his face when he realized we thought he could be a suspect. All of a sudden they weren't buds anymore."

Crawford was framed in the doorway when they backed the Cherokee around to head out. He raised one forefinger in a tentative Montana salute.

"Worried man with a worried smile," Stranahan said.

Ettinger grunted, submerged in thought.

PART THREE

THE MOST DANGEROUS GAME

It had to be the Indian, the ponytail a dead giveaway even at half a mile. The Indian was pausing at the trail junction. He was in the shade of trees, only his red headband visible. Then the Indian turned up the trail toward the saddle, into the sunlight. The watcher waited until the man had hiked out of sight and then he set down the binoculars. His hand went automatically to the dog, his fingers worrying the fur.

Unlike the hiker he'd seen on Sunday and could not be sure he recognized, the Indian he'd seen before. It had been on Monday, the second morning of his arrangement with the simian man, the man having failed to show on the first day. The watcher had been overlooking the trail when a party of hikers appeared below him. The Indian was accompanied by another man and two women, one with a dog at her heel and the other appearing to wear some sort of uniform. There had been an air of authority about the group that gave the watcher concern. Now, only three days later, a member of that party was again coming up the trail.

The watcher ran his tongue over his cracked lips. He sucked at his mustache. Had he dropped or left something on the bench, a cartridge case, maybe the butt of one his handrolled cigarettes? He knew he'd dropped a cartridge case last summer when the Mexican had fired and missed and he had run to keep abreast of him and, running, had tried to finger a spent cartridge case out of the breech of the big *double rifle and dropped it. He'd fumbled in a loaded cartridge and fired as the man crossed a break in the trees, the man stumbling at the shot. The watcher had followed the blood trail into the lodgepoles to the lee of a big rock where the Mexican was sitting down, blowing a bubble of blood out of his mouth. The man had looked at him with unfocused eyes, one long rattling exhalation collapsed his chest, and then the chest heaved to breathe and the breath caught and the Mexican's eyes swam out of his head, and when the last, long, gurgling exhalation followed, he was already dead. The Mexican had been dying for ten minutes until the watcher walked up on him and was holding a Spanish-language Bible open in his right hand, a crimson ribbon folded into the crease between the pages.*

For a long minute the watcher experienced a remorse so deeply felt that he could not draw breath. Finally he had gulped air like a man surfacing from a cliff dive. Shuddering gasps escaped him and he sobbed, not wiping at the tears. "What have I done?" he said aloud. He sat rocking back and forth with the Mexican's head in his lap, cleaning off his mouth and stroking his hair with his callused palm. Then he took off his boot and sock to put his big right toe into the trigger guard of the rifle. For minutes he'd sat with the twin barrels pressed to his temple. But crying had emptied him of the resolve to press the five ounces of resistance that would trip the right-hand sear.

Back at home, he dug the Mexican's Bible out of his saddlebag and opened it to the crimson ribbon. Job 1:21 was underlined in blue bottle ink. Being unable to read Spanish, he set the book down and found the King James version on his bedstand.

Naked came I out of my mother's womb, and naked shall I return thither: the Lord gave, and the Lord hath taken away; blessed be the name of the Lord.

"I'll be," he muttered aloud, for it was a passage he'd read many times, first thinking that the mother was the literal mother and then

with the understanding that "mother" referred to the lifeblood of Earth. It was the end he intended for himself, to be buried back into the mountain breast. But the Mexican had missed his shot and he hadn't, it was that simple. It was the next morning before he realized he had left an empty cartridge shell somewhere on the bench. He'd gone back but had been unable to find it.

It had seemed to matter, and then as the summer passed it hadn't, and now, a year later . . . well, almost nothing mattered now. The disease was flexing its muscles, playing with the power of its grip. It had advanced to the point where seeing the Indian caused no more than a flicker of concern. It would not interfere with his arrangement if, in fact, there was still a chance of death with honor. But the simian man had not come on the appointed day, nor the second, nor the third, nor now the day after that. The watcher glanced around where his grandfather's buffalo gun leaned against a tree trunk. Beyond it rose a wisp of smoke from the ashes of his cooking fire, and in the dappled shade of the pines, his horse with one leg up dozed. He shook his head.

"We've got enough beans for one more day, girl," the watcher said, and his hand jumped on the dog's neck.

CHAPTER TWENTY-FOUR

The Decoy

When Martinique opened the door, she was still wearing the sailor uniform she'd worn to work and had her hair pinned up under a cap tilted jauntily to the side.

Stranahan was taken aback for a moment, then said, "Permission to come aboard?"

"I like the sound of that," she said.

"Isn't that outfit a little demure for Lookers and Lattes?"

"Not if I unbutton it," she said, unbuttoning two buttons.

"I know it's hopelessly old-fashioned of me, but I really wish you had a different job."

Martinique gave him a look and rebuttoned the buttons. "Sean, we've been through this. If you can find me a four-hour shift that pays as well, I will. But right now the most important thing is my studies and I need time for that. I can't have a full-time job."

"Didn't Jeff Svenson offer you something?"

"Jeff Svenson offered me the privilege of working beside him at his clinic for free. And I'm going to start doing it a few hours a week because a couple years from now he might want to take on another vet, and if he likes my work, I could have a job when I graduate. Wouldn't you like me to come back to Montana?"

"I guess we never talked about it."

"You know I have to do my last four years in Oregon. I'll have to move back at the end of January."

"I know. But everything was so easy, I was still taking it a day at a time."

"Did you ever think there's a reason it's easy? It's not like it's happened this way before, relationships with men. You and me, we just fit. Don't we?" She looked down. "I thought we did."

"Hey, where's my smile?" Sean said. He put his fingers under her chin and she looked up. Her eyes glistened.

"I'm sorry," she said. "I didn't mean to bring this up. I don't want to scare you away."

"You aren't." He kissed the tip of her nose.

"You can do better than that," she said, and ran her fingers through his hair and looked seriously at him, and closed her eyes and kissed him, her lips parting and the kiss saying the unspoken words that waited for the moment.

"You smell like something," she said, pulling back from him. "What is it?"

"Gunpowder. Among other things."

"Why don't you wash up? We're cooking outside tonight. Sam Meslik's coming by to grill something he called speedy goat. I'm making a salad. What's speedy goat?"

"Pronghorn antelope. This is . . . ah, I didn't think you'd met Sam."

"He came by the hut when I was closing up. He said it was about time he introduced himself on account of he'd lose his fishing buddy if I didn't approve and just heard lies about him."

"Do you approve?"

"I do. I like men who are bigger than life. My dad was, when he'd come home from work wearing that big stag shirt and smelling like pine sap and sawdust, it was like six people came into the room. Our house never had a lock, did I tell you that? Everybody was welcome, all these brute loggers who'd leave their caulks on the stoop and wore suspenders. They all had nicknames—Ham Bone, Four-Fingered Ollie, a guy who called himself the Pope. Your Sam would have fit right in. They'd come over for Sunday afternoon potlucks."

"Sam's a good cook."

"So he told me."

They turned in unison to the crunch of gravel in the drive.

"Here he is. He's got Killer riding shotgun. Are your cats in?"

"They're up in the bedroom. I'll shut the door."

"**K**imosabe," Sam said, pushing by Stranahan with packages under both arms, glancing around for the kitchen and slapping a plastic bag of bloody meat on the granite countertop.

"I seen this place a hundred times and wondered what it looked like inside. Sorta like living inside a rocket made out of barn wood. What do you have to do, climb the stairs outside to get to the loft up there?"

Stranahan nodded.

Sam craned his head to see the cupola six stories up. "Far fucking out." He pried the caps off three bottles of Moose Drool with the back of his folding knife.

"Just take over the kitchen, why don't you?" Stranahan said.

"I wouldn't want to displace you."

Martinique came down the steps. She'd let her hair down and changed into jeans and a blue cotton shirt with white stitching.

"The lovely Cannelle," Sam said, handing her a beer. "Don't worry about Killer. He'll stay in the bed of the truck."

"Thank you, good sir." They touched bottles.

"What have I missed?" Stranahan said.

"My birth name is Cannelle," Martinique said. "Sam pried it out of me. He's very persuasive when he wants to be."

"I told her there's a law in Montana against any name that makes you think of palm trees and piña coladas. It puts the natives at a psychological disadvantage."

"Why didn't you tell me?"

"Well, Martinique is what my mother called me, I told you why, and it stuck. My father had a grandmother named Cannelle back in Provence, in a place called Carpentras. Cannelle means cinnamon. My dad said I smelled like cinnamon so all the boys would be after me."

"And I bet they were," Sam said.

"Well, I was just a tomboy then with gangly legs and a big forehead."

"Before you traded your jumper for the sailor uniform."

"Well, I wouldn't have had anything to put in it then."

"Anybody tell you there's something to put in it now?"

Martinique blushed, but recovered quickly. "Anybody say you look like a timber wolf with a mane?"

"Did your boyfriend tell you some of my wolf blood saved his life last year?"

"He did. Lucky for him it doesn't show."

Stranahan thought, *A few minutes ago she's kissing me with tears in her eyes, talking about how well we fit, and I didn't even know her name.* He went out the back door to light the coals. Crows were mobbing a red-tailed hawk, flocking toward the Bitterroot horizon, indigo clouds rimmed in lemon neon. He heard the screen door creak.

"You two seemed to have hit it off," he said without turning around.

Sam grunted. "I like her a sight better than that Beaudreux woman last year. She was exotic as a mynah bird, but you got the feeling there was a bubble around her and nobody could get in there but her. So you ever hear from her?"

"She called a couple months ago." Stranahan doused a mound of coals with lighter fluid and shot a match at it. "Middle of the night, like always."

"And . . . ?"

"And nothing. She creates this world that's just the two of you, like you're the last lovers on earth, except that for some reason she just can't see you in person. Then in the morning it's like she was never there in the first place. But Martinique's for real. She's right in front of you. You get all of her."

"Except for her name," Sam corrected.

"That minor detail."

"How does a fuckup like you get a babe like her?"

"Because I like cats, I guess. You have no idea how much nerve it took for me to talk to her at the kiosk. I know how lucky I am."

"Well, before you jump down my throat for ruining any romantic plans you had for the evening, I have something to tell you. I invited myself over 'cause you got no cell service here and this can't wait."

"And . . ."

"Well, I can't tell you yet 'cause I don't exactly know. Peachy was going to call and tell me, but then I'd have no way to get a hold of you because I figured you were out here and gonna spend the night. But then I stopped by the hut and Cannelle said she's got email, so I called Peachy back and gave him the address. He says he'll send a message to her computer sometime tonight. So anyway, that's why I invited my ass over. Plus I got this goat defrosted and Darla bailed on me."

"Are you two back together?"

"I don't know. She told me she missed the hugs, but she doesn't re-gard me as quote, 'relationship material.' So I guess that's a way of saying we're fucking." Sam took the tongs from Stranahan's hand and scraped the coals to either side of the grill. "I never thought I'd say it, but I'm getting to a point in my life where I want more."

"You're just finally growing up."

"Shoot me if I ever do."

"What's this about Peachy? It has something to do with earlier to-day, doesn't it?"

"Peachy says the chimp didn't tell you and the sheriff all there was to know. But he hinted to Harriet after you'd gone and now she's try-ing to get him to open up, and Mel says he will but not if she tells the sheriff. So they're at a standoff. But she's got the tool to make him talk and I'm guessing the longer she keeps her cat under cotton, the quicker he hollers. That man's about starved for poon. We boot up the computer in an hour, there's going to be a message."

"Let's check right now," Stranahan said.

There was no message.

Martinique said, "What are you two up to?" Her voice from the kitchen.

"Can you tell her about it?"

"I don't know."

"Tell me about what?"

"It's nothing," Stranahan called back.

"So," Sam said, lifting his beer bottle when they were sitting at the picnic table, "here's to love that's a thousand miles long and comes in ten-inch installments."

"You wish," Martinique said.

The message from Peachy Morris was boldfaced in the inbox when Stranahan checked at eleven. He asked Martinique for the closest place he could get a bar off a cell tower. She said two miles east on the old Amsterdam Road. And he was out the door.

Sam sat at the desk where Martinique had plugged in her laptop, the message staring at him while Martinique read it over his shoulder:

Harriet says that everything Mel Kauffeld said was true except it wasn't the whole truth because the guy Wade said he would keep coming back if Mel didn't show up the first or second day. In case Mel felt bad or something he'd have a little more leeway. She tried to pin him down on how many days and Mel said four but she thinks he was maybe just throwing out a number to get her off his back about it. Anyway, he didn't tell the sheriff because he didn't want Wade to get caught or die in a shoot-out but Harriet convinced him he's guilty of withholding evidence in a murder investigation if he didn't come clean. So that's all I know. Hey are you booked day after tomorrow? I got four people want to fish and need a second boat for a lower Mad run. They're yours if you want them. Meet me at Crapper Corner at six or if you can't maybe Stranny? But let me know one way or the other or I'll have to give them to Whitefish Ernie. Peachy.

"He could learn how to use a comma," Martinique said. "So this is what was nothing, huh? Doesn't sound like nothing. What's it mean, Sam?"

"I can't make it," he said absently. "The float Peachy mentioned, day after tomorrow. You'll have to ask Sean if he can cover for me."

She repeated her question.

Sam came back from somewhere else. "It means something that looked like it was over isn't over. Maybe."

"Now you've got me worried."

Sam grunted, trying to think three steps ahead of the page that faced him. His face was grim.

The last time Stranahan had been to Martha Ettinger's house after sunset, he had heard the four-note inquiry of a great gray owl. But it was nearly midnight, the owl silent in the bottom of Hellroaring Canyon, nothing but the murmur of the creek. When he came to the section that Ettinger had mentioned was for sale, he shut off the motor and rolled down the window to listen. And thought, *I could live here.* He allowed himself to expand on his reverie, subconsciously understanding that it could be the last moment of reflection he might enjoy in some time. He pictured the small log home he would build. He pictured stringing a rod and hiking down to the creek to catch brook trout for supper. He saw himself sitting on a porch swing. And Martinique was there.

He turned the key to crank the starter. "Would that I could," he said.

Ten minutes later he was sitting in Ettinger's kitchen, declining her offer of tea.

"Not if I want to sleep tonight. Or is that why you're offering? You need me to stay awake."

"I don't know. I've put everyone into place except you and Harold, and he's off the rez, so to speak. Or rather off to the rez. He checked in after climbing the mountain this afternoon and said he had some personal business in Browning. A family matter." She shrugged and took a sip of tea. "You get out of town up there, you might as well throw your cell phone out the window for the good it will do you. I tried calling him a couple times."

Stranahan listened impatiently, his mind jumping ahead. "So what are you thinking? Send somebody up to the Sphinx with a red hat and a rifle and see if you can trick this guy into making his move?"

Martha compressed her lips. "I've been back and forth on it. I don't like the idea of painting a bull's-eye on somebody's back, but I can't see any other way. Not if we're going to get enough evidence to stick."

"It might be easier if we knew who was going to be waiting there with a gun. Buster Garrett didn't seem the type when I met him, but he's the only person who fits the description Melvin Kauffeld gave us. Think about it. He outfits on Sphinx Mountain. He's aware of 'The Most Dangerous Game.' And he knows Crawford. It's three strikes. I don't know how he got ahold of Crawford's gun, but he must have. I know we had our doubts about him—"

Ettinger raised her hand to stop him. "I don't need convincing," she said. "There's something you don't know."

Stranahan waited.

"Buster Garrett has cancer."

Stranahan let it sink in. "You're sure?"

"Mmm-hmm. Judy located his sister over in Darby. I called her as soon as I put down the phone talking to you. I apologized for the hour and said we'd questioned her brother about a game violation last week and needed to complete his file. We couldn't locate him, but we needed to know if he had any outstanding medical conditions we should be aware of, because we couldn't interview him again without doctor's approval, depending on the severity of his condition. It's true, actually. Technically, anyway."

Stranahan arched his eyebrows.

"I wasn't proud of myself. But tomorrow could be our last chance.

Under the circumstances it seemed justified. And guess what? He's got prostate cancer. The sister says he goes to Deaconess as an outpatient."

"So if Garrett and Wade are one and the same, it backs up Kauffeld's story. The motive rings true."

"I don't care about motive one way or the other. The thing that matters is we have evidence to arrest. Judy got confirmation this afternoon that the DNA on the bullet is a match with the second body, but we can't get the gun in possession because Crawford sold it and it's in Texas. Dusting a useful print at this date is unlikely. So what we have to count on is that Garrett will go back up there tomorrow, hoping that Kauffeld will show, and he'll respond to the hawk call. That's powerful circumstantial evidence. Plus we have Kauffeld's ID once Garrett's in custody, Kauffeld's eyewitness account of their first meeting, and, if the stars line up, we can corroborate with handwriting analysis on the note. It's enough for the DA to build a case, especially if we can get the Living at Last people to place Garrett at a retreat where he could have met Gutierrez. But"—she paused and looked at Stranahan—"if he's up there overlooking the trail with binoculars, like he told Kauffeld he would be, then everything hinges on the decoy. If Garrett doesn't buy the decoy, then we'll have scared him away for good."

Stranahan looked at her levelly. "Why don't you just say me when you say 'the decoy.' It's me or I wouldn't be here."

Martha shook her head. "I'd rather have it be law enforcement. But Harold's out of the equation. I'd send Warren, but he's too short and . . ."

"No, it's got to be me," Stranahan said. "I have the height and build. Besides, Warren wouldn't agree to shave his mustache."

Martha allowed herself a brief smile. "You're right," she said. "He probably wouldn't. But he'll have your back, trust me on that. So will I. But I want you to know what you're getting into before I deputize you." She got up from the table and led him to her home office in the main room of the old farmhouse. She switched on the overhead track lighting system. Two maps were spread across the urethane surface of the sawn stump that served as her desk. One was a standard Montana road map, the other a USGS quad for Sphinx Mountain.

"Ever got around to counting the rings?" Stranahan said.

"I haven't been bored enough yet. I was told it's eight hundred years old; did I tell you that?"

"Last summer. You said it was a Ponderosa pine."

"Yeah, well I had other things on my mind that day. You did, too, if you recall."

"Like now."

"Déjà vu, as Walt would say." She pointed to the road map. The route from Big Timber, where Buster Garrett lived, to the trailhead at the Bear Creek Forest Service Station was highlighted in chartreuse marker. Ettinger told Stranahan that the Sweet Grass County Sheriff's Department had agreed to post a deputy at Garrett's house. The deputy would call with a vehicle license and description as soon as Garrett was on the move

"How do you know he's home?" Stranahan said. "Why couldn't he be on the mountain tonight, camping out above the trail? That's the way I'd do it."

"Well, his truck's at home, the one you saw him driving, and the house lights are out, but no, we don't know for sure. Just like we don't know for sure that it's Garrett in the first place. You only called me an hour ago. Right now I'm trying to set this up with overworked people who are dressed in pajamas. You want to object or do you want to listen?"

Stranahan acquiesced by steepling his fingers.

Ettinger took him though the strategy she'd devised, referring to the topographic map. It seemed simple enough. The GPS coordinates for the arrangement, which Kauffeld had received in the note he'd recovered under the bridge, marked the bench of timber where the first body had been recovered. There were two trails leading to the saddle below the bench, both starting from the same trailhead. One followed the Trail Fork of Bear Creek—this was the path the body recovery team had taken and, later, that Sean and Katie Sparrow had taken when they used the metal detector to find the bullet. Kauffeld had been instructed to hike up this trail. It was presumed that Garrett would station himself where he could overlook it. Ettinger traced the trail with a yellow highlighter. "That's your route," she told Stranahan.

The other approach to the saddle was a trail up the Middle Fork of Bear Creek, along the northern side of the Helmet. It was about the same distance, but the going was more difficult, with several iffy creek crossings. Ettinger marked it in pink highlighter. This was the route she and Warren Jarrett would take. It would keep them out of sight of anyone watching the other trail, and they could then meet up with Stranahan on the saddle, a few hundred yards below the bench. She gave Stranahan the coordinates of the meeting place to program into his GPS.

"Okay then," she said, "once we rendezvous, we'll climb as a team to the bench and take cover. You'll give the hawk call. We'll let Garrett come to us. Warren will apprehend. We'll back him up. No cowboy-hatting. You got that?"

Stranahan nodded.

"Can you drive a different car to the trailhead? Garrett knows your Land Cruiser. He shouldn't be in any position to see the trailhead by the time you arrive, but why take the chance?"

Stranahan nodded again.

"So, what do you think?"

He caught the note of uncertainty in her voice. "I think it's like boxing," he said. "Everybody has a plan until they get hit."

"Meaning what?"

"Meaning things don't always go to plan."

"They never do. Anyone who's dealt with an Adam Henry can tell you that."

Stranahan inclined his eyebrows.

"Adam Henry. An aggressive and hostile suspect. So are you in or out?"

"I'm in."

Ettinger began to speak and then snapped her middle finger against her thumb and held up her forefinger. "Ssshh. Listen."

It was the owl's low-pitched call—"whooo-ooo-ooo-ooo."

They were quiet, waiting, and then it came again, the silence of the forest profound when the last note died. After a time the sound of the creek came back.

Martha's voice was thoughtful. "Do you know the great gray owl is called the gray ghost of the north? A coincidence, huh? I never thought of it until now."

"Maybe it's an omen," Stranahan said.

"Yeah," Martha said. "But a good one or a bad one?"

"I guess we'll find out tomorrow."

"I guess we will. Now raise your right hand before I change my mind."

CHAPTER TWENTY-FIVE

A Strike from the Bucket List

A cool and absolute stillness that was more of an emotion than a quality of atmosphere smothered the trailhead the next morning. Stranahan glanced at his watch—eight-fifty. Warren Jarrett's unmarked Toyota Tacoma was there, but no other vehicles were parked at the trailhead or in the adjacent campground. Nor had he received any messages on the powerful FM radio that Ettinger had lent him. If the Sweet Grass County troll who'd been posted at Garrett's house had anything to report, it hadn't reached Stranahan's ears. He thought of Martinique, burying her face in his neck when she'd seen him out the door an hour before. Maybe there was no need for her to worry after all.

He walked around to the back of the Datsun, the lift struts of Martinique's hail-damaged hatchback so shot he had to hold the trunk open while reaching down for Kauffeld's .300 Savage. Ettinger had pressed the rifle into his hands the night before, along with the hawk call and the red hat. He leaned against the hood and stretched his legs. A few drops of rain, a promise of more. He tied the arms of a rain jacket around his waist, shut the hatch, and started hiking, feeling about as naked as he ever had, despite the reassuring weight of the rifle hanging by a sling from his shoulder.

For two miles the trail dipped into and out of forest, into and out of a drizzling rain. It was in the wildflower meadow at the trail junction, where the path to the saddle veered to the left and began to zigzag up, that Sean had felt the hair on his forearms prickle the last time he'd hiked here alone. Then he had been able to dismiss the feeling, but it was not so easy while wearing a target in the form of a red hat, and with the suspicion that he was being watched from one of the openings in the timbered slopes that rose sharply on either side. He resisted the urge to glance around, but instead trained his eyes on the massive extrusion of limestone on the Helmet, the plume-like peak resembling the brush of horsehair topping a Roman general's hat. He bent forward as he walked, swinging his arms in an attempt to emulate Melvin Kauffeld's distinctive stride. And felt his heart pound against the binoculars that bobbed on his chest.

But nothing happened and the feeling of impending doom gradually receded. An hour and fifteen minutes later he reached the place on the saddle where he'd been instructed to wait for Ettinger and Jarrett, and ten minutes after that he heard a branch break to the north, from the direction of the Middle Fork. He was gripping the rifle tightly as Ettinger and Jarrett rounded a bend in the path. Ettinger put a finger to her lips and motioned Stranahan back into the trees, where they squatted in silence.

The sheriff's sergeant spoke first. "Did you tell him?"

"Tell me what?" Stranahan said.

Jarrett explained that Buster Garrett had been spotted walking outside his house at six a.m. wearing boxers, scratching his belly, and urinating in his yard. He'd gone back into the house and had come out again at seven and driven off in his truck, heading west on the highway.

"His truck wasn't at the trailhead when I drove in," Stranahan said.

"He could be coming late," Jarrett said.

Ettinger didn't want to argue about it. She turned to the sheriff's sergeant. "Okay, Warren, it's your show."

Jarrett told them to check their rifles. One in the chamber, safeties on.

Stranahan eased open the lever of the Savage, caught the reassuring glint of a cartridge, and closed the action.

"Here's how it goes down," Jarrett said. "We climb to the bench single file; Sean, you're last. I'll choose our cover. You two will spread out to either side of me, how far depends upon the nature of the cover. We settle down, wait for everybody's pulse to return to normal. You have that hawk call?"

Stranahan pulled the call on the neck lanyard from under his shirt.

Jarrett nodded. "I'll wait till exactly noon, per the instructions Kauffeld gave us. When I put my fingers to my mouth, you give the call. Then we wait. If somebody comes in with a weapon, I'll identify myself and command him to drop it. All three of us will stand and show arms, so he knows we have superior force. Nine times out of ten if you have superior force, the subject drops the weapon. Protocol is if he raises the weapon, makes any move to point it in our direction, then we shoot to kill. You got that?" He looked at Stranahan.

Stranahan said, "What if he runs?"

"If he runs and I consider him an armed suspect, I have discretion to use reasonable force to stop him."

"We shoot him?"

"I shoot him. Only if he threatens us with a weapon do you or Martha fire." Jarrett stood up. "That's it. That's my speech."

"Then it's showtime," Ettinger said.

As the party climbed upward, the drizzle became constant, slanting rain. Ettinger caught Stranahan's eyes and raised her own to the leaden sky. The rain meant the call of the hawk wouldn't carry as far. But there was nothing to be done about it, and the call sounded loud enough when Sean blew it a few minutes after they'd reached the bench. The tension among the team was palpable. Sean could hear Warren Jarrett breathing ten yards to his right. His hands on the rifle were slick with sweat. But nothing happened, and nothing happened after he'd blown the call for the second time a half hour later. As the afternoon advanced, legs became cramped, clothes soaked through, spirits were deflated. Finally Ettinger made a cutting motion across her throat. It was a weary and very wet team that stumbled down the trail and gathered for dinner at the Ennis Café.

"You notice we never saw the shovel," Jarrett said. "We were within fifteen yards of the coordinates. You'd think we would have seen it if the game was on."

"The shovel would have been nice," Martha agreed. "We might have dusted a print from it." She held up a finger, reached for the cell phone vibrating in her pocket. "Ettinger." She listened, said "uh-huh." She ran her forefinger across the face of the phone.

"That was Sweet Grass County. Buster Garrett returned to his house at noon, hasn't gone out since. He must have just been working a job this morning." She blew out a breath, her lips making a bubbling sound. "I never did think it was him, even after his sister said he had cancer. I just let myself hope it was him."

"What about going back tomorrow?" Stranahan said.

"What about it?" Ettinger said. She cut into her chicken-fried steak.

"Well, the sound of the call couldn't carry in that heavy air. Maybe he'll come back tomorrow, give it a last chance."

Jarrett combed his fingers through his wet hair. "I think if anybody comes back to the bench tomorrow it's that sow grizzly what chomped on Harold. I could smell her in there today."

"Listen, Sean," Ettinger said. "Today was the fifth day. If this fellow Wade"—she made quote marks in the air to emphasize the name—"if he didn't come on a day he said he would, then he isn't coming on a day he said he wouldn't. He probably wrote Kauffeld off as a player after the first no-show. Now it's on to the next pigeon. It's over for him, this time anyway. It's over for us, too."

Back at the grain elevator with the churring lament of a nighthawk pouring in the open windows, Martinique proved to be equally dismissive—and adamant—about his not returning the next day. She said if he absolutely had to experience a more elevated heart rate, she could do something about it. He asked her what that could be. She led him up the stairs and showed him.

Remember Sam has you lined up for that float in the Bear Trap. You have to meet Peachy at six."

"I know. I'm getting up." He sat up in bed. "Martinique, you look . . . indescribable."

Readying herself for a double shift, Martinique was applying patches of double-sided tape to a gauzy peasant blouse, just above and below the dark circles of her nipples. She pulled the heavy Weyerhaeuser suspenders clipped to her jean cutoffs up over her shoulders and pressed them over the tape. It was the extent of her outfit. She gave a businesslike bounce to make sure the straps would stay in place.

"These were my dad's logging suspenders," she said.

"Wouldn't he be proud?"

"Don't go there, Sean. We agreed, remember?"

"You agreed, but I'm not going to argue with you this morning. I do wonder, though, why you signed me up for a float today without consulting me. It just seems . . . out of character, you being so independent yourself. I can't imagine your reaction if I did the same thing, commit you to something without asking."

"Oh, baby, don't you know?" She sat on the edge of the bed and took his hand.

"No, I don't think I do."

"I know it isn't logical, but I thought if I . . . how do I put this?" She turned his hand over and rubbed his palm, looking down. "Yesterday, when you left and I knew you were going up into the mountains, I didn't know if you were coming back. So I thought if I signed you up to fish today, then you would have an obligation. You'd have to come back. 'He can't die, because he has to do this float. Sam's depending on him.' You understand?"

"I do." He pulled her to him. The metal clasps of the suspenders were cold against his chest.

"I better go make breakfast," she said. Her voice assumed a self-mocking tone. "Then this little logger chick is off to pour coffee."

"Your nipple's showing."

She looked down. "We can't have that," she said. "Your sheriff would throw me in the hoosegow."

Stranahan tried to mask his surprise when he saw Melvin Kauffeld and Harriet Langhor standing beside Peachy Morris's Explorer at the boat ramp. He hadn't known who his clients would be, only that they were from the Double D.

"Where's Peachy?" he said, taking the cold hand that Kauffeld extended and then Harriet's, whose grasp was hard as any man's.

"He put in ten minutes ago," Kauffeld said. "You cover your surprise well, Mr. Stranahan."

"Sean."

"Sean. But look at it from my point of view. Harriet's conference lasts until Sunday. I'd be a fool to leave her before I absolutely had to. And Peachy seemed quite keen on taking the two young women from Oklahoma, which leaves us with you. He said you're a fine fisherman, that you don't catch a lot of trout but you know how to catch the big ones. I'd like to catch a twenty-inch trout. Do you think you could grant one wish from a dying man's bucket list?" He crinkled his eyes, which disappeared into their deep sockets.

To Stranahan, the display of bravado seemed forced. But then, he thought, so would most attempts at levity by a man with Kauffeld's prognosis. He said, "I've put anglers into fish that size in six runs between here and Greycliff. We'll go with articulated streamers, but the thing about slinging artillery is you might not catch anything at all—that's the trade-off."

"Sean, just waking up this morning was a blessing. I was kidding you about the wish."

But he got it, anyway, about an hour into a cold float with a brisk wind lifting spray from the riffles. The trout, a rainbow fat as Finnegan, took an olive streamer tied from dyed Finn raccoon fur, a pattern of Stranahan's that had paid off before in the lower river. After taking the obligatory photos and releasing the trout, the anglers admired a pair of ospreys that peered regally down from their throne on a pinnacle of cliff.

Kauffeld said, "You two keep an eye on the birds. I drank too much coffee this morning." He started to wade downstream, toward a bay that was out of sight.

Stranahan felt Harriet grip his arm. "He's putting up a front," she said, her accent thicker than Sean had remembered. "Something was bothering him yesterday. I told Peachy we wanted to float with you, so I could tell you."

"Tell me what?"

"He sent you on a goose chase yesterday." She unzipped a top pocket of her wading vest and opened a cell phone. "Mel's phone. He doesn't know I have it." She tapped keys. "I turned the volume down. Put it to your ear."

A voice message, the voice muffled, Stranahan thought deliberately so: "I know you're at the Double D. I followed you to the airport . . . Last chance, pardner. Be a man."

"Look at the time," she said. The banner readout scrolled from left to right: *Wednesday, July 16, 2:20 p.m.*

"Yesterday afternoon we were on the mountain," Stranahan said. "We were where they were supposed to meet."

"I think you were in the wrong place. Mel told you he didn't have a map, but I went through his clothes. I found this." She handed him a folded paper from the same pocket of her vest. It was a computer copy of a *National Geographic* map page. Stranahan identified Sphinx Mountain and the Helmet. There were circles on the map. One, in red marker, circumscribed the timber bench where the bodies had been found, where Stranahan had met Ettinger and Jarrett the day before. The other circled a lower slope of a ridge a couple miles west of the saddle. Sean marked it as being not too far from the meadow at the trail junction. A shorter and much easier hike from the trailhead. In addition to a set of penned GPS coordinates beside the X that marked the center of each circle, there were sequential numbers separated by hyphens: 13-14-15 inside the circle that marked the saddle; 16-17 inside the circle that marked the lower slope.

"They're dates, don't you think? You went here"—she pointed— "but Wade was at this other place then. I am right, yes?" Her intense eyes shifted from the map to Stranahan.

Stranahan nodded. He was thinking that the second circle was the contingency plan, in case an older and infirm man decided he couldn't hike as far as the saddle. He folded up the map as Kauffeld bucked the current, wading upstream toward the boat.

"Don't tell him you gave me this," he whispered.

"What should I do?"

"Nothing. It's obvious Mel was communicating with this man more than he let on. If he suspects anything, he might warn him. So just go about the day and try to keep the phone away from him."

"Are you going to call the sheriff and go to this other place? Today's the seventeenth."

"Hey, what is this, a conspiracy?" Melvin Kauffeld's baritone boomed over the sound of the current and the sloshing of his waders.

"You caught us," Stranahan said, holding up his hands. "We were just talking about reassigning you to the back of the boat so that Harriet has the next chance at a big fish."

Kauffeld climbed onto the aft seat of the raft and rummaged around in his waterproof gear bag. He extracted a thermos and poured a cup of coffee, to which he added a dollop of whiskey from a gunmetal flask. A drop of liquid suspended from his red nose, then dropped with an audible plop into the cup.

"A dash of bitters won't do any harm," he said. "Did you know that Irish coffee was born on a day like this one? Just after the war, in Foynes, Ireland. At the airport there, the planes were always having to turn back in heavy weather—I've been to Limerick, that's how I know the story—and one day the chef at the hotel prepared this drink to revive the spirits of the returning passengers. Somebody said, 'Is this Brazilian coffee?' and the chef said, 'No, it's Irish coffee.' To make it right you add cream on top, you pour it over"—his voice began to quaver—"a . . . spoon." He heaved a sigh. "Oh God, what brought this on? I just caught the biggest trout of my life and I'm with the woman of my dreams and I'm on the Madison River and I'm ready to cry." Kauffeld shook his head as if to clear out what was in it.

"We're here with you, Mel," Stranahan said.

Kauffeld gathered himself. He conjured a smile after a short struggle, one side of his mouth having to work at it. The lopsided gesture struck Stranahan like a fist. For a few seconds he wasn't sure what he was seeing as faces blurred in his memory, then he was seeing one face very clearly, the left eye and cheek clenching tight, as if it had been stung by a bee. *Of course*, he thought. *It makes sense.*

Kauffeld was blinking away his tears. He said, "I don't mean to be a killjoy, but here's to what's left of life." He raised the mug, the steam dissipating into the air.

For Stranahan, what was left of the float was an exercise in patience. His mind was on the second circle on the map, trying to envision the country. He knew what he had to do, had an idea how to go about it, had a very good idea whom he'd meet there. But he was on the fence about going in alone. It was hard to think of that and fishing, too. A half dozen more strikes, a couple smallish browns for Harriet, a few snapshots to remember the day, and finally they were at the take-out. Peachy had beat them and was loading his boat onto his trailer. A driver for the Double D had shuttled the rigs and was waiting beside a van to take Kauffeld and Langhor back to the ranch.

After helping Peachy with his boat, Stranahan waved him to the far side of the rigs, where they could speak in private.

"I got a big favor to ask. Do you have a rifle back at your cabin that

I could borrow?" He'd returned Kauffeld's Savage rifle to Sheriff Ettinger when they came off the mountain.

"No, man. My Weatherby's at Rocky Mountain Sports in Ennis. The floor plate was opening under recoil and spilling ammo onto the ground. They're putting in a stronger spring. It's done, but I haven't picked it up."

"When you get back in cell range would you call and tell them I'm picking it up? I'll have it back to you later tonight."

"Sure. If you can pony up for the bill, I'll pay you back. It's a .338-06. I got half a box of handloads in the truck. She's sighted an inch and half high at one hundred yards, groups in a nickel from the bench."

No hesitation, no question why Stranahan needed the rifle. Nowhere else he'd lived would such a conversation take place. Peachy gave him the cartridges as Kauffeld walked up, unfolding a thick wad of bills. Stranahan firmly closed his fist over the man's hand.

"It's not every day I get to grant a wish from a bucket list. I'm not going to taint the morning by taking your money."

Kauffeld insisted on paying fifty dollars toward Stranahan's gas. Thinking of the drive ahead of him, he hesitated only a moment before pocketing it.

In Ennis, he collected the rifle, bought a turkey locator call that included instructions for the scream of a red-tailed hawk, and found a red cap with the logo of the Kingfisher Fly Shop. So armed, he motored through the town and then stopped by the bridge and got out to look down at the Madison River.

Stranahan was an instinctive person who felt his way toward decisions and found that water helped when the level was balanced, that the current shifted the weight in some inscrutable way so that he felt the decision in his heart without knowing why or how the balance had tipped. He'd be out of phone communication in another few miles, so the question was should he call Ettinger. He knew her reaction would be skeptical. Even if she was persuaded by the phone message and the map, she would insist on a group operation, which translated into time lost, not including the drive down from Bridger. Already it was noon. Who knew how long the man would stay up there, given that this was the last day and long odds on anyone showing? But against his going up there alone was the chance of being shot. He recalled Warren Jarrett's comment on overwhelming force. Stranahan knew he would be running a grave risk. He also knew it wouldn't have mattered so much a year before. He was not building a life then so much as running from one. Now there were people he cared about, a future he cared about. Not to mention a section of land on a creek, haunted by an owl in a cottonwood bottom.

But the face of the river gave him nothing. When he got back behind the wheel, he just sat there, looking within for the answers the water had refused him.

CHAPTER TWENTY-SIX

The Courtly Cowboy

A woman with crow's wing hair, gray roots painting a stripe down the middle of her part, stood on the porch of the small frame house by the railroad tracks in Wolf Creek. Bird-chested, her face pinched and severe, she was an Appalachian vision in a sack dress. She folded her bony arms across her rib cage.

"Ma'am, my name is Harold Little Feather. I'm with the Hyalite County Sheriff's Department? I called you earlier."

"You're an Indian." It was a statement.

"Apparently," Harold said. "Can I come inside? I'd like to ask a few questions about your husband."

She hesitated. Harold could hear a truck shifting gears up on the highway, then the undertone of Prickly Pear Creek. The woman opened the door and let him in. "Webster, there's an Indian in the house with his arm in a cast." She moved her chin up and down in agreement with herself. "He's a lawman."

As Harold's eyes became accustomed to the darkness he saw that the house was sliding south, the furniture solid where you could see it under piles of clothing and newspaper, but the wood floors stained black, the boards spongy underfoot. A vaguely houndlike mutt lay on a couch littered with magazines. It opened one eye and the eye found Harold, lost its focus, and skinned back over.

The woman said have a seat, indicating the dogless end of the couch. "Where's my manners?" she said. "I got Folgers. I just opened a can."

Harold nodded. "Black," he said.

As the woman rummaged out of sight in the kitchen, he glanced up at a shoulder mount of a bull elk on the knotty pine wall. Mabel Webster's husband had been a hunter. Had been because he was presumed dead, having disappeared in the Big Belt Mountains the previous November. Martha Ettinger had flagged his name while searching for lost hunters who might match the unidentified bodies buried on Sphinx Mountain. Webster, a retired railroad conductor for Burlington Northern, was in the ballpark for age, mid-sixties, wore hunting clothes, and had disappeared at about the time the remaining John Doe was presumed to have been buried. But the Big Belts were two hundred miles north of the Madison Range and the department's investigation into Webster's disappearance had been shelved when his wife, in a phone interview, denied that her husband suffered from pancreatic cancer, contradicting the autopsy report. He was "fit as an Arkansas fiddle," she had said.

The truth was Harold doubted that interviewing Webster's widow would reveal anything worth knowing, but his trip back from the reservation was right down the I-15, putting him in the neighborhood, and was a step toward getting back into Martha Ettinger's good graces. She'd been none too pleased when he had called after being out of communication for a day and a half. His explanation, that he'd had to intervene in a family crisis—his brother, Howard, not a day off the wagon before being accused by his wife, Bobby, of slapping her, when it turned out that he hadn't slapped her but had slapped the table so hard the dishes jumped onto the floor, after which Bobby had hit him with a broom, breaking his finger—anyway, the explanation hadn't gone over too well. Ettinger's only comment had been, "So was there a phone in that house, or wasn't there?"

Harold heard the widow's voice muttering from the kitchen and returned to the present. He caught the word "Webster" as she walked back into the living room.

"Is your husband still alive, Mrs. Webster?" he asked.

She handed him a cup and settled herself on a turned-around ladder-back chair, her legs straddling the seat. "For pity's sakes, young man, of course he is. Didn't he say so?" Her hands fluttered over her face like anxious birds.

"What do you mean?"

"Why, he wrote it in a letter. I read it every night. It's in my Bible." Then she seemed to lose track and opened her eyes to his presence as if she had never before seen him. She turned her head toward the kitchen, her clavicles straining under the membrane of skin. "Webster, there's an Indian in the house," she said.

There was nothing malicious or condescending about it, Harold thought; she was just repeating a fact, talking the way the crazy people do on the sidewalks of big cities like Billings. Or Browning. He couldn't deny the reservation had its share of crazies.

His coffee drunk and a second cup making a sweat ring on the coffee table, Harold had the woman's confidence and the letter, the one she hadn't told anyone about at first. She certainly hadn't told that nosy woman from the Meagher County Sheriff's Department who had peppered her with questions after Webster didn't return from his hunting trip.

My darling Mabella,

Do not worry about me if I go away for a while. I'm just tired with the sickness and want to lie down where no one will disturb me. I wish you could come with me, but you must live your life here before we see each other again, in that place we have been promised. You have slipped away from me as I am slipping away from this existence, and I pray that the Lord takes you when you still know who I am and how much I love you. I am so sorry I could not give you children. They would have been a comfort to you now. But we had each other and it was a good life, all I could ask for and more. Don't try to find me. I will find you.

Your loving husband,

Webster

"See, he calls me Mabella. Ever since we was kids."

"It's a beautiful name," Harold said absently. He had seen a number of suicide letters and was often struck by the eloquence. You looked at people and it didn't show, that poet's soul. It was as if it took sickness or a shock to the system to remove the skins of age and habit and write with such candor.

"Who else have you shown this to?"

"I showed it to my reverend. I showed it to Missy Watkins."

"Not the sheriff when Orvel went missing?"

"Nobody called him that. He was just Webster. And Lordy no, I didn't tell anybody then. Not that woman, all her questions." Her hands fluttered.

Harold worked a forefinger between the braids of his hair. "Where did your husband say he was going hunting?"

"He liked that Tenderfoot Creek country up in the Belts. I used to go with him in the big wall tent. Did the cooking on a sheepherder stove. Webster and his cousins on the Brady side. Those were good times. Are you a hunter, Mr. Feather?"

"I am."

"It's an Indian thing, I suppose."

"When the last buffalo falls on the plains I will hunt mice, for I am a hunter and must have my freedom."

"That's like a poem."

"It's what Chief Joseph said when he was exiled from his homeland in the Wallowas."

"You people have a way with words. My Webster was a silent man. But my he was strong. And bullheaded? He got a mind to do something, you could'na stop him."

Harold took a sip of his coffee. "That's a big elk on your wall. Did Webster shoot it in the Belts?"

"No, he got that one downstate. He wasn't so strong anymore and got himself a guide and they went on horses. A place with a name like a fossil. My brain's like a sieve sometimes. It's there on the plaque."

Harold set down the cup and walked over to the mount and read the brass escutcheon on the dark wood plaque.

TAKEN BY ORVEL WEBSTER WITH E. J. CUMMINGS
Specimen Ridge, Gravelly Mountains, Montana

"I don't see a date on this, Mrs. Webster. When was it?"

"Three or four years ago. He was in remission. That cancer, it's a terrible thing."

"Who's E. J. Cummings?"

"He was the guide with the horses. Webster said he was a nice man. He called him something like a title—the courtly cowboy. Yes, that was it. On account of him being so polite. 'The courtly cowboy.' He said he lived down in the Madison Valley where that man lives who has the big boil on his neck. You see him on the TV."

"Weldon Crawford," Harold said, sitting back down at the table. He was no longer thinking about Martha Ettinger's good graces.

"That's him. Webster said except for the Old Faithful Inn, that was the biggest log house he'd ever seen."

Harold stirred a spoon in his coffee and watched the surface tremble. "I don't suppose there's a chance he was hunting down there last year when he disappeared."

"He never said where he was going hunting, but everybody thought Tenderfoot Creek. That's where those search-and-rescue people looked. I told them they would'na find him."

"Why did you tell them that?"

"I just had a feeling, like when you . . . well, you just know something, like somebody's in a room and you can't see them but you know they're there."

"Like Webster is, you mean?"

"Yes. See, you know he's here, too."

"Ma'am, I'm just going to step out on your porch and make a couple phone calls."

"Do you want me to heat up your cup? Or make you a lunch? I've got some bean soup. I don't get many visitors."

"Thank you. Just the coffee."

Jittery with caffeine, Harold punched the wrong numbers into his phone twice before hearing the ring.

He muttered to himself, "Imagine that—an Indian who can't handle his coffee. What's next, alcohol?" Stranahan's voice mail picked up and Harold left a message. Ettinger was on speed dial, one finger tap away. He managed it. She picked up on the second ring.

"I'm at Orvel Webster's place outside Wolf Creek, with the widow. He's our John Doe, good chance." Harold told her why before she could ask. "Another thing—a couple-three years ago he went on a guided elk hunt on Specimen Ridge with an E. J. Cummings. The woman says Cummings is a neighbor of Weldon Crawford."

"I know the name. Sean Stranahan mentioned him."

"That's what I remember, too. Did Sean file a report?"

"No, it was in connection with looking for that missing trout fly. He met a few of the neighbors. I think Cummings was caretaker of some places, a year-round resident there. His first name's Emmitt. Are you thinking what I think you're thinking?"

"Well, the man guides on Specimen Ridge, I'd lay odds he knows Sphinx Mountain. One throws its shadow on the other. Plus Cummings knew Webster. Maybe they talked on that hunt, both of them looking at the end of a short road, and a couple years later got together for the so-called arrangement. *And* he's Crawford's neighbor. Not a stretch he could have laid his hands on the congressman's gun. Be worth seeing if Cummings fits the description Kauffeld gave us, the guy he called Wade."

"Seems a coincidence, Stranahan stumbling into him like he did."

"You said it yourself. Sean's a guy who manages to step in shit even if there's only one cow in the pasture."

"I think I better talk to him. And I think you better get down here."

"I tried his number just before calling you," Harold said.

Ettinger heard him sigh audibly. "Are you okay, Harold?"

"I'm jittery or tired. Take your pick. I slept on the couch at my brother's and listened to the two of them make the beast with two backs half the night. They were banging that headboard louder than Howard slapped the table, I'd lay odds on it. Sometimes I think they fight just for the makeup sex."

Ettinger grunted, a stab at sympathy. She was still thinking about Stranahan. "I'll call his guide buddy, Meslik," she said.

"Best bet would be look up his girlfriend. Her name's Martinique. She works at Lookers and Lattes."

"I didn't know that."

"Then you're the only one."

When she swung the department Cherokee up to the window of the kiosk, Martha felt the air go out of her lungs. She'd been hoping the barista would have a tramp stamp peeking above a thong or lipstick-smeared teeth, someone she could feel superior to. A "butterface," as she'd heard Walt refer to a waitress at Josie's who had the profile of a smoke jumper's Pulaski. Everything *but-her-face.* But the tall woman with the flashing dark eyes had a face you looked into and kept on looking. A brunette to make a bishop forget he'd cried over a choir-boy, to use another of her deputy's euphemisms. Martha knew she wasn't unattractive herself, but this wasn't fair. Why did Sean's girl-friends have to be so beautiful?

"What can I get for you, ma'am?"

Martha felt her shoulders slump. *Ma'am?* Had she fallen so far she was a ma'am?

"I thought you used suspenders to hold up your pants," she said dryly. *Just a quarter moon of areola*, Martha thought, *and I'll cite her for indecent exposure.*

Martinique crossed her arms over her chest.

"I'm looking for Sean Stranahan. It's department business." She relented. "I'm sorry. You have the right to make a living any way that's legal."

"You're Martha Ettinger. Sean says nice things about you. It's a pleasure to meet you."

They awkwardly shook hands, Martinique leaning out the window of the kiosk.

"Sean guided on the lower Madison this morning," Martinique said. "It was that man you interviewed about the bodies on the mountain. Melvin Kauffeld and the woman he's with, from the teachers' convention at the ranch. He just called me from Ennis."

"Who, Sean?"

"Yes."

"What did he say?"

"He told me about the float. Then he said something about looking at water for the answers to life's persistent questions. Only this time it wasn't working."

"Do you have any idea what he meant by that?"

"No. It was just something he said. Like he was making fun of himself."

"Did he say anything else?"

Martha saw Martinique's face color.

"He told me he loved me."

Martha felt herself breathing. "Is that . . . is it something he says often?" She watched the woman's face color again.

"It was the first time."

"Did he mention where he was going?"

"Like back to Sphinx Mountain? No, nothing like that. I tried to call him back a few minutes ago. I'm worried about him."

"Oh, I wouldn't be," Ettinger said. But she could feel the artery throbbing in her neck. She drummed her fingers on the steering wheel. "I think I'll take a coffee after all."

CHAPTER TWENTY-SEVEN

Loose Ends

Stranahan wiped the sweat from his face and squatted to examine the leaf. The spot of blood was the size of a dime. He placed it on his palette as being the same hue, but a half shade darker than the Indian paintbrush that bloomed along the trail. Dry but not dry dark. He glanced at the GPS readout on his Garmin. He had passed the trail junction and was exactly .46 miles west and a little south of his objective, the slope of timber encompassed by the second circle on the map. A fifteen-minute hike, twenty when you took into account the contour lines, indicating an uphill grind at the end.

One thing Stranahan had learned from Harold Little Feather was that the tail of a blood drop points in the direction of travel. The tail pointed downslope, toward the Trail Fork of Bear Creek, not far from where he'd fished it the day he'd hiked up here alone. Looking toward the creek, he spotted a clump of grass with a single crimson stalk. The blood trail could have been left by a deer that had escaped a mountain lion, all but one of its claws. Or it could be from a squirrel dripping from the jaws of a pine martin. Or—Stranahan swung the Weatherby rifle off his shoulder—it could be human.

He dialed the variable scope down to two, its lowest power but with the widest field of view. Forty yards to the creek, the bottom so overgrown with thistle and chokecherry that he could hear but not see the water. Stranahan kept the muzzle up, so as not to tangle in the brush. Twenty yards below him the slope became convex, the country it concealed inching into view as he stalked down the hillside. Stranahan stopped. Ahead of him the undergrowth was flattened over a considerable area, as if a heavy animal had fallen. A sour dog smell invaded Stranahan's nostrils and he felt his insides contracting. He trained the muzzle of the rifle on the flattened brush and said, "Hey, bear." Nothing. He glanced down, found a rock, and heaved it into the creek bottom. It made a hollow cracking sound as it smacked onto the loose shale on the bank.

Stranahan pushed through the branches. Thorns wicked as a goshawk's talons tore at his skin. Something wet and cold traced his cheek and clung there. It was a finger of clotted blood, suspending from a thorn. Wiping it off his face and looking straight ahead, he almost stepped on the dog. The animal was on its side, its eyes staring ahead, its upper body matted with blood. Its flanks were shivering and Stranahan could detect shallow breathing. For a moment his hands relaxed their grip on the rifle. Bad enough, but he had expected far worse. Breathing deeply, he glanced around before bending to examine the dog. A dark bird fluttered its wings a few feet away. Or was it a bird? As the shape resolved into focus, Stranahan saw that the "bird" was a strip of cloth dangling from the branch of a willow that shielded the creek. He fingered it—charcoal-colored denim, purple wet with blood. He felt a constriction in his chest and parted the willows with the rifle barrel. He thought he was prepared for what lay crossways to the current, changing the song of the creek. He wasn't. When his stomach was empty, Stranahan forced his way upstream and with his back turned to the mangled remains washed his mouth out with water. *Christ.* He steeled himself and turned around.

You couldn't even call it a body. The lower half at best, backside facing up. The jeans were ripped and one foot had been bitten or hacked off at the ankle. Sean patted the back pockets for a wallet, noticing the left one had a ring worn in the fabric in the shape of a snoose container. He rolled the body over. A belt buckle glinted under the gray coils of eviscerated intestines. Stranahan felt his gorge rise and turned his head. He patted the right front pocket, felt something hard, and fingered out an unfired rifle cartridge nearly five inches long. He glanced at the numbers stamped onto the base—.475 No. 2 N.E. It was the caliber that matched the bullet he and Katie Sparrow had found in the tree root. He pocketed the cartridge and patted the other front pocket. Nothing. It didn't matter. He'd seen the buckle before, big as an elk's hoof, the bucking bronc embossed in copper on a pewter background. It was Emmitt Cummings's belt.

When he returned to the dog, its up eye was swimming in the socket and for a second focused on him. Stranahan unwrapped a space blanket he carried in his daypack and gently tucked it around the dog's body. The dog was small with a collie face and a white coat puzzled by sable and iron gray patches; the eye staring at him was blue. Despite the dog's being covered in blood, there was no obvious indication of injury. He left it and climbed back to the trail. He looked uphill—the direction from which the wounded man must have stumbled down to the creek. On the other side of the meadow and about three hundred vertical feet above it was an outcrop of white rocks he'd noted on that earlier trip. Stranahan crossed the meadow and began to climb, only the occasional blood drop to keep him on course, his finger on the button safety of the Weatherby. The snort froze him. It didn't *sound* like a bear, but he was taking no chances and slowly began to back down the slope. The snort came again, loud in the enclosed space of the trees. Stranahan felt the tension flood out of his body. This wasn't the cough of a grizzly bear readying to charge, but a phlegmy vibrato whinny. Less cautiously now, he climbed, arriving at a bench of more or less open ground above the rocks. The brown eyes of a horse regarded him with wild trepidation. It backed warily away, a rope lead dragging between its hooves.

"It's all right, Sally Ann."

His eyes took in the camp: a canvas A-frame tent, mildew-spotted, probably as old as the man who'd pitched it, a fire ring of blackened stones with the butts of two handrolled cigarettes in the ashes. Thumb-thick kindling was neatly stacked to one side. A blackened iron cook pot suspended over the fire from a stick driven into the ground at an angle. A pack saddle was draped over a lodgepole stringer; hanging off one of the pack forks was a jute coffee bean bag half filled with oats. It was an organized camp. Stranahan's eyes caught a gleam of light. Twenty yards from the tent, on the lip of the rock outcrop, a pair of binoculars suspended from a branch stub under a Ponderosa pine. The duff under the tree had been heaped up to make a soft seat. Stranahan set the rifle against the tree trunk and sat and brought up the binoculars. He looked down at the trail winding in and out of sight below him.

From this vantage, the watcher would have had a clear view of anyone turning onto the trail that led to the saddle between the mountains. The observation post had been picked with care and for a minute Stranahan was puzzled. Why hadn't Cummings seen him coming up the trail yesterday? Then he remembered that it was raining and the meadow at the trail junction was smothered in fog. Cummings could not have seen him from this vantage, and in any case, he was expecting Kauffeld, if he came at all, to be guided by the coordinates marking the second circle on the map. Cummings might well have waited for him there, while Stranahan, along with Ettinger and Jarrett, was waiting at the other location. No wonder he hadn't come to the call.

Since stepping onto the bench, Stranahan had not noticed any blood, but then his eyes hadn't been on the ground. As he made a second tour of the camp, the chestnut quarterhorse clopped along a few yards behind him, keeping its distance but obviously wanting the assurance of companionship. Stranahan spoke to it in low tones and approached the tent. One front flap was loose, the other held open with a string tie. A single ray of sunlight bisected the interior shadow of the tent. Stranahan puzzled over it, arriving at the conclusion that it had to be admitted by a hole in the back of the tent, since that side faced the sun. He suspected what he'd find before he found it, the shot spray of blood on the interior tent wall. There was more blood inside the entrance and a long smear on the open side of the tent flaps. A military surplus sleeping bag was soaked through. A leather rifle scabbard embossed with roses lay beside it, but no rifle. There was nothing else in the tent but a Coleman lantern tipped on its side, a leather-bound Bible, the cover smeared with bloody fingerprints, and a pair of reading glasses. Stranahan pulled the sleeping bag aside and found a vial of pills. XENAZINE (*tetrabenazine*). Prescribed to Emmitt James Cummings. "To suppress chorea and associated involuntary body movements."

Stranahan tried to picture how it happened. Cummings had been in the tent when the shot was fired—that much was obvious. Probably early, dawn or shortly after. Wounded, he had struggled out of the bag and fled across the bench and down the hill. Running would account for the scarcity of blood drops, the skin and clothing shifting over the entrance and exit holes in his body. Where Stranahan had seen the matted grass was where the man had fallen. Then he had got up and made it as far as the creek. There he'd died, or possibly been followed and shot again by his murderer. The grizzly had come along later, following her nose for the windfall as she'd done once before on Sphinx Mountain. She had a long memory and an appetite made ravenous by the cubs depending on her. She had probably knocked the dog aside as it sought to defend its master. Then she'd dismembered the body and carried half of it away, possibly as a reaction to having been blasted with pepper spray in the vicinity only two weeks before.

Ever since floating the river with Melvin Kauffeld, Stranahan had been shifting pieces of a puzzle in his head. He had made them fit well enough that the watcher's identity didn't come as a surprise. In fact, he'd counted on it. It was one reason he had not called Ettinger before driving to the trailhead. Cummings he read as a man who lived by a code. Cummings wouldn't shoot a man in cold blood.

The puzzle piece that he'd had to force into place was the voice mail left on Kauffeld's phone. Although muffled, it didn't drawl like Cummings's voice and the fact of it seemed out of character. It was a transgression of the arrangement, and the taunt at the end—"Be a man"—seemed out of character. It betrayed desperation, a last attempt by the caller to meet up with a man who at that point obviously wasn't coming.

He's tying up loose ends, Stranahan thought.

He ducked out of the tent and moved into the cover of the trees, where he sat down. He'd been up since five and the day was catching up to him. The horse clopped up and showed him the dominoes of her teeth and then put her big tongue on his head.

"I'm sorry, girl," Stranahan said, reaching up to stroke her cheek, "but he isn't coming back." He was thinking of the one time he'd met Cummings. Cowboy through and through, not the western cliché but something better: a man of clear and shrewd eyes, as forthcoming and kind as he was stoic and tough-minded, as gentle with his animals as he was hard on himself. It was a lot to infer from a twenty-minute conversation, but Stranahan felt an empathy toward Cummings that he knew was not shared by Martha Ettinger. Ettinger saw the world in black and white. Cummings's "arrangement" with Melvin Kauffeld and the ones who preceded him were shaded a gray that she couldn't come to terms with. But Stranahan accepted the apparent contradictions. As far as he was concerned, any crimes perpetrated from this camp were set in motion by consenting adults and paled in malice compared with the one that had been committed here only a few hours ago. Cummings had not died in a fair fight, but had been shot through a tent wall while in his sleeping bag. The shooting was an act of cowardice perpetrated by someone who was now, very probably, lying in wait—he punched buttons on his GPS—exactly .43 miles due east. That man would be waiting to align his sights on a man who wore a red hat. Stranahan was unsure what threat the man in the red hat represented to the killer. His understanding was that there had been no communication between Cummings and Melvin Kauffeld that hinted at the involvement of a third party. But maybe Cummings's killer couldn't take that chance.

Stranahan knew that if he turned and hiked back the way he had come, the man who lay in wait would walk out of the mountains free from the consequences of his actions. Stranahan had noted the license plate of the champagne-colored Toyota Highlander that was parked at the trailhead when he arrived. Presumably the owner could be traced and the vehicle would place him on the mountain on the date Cummings was shot. But unless a bullet could be found, and a rifle found that shot it, there would be no evidence of murder. And Stranahan doubted there was a bullet. If it remained in the body, it was probably in the upper half that had been carried away by the bear. Quite possibly it was now inside the bear's gut system. It would be excreted on a distant slope of mountain, just another hunk of lead to poison the earth.

"I'll be back, old girl."

Stranahan stood. He lifted the bolt of Peachy's rifle, pulling it back just far enough to show the glint of the cartridge. No time to regret not having test-fired the weapon before driving to the trailhead. He replaced the bolt and thumbed the safety off. He slung the binoculars hanging from the tree branch around his neck. Then he started off on a contour that would take him into the country inscribed by the red circle on the map, his focus narrowing as he lost himself to that throbbing pulse of blood that is the hunting instinct, still intact under the pallor of modern skin.

Harold Little Feather felt the phone vibrate in his jeans pocket. He shifted his hips and reached it, keeping his left hand on the wheel.

"Martha, my dear."

"I forwarded the website for Cummings's outfitting business to the Langhor woman. Kauffeld ID'd the photos as the guy he knew as Wade. I got Crazy Conner to sign off. I'm on my way with the warrant right now."

"I'm just past the turnoff to Pony."

"Then I've got you by twenty miles. There's a pullout where you can see the wagon ruts of the Bozeman Trail. Up on the pass?"

"The path of the great white snake. I always spit out the window driving by. We should go in my truck, don't you think? It's unmarked."

"Just get here," Ettinger said.

"Montanan my livelong life and I can't remember driving to a single ranchstead without a dog yapping at me." Ettinger pulled the slide of her sidearm to jack a shell into the chamber. "I got a feeling we're too late," she said.

No one answered the knock at Cummings's door. They cleared the one-story cottonwood cabin, Ettinger frowning at the disorder.

"It's been tossed," Harold said.

"Or maybe he's just a pig." She worked her chin.

"No, a hand went through it. He was looking for something small, like in a drawer."

"How can you tell?"

"You want a lecture in crime scene investigation or do you want to get to the Sphinx?"

"You think he's up there, don't you?"

"One way to find out," Harold said.

CHAPTER TWENTY-EIGHT

The Scarecrow

Stranahan checked his GPS. He'd been sidehilling the mountain for ten minutes, had jumped across three creeks that spilled in miniature waterfalls down the slope, and was still a couple hundred yards away from the coordinates marking the X at the center of the second circle. Much closer, he thought, and he could be walking into a bullet. He knew the man lying in wait would give him no more chance than he'd given E. J. Cummings a few hours before.

He carefully toed out onto a shelf of rock and looked down. Two hundred feet below, a cliff face ended in a scree slope, at the base of which a few acres of flat ground were grown up in lodgepole pines. He brought up the binoculars he'd taken from Cummings's camp and scanned the country to the east, almost immediately registered a distant glint that on examination appeared to be a shovel. So the game was on. Or rather, it had been on until Cummings's murder. Now it was a different game, there were different players, and there were different rules.

Stranahan found an elk trail that zagged to the bottom of the cliff. Most of the trees had rusted brown from the ravages of pine beetle infestation. Several rocks studded the bench, the largest a lichen-covered boulder streaked with rose quartz. He took cover behind it and again scanned the country until he was certain that he was alone. Twenty yards from the boulder a tree had toppled over, cracking the lower branches from the trunk with the impact. One of those branches Stranahan wedged upright in a fork of the downfall. Taking off his shirt, he draped it around the branch and then placed the red cap on top. Anyone coming to investigate would have to stalk within sixty or seventy yards before coming into sight of the decoy, and Stranahan paced the distance off and then looked at his handiwork through the rifle scope. It looked like a hat propped on a stick. He went back, wove some pine boughs around the branch to fill out the chest area, and constructed a face from loose bark that was the color of cork next to the cambium of the tree. Then he screened the decoy with branches to deliberately obscure its outline and again paced off sixty yards. It still looked like a scarecrow, but then he knew what it was. It would have to do.

On his way down, he'd noted where elk had pawed a wallow at a seepage spring. Detouring to it, he coated his arms and bare chest with mud that reeked of elk urine. He walked back to the rock and lay prone beside it. He streaked his cheeks with the mud on his arms and then rested the fore-end of the rifle over his daypack and trained the crosshairs on the far end of the bench. Without moving his eyes from the scope, he placed the reed of the hawk call between his lips and blew it sharply.

Silence.

Cheeeeeeee. The answering call rose and died on the mountain walls. From somewhere to the east, he thought. But not distant. Stranahan felt his heart beat against the floor of the forest.

The shadow shifting at the periphery of his vision was nothing more than a suggestion of movement. There. But gone as quickly as it registered. Sunlight penetrated the canopy of the forest, striping the ground abstractly. Stranahan stared through the scope until his eyes began to water. Very slowly, he set the rifle aside and reached for the binoculars. Mentally dividing the field of view into quadrants, he searched each individually without moving the glasses. In the lower left quadrant, an oblong shape interrupted the downfall littering the ground. He focused on it and it moved, amoebalike, a sack of dappled shadow that, when it stopped, so perfectly matched the pattern of the understory that the edges melted into the background. But the lump was still there, and now Stranahan could see the stick beside it that was not a stick. The shape shifted again, seemed to double up, and just as Stranahan saw the pattern of digital camouflage for what it was, the stick jumped and a fraction of a moment later the concussion of the rifle blast jarred the mountainside.

Harold Little Feather held up a hand. Ettinger, who was looking down at the blood drop on the leaf at the edge of the trail, took a step and stopped beside him.

"Hold your breath," Harold whispered. He saw the artery pulse in her throat. Her face began to redden.

Karoooom! A second shot echoed through the canyon.

He canted one ear toward it, nodded. He'd been holding his breath for half a minute and inhaled, smelling his own dark odor.

"Jesus," Martha said, her chest heaving. "What kind of gun is that?"

In the enclosed area of the bench, the shot was deafening. The sensation in Stranahan's head was the same he'd experienced taking a counter right hand in the quarterfinals of the Lowell Silver Mittens tournament. He'd survived the round and won the fight, but an insect had droned in his head for a week after. At the second shot, Stranahan heard the bullet impact against the decoy and saw it snap backward. The decoy fell out of sight behind the deadfall tree, exactly as Stranahan hoped it would. The man would have to come close to make sure. Now the figure he'd been watching stretched and unfolded until it was upright. A man garbed in military camo began to walk forward, his face hidden by an olive mesh mask with eye cutouts. Forty yards. Thirty. Stranahan felt sweat sting his eyes. His breath was coming in shallow pants.

Ten yards away, the man came to a stop. Stranahan knew the man could see the red hat now, the empty sack of the shirt. The man froze in place with his rifle raised in the direction of the decoy.

". . . fuck is going on." The voice was muffled by the mask, a mumble.

Then, clearer: "Kauffeld?" Silence. "Who the fuck is out there? Be a man, goddammit. Show yourself."

Stranahan wanted to wipe the sweat out of his eyes, but didn't dare move. *Just wait him out*, he told himself.

As if hearing his thought, the man turned directly toward Stranahan, the muzzles of the rifle sweeping to cover him and then continuing their arc as he turned completely around, facing the way he had come.

"Drop the weapon," Stranahan commanded. "Don't turn around. Drop it."

The man hesitated.

"Drop the weapon now!"

"Fuck you." But he didn't turn around.

"We have you covered. Drop the weapon."

"Why you're . . . shit . . . I know your voice, Stranahan. You don't have the guts. I could walk right up and slap your face silly. But that's not what I'm going to—"

The man whirled round and Stranahan, lying prone, saw the blur and fired, the rifle bucking up against his cheek so that he lost sight of the man through the scope. He heard the man's rifle, though, like a detonation, and rose to his knees to see the camouflaged figure bowed forward crookedly, the big African double rifle jammed muzzles first into the ground and the earth cratered around it. The man extended a hand that was a bloody claw toward the buttstock.

"Don't," Stranahan said.

The man looked up as if seeing him for the first time. He raised both hands and dropped to his knees. Stranahan, his ears ringing, walked up and wrenched the muzzles of the rifle out of the earth. The right barrel had split and the stock was splintered, with a chunk of wood blown out in back of the pistol grip.

"Are you hurt?" Stranahan heard his own voice as if from under water.

"You shot my fucking finger off. I fell on it, the rifle . . ."

Stranahan tossed the rifle aside and slowly circled the man, looking for signs of injury other than the hand. He realized that the bullet from Peachy's Weatherby, after hitting the stock of the safari rifle, must have glanced off course, missing the body. The man's rifle had fired accidentally, the sear tripping as he fell and jammed the muzzles into the earth.

"You're lucky to be alive," Stranahan said.

The man didn't seemed to hear. "God," he said. He had gripped his right hand in his left and was rocking back and forth.

"You can take off your mask, Weldon," Stranahan said. "It's all over now."

"My lawyer will make you wish you were never born."

"Where's the other rifle? The one you took from E.J. after you shot him in his sleep."

"I don't know what you're talking about. I came up here when I found out what he was doing. Jesus fucking Christ that hurts. I was . . . I was trying to stop him, but then he pulled down on me and I had to shoot him. He ducked behind the tent . . ."

"So he had a rifle. You're contradicting yourself."

"No. I mean yes, he had one. I . . . he ran down the hill with it and . . . must have dropped it. I was just trying to stop him, I'm . . . I'm a United States congressman . . ." His voice trailed off.

"Who just shot what he thought was Melvin Kauffeld and fired a weapon at an officer of the law."

"You're no . . . officer."

"I am," Stranahan said. He saw Crawford's shoulders slump. He sat back on the ground. Slowly, as if it took great effort, he pulled the camouflage mask off his face. His hair, which had been parted as if by a razor on each occasion Stranahan had seen him, was stringy with sweat and plastered to his forehead.

His voice was heavy with defeat. "What do you want? Do you want money?" Then he laughed, a bitter bark of a laugh. "You just blew up eighty grand. I could give you the Rigby, see what you can get for it now." His tone becoming bitter. "Serve you right, you son of a bitch."

"I'm listening," Stranahan said.

"Really?" Crawford had seen a ray of light. "There are options here. We can work something out."

"Tell me what happened. Why did you kill E. J. Cummings? What did he know that was so bad he had to die?"

"What's it matter if I can make you a rich man?"

"You just did your damnedest to kill me. I want to know why. What did E.J. have on you?"

"Have on me? You mean what did I have on him. I knew all about the games he'd played up here, his 'arrangements.' Hell, it was me who gave him . . ." He stopped. Sweat was beading up on his forehead. His face had turned white. "Jesus." He clutched at his stomach with his right hand. "The fuckin' bullet hit me, man. I'm leaking blood." He was pulling up his shirt, digging his fingers into thin rolls of fat sprouted with gray hair.

"The blood's from your hand," Stranahan said. "You aren't hurt. You're just going into shock."

"I need a fuckin' doctor. I'm not saying another . . . word. Not until . . . until you get me off this mountain."

Stranahan sat down on the ground twenty feet away, the bore of the Weatherby rifle pointed at Crawford's chest. He made a show of making himself comfortable. "I got nowhere I have to be," he said.

"All right, goddammit. It was . . . I showed him the story."

"'The Most Dangerous Game.'"

"Yes. When I found out he was sick, I, he . . . how the hell was I supposed to know he'd do what he did? Take it to heart that way."

"What did you do, give E.J. your rifle so you could live vicariously, be in on the kill while you were drinking whiskey in your mansion?"

"No." Crawford's voice was indignant. "Hell, no. He knew about the bookcase, he saw me pull it open when he was doing some plumbing and I didn't know he was in the house. Stumbled in on me.

I didn't think that much about it. You had to know him, he'd see the devil drop a dime and pick it up for him. The man didn't have a crooked bone in his body. The last thing I worried about was he'd steal a gun. But he'd shot the double, you see, we used to shoot out on my range, and I think, the African connection, the romance of the big gun. He said he was just borrowing it. That was later. I didn't even know it had been gone until he told me, 'cause he replaced it in its case, you see. And then he held that over me. That's why I had to sell it. I couldn't keep a murder weapon in the house."

"I thought it wasn't murder. Or did your tongue just slip?"

"You know what I mean, a gun that killed somebody. You'd have done the same thing."

"I'm not the one you have to convince, Weldon. Why did you kill E.J.?"

"I told you. I had to stop him. I didn't hear about the others until after, I couldn't prevent them, but this one, Kauffeld, E.J. got some whiskey in him and one night he talked. Once I knew, the blood would be on my hands, you understand. You got to believe me."

"And Kauffeld, what made you so desperate you needed to kill him, too? How did he even know you were involved?"

"He's . . ." He stopped and breathed. He coughed, hacking, and at once Stranahan saw that it was theatrics, that Crawford was thinking what to say and anything now would be building a story, not relating one. "I, ah, E.J."—he coughed again—"he said he'd told him about me, that Kauffeld knew about me. He lied, you see, he told him it was me, that I was behind it, the arrangements. I . . . I'm innocent here. All I did was show a man a book. I couldn't let him . . . Kauffeld, if he ever talked."

"Well, he has talked," Stranahan said. "And he's going to talk more. We'll see what he knows."

"No, no, it would all be lies. We have a deal, I can get you more money by tomorrow than you can make rowing a guide boat the rest of your life."

"Save the money for your lawyer," Stranahan said.

"But you— Come on, man. We had a deal."

"All I said was I was listening. Get up, Weldon. Get up and walk."

"Be smart about this, Stranahan. It's your word against mine. I'll deny. I'll say you forced me to come up here, that you set it up, all of it."

"Even your bloody fingerprints on E.J.'s Bible? Are those a lie, too?" It was a shot in the dark. He didn't know if the prints were Crawford's or from Cummings's clutching the book after he'd been hit. But Crawford's shoulders fell at the mention of them. It was as if the life went out of him, that after building a sandcastle of lies and fooling even himself, this one irrefutable piece of evidence had driven like a knife into his deceit and he saw, finally and with utter clarity, that it was hopeless. He seemed to shrink away within the suit of camouflage until it was just the shapeless sack that Stranahan had first seen.

Stranahan stood and motioned with the gun barrel. *Up.* Crawford nodded. It was an old man Stranahan saw getting to his feet, and for a moment his mind flashed to Polly Sorenson, the fly tier, and another piece of the puzzle found its place.

"Satisfy my curiosity," Stranahan said. Crawford raised his head, his expression resigned.

"What was the deal with Polly Sorenson? Was your job to recruit him for E.J.'s next arrangement? Is that why you invited him up to your house?"

"I suppose you could say I was baiting the hook. But not for E.J. One way or the other, E.J. was going to be out of the way." Ego seeped back into his voice. "I was going into business for myself. I was saving him for me."

"But he didn't bite."

"No, but he might have a couple months from now, or next year, when it was getting harder for him to breathe. You see I'd put a . . . I had a plan."

"What was your plan?"

"Don't you know? I thought you were a smart fellow."

"Tell me."

Crawford's eyes narrowed. He stood up straighter. "No, I'm not going to give you that satisfaction."

The defeat Stranahan had seen in Crawford's posture had once more been replaced by defiance. Stranahan sought to shatter it. He said, "You know what I see when I look at you? I see a man who doesn't have the balls for a fair fight. Not even with a sick man like Polly Sorenson. All that talk about facing up to old m'bogo, it's just an act. I'll bet if I talked to any professional hunter you hunted with, he'd tell me how you ran when the charge came. Admit it. The only thing you have the courage for is putting bullets into a paper buffalo." He paused. "Or a sleeping man in a tent."

A sound that was a cross between a howl and a growl came out of Crawford.

He sneered, his teeth showing whitely. "Try me," he said. His voice was guttural. The animal in him, the heat and concentration of dark energy that radiated from the man, seemed to engulf Stranahan. "Drop your gun and try me right now."

The forest was dead silent. "Now who's the coward?" Crawford spat out the words. He turned his back. "I'm going. I'll take my chances with the courts." He started to shuffle away toward the edge of the bench, in the direction from which Stranahan had first seen him. It looked to be as easy a way down to the main trail as another and Stranahan followed him without comment, staying ten yards behind, his finger tense on the trigger.

They had proceeded fifty yards or so when Crawford tripped over a stone and fell heavily, swearing as he writhed on the ground. Stranahan wondered if it was an act, an attempt to get him to drop his guard. He wasn't going to be fooled that easily. "Get up," he said.

Crawford rubbed vigorously at his knee with his uninjured hand. "I can't seem to get my balance," he said. He shuffled off again, a drag to his left foot.

"Stop right there," Stranahan said. Something was bothering him, but he couldn't place it.

"You're not cut out for this." There was bravado in Crawford's voice now.

"Shut up." His instinct told him something was wrong. *What was it?*

"You're beginning to think, aren't you? You're making a mistake. You'll wish—"

"Just walk."

Crawford started off, dragging his leg, and just as Stranahan registered that it was the other leg that he'd hurt when falling, the right, not the left, Crawford stumbled again, then made a lunge forward.

To Stranahan it seemed to happen in slow motion, Crawford's body pitching forward over the fallen trunk of a pine tree. He was there, then gone from sight, gone like that, and as Stranahan raced forward he saw a glint, a flash like metal beyond the rusted needles of the dead tree. Crawford had a rifle in his bloody hands and was raising it, the muzzle climbing, and Stranahan, trying to raise the Weatherby, felt as if he were trapped in a dream where you can't will your body to move. Then the air split with thunder and he didn't feel the gun jump in his hands or even know that he'd shot. An image froze: Crawford's head jerked to the side, his cheek an explosion of red, bulging outward.

Stranahan felt a hot spray against his neck as Crawford collapsed, his head and chest draped over the bole of the fallen tree. Crawford's left eye, bulging out of the socket, stared obscenely at nothing. Stranahan reached out and touched the eye with the muzzle of Peachy's rifle, the way Sam had told him you touched an elk's eye to make sure it was dead. He was dead all right. On the far side of the tree, the rifle Crawford had gripped lay on the ground. It was a single-shot with an exposed hammer, a plains rifle, something you'd see in an old western. He realized it must be the rifle Crawford had taken from Cummings's camp, that he'd ditched it behind the log when he stalked forward toward the sound of the hawk call, before shooting at the effigy Stranahan had constructed.

It puzzled him a moment. The cartridge he'd taken from Cummings's pants pocket was one that fit the big African double rifle that had killed Gutierrez. Well, that was something to think about later. Stranahan lifted the bolt of the Weatherby to extract the spent shell. The cartridge jacked onto the ground and he saw that it was intact, the bullet still seated in the neck of the cartridge case. He hadn't felt the jar of recoil because he hadn't fired. As he stared at the cartridge, a sound penetrated the buzzing sensation inside his head. A shout.

"Sean, are you all right?" Below him, he saw Martha Ettinger climbing over the lip of a ravine. Harold Little Feather appeared moments later. Both were carrying rifles. Stranahan waved them up.

They came at a trot, breathing hard, up to the log. Harold leaned his Winchester lever action against it. Ettinger, her elk rifle slung over her shoulder, bent over and put her hands on her thighs. She hung her head a few moments and then glanced at the body. The bullet had entered just above and a little forward of the boil below Crawford's right ear, blowing off the far side of the cranium. Nobody said anything. Finally, Harold said, "He seems to have lost his looks."

"Jesus, Harold," Martha said, and walked away a few feet and was sick.

"Who do I thank?" Stranahan said. He reached up to wipe blood and brain matter off his neck.

Harold jutted his chin toward Ettinger. "She had her scope on him ever since he spun on you the first time. But you were in the line of fire then. You weren't this time."

"So you heard?"

"We got the drift of it," Harold said. He walked over to Ettinger and put his arm around her. She turned and buried her face in his chest.

"I never shot a man before," Stranahan heard her say.

When she disengaged from Harold, she was Martha again. "I don't know which of you smells worse," she said.

"I just smell like a man," Harold said. "It's Sean smells like an elk pissed on him."

It took hours to get off the mountain. Ettinger radioed the office and got through to Walt, just back from his trip to Chicago, who drove down to take preliminary statements and video the scene. Then they backtracked Stranahan's footsteps to Cummings's camp and from there visited the carnage in the creek bottom, getting their ducks in a row regarding the facts and their initial assessment of what had transpired. At one point, Ettinger said, "I just shot a man who carried the county by two thousand votes in a national election. I'll be lucky to work animal control next term." No one argued with her assessment.

It was a bedraggled group that filed the last two miles down to the trailhead. Harold was leading Sally Ann. Stranahan and Walt traded off carrying the dog. It was still alive, and once when Stranahan clutched it to his chest during a creek crossing, it had lifted its head and licked his face. Martha lagged behind them, lost in her thoughts. What she was thinking about was the Moleskine notebook she'd discovered in the bottom of the feed bag of oats. It was Cummings's journal, the first entry dated July 10, three years before. The first line, in a very small and precise hand, began, "Yesterday I learned I was going to die." There had been no time to read the journal, but her hopes were high that the story it told would shine a light into shadows not yet lifted from the mountain behind them.

As they rounded the final bend, Stranahan saw Sam's pickup in the turnaround. When the big man opened the door, the cab light came on and he could see Martinique on the bench seat. She was setting aside the mangy Maine coon cat that Stranahan had twice seen lurking at the trailhead. Leave it to Martinique to have coaxed it out of hiding.

"I see the cat lady has found another one," he said in an attempt at levity.

"Just hold me," she said.

Later, when they were sitting at the table in the grain elevator, Stranahan still riding an adrenaline rush, she said, "I'm going to call him Sphinx." The cat, wild-eyed, big as a yearling bobcat, crouched on the stairs, staring at them.

Stranahan said, "I'm not sure what I'm going to call her." They had dropped the dog off at Jeff Svenson's veterinary clinic on the drive back. He'd told them it had a collapsed lung and damaged right eye, but would live.

"She's got a name," Martinique said. "Someone will remember. But you're sure about it? Shelties can be a handful."

"I don't know," he said. "Cats and dogs, I don't want them to come between us."

"They'll sort it out," she said. She looked at him, her eyes shining. "This is where you say, 'We will, too.'"

CHAPTER TWENTY-NINE

Return of the Past

By the time Martha Ettinger attended to her cats, fed Goldie and brushed down Petal, and shut the barn door for the night, the tears on her cheeks were almost two hours dry. She looked at the waning moon above the horizon. She'd known it couldn't last with Harold. They'd been having ups and downs for weeks. But why did it have to happen on the night she'd shot a man? As if that weren't enough of a bad day. It wasn't television, where you put killing the bad guy behind you with a wisecrack. It would haunt her for months, she knew it. And to have it happen with Harold the way it had, right there on Main Street in Ennis, with the jukebox blaring from the Silver Dollar, the crowd spilled onto the sidewalk, ranch hands and trout fishing guides drinking their PBRs and longnecked Buds.

She'd assumed Harold would caravan with her back to her place after they picked up the department Cherokee, which she'd left outside the bar before climbing into Harold's truck to drive to Cummings's ranch house that afternoon.

"I'll see you there, huh?" she had said. And Harold, leaning back against the hood of his pickup with his arms crossed so that she could see the weasel tracks circling his upper biceps, said, "About that, Martha. I think I'm just going to go crash at my sister's in Pony."

Martha had sensed there was more. "What?" she said. "You think because of what happened up there today, that I won't be in the mood? Why make the drive if the most you can expect is a peck good night?" Trying to make the remark light but hating herself, knowing how it sounded.

"It's not that."

"Then what is it?"

"You know when I drove to Browning, I said it was personal?"

"Yeah. Your brother had a drink. Dishes were broken."

"Well, there was that, and then, Lou Anne, she wanted to see me."

Lou Anne was Harold's ex. Martha had never met her, but she'd heard the tone in Harold's voice when he had talked about her and she felt it coming, felt her heart beating and reached up and placed two fingers on her throat.

"Are you . . . seeing her again, Harold?"

"Well, you know the past, it keeps coming back sometimes." He shifted uncomfortably, the weasel tracks changing their shapes.

"You weren't dwelling on the past a couple nights ago. They're still on the sheets, the petals of that white rose you bought me." She felt the heat rise in her face.

"This doesn't have anything to do with you, Martha."

"Obviously."

A bottle broke on the sidewalk outside the bar. She heard the doors bang open, voices raised. "What the fuck, Bob?" she heard someone say. And someone, maybe Bob, say, "First cousin, man. I swear I didn't know 'til I opened my eyes. She was riding me like the Pony Express."

Martha sighed. *Men.*

"So what now?" she said. "We don't see each other?"

"For a little while, while I sort this out." Harold stubbed the toe of his cowboy boot, turned over a pebble. "Shouldn't change anything at work, though, right?"

"Sure, Harold. We're all adults here." And she'd felt the weight behind her eyes and held the tears in until she drove off, because she was damned if she was going to let him see her cry, and then all the way back she'd been hoping to find his headlights in the rearview, wanting them to blink her to a stop and Harold to walk up and say that it was more than maybe it had been, that she hadn't been just fooling herself thinking that it was.

She took off her uniform and got into bed, but she wasn't going to sleep no matter how tired her body was, and so she got up and went into the bathroom and found the box of latex gloves. She pulled on a pair and unzipped the plastic bag containing E. J. Cummings's journal and sat down in the stuffed chair her cats used as a scratching post. Tomorrow, the notebook would be entered into evidence and dusted for prints.

An hour passed and she made herself a cup of chamomile. She sat back down and stared into the distance until the tea cooled a bit and took a sip. When she finally zipped the notebook back into the plastic bag and set it aside, she could hear the first of the morning's robins outside the window. She would never think about E. J. Cummings again without feeling his confliction nor the immensity of his loneliness, nor think of Alejandro Gutierrez or Orvel Webster as bones in the ground.

The bedroom was still dark and she turned on the lamp and set her watch alarm for two hours. She felt a magazine under her and lifted her hip to push it aside. The night before she'd been reading an article by a celebrity doctor on the health benefits of sex. A study revealed that women who had one hundred orgasms a year lived 6.5 years longer than those who didn't. Martha grunted, thinking back on her failed relationships and the gaps in between. She scratched Sheba's cheeks, the Siamese coming to lie down by her head. "At my rate," she said to the cat, "I live to forty I'll consider myself lucky."

Then she reached up and switched off the lamp.

Death with Honor

Melvin Kauffeld pinched out his lips, thumb and forefinger on either side of his mouth, studying the photo Ettinger had handed him.

"You see the boil on the side of his neck?"

Kauffeld nodded. "I see *it*, but no, I don't recall ever seeing *him*."

"Take a good look. This is the gentleman who was going to kill you on Sphinx Mountain."

He shook his head. "My arrangement was with Wade. This . . . Crawford, he must be twenty years older."

"Wade, er, E.J. was killed early yesterday morning while he was waiting for you. Weldon Crawford shot him in cold blood. Crawford was actually hoping you would kill Cummings for him; that way he could have kept his hands clean. When you didn't show up, he became desperate. That's why he left the message on your cell phone."

"How do you know about my phone? I didn't talk to anyone about that." He looked away from Ettinger, who was sitting across the table from him, to Harriet Langhor, who was leaning on the log rail at the other end of the cabin porch. Langhor stubbed her cigarette out on the rail and sat down beside Kauffeld. "Look at me," she said, leaning close to him and taking his hand. "I'm the one who found the voice mail on your phone. I played it for Sean Stranahan the morning we went fishing."

He shook his great head, his jowls sagging. "I trusted you."

"Didn't you hear the sheriff, Mel? That man you were trying to protect was murdered."

He was silent a few moments, looking at her, then away.

When he spoke, his voice had lost its indignation. "The phone message bothered me. It wasn't Wade's voice. And I had never given Wade my number. Our arrangement was on paper."

"We don't know how Crawford got your number," Ettinger said, "but we do know that he was in communication with Emmitt Cummings."

"Have you arrested him?"

"He's dead," Martha said flatly. She gave him an abbreviated version of the confrontation on the mountain. "I released a statement to the press this morning. We were hoping you could help us with our investigation."

"I have no obligation to this man. I'll cooperate any way I can. Wade, ah, Emmitt—it's hard to think of him by that name—he never mentioned Crawford. I just don't know how I can help." He looked from Ettinger to Walter Hess, who had arrived at the ranch cabin late, after helping with the recovery of the bodies early in the morning.

"What about the bullet, Mel?" It was Langhor.

Ettinger's eyebrows knitted together.

Kauffeld nodded to himself. "Maybe. I'd completely forgotten. Wade told me, and this was way back when I met him in Michigan, that if I was the one left standing, then I should look in his pockets for a rifle cartridge. I'd be able to pull the bullet out of the case and there would be a note inside it, instructions on what to do in the event of his death. I assumed . . . well, the truth is I don't know what I assumed. I thought I was the one who was going to die. I never gave the cartridge much thought."

Ettinger looked sharply at Walt. "Did Sean give you the bullet to enter into evidence?" Stranahan had told them about the cartridge he'd found in Cummings's front pants pocket.

"He didn't give it to *me*."

"Shit," Martha said. "We dotted every fucking T but that one."

"You mean crossed every T."

"That's what I said."

"No, Martha, I believe you said—"

"Oh, for Chrissakes, Walt, drop it." She stepped from the table, punching numbers into her phone. She drummed her fingers on the butt of the semiautomatic holstered on her hip. "Sean said he wasn't guiding today. He must be at his girlfriend's house. There's no reception there." She jerked her head toward Walt. "Can you finish up here? I have to find him."

"Nice place, isn't it?" Stranahan said.

Ettinger, hands on her hips, was craning her head to see the cupola on top. "I don't know. It looks like a grain elevator to me. Anyway, I didn't come here to admire the architecture. The bullet you found on Cummings's body, where is it?"

"It's, ah, Jeez. It must still be in my jeans."

She followed him inside. "Where's the missus?" she said.

"If you mean Martinique, she's over at Jeff Svenson's clinic. She's a second-year veterinary student, she'll have her doctorate in a couple years."

"Humph," Martha said. "When I saw her she was nekked under her suspenders. I guess appearances can be deceiving."

She hadn't been naked, technically, but Stranahan let it go and got the cartridge and held it out to Martha by the rim. "I tried to be careful but my prints might be on it," he said.

"I understand the circumstances." She walked over to the kitchen counter, got her Swiss Army tool out, and used the pliers to pull out the bullet, taking care not to touch the brass casing with her fingers. She set the bullet upright on the counter. She'd lost the tiny tweezers on the tool and asked Stranahan if he had any.

He walked outside and got a similar tool from the repair kit on his raft. "When I was in college we'd always be losing these things," he said. "You'd use your tweezers to smoke the roach and then you'd be stoned and forget where you put them."

"I'm going to pretend I didn't hear that," Martha said. She had pinched the edge of a piece of paper inside the cartridge case and was pulling it out. She immediately recognized it as the same unlined, off-white paper in Cummings's journal. The powder had been dumped and the paper rolled tightly to fit inside the case.

"Are you going to tell me about this?" Stranahan leaned over her shoulder.

"It's a note Cummings meant Kauffeld to find in the event he was killed up there. Here, help me hold it open." Stranahan held down the outside curl of the paper with the blade of his tool while Ettinger unrolled it using the tweezers. The paper was two inches square. Four words—*Under The White Rock*. A set of GPS coordinates: 45 22.812 N; 111 10.932 W.

Stranahan got his Garmin and they walked outside and waited for the GPS to acquire the satellites for triangulation. Stranahan inserted the coordinates and pushed the "Go To" button. The liquid crystal numbers on the screen indicated that their destination was 29.7 miles to the southeast.

"Somewhere along 191 in the Gallatin Canyon, maybe," Martha said.

"The bridge," they said as one.

The GPS had registered the distance in a straight line. By road it was forty miles and change. Ettinger's foot was heavy on the pedal.

"What's the hurry, Martha?" Stranahan said, looking back to see a river of dust raised over the lower half of the grain elevator. "They're both dead. No reason to kill us, too."

"The hurry is because I blew the head off a congressman and I have to give a statement this afternoon. You can bet the Crawford clan is polishing up their incisors. Like Walt says, they only own half of Flathead County and enough cattle to flip Whoppers for every Indian in Delhi . . . well, if Hindus ate beef. The point is I have to have the facts on my side. This man was a national figure. There's going to be a coroner's inquest, that's a given. Yours truly will be grilled like a sirloin steak. Even the FBI could get involved. So I'm nervous, okay? That journal was a help, but it didn't clear up everything."

"Okay. Slow down and tell me about the journal."

Ettinger grunted. "I'll tell you what it isn't. It isn't 'who, what, why, when, and where.'"

"Then just tell me what it is."

"Well," she said, and a mile went by and finally she made a clucking sound with her tongue and drummed her fingers on the steering wheel. "The gist is Cummings had Huntington's disease, like Kauffeld said. Those pills you found were to control the muscle spasms, which get worse until you lose control of your body. I don't exactly know how you die, but you've forgotten who you are by the time you do. Hereditary, so no doubt someone in his family had it. You get that first twitch, you know the rest of your life isn't going to be very pretty."

Stranahan was nodding his head. He said, "He did this thing where he clenched up the side of his face. I noticed it the first time I saw him."

"I think it was considerably more advanced than that. Anyway, three years ago the symptoms popped up and that's when the entries start in the journal. At first it's about suicide, how he'd like to go out. There's one page where he lists ten methods he was considering; number one was climbing the Chinese Wall in the Bob Marshall Wilderness and throwing himself off the cliff. Manly stuff—provoking a charge from a grizzly bear, prodding a den of rattlesnakes. Anyway, skip ahead and the phrase "Death with Honor" starts cropping up, and then there's this entry marked on the summer solstice, two years ago June. No date, it just says summer solstice. He writes, and this is word for word, 'It's done, but he done it, not me. I thought I'd found a man, but I was wrong.' No name, no detail, nothing about making an arrangement with anyone, none of that, but the entry was written from a really dark place. And the handwriting was almost illegible, letters written on top of each other like he was writing at night without a light. My gut tells me he killed somebody, or maybe some guy he had an arrangement with turned the gun on himself. Either way, this would be a full year before Gutierrez and Webster."

"Did he mention Sphinx Mountain?"

"Not that time, but in an entry about a month before he writes about riding his horse up on the Buck's Nest. 'Took Sally Ann up on the Buck's Nest, some good flat benches to either side of the ridge, looked as good a place as any', words to that effect."

"I know where that is," Stranahan said.

"Then you know it's behind his place. Up on the east side of the Gravellys. What I'm thinking is he did his first one in his backyard, only a few miles away, and then thought better of it and went across the river to the Sphinx for the later ones. So we might have another pile of bones up around the Buck's Nest, not that it's of the utmost concern at the moment. The later guys, he goes into considerable detail. He calls them his 'fellow travelers.' Gutierrez he met at one of those Living at Last retreats in Fresno, California. Same method he used to meet Kauffeld. He also writes about flying to Portland, where there was a retreat on the coast at Cannon Beach, and down to Taos, New Mexico, but he couldn't find any takers in either place. Webster, he'd known personally from their hunt together. Seems like they made a pact. Both of them were in the early stages of their illnesses then and decided they'd get back together for the final act if and when it became apparent that time was running out."

"When does Crawford enter the picture?"

Ettinger downshifted as they neared Four Corners, then ran through the gears as the Cherokee growled its way south up the Gallatin Canyon. "That's just it," she said, flicking her nails against her jaw, "he doesn't. The closest he comes to incriminating Crawford is an early reference to 'The Most Dangerous Game.' He writes that he took the idea from it. You and I know it was Crawford who told him about the story, but it's a long way from lending someone a book or telling someone a story to being complicit in crimes that result from it. My suspicion is that Crawford also gave him the money to fly to the retreats. There's a chance the plane reservations are in his computer. I also suspect Crawford lent him the double rifle to kill Gutierrez. It was his way of living out his fantasy through Cummings."

"Maybe Crawford isn't mentioned because E.J. considered him a friend. He didn't want to implicate him if the journal fell into the wrong hands."

"At first, yes, I'd say that. But at some point the friend became the accomplice. Once Crawford headed down that road, it was only a matter of time until he killed Cummings. He'd put himself in a position where he had to. We're talking about a man with political aspirations, maybe the governorship. Cummings knew too much. But this is all conjecture, we have no solid evidence linking Crawford to anyone who died on Sphinx Mountain."

"Martha, you're being paranoid. We have a cartridge from a rifle Crawford owned that was in Cummings's possession. If we're lucky, we'll be able to match DNA from Gutierrez to the bullet in the root. Those were Crawford's fingerprints on Cummings's Bible, that's more than a maybe, we have Crawford with a rifle in hand in a place that only the killer and Kauffeld knew about, plus he shot a dummy I put up to look like Kauffeld. We might even be able to match Crawford to the voice on Kauffeld's phone message."

"What I'm hearing is 'if, maybe, and might be.' So you see why I'm anxious to find the rock."

The rock under the west pylon of the Squaw Creek Bridge was rectangular, heavy enough that Stranahan had to use all his strength to roll it over. Underneath, an inch of sand covered an olive drab ammo box with military stenciling.

"Let me have the honor," Ettinger said. She pulled on a pair of latex gloves.

The box contained three items. What looked to be a book was wrapped in layers of opaque plastic grocery bags and bound with rubber bands. A clear plastic Ziploc bag contained a half-inch-thick bundle of photocopied pages of handwriting—Cummings's journal if the top page was consistent with the body of the package. The third was the thinnest, another Ziploc containing only an unsealed envelope. Inside was a letter written in ink on a single sheet of copy paper.

Fellow traveler,

If you are reading this I am dead by your hand. I want you to know you did the right thing by bringing both of us alive on the mountain. Others will judge us as they will. I'm here to say you did me a favor, pard, and no doubt about it. You gave me some peace the earth wouldn't and picked up the sword I laid down. Go forward in your own way now and God be with you. I'm giving you my journal. It may give you some comfort to know the pain I have been through and the mental struggle that led to our arrangement. Maybe comfort isn't the right word but perspective. The big package is a book with some notes and other things inside. I would like you to mail it to the Sheriff's office in Bridger, along with the cartridge and everything else in this box. As you'll see there's nothing will betray you, even your fingerprints unless you have a record. But I have become a victim of some blackmail and this man who is feeding off me has a black heart. He will be punished in the next world but I would not mind to see him have his due in this one, either. I wish you well and thanks for giving this old horse a rest at the end of a long ride.

Dead with Honor,

Emmitt James Cummings

At the bottom of the letter was the address of the sheriff's office. Seeing her name misspelled at the top of the address—*Entinger*—brought a grim smile. Martha looked at Stranahan.

"Do we open the package?" he said.

Martha brought her fingers to her throat. "No, I don't want any chance of blowback. What we do is give it to a crime scene investigator, not Harold, because he was involved in the investigation. Someone with a sterling reputation, like Georgeanne Wilkerson out of Custer County. She's in Bridger conducting classes this week. Let Ouija Board Gigi cast her spell and open its secrets. Then this afternoon we'll look at it when there's no question of tampering and hope it's what we think it is."

It was. The dog-eared Grayson edition of *Stories for Men* that Wilkerson, a sunny speed talker whose eyes were magnified by strong prescription glasses, released to Ettinger after lifting the prints had Weldon Crawford's name scrawled in a loopy, young boy's longhand inside the cover. "The Most Dangerous Game" was the fourth chapter of the book. Inserted between the pages were Cummings's notes detailing his relationship with the congressman, starting with a conversation between the two men in Crawford's Africa room, where Crawford had first introduced him to the short story. The notes, eight pages of college-ruled paper stapled together, made it clear that Cummings felt honored to be the acquaintance of such an important man, and that while the story was indeed the inspiration that led to the arrangements, Crawford had played no part in Cummings's first encounter on the Buck's Nest with a mentally failing World War II veteran. That botched confrontation—for the old man had taken his own life rather than play the game—had gnawed at Cummings's gut and led to his confession of the incident to Crawford during an evening "when I crawled into the neck of a whiskey bottle." Cummings wrote that Crawford had "snaked it out of me, the bastard sure knows how to pull a man's string." In a sort of joking manner, Crawford had wondered aloud if he should report the matter to the authorities, all the while saying that he probably wouldn't. He'd let Cummings sleep on the implied threat and then had used the confession to leverage his way into sharing the planning of future arrangements.

"Though I considered him a friend, having none other, he had me over a barrel," Cummings wrote. As Ettinger suspected, Crawford had funded Cummings on expeditions to at least three Living at Last retreats through the spring and early summer of the previous calendar year, until he found a cooperative party in Alejandro Gutierrez. Crawford had then insisted Cummings use his double rifle, the big .475 No. 2, which he had subsequently sold after its return, getting a retroactive case of cold feet. Cummings, however, had had the foresight to save the fired cartridge case, as well as several loaded ones, as insurance against "eventualities."

After watching the breath rattle out of the Mexican, Cummings had no stomach for future arrangements, but then by chance he had met Orvel Webster at a gun show in Helena. "Remember what we talked about a couple years ago?" Webster had told him. "Well, it's time." And Cummings had agreed, for here was a man whom he did not have to coax, but who was an equal partner in the planning of their arrangement. Cummings found a purity in his confrontation with Webster that gave him the strength to keep it a secret from Crawford, but it did not grant him the fortitude to turn his back on the bottle, or to stave off the depression he'd suffered every winter since Huntington's had begun to toy with his synapses. He had recurring nightmares about Gutierrez and Webster, whom in retrospect he had come to regard as victims of his own misguided obsessions. In the dreams, the old men tried to rise from their graves and he had to keep climbing back up there and pushing them down and putting more dirt on them. "I don't know if they were trying to get back at me or just turn their souls loose on that mountain, but I was wearing out boot leather and it wasn't going to end soon, no sir."

When Crawford paid an unexpected visit to his summer mansion in February, Cummings was in the depths of despair and once more found himself weakening under the force of the congressman's personality. He reluctantly agreed to the trip to Michigan, where he met Melvin Kauffeld, being ambivalent about it, but then as the date of their arrangement neared, he found that the preparations lifted him out of his depression. More than that, in Kauffeld he thought he'd found a worthy successor to Orvel Webster, one who might finally grant him death with honor. He had long ago disclosed his physical affliction to Crawford, and Crawford hinted that maybe it was time he let someone get the drop on him in an arrangement. It began to dawn on Cummings that Crawford wanted him out of the picture and would kill him if he had to, that if Kauffeld's bullet missed the mark there would be another coming, no doubt from one of the big African rifles. "And I'd have welcomed it," he'd written, "had it come from another man's barrel." It was this growing unease and his determination that Crawford get his comeuppance that led him into penning the notes and placing them where Kauffeld would find them in the event of his death.

Ettinger slipped the notes between the pages of the story and sealed the book back into the evidence envelope. She clasped her hands behind her head and leaned back in her office chair. She regarded Stranahan through slitted eyes.

"It must have been a strange relationship," she mused.

"Well, he was a charismatic man, Crawford," Stranahan said. "He had a sort of force field that repelled you and drew you in at the same time. You found yourself talking to him even if you didn't like him. Maybe it was a politician's trick, but it felt like intimacy. And Cummings was all alone on the planet. It's an odd couple but I can see it, the two of them sharing their brandies in Crawford's study with the snow on the sills, finding their common ground in hunting and 'The Most Dangerous Game.' Oiling the heavy rifles. I can see Cummings taking the concept of death with honor and running with it, turning this adolescent fantasy of Crawford's into reality. Crawford gave him the seed, Cummings watered it and saw it bloom, then Crawford poisoned the plant when he found out about it; he fed his own sickness with it."

Martha compressed her lips. "Aren't we the psychologist?" she said. "I never heard you talk like that before. Makes me wonder if it's me who doesn't know you."

"Well, I've had some time to think about it. I've also had time to think about something else," he said, thinking of the something else. He glanced at his watch. "It's still early. If you don't need me this afternoon, I'm going to take a drive up the valley."

"Mmm," said Martha. "You do that. Meanwhile, I'll just sit here and deal with the fallout. Do you know how many interview requests Dispatch logged since I gave my statement yesterday? Forty-seven. *Washington Post. New York Times.*" She rolled her eyes. "The *Enquirer.* I'm the woman sheriff who gunned down a congressman in the old Wild West. Oh yeah, and with her trusty Indian tracker at her side. Hmpff. I'll tell you what. Five o'clock comes around, I'm going to drive back to my place and take the phone off the hook. You take care of your business up the valley, why don't you come join me? I have a feeling I'm going to need a sympathetic ear." She hesitated. "'Course, you might rather be with your barista. I can't fill out a pair of suspenders like she can, so I'll understand."

Stranahan looked at her.

"That was supposed to be a joke," she said.

"It's not going to be as bad as you think, Martha. You'll end up being the hero." He stood up. "I'll bring the beer," he said.

"Good luck finding those flies, Sean."

"How did you . . . ?" Sean looked at her sideways.

"Give me a little credit," she said. "Why else would you be burning thirty bucks of gas on a day you aren't fishing? Besides"—she waited a beat—"you said it in your sleep when we were driving back from the bridge. You said, 'The ghost. I know where the ghost is.'"

"What else did I say?"

"I think I'll save that card for when I want to play it," Martha said.

CHAPTER THIRTY-ONE

The Mystery of White People

The Sheltie pressed its nose to the window as the Land Cruiser passed the ruts to Cummings's old place, but did not make a whimper. When they reached the clubhouse, Stranahan told it to stay on the porch and put his knuckles to the door.

Patrick Willoughby was wearing a sweater.

"Since when do you feel the need to knock?" he said. "Come on in. I was just about to strike a match to our first fire of the fall, though it's still July if you can believe the calendar. Isn't that the damnedest news about our neighbor, though? But I guess we should never be surprised by our politicians. Polly," he said, gesturing toward the elder statesman of the club, who was in his customary seat at the fly-tying table, "just look what the dog dragged in." And to Stranahan, "About that dog. Isn't that Emmitt Cummings's collie? Hard to believe E.J. was mixed up in something like that. Very hard to accept. I'll not judge the man. I liked him."

In the few days that he'd had it, the little Shetland sheepdog had become Stranahan's constant companion. One eye was bandaged where it had popped out of the socket when the grizzly swatted it—time would tell how much vision was permanently lost—but otherwise the dog was well on its way to recovery.

"I seem to have adopted it," Stranahan said. "You wouldn't know its name, would you?"

"Something Indian, I think. Not native, but 'Jewel in the Crown.' Do you remember what it was that E.J. called his dog, Polly?"

"Choti," Polly Sorenson said. "It means small." He flipped up the magnifying lenses from his glasses and peered at Stranahan. "Good to see you again, Sean. I'd get up but this damned arthritis . . ."

"It's good to see you, too. What are you tying?"

"A Lady Amherst. It's one of the few salmonfly patterns to originate in Canada. A spare tie as you see, but not the easiest to turn out of your vise, not at all." He lifted his eyebrows. "But then my fingers find all the classics a challenge now. This age they call eighty, it isn't for sissies, I'll tell you that."

"Where are the rest of the boys?" Stranahan asked.

"The boys as you call them have gone home," Willoughby said. "Robin Cowdry left only yesterday. But Kenneth Winston has flown in for the week and I'm sure he'll be tickled to see you. Drink? I seem to recall that the George T. Stagg bottle still has a few inches of dew in the bottom."

"I would, but there's something I'd like to talk to Kenneth about first. Is he on the river?"

"You'll find him down in that slick below the log jam. Into a fish, if I know Kenneth."

He was releasing one when Stranahan called out his name. Winston saluted with the hand not holding his fly rod. "Give me some of that pure cane sugar," he said as the men embraced on the riverbank. "I was hoping you'd come down."

"Take a walk with me," Stranahan said. "I might have a surprise for you."

They passed the clubhouse and walked up around the bend. The boy was where Stranahan had seen him when he was driving in, when he crested the bluff to see the river sparkling before the road dipped to the clubhouse. He was standing in the shallows, facing upstream. He didn't hear the men approach.

"Good cop, bad cop," Stranahan whispered.

"Which one am I?"

"You're the good cop."

"You really aren't going to tell me what this is about?"

Stranahan just smiled. "Hello, Sid!" His voice was a shout.

The boy, startled, turned and slipped on the slick boulders. He abruptly sat down in the water. Winston got him by the arm and helped him climb up the bank. He walked back and retrieved the fly rod the boy had dropped.

"You seem surprised to see me," Stranahan said.

"I thought you were going to be around more," Sid said. His eyes darted to the slim man holding his fly rod. "I never seen a black fisherman."

Winston arched his pencil-thin eyebrows. He held out his hand, which the boy shook tentatively. "I'm Kenneth," he said. "It's a pleasure to meet such a nice young man. Sean has told me what a good fisherman you are."

Stranahan spoke seriously to the boy. "I'm afraid you've done a bad thing, Sid."

"What? I didn't do nothing."

"Don't look at me like that, son. I know you found the key to that cabin down the river there. I know you pushed the stump where you could climb up and get to it. Probably saw one of the men reach up there, right?"

"No, I never."

Winston spoke up. "Now Sean, if the boy says he didn't, maybe it was somebody else."

"No, it was you. What did you steal? Rods? Reels? Money?"

"I didn't take no money." He had edged a step toward Winston.

"What rods did you take?"

"I only got this rod." He pointed to the rod that Winston held. It was the same cheaply made rod he'd had when Stranahan had first seen him. One of the stripping guides was held on by duct tape, and a sloppily glued tip-top showed where the upper section had snapped.

The boy saw Winston examining it. "I only lost about two inches off the end," he said. "It still casts good."

Winston removed the fly from the cork. It was, or had been, a Trude. Most of the white wing was missing. He pulled a few yards of line from the reel and backcast the line forty feet behind him, not looking, the river over his shoulder, the loop of line tight and then unfurling to drop the fly like a thistle onto the surface.

"Passable stick," he said. "Not a bad rod at all."

"Mister, you're an awful good caster. He's better'n you." He turned to Stranahan, his chin out. *So there.*

Stranahan had to hand it to the kid. He had spine, as his grandmother might say.

"Here's the deal," Stranahan said. "You turn over everything you stole from the cabin and I'll call the sheriff back and tell her not to come."

"Sean, you didn't have to do that." Winston looked at Stranahan and raised his brows, the purpose of their visit with the boy becoming clear. He squatted down and crooked his finger. "Come here, Sid," he said in a gentle voice. "If Sean doesn't call the sheriff off, then I will, don't you worry. I know all you took were some trout flies. It's just that a couple of those flies are like antiques. They're not very good for fishing. Those old hooks are brittle and if you hooked a fish they'd probably break."

"I caught—" The boy stopped himself.

"Did you catch a fish on one? I'm surprised."

Sid looked down at his feet. "There was so many boxes I didn't think anybody would miss one. My uncle, he won't let me buy any flies, so all I got is some old ones that the thread unwinds right away. I'd like to learn how to tie flies, but it takes a lot of money."

"I'm a fly tier," Winston said. "You know what I'll do? I'll put together a kit for you: vise, hooks, feathers, everything. If you have time, I'll even teach you how to tie."

"You'd do that?"

"I surely would. But I'm going to have to ask you to give those flies back. There's two of them that have what you call sentimental value. Do you have them?"

Sid's eyes were on his wet tennis shoes. He didn't look up. "The silver box I took, I give it back. I give the box to that man . . ."

Stranahan was confused. He thought the boy had taken a few flies from the box, not the box itself. The box wasn't missing.

"What man?" he said.

"He saw me gettin' the key. I tried to run, but he caught me. He said he wouldn't tell no one."

"Who?"

"The man in the big house."

"You mean Mr. Crawford?"

"I don't know his name. He had this big lump." He pointed to the side of his neck.

"And he took the box from you."

Sid nodded.

"And you didn't take any flies out of the box?"

He shook his head. "I took some other flies a few days ago." Stranahan thought of the moved block. "I waited till the car was gone."

"What exactly did the man do, the one with the lump?"

"When he come running down the hill, his face was redder than my uncle's."

"Did he hit you?"

"No, he just took the box and cussed me out. I thought his head was going to explode."

Stranahan looked past the boy, up the draw to the hexagonal mansion on the bench. "Sid, you go on home," he said presently.

"I thought your friend was going to teach me to tie flies." The boy's voice was accusatory.

"Why don't you come to the cabin tomorrow about this time," Winston said.

When the boy had gone, dragging his shadow up the hill, Winston traced his mustache with his right thumb and forefinger. "That young fella reminds me of me at that age," he said. "A rapscallion, as my mother would say. You'd have thought he'd be nervous as a two-tailed cat on a porch full of rocking chairs, but he doesn't scare for long, does he?"

Stranahan had a set to his jaw and the words washed over him, as incoherent as the murmuring of the river. *If Crawford took the flies from the box, how did he know which two to take? And what was the point of taking them in the first place?* The answer was there, swirling out of reach, like a trout rising beyond the length of your farthest cast. If he could just reach a little farther into the ether of his sub-conscious, wade a little deeper in order to make the cast. And . . . and it was there. The fly drifted into the saucer where the trout rose and he had the answer. Or rather, he knew who would give it to him.

"I don't get what a man like Crawford would want with a couple trout flies." Winston shook his head in wonder as they started back to the clubhouse. "White people," he said, "they're a mystery."

Stranahan swam out of his reverie. "He didn't care about the flies, Kenneth. He only took them so he could return them to Polly Soren-son and purchase his friendship. He was just waiting for the right moment."

"I don't mean to say my mother raised a fool, but Polly? I'm afraid you've lost me."

"It'll be clearer in about ten minutes," Stranahan said.

When it was, when the arthritic old fly tier with the whispering breath admitted that he'd shown Weldon Crawford the Quill Gor-don and the Gray Ghost the day he'd invited him in for a drink, had talked at length with the congressman about their value, both senti-mental and monetary, had mentioned the plan to put the flies in the box until the other club members arrived, but hadn't told Wil-loughby about the conversation because he was embarrassed how easily the congressman was able to insinuate himself into his confidence, after the shine came to the rheumy eyes and Willoughby had said, "Now, now, Polly, there's nothing to be ashamed of," Stranahan looked at the songbird clock on the wall, the hour hand still shy of the tufted titmouse that stood for the number five, and called Martha Ettinger at her office.

CHAPTER THIRTY-TWO

Return of the Gray Ghost

Her first words were, "This had better be good."

Ettinger ushered Stranahan into her home office, where she had cleared space on her desk for Weldon Crawford's Rigby double rifle, the one Stranahan had shot at the charging buffalo target and later Crawford had carried to Sphinx Mountain to shoot Emmitt Cummings through the wall of his tent. As Stranahan had remembered, the right barrel was split where the rifle had accidentally discharged when Crawford fell on it, driving the muzzles into the ground, and there was a chunk of the wood missing near the pistol grip. Despite the damage, the rifle remained a potent instrument of death, incongruously beautiful in repose, the Circassian walnut stock gleaming under the overhead lights.

"I checked it out of evidence like you asked," she said. "Now what's this about?"

"The final piece of the puzzle, or at least that's what I'm hoping," Stranahan said.

"Maybe you better explain."

"I'll try, but can we go out on the porch? I left the dog in my rig and he gets antsy when he can't see me."

"You know what you are, Sean? I thought about it when you took up with that riverboat siren last summer. You're a taker-in of strays. Stray women, stray men like your buddy Meslik, who's so feral he'd just as soon use a litterbox as a toilet, stray dogs, stray anything."

"Does that mean you're a stray, Martha?"

"No, I'm a misfit. There's a difference."

They moved to the porch. "Speaking of puzzles," Martha said, "there's something you'll want to know. Remember how we never found Cummings's pickup at the trailhead. That bothered me. Well, we found it. He'd parked down at Indian Creek and ridden in from there. That's a long way around."

"Careful man," Stranahan said.

"He wound up dead all the same. So back to your puzzle, tell me about it."

"When I left your office this afternoon," Stranahan said, "I thought this boy I'd met on the river had stolen the flies. I'd seen where he pushed a stump so he could stand on it to reach the hidden key to the clubhouse. And my hunch was right. But then when I confronted the boy this afternoon, it turns out our good congressman had caught him stealing the fly box. Crawford had returned it to Willoughby's vest, where the boy had found it. But first he'd removed two flies from the box, the valuable ones—the Quill Gordon and the Gray Ghost."

"Crawford or the boy took the flies out of the box?"

"Crawford."

"I'm with you. I've got my doubts about where you're going with this, but I'm with you."

"Just hear me out," Stranahan said. "Crawford had no interest in the flies, but he did have an interest in one of the club's members." Stranahan told her about Polly Sorenson and his illness, the prospect of dying in a hospital bed fighting for breath, and how he'd confessed his condition to Crawford the previous summer. "'A man who rubs you two ways at once' is what Polly called him. There were things you didn't like about Crawford, but you found yourself wanting him to like you. He'd get you under his thumb, watch you wriggle, listen while you said things you hadn't meant to reveal, then get you to do what he wanted you to do, even if it wasn't in your best interest."

"He wanted Sorenson to play the Most Dangerous Game," Ettinger said.

"Exactly. Crawford wanted to find out what it was like, hunting down a man. He'd lived it vicariously through Cummings. Now he had an itch to use his own finger to pull the trigger. And Sorenson was a prime candidate. He had a terminal illness, but he was strong enough to get around. Plus he was right here in the valley. So what I think is, when Crawford took the fly box from the boy, it occurred to him that if he removed the flies, he'd wait for a moment when he had Sorenson alone, and then he'd return them to him, say the boy had stolen them and he'd caught the little thief. He'd use the flies as leverage to worm his way into the old man's confidence. Then he could exercise his powers of persuasion, butter him up for the kill. I doubt it would have worked. Polly has a wife back east, a married daughter and two grandchildren. I think the family is close-knit. But Crawford had an ego the size of his mansion and thought he could pull it off."

Ettinger scratched at her throat. "That seems like a lot to infer," she said.

"Not really. Crawford told me as much on the mountain. When I asked him if he was recruiting Polly Sorenson to be Cummings's next arrangement, he corrected me, told me he was going into the arranging business for himself. 'I suppose you could say I was baiting the hook' is the way he put it. He said he was working on Sorenson, that he had a plan and I should be smart enough to figure it out. I think the flies were the plan, to insinuate himself with the victim."

Ettinger slapped at a mosquito. She wiped the smear of blood from her forearm. "So where are they?" she said.

The trapdoor that accessed the compartment in the buttstock of the rifle was so closely fitted to the buttplate as to be virtually invisible. The recessed lever that opened it required a small, sharp instrument. Ettinger handed Stranahan a fork from a kitchen drawer and he inserted a tine under the lip of the latch.

"Moment of truth," he said. "When I asked Crawford what was inside, the question caught him off guard. He seemed nervous, said something about hoping it would be a ruby, but it was only a set of firing pins. Then when I changed the subject, he relaxed. Crawford was a romantic. What better place to keep the flies that he hoped to lure Sorenson with than in the rifle he was going to use to kill him?"

"Quit stalling."

The recess in the buttstock was the size of a pack of playing cards. Stranahan tried peering inside, but the recess was dark. He turned the buttstock over and shook it. The dry fly drifted like thistledown to settle on its hackle points on the stump. Stranahan shook the stock again. Then he worked his forefinger into the compartment. The hook point of the Gray Ghost had stuck into the wood. Stranahan freed it and the graceful streamer fly joined the Quill Gordon on the polished wood.

CHAPTER THIRTY-THREE

Too Blue to Fly

Though little more than a month had passed since Stranahan first visited the Madison River Liars and Fly Tiers Club, the season had subtly shifted. The solstice was many casts behind him now, the nights were longer, the first of the riverside willows wore crimson leaves. He used the hidden key to let himself in and stood for a minute until his eyes adjusted to the dim light. The plaques and glass domes that had held the club's fly collection were gone from the shelves and the walls, packed up and shipped east for the winter. The pegs where the members had hung their vests were bare. The buffalo skull with the tuft of sweetgrass in its nasal cavity stared with empty eye sockets at the light film of dust covering the fly-tying table.

Stranahan pulled the letter he'd received at his studio in Bridger from his hip pocket and read it again, standing up.

Dear Sean,

I'm sorry to bear the sad news of Polly Sorenson's passing. He died of a heart attack on August 4 while fishing in the Neversink River. I've enclosed a copy of the obituary. All the Catskill rivers ran high this summer and apparently he had fallen in, for his clothes were wet, perhaps prompting a coronary. Polly died the way I'm sure he would have wanted, not in a hospital from the congestion of his lungs, but in his waders, fishing a Light Cahill tied by his own impeccable hand. His wife found him on the riverbank. She said he looked peaceful. I hope he was. He was one of the finest men I have ever known.

As you know, we are all very grateful for your assistance in returning the flies. They are, in fact, on the wall of my den from which I am writing you this letter. In one of my last conversations with Polly, he brought up the possibility of rewarding you in a unique way. You may recall that we often talked about fishing for bonefish in the Bahamas. The club leases a cottage for three weeks each winter on the Atlantic side of an island called Eleuthera. In accordance with Polly's wishes, we would like to fly you there to fish next January. None of us can make the week of the 7th–15th, so it would be only you and, of course, Martinique. You are still in her good graces? Quite frankly, I believe Polly was thinking as much of her as he was of you when he proposed the idea, and thought that it would do her good before starting her studies in Seattle. A friend of ours, Paul Thackery, will pick you up at the airport at Governor's Harbour and give you the scoop on the tides and the fishing, but for the most part you'll be on your own, which I know is how you like it. You will have the keys to our Jeep and please use the kayak in the garage, as it will open up many flats that are cut off from the shoreline by channels.

We need to reserve your flights so please call me at your earliest convenience and really, don't bother arguing. We won't hear a word of objection. This is what Polly wanted.

I expect to hear from you very soon.

Best regards,
Patrick Willoughby
President, The Madison River Liars and Fly Tiers Club

PS The Jock Scott salmon fly that Polly tied for you is in the top drawer of the desk. He meant to give it to you before he left, but you were rather preoccupied, all that derring-do on Sphinx Mountain. It is still difficult to accept that our club was involved, even if tangentially and in so small a manner as missing trout flies. As you have been elected an honorary club member, a chair at the poker table is reserved for you next summer. Until then, tight lines and singing reels and beware—on Eleuthera, they drive on the wrong side of the road.

Stranahan folded the letter and found the shadow-box in the drawer, with the regal Jock Scott mounted in the indentation and an inscription underneath. *Tied for Sean Stranahan by Polly Sorenson.* He decided it would hang on the wall in his studio until the cabin he intended to build on the three acres along the creek was finished. He'd put the down payment on the property only a few days before, after the check cleared from the sale of his grandparents' house in Massachusetts. When his grandmother had succeeded his grandfather in death the previous December, Stranahan and his sister inherited; it was Karen who had arranged the sale. Stranahan hated to say goodbye to the old place, so many memories, listening to his father and grandfather tell stories while their pipe bowls glowed cherry red amid the smaller lights of the fireflies, night-fishing on the pond for largemouth bass, sketching bullfrogs and garter snakes in the reeds. But he had known for some months now that his life was here, along the ribbons of river that reflected the clouds and the peaks and the deep autumn blue of Montana skies.

He celebrated the purchase of his small corner of this paradise with a glass of Martha Ettinger's homemade hard cider on the first Sunday in September, the two of them sitting on Ettinger's porch while the little Sheltie and Martha's Australian shepherd sniffed each other and got acquainted. It was one of those early autumn twilights when the mosquitoes are gone and the evenings chill enough to drape a jacket, or, the way Stranahan read weather, when the summer mayflies had folded their tents and the trout had turned on to hoppers.

The coroner's inquest of the shooting on Sphinx Mountain had cleared the sheriff of wrongdoing, Stranahan too, for that matter, and the silence as they drank their cider was one of the easiest they'd shared in several weeks. But if the department was off the hook with the long arm of the law, the sheriff's celebrity had not been so easily shed. The story had run its course in newspaper ink, but a *Vanity Fair* article had yet to be published and the Pulitzer Prize–winning author who'd penned it was said to be considering expanding it into a book.

Ettinger shuddered to think of it. "If I didn't have this place to get away from it all, I'd have gone crazy a month ago." She drained her Mason jar in a long swallow and set it on the porch rail. "Once you get your cabin built, you'll know what I'm talking about. You come out here after a day in the uniform and you step back in time a hundred years. What are you, still a couple years away from building?"

"Actually," Stranahan said, "I'll be moving next spring. I probably won't even have the foundation dug, but Harold said he'd lend me one of his tepees to live in. A big one—eighteen poles. Be like camping out, but it's still a step up from sleeping on the futon in my studio."

"Harold," Martha said in a reflective voice. "I guess you know we're taking some time off from each other."

Stranahan nodded.

"Martinique? I assume you're still with her?"

"I am."

"How involved are you?"

"Pretty involved."

Martha tried not to let anything show in her face, but couldn't hide the trace of bitterness that crept into her voice. "One thing I've learned about men," she said. "Give them a little time and they tend to become uninvolved." She looked away, not wanting him to see the slight quiver of her jaw. *Was this the way it was going to be even when they were neighbors, the man and woman who could have been, who watched each other form other attachments when they should have been, who grew old and never were?*

She composed herself and changed the subject. "I haven't heard that great gray for a while. This is the time of night you usually hear him."

She fingered the button on her shirt pocket and drew out her harmonica, the Hohner Big River that had been a gift from her father. She'd grown up listening to his old vinyl records—George Jones, Loretta Lynn, Patsy Cline. Patsy had a voice that was as clear as water from the mountain, but every time Martha opened her mouth, just squawks came out. Once, she'd overheard her father saying his little girl wanted to sing like a nightingale but she'd be more at home in a nest of baby blackbirds—*acht, acht, acht.* She'd heard her mother laugh in spite of herself. "You shush now, Martin Ettinger. That's cruel." Martha, all of ten years old, had cried herself to sleep.

"What's that you say?" She came out of her reverie.

"I said I didn't know you played."

"Like I keep telling you, there's a lot of things you don't know about me."

She ran a scale on the harp, wetting her lips. "Any requests?"

"How about a little Hank Williams. 'I'm So Lonesome I Could Cry.'"

Story of my life, Martha thought.

"If you don't know it, then anything's fine."

"No, it's one of my favorites." The first of the plaintive notes bounced around the rock walls of the canyon. They quavered and died there, like the whippoorwill of the song, too blue to fly.

Epilogue

Stranahan pinched a Crazy Charlie he'd tied in his art studio between the thumb and forefinger of his left hand. Loops of fly line trailed in the water as his wading shoes lifted puffy clouds of marl from the bottom of the flat. Forty yards away, the surface shivered, marking a school of feeding bonefish. He turned to point out the nervous water to Martinique, who was a vision in her turquoise bikini on the pink sand beach. The cat woman who had been named for a Caribbean island but had never seen one had spent the day snorkeling and had her nose buried in a book.

Stranahan watched her turn a page and deliberately crossed his eyes until a shadow image separated and he was looking at two of her. She would be moving to Corvallis less than a week after they returned to the States. The drive from Bridger to western Oregon was fourteen hours, which he could ill afford to undertake very often with the cost of gasoline and the unslakable thirst of his Land Cruiser. He was thinking about trading the beloved beast for a hybrid to make a long-distance relationship feasible, but then he wasn't sure convention permitted a fisherman to operate a Prius, or how he would haul his raft with one. Sam, he knew, would never let him hear the end of it.

It was Sam who was petsitting for them. He'd balked at taking in the three cats and the dog, warning Sean that Killer would have them for breakfast. But when Stranahan had checked in with him from the club's beach cottage, Sam told him it was Killer who'd been put in his place. Extending an inquisitive muzzle toward the coon cat, he'd received a swat on the nose and dripped a trail of blood into Sam's bedroom, where he'd cowered ever since. "I never thought I'd say it, Kimosabe, but my dog's been pussy-whipped. You paintbrush-pushing excuse of a fly fisherman"—as a New Year's resolution Sam had decided to swear off swearing, "on account of it's time I started sounding more like a fucking human being"—"I'm cleaning kitty litter and freezing my coconuts off while you're fishing in your skivvies."

"Coconuts, Sam?" Stranahan told him to curl up with the cats and was laughing when he put the phone down. He'd made a note to bring the big fella a bottle of Old Nassau rum.

When he refocused so that Martinique was no longer an abstraction and turned toward the ocean, the school of bonefish had moved out of casting range. A midget barracuda regarded him with a carnivorous grin and Stranahan held its stare. When he lifted his head, there was something different about the flat and he swept his eyes back and forth, the polarized lenses of his glasses cutting through the surface mirror to search for the secrets beneath. *There.* A smoke-colored stick protruded from the flat, a vague shadow wavering underneath it. *A stick that wasn't there before?* Although Stranahan had never seen a tailing bonefish, he knew the stick was the top lobe of its tail, tilted up as the vulpine head rooted in the marl for penaeid shrimp and spider crabs. The tail waved at him, beckoning like a languid finger as Stranahan roll cast the loops of line off the surface, double-hauled, and shot a cast that dropped the fly three feet in front of the tail. He pulsed the Crazy Charlie, the tail folded over and disappeared, pulsed the fly again, the tail came up, and he felt the weight and lifted his hand into the smooth power of the bonefish. The line snapped tight against the arbor of the reel and then began to unspool, the line lifting a sheet of water, and Sean Stranahan, looking out to sea, forgot about secrets unearthed on a Montana mountain, forgot about a cabin unbuilt on a brook trout creek, forgot even about Martinique. He forgot about everything but the bend of the rod and the singing of the taut line and the phantom of the Eleutheran flats.

AUTHOR'S NOTE

Last summer, during a Fourth of July celebration, I discovered four baby blackbirds in a nest. The nest had been driven on a flatbed trailer some 150 miles, and it was only after the planting of the tree, a densely branched fir that a friend ordered from a tree farm, that anyone realized a family had been uprooted as well. This occurred in the Madison Valley that is the setting for this book, and I was well into the writing of it when I first heard the nestlings squawk.

With twilight casting a spell over the Gravelly Range, I took a shovel to the river to dig worms. Until that night I had never bought into the concept of novelists as people who lead interesting lives, as writing is largely a business of going into a room and shutting the door and telling lies that would put a politician to shame, engrossing enough to the one doing the lying but hardly the stuff of envy. But as I returned from the river to drop worms down the greedy mouths, I suspected that the writing of *The Gray Ghost Murders* might prove an exception. That was made abundantly clear when I contacted the nearest wild bird rescue person, who told me to call her Captain Marvel. When I asked Captain Marvel if she would take over the rearing of the nestlings—after all, that's what these people do, I naively thought—she said, "Honey, that's how we all start."

So began the most demanding artistic endeavor of my career, for nestlings must be fed every fifteen minutes and heretofore I had aligned myself with that school of writing championed by Oscar Wilde, whose idea of a morning's work was to insert a coma, and in the afternoon to take it out. With the birds summoning my attention—and the squawking of a Brewer's blackbird is not to be ignored—I found that in order to avoid feeling a total failure I had to insert more than punctuation during the intervals of silence. And so, sitting under a sun umbrella near the chicken-wire enclosure I had built to house the little darlings, *The Gray Ghost Murders* was coaxed to life, and, in the process, I discovered that if you actually put words down as they come into your head, so that you might weigh and weed them later, rather than endlessly editing in your mind before committing so much as a period to the screen, then writing need not be a tortured bloodletting of a drop at a time, but could move and sing through your veins, or at least emerge onto the page in complete sentences.

In three weeks the birds had feathered over to become the terror of the neighborhood, soaring to parts unknown every evening, but usually perched on the top branch of a giant spruce in the morning, four little sentinels sitting side by side. For another month they continued to need supplemental feeding, and I would have to place a hand over my head to avoid being mobbed the moment I walked out the door. But what started as an act of mercy became a privilege as the summer grew short, for not only had these birds taught me a lesson about my craft, but they gave me a gift rarely awarded human beings, a personal glimpse of that indomitable wildness of spirit that is the wonder of nature, and that can be heard not only in the voices of wolves and elk in the mountain folds, but in the songs of our backyards.

By fall the siblings had become part of a larger flock wheeling in the sky, peeling off to visit me once or twice a day, the runt I called Blackie still hopping onto my laptop to take mealworms from my fingers. On October 12, I saw them together for the last time, and two days later Blackie came alone. He spoke in a querulous voice I had never before heard from a blackbird and then he, too, was gone. In the span of several days the raucous singing of the flocks was stilled, as thousands of blackbirds darkened the sky, and were seen no more. I finished the novel later that week.

And so it has been with an eye to the sky that I have worked this summer, hoping for their return. Blackbirds are colony nesters and do not invade town to forage until they have raised their broods; but as the fireworks of Independence Day burst forth and died, my hopes began to fade, and when I sat down to breakfast on July 7, I was resigned to the likelihood of never seeing them again. Compared with most songbirds, a blackbird's voice is unmusical, but to me it is as lovely as the whistling of a thrush, and with the first grating *aawk* I was running to the door. Blackie was perched on top of the cage, showing me his bold white eye. I wanted to tell him that the book was finished and that he and his two brothers and sister deserved credit, but he no longer had much use for a being who couldn't fly, and after letting me admire his iridescent plumage, he flew to the top of the spruce where I had so often seen him herald the dawn. I had but a fleeting glimpse, his fearsome countenance silhouetted against the sky, and then he was gone, this time, perhaps forever.

Keith McCafferty
August 14, 2012

The next novel in the
Sean Stranahan mystery series
is now available from Penguin Books.

Read on for the third chapter of

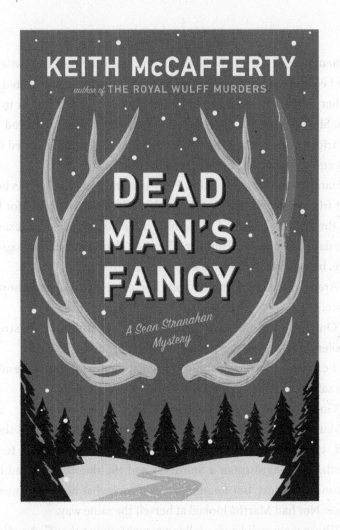

KEITH McCAFFERTY

author of THE ROYAL WULFF MURDERS

DEAD MAN'S FANCY

*A Sean Stranahan
Mystery*

CHAPTER THREE

Reading the White Book

When Martha saw a light flicker up the mountainside, she switched the beam of the tracking light on and off a few times. She waited until her signal was answered, then her eyes fell to the revolver in her lap. She fingered the latch to swing out the cylinder, removed one cartridge and replaced the cylinder so that the hammer rested over the empty chamber. She holstered the revolver.

Harold was riding his paint. He dismounted and pulled his braid out from under the collar of his jacket. Martha made room for him on the log. She breathed in Harold's odor that wasn't sweat exactly, but dark and organic. Familiar. They had shared more than logs before, before Harold took back up with his ex-wife.

"Aren't you going to tie off your horse?" she said after a short silence.

"Only white people lose their horses." And after another stretch of silence: "I see you're packing the Ruger again."

"I can shoot it. I can't shoot those damned semi-autos. Besides," she said, "I'm a Western sheriff, I have to look the part."

"Got to please your public, famous woman like yourself."

Martha grunted. It had been more than a year since she'd shot a U.S. congressman in these mountains some twenty miles to the north, the congressman a murderer and the shooting cleared by a coroner's inquest, but no one had ever looked at her the same way since. Nor had Martha looked at herself the same way.

"Those wolves did some talking tonight, didn't they?" she said. "I thought one of them was going to walk right in on me a while back."

She put nonchalance into her voice, but felt her heart beat waiting for Harold's reply, wondering if he'd heard her screams a half hour earlier.

"My understanding was FWP wiped out that Black Butte Pack," Harold said. "Back when they got into the cattle that last time. Looks like a new one moved in."

He wouldn't say if he had heard, Martha thought.

"You want a piece of corn cake?" Harold was unfolding a square of wax paper on his knee. Martha told herself to let him get around to it in his own time. Talking about anything other than what brought two people together under unusual circumstances was a trait shared by many Westerners, but perfected to an art form by Native Americans. Harold retrieved a thermos of tea from a saddlebag and they sat in easy silence, trading sips from the screw-on plastic cup.

"You make good tea," Martha said. "What is it?"

"Whatever was in the cupboard at my sister's. Why don't you tell me what you saw tonight, starting with that horse wandering into your camp?"

"Did Jason tell you about the guy with the elk antler sticking out of his gut?"

"He did. I can smell the blood. But we'll be able to read the white book a whole lot better in an hour or so. Just muddy up tracks if we go in now."

So she told him, omitting only the scream. Harold refolded the wax paper and put it in his jacket pocket. "Couple things," he said. "Did you notice any other tracks besides the horse's? Wolf? Human?"

Martha said no, but that didn't mean they weren't there. Once her light registered the bloodbath, her attention had centered on the body.

Harold nodded. It was gradually growing light. Martha could see the barred blue grouse feather that Harold wore in his braid flutter in the wind.

"Okay, last question. Did you circle around to see where the horse entered this stand of trees?"

Again, the answer was no.

"Then that's the first thing we'll do. I need to know if the horse was already running, which means something up above spooked him, or if he was walking. If he was walking, then what made him bolt was the kill. Horse coming from upwind, he could have stumbled right into the blood before it registered. Things go sideways in a hurry when a horse smells blood."

Reading the white book" was an expression that Harold had picked up from his grandfather, who'd taught him to track on the escarpments of the front range that bordered the Blackfeet reservation. It was the skill of deciphering stories written in snow, the pages turning as each animal went about the business of his day. Who came here, what was his name, whom did he fear, in whose teeth did he die? In early autumn, many pages in the white book were blank, while others were written in a disappearing ink, for the snow came and the snow went, often in the same day. When Harold and Martha circled the trees to find where the horse had entered them, Harold figured he had several hours before the snow melted and the book shut. He examined Martha's boot tread so he could identify it and told her to follow two steps behind, placing her boots exactly in his own tracks.

The horse had entered the copse of pines at the upper northeast corner, where the trees were sparsest. Harold pointed with a stick. The pockmarks were spaced at regular intervals, faint scoops in the vanilla swirl.

"He was walking, huh?" Martha said, and cursed herself for commenting on the obvious. Notwithstanding the personal baggage of their relationship, she always felt inadequate following Harold while he tracked. He didn't suffer fools and was disinclined to honor any but intelligent questions with an answer.

She followed him down into the thicket. Harold pointed again. "See where he crow-hopped?" The horse had kicked up dirt over the snow where it jumped. "And here, here's where the rider bailed." He was pointing to two narrow impressions—the snow-covered tracks of a man. "He landed on his feet." Harold's voice was matter-of-fact. "Good horseman."

Martha felt the quick tremor of a vein in her neck. She rubbed at it and put her hands on her hips. The corners of her mouth turned down. "If he was bucked off here, how does he end up on the sharp end of an antler yonder down the hill?"

A momentary tightening of his cheeks was Harold's only response. He tucked his braid under his jacket collar and pushed through the wall of branches. As Martha followed him, she watched where his stick tapped the snow, but if there were tracks she couldn't see them. When they reached the edge of the clearing, Harold motioned to Martha to stay put while he conducted a perimeter search and disappeared into the trees. Martha squatted twenty feet from the elk carcass. It didn't look as ominous in the dawn. The face of the wrangler was hidden by the bulk of the elk and most of the blood was at a remove under the snow. *I should be tired*, she told herself. Instead, she found herself snapping her fingers, sending Harold telepathic signals to hurry.

Harold was back. He drew his belt knife before squatting next to her and whittled a stick into a toothpick. It shifted around as he worked it with his teeth.

Martha fought her impulse to break the silence. And lost. "What's the book tell us?"

Harold spit out the stick. "The pack that took down the bull is four, maybe five strong. They've probably been feeding on it couple days, hanging about the vicinity. They left just after it started snowing."

"I didn't see any wolf tracks."

"You wouldn't. They're more shadows than anything physical."

"Did the wrangler spook them when he rode in? Maybe that's why the horse bucked."

"No, I'd say the wolves left about an hour before the wrangler got here. But it wasn't just the wrangler. There were two others."

"Two?" Martha felt the breath slowly leave her lungs. Her lower ribs pressed against the muscles of her abdomen.

"They came in an hour or so after the snow started and it was snowing for a couple hours after they left, so we're talking dents. You look close, half the dents are about two inches longer than the others. And neither has a square heel. Wrangler's boot has a square heel. That tells me two other people were here."

"Were they together?"

"Same time frame, but I don't think so. The wrangler, we know he came on horseback. He stumbled into the opening from above. Call him person one. Person two came on foot from the timber flank there"—he pointed with his stick to the south—"ninety-degree angle to the route the wrangler took. Left the same way. His track's wider than the wrangler's track. The smaller track, person three, came in from the north, opposite direction from person two. Also on foot. Also left on his backtrack. Spacing says he was running on the way out. Tripped and fell down once, down below in the trees. Running blind, down timber all around, no more sense than the horse."

"Or a woman." Martha scratched the soft skin under her chin. "You said the third set of tracks are shorter. Why couldn't they be a woman's? That's who's missing on this godforsaken mountain."

"Could be at that. Make sense if she came onto the scene, saw him dead like this."

"I damn near bolted myself."

"No, Martha, you didn't. You just walked out to the edge of the trees where I found you and threw up and kicked some snow over it."

"Damned white book," she muttered under her breath. "Any idea where number two and three came from?"

Harold shook his head. "Once you get in the open, the tracks are windblown. Odd thing, though. There's a drag mark near the elk carcass, a little dirt kicked up. Like someone dragging a heavy branch. Hard to tell with the snow cover."

Martha fingered the point-and-shoot in her breast pocket.

Harold shook his head. "Pictures will just wash out, all that light bouncing off the snow."

"I know that. I'm not taking pictures of the tracks. This is just my way of telling you to finish up so I can take the scene photos. If you haven't noticed, there's a man over there who's cooling down to room temperature and he has an antler sticking out of him that's long enough to hang a hat on."

"That's what I miss about you, Martha."

"What?"

"Oh, just you being you."

"That was your choice, Harold."

"My wife had something to say about it."

"Your ex-wife."

Harold looked away. Martha felt her shoulders sag.

"I'm sorry," she said. "What's going on with you and Lou Anne, it's none of my business. Except . . ." All right, she told herself, I'm just going to say it. "I don't know, you and me, I thought we had something. I keep asking myself what I did to screw it up."

"You didn't do anything. Lou Anne and I have known each other since we were kids. She's my people. She's got a problem with depression; she wanted to talk about it. I thought I could deal with it without getting involved, and I couldn't. I wasn't going to be two-timing you. You mean too much for me to be anything but honest." He swept his arm, encompassing the opening in the trees, the pines beyond, putting on their colors as the country came awake. "All this, there's no place I'd rather be than working a story in the snow with you looking over my shoulder, tapping your foot and telling me to get off Indian time."

"Yeah," Martha said drily. "We ought to do this more often, get together on a mountain drenched in blood."

Suddenly she *was* tired, her voice was tired, everything about her was tired. "I better radio Walt," she said. "He'll be waking up to three horses and wondering where the hell I am."

"Don't bother. I spotted him when I was searching the perimeter. He's following your tracks, humping it about as fast as a Scotsman reaching for the check." Harold got his feet. "I'm going to need some time here alone. Keep him out of my kitchen. Same if Bucky Anderson shows up. Jason radioed him the coordinates same as me. He should have been here." He reached into his jacket pocket and brought out an apple, took a quarter of it in one bite and handed it to Martha. "Give it to Snow. Mind your fingers."

Now he's telling me how to feed a horse, she thought.

Back on the open mountainside, she clucked to the paint. "Hey there, Jerry Old Snow," she said, and offered him the apple on the flat of her hand. She could see Walt coming up from below and waved her hat to draw his attention.

"Walt, I'm sorry about this. I should have called in earlier," she said as she stepped down the slope. She could hear his labored breathing and held out a hand, but he waved her off. "I made it this far. Point of pride to finish the climb."

"Jesus, you're leaking blood." She wiped the snow off the log so he could sit at the lower end. "Let me see the damage."

He held up his left foot. He'd cut the toe off the boot. The sock was torn and his big toe curled out like a plum.

"I thought I heard a scream 'bout fifty minutes ago," he said. "I was on your track already, but after that I come fast as I could."

"Those were just the wolves."

"Then there must have been a werewolf with 'em 'cause it sure sounded human."

Martha felt a wave of emotion. For all his faults, Walt was the most devoted to her of anyone on the force. She could count on him having her back, even if it meant showing himself in a disadvanta-geous light. The fact that they had nothing in common beyond the job and that she betrayed her exasperation with him on a daily basis made no inroads on his loyalty. She poured him the last of the tea.

"Jase fill you in?"

He took a sip and nodded. "I take it that wrangler's got himself impaled on an elk antler."

Martha grunted. "Or maybe he had help."

Walt frowned. "What makes you think that?"

"Harold says there were two other people here last night. He's working out the tracks."

"Speaking of the red man," Walt said.

Harold had materialized at the edge of the trees. He inclined his head for them to follow. "I've tracked lung-shot elk that didn't leave a blood trail as heavy as yours, Walt," he said, the words tossed over his shoulder. "We finish up here, I can build us a fire and cauterize that toe."

"Say what?" Walt said.

"I said I got a clean, sharp blade. I can take that toe off, once we're done here."

"Funny," Walt said. He hopped to follow Martha into the trees.

"Oh Jesus." Martha sucked a lungful of air as she looked at the wrangler's body.

"You didn't notice last night?" Harold said.

Martha shook her head. "I couldn't see this part of his face. What do you think? There was a fight?"

"I don't know. You get punched in the side of the head, this is what it looks like, like Walt's big toe there. But snow would tell me if someone was knocked to the ground and the bruising looks more than a few hours old. Something else." He pointed to an ankle-high cut in the leather of the man's right cowboy boot. The cut looked fresh, the leather lighter in color at the edges where it was sliced.

"Maybe when he bailed, his horse stepped on him," Martha said. "Like Big Mike stepped on Walt."

"Maybe." Harold's voice sounded doubtful.

"Hurt like the dickens if it did." Walt was nodding his head. "That's a trophy elk, I ever saw one. Look at the length of those G4 tines."

Martha gave him a withering look. "We got a man twisting on the spit and that's all you have to say, it's a big bull?"

"Score three-sixty, maybe three-seventy. What do you think, Harold?"

"At least," Harold said. "You look at the brow tines, good length on the main beams, hardly any points subtracted for asymmetry, he's maybe not Boone and Crockett but the Montana record book for sure."

Martha looked from one to the other. "Let's . . . focus . . . here."

They stood in silence over the body. Martha's fingers reached for the pulse in her neck. Harold crossed his hands over his belt buckle.

"That G4," Walt said, "They don't call it the sword point for nothing, do they?"

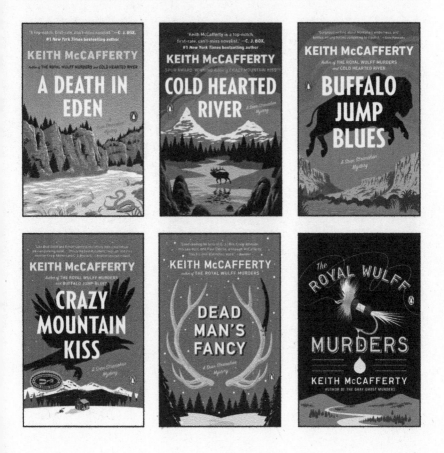